Rosamond Lehmann was born in Buckinghamshire and was educated privately and at Girton College, Cambridge. Her father was an M.P. and a contributor to *Punch*, and her brother John Lehmann is also a writer. Her recreations are reading and music, of which she is an absorbed student. *Dusty Answer* was her first novel and received great critical acclaim. It was followed in 1930 by *A Note in Music*. Her other publications include *The Weather in the Streets* (1936), *The Ballad and the Source* (1944), *The Echoing Grove* (1953), *The Swan in the Evening: Fragments of an Autobiography* (1967) and *The Sea-Grape Tree* (1976). Miss Lehmann has also translated Cocteau's *Les Enfants Terribles* for the Penguin Modern Classics. In 1982 she was awarded the C.B.E.

Several of Rosamond Lehmann's novels have been published in Penguin.

ROSAMOND LEHMANN

DUSTY ANSWER

Ah, what a dusty answer gets the soul
When hot for certainties in this our life!
— GEORGE MEREDITH

PENGUIN BOOKS

Penguin Books Ltd, Harmondsworth, Middlesex, England
Penguin Books, 40 West 23rd Street, New York, New York 10010, U.S.A.
Penguin Books Australia Ltd, Ringwood, Victoria, Australia
Penguin Books Canada Ltd, 2801 John Street, Markham, Ontario, Canada L3R 1B4
Penguin Books (N.Z.) Ltd, 182–190 Wairau Road, Auckland 10, New Zealand

—

First published by Chatto & Windus Ltd 1927
Published by Collins 1978
Published in Penguin Books 1936
Reprinted 1981, 1982, 1983, 1984

—

—

Made and printed in Great Britain by
Richard Clay (The Chaucer Press) Ltd, Bungay, Suffolk
Filmset in Monophoto Ehrhardt by
Northumberland Press Ltd, Gateshead, Tyne and Wear

To
George Rylands

Part One

I

WHEN Judith was eighteen, she saw that the house next door, empty for years, was getting ready again. Gardeners mowed and mowed, and rolled and rolled the tennis-court; and planted tulips and forget-me-nots in the stone urns that bordered the lawn at the river's edge. The ivy's long fingers were torn away from the windows, and the solid grey stone front made prim and trim. When the blinds went up and the familiar oval mirror-backs once more stared from the bedroom windows it seemed as if the long time of emptiness had never been, and that the next-door children must still be there with their grandmother, – mysterious and thrilling children who came and went, and were all cousins except two who were brothers, and all boys except one, who was a girl; and who dropped over the peach-tree wall into Judith's garden with invitations to tea and hide-and-seek.

But in truth all was different now. The grandmother had died soon after she heard Charlie was killed. He had been her favourite, her darling one. He had, astoundingly, married the girl Mariella when they were both nineteen, and he just going to the front. He had been killed directly, and some months afterwards Mariella had had a baby.

Mariella was twenty-two years old now, Charlie's widow with a child Charlie had begotten. It seemed fantastic when you looked back and remembered them both. The grandmother had left the house to Mariella, and she was coming back to live there and have a gay time now that the war was well over and Charlie (so you supposed) forgotten.

Would Mariella remember Judith next door, and how they used to share a governess and do the same lessons in spite of Mariella's four years' seniority? Miss Pim wrote: 'Judith is an exceptionally clever child, especially about essays and botany. She laps up knowledge as a kitten laps milk.' The letter had been left on Mamma's desk: unforgettable, shameful, triumphant day.

Mariella on the other hand – how she used to sit with her clear light eyes blank, and her polite cool little treble saying: 'Yes, Miss Pim,' 'No, Miss Pim' – and never be interested and never understand! She wrote like a child of six. She would not progress. And yet, as Miss Pim said, Mariella was by no means what you'd call a stupid girl ... By no means a stupid girl: thrilling to Judith. Apart from the thrill which her own queerness gave, she had upon her the reflected glory of the four boy-cousins who came for the holidays, – Julian, Charlie, Martin and Roddy.

Now they were all grown up. Would they come back when Mariella came? And would they remember Judith at all, and be glad to see her again? She knew that, anyway, they would not remember so meticulously, so achingly as herself: people never did remember her so hard as she remembered them – their faces especially. In earliest childhood it was plain that nobody else realized the wonder, the portentous mystery of faces. Some patterns were so pure, so clear and lovely you could go on looking at them for ever. Charlie's and Mariella's were like that. It was odd that the same bits of face shaped and arranged a little differently gave such deplorable results. Julian was the ugly one. And sometimes the ugliest faces did things that were suddenly lovely. Julian's did. You dared not take eyes off a stranger's face for fear of missing a change in it.

'My dear! How your funny little girl stares. She makes me quite uncomfortable.'

'Don't worry, my dear. She doesn't even see you. Always in the clouds.'

The stupids went on stupidly chattering. They little knew about faces. They little knew what a fearful thing could happen to a familiar face – Miss Pim's for instance – surprised off its guard and broken up utterly into grossness, withered into hatred or cunning; or what a mystery it was to see a face day after day and find it always strange and surprising. Roddy's was that sort, though at first it had seemed quite dull and flat. It had some secret in it.

8

At night in bed she invented faces, putting the pieces together till suddenly there they were! – quite clear. They had names and vague sorts of bodies and lived independent lives inside her head. Often they turned out to have a likeness to Roddy. The truth was, Judith thought now, Roddy's was a dream rather than a real face. She felt she had never seen it as it actually was, but always with that over-stressed significance, that haunting quality of curiousness which a face in a dream bears.

Queer Roddy must be twenty-one now; and Martin twenty; and Julian twenty-four at least; and beautiful Charlie would have been Mariella's age if such an incredible thing had not happened to him. They would not want anything to do with her. They would be grown up and smart, with friends from London; and she still had her hair down and wore black cotton stockings, and blushed wildly, hopelessly, eternally, when addressed in public. It would be appalling to meet them again, remembering so much they had certainly forgotten. She would be tongue-tied.

In the long spaces of being alone which they only, at rarer and rarer intervals, broke, she had turned them over, fingered them so lovingly, explored them so curiously that, melting into the darkly-shining enchanted shadow-stuff of remembered childhood, they had become well-nigh fantastic creatures. Presumably they had realized long ago that Charlie was dead. When they came back again, without him, she would have to believe it too. To see them again would be a deep wrenching sort of hurt. If only it could be supposed it would hurt them too! . . . But Charlie had of course been dead for years; and of course they did not know what it was to want to know and understand and absorb people to such a degree that it was a fever. Or if they did, it was not upon her, trifling female creature, that they applied their endeavours. Even Martin, the stupid and ever-devoted, had felt, for a certainty, no mysterious excitement about her.

When she looked backwards and thought about each of them separately, there were only a few odd poignant trivialities of actual fact to remember.

Mariella's hair was cut short like a boy's. It came over her forehead in a fringe, and beneath it her lucid mermaid's eyes looked out in a blind transparent stare, as if she were dazzled. Her skin was milk-white, her lips a small pink bow, her neck very long on sloping shoulders, her body tall and graceful with thin snakey long limbs. Her face was without expression, composed and cool-looking. The only change it ever suffered was the perfect upward lift of the lips when they smiled their limited smile. Her voice was a small high flute, with few inflections, monotonous but soft and sweet-tempered. She spoke little. She was remote and unruffled, coolly friendly. She never told you things.

She had a Great Dane and she went about alone with him for choice, her arm round his neck. One day he was sick and started groaning, and his stomach swelled and he went into the thickest part of the laurel bushes and died of poison in half an hour. Mariella came from a French lesson in time to receive his dying look. She thought he reproached her, and her head, fainting in anguish, fell over his, and she said to him: 'It wasn't my fault.' She lay beside him and would not move. The gardener buried him in the evening and she lay on the grave, pale, extinguished and silent. When Judith went home to supper she was still lying there. Nobody saw her cry, and no one ever heard her speak of him again.

She was the one who always picked up naked baby-birds, and worms and frogs and caterpillars. She had a toad which she loved, and she wanted to keep a pet snake. One day she brought one home from the long-grass meadow; but Miss Pim had a faint turn and the grandmother instructed Julian to kill it in the back yard.

Charlie dared her to go three times running through the field with the bull in it, and she did. Charlie wouldn't. She could walk without a tremor on the bit of the roof that made everyone else feel watery inside; and she delighted in thunderstorms. Her hair crackled with electricity, and if she put her fingers on you you felt a tiny tingling of shock. She was elated and terrifying standing at the window and smiling among all the flashes and thunder-cracks.

Julian was the one she seemed to like best; but you never knew. She moved among them all with detached undemanding good-humour. Sometimes Judith thought Mariella despised her.

But she was kind too: she made funny jokes to cheer you up after tears. Once Judith heard them whisper: 'Let's all run away from Judy' – and they all did. They climbed up the poplar tree at the bottom of the garden and made noises out of it at her, when she came by, pretending not to be looking for them.

She went away and cried under the nursery sofa, hoping to die there before discovery. The darkness had a thick dusty acrid smell, and breathing was difficult. After hours, there were steps in the room; and then Mariella lifted the sofa frill and looked in.

'Judy, come out. There's chocolate biscuits for tea.'

With a fresh burst of tears, Judith came.

'Oo! You do look cry-ey.' She was dismayed. 'Shall I try to make you laugh?'

Mariella unbuttoned her frock, stepped out of it and danced grotesquely in her holland knickers. Judith began to giggle and sob at the same time.

'I'm the fat man,' said Mariella.

She blew out her cheeks, stuffed a cushion in her knickers and strutted coarsely. That was irresistible. You had to squeal with laughter. After that the others came in rather quietly and were very polite, not looking till her face had stopped being blotched and covering her hiccups with cheerful conversation. And after tea they asked her to choose the game. So everything was all right.

It was autumn, and soon the lawn had a chill smoke-blue mist on it. All the blurred heavy garden was as still as glass, bowed down, folded up into itself, deaf, dumb and blind with secrets. Under the mist the silky river lay flat and flawless, wanly shining. All the colours of sky and earth were thin ghosts of themselves: and on the air were the troubling bitter-sweet odours of decay.

When the children came from hiding in the bushes they looked all damp and tender, with a delicate glow in their faces, and wet lashes, and drops of wet on their hair. Their breath made mist in front of them. They were beautiful and mysterious like the evening.

The happiness was a swelling pressure in the head and chest, too exciting to bear. Going home under the willows in the little connecting pathway between the two gardens Judith suddenly made up some poetry.

Stupid funny serious Martin had red cheeks and brown eyes and dirty knees. His legs were very hairy for his age. He had an extremely kind nature. He was the one they always teased and scored off. Charlie used to say: 'Let's think of a sell for Martin,' and when he had been sold, as he always was, they danced in front of him shouting: 'Sold again! Sold again!' He never minded. Sometimes it was Judith who thought of the best sells, which made her proud. She was very cruel to him, but he remained faithful and loving, and occasionally sent her chaotic sheets of dirt and ink from school, signing them: 'Yrs truly, M. Fyfe.'

He loved Roddy too, – patiently, maternally. Sometimes they went about each with an arm round the other's neck; and they always chose each other first in picking sides. Judith always prayed Charlie would pick her first, and sometimes he did, but not always.

Martin had coagulated toffee in one pocket and hairy acid drops in the other. He was always eating something. When there was nothing else he ate raw onions and stank to Heaven.

He was the best of them all at running and chucking, and his muscle was his fondest care and pride. What he liked best was to take Roddy or Judith in the canoe and go bird's nesting up the creek. Roddy did not tease him about Judith – Roddy never cared what other people did enough to tease them about it – but the others were apt to, so he was rather ashamed, and spoke roughly and pushed her in public; and only showed he loved her when they were alone together.

Once there was hide-and-seek and Charlie was he. Martin asked Judith to hide with him. They lay in the orchard, under the hay-stack, with their cheeks pressed into the warm sweet-smelling turf. Judith watched the insects labouring over blades of grass; and Martin watched her.

'Charlie's a long time coming,' said Judith.

'I don't think so. Lie still.'

Judith dropped back, rolled over and surveyed him out of the corner of an eye. His face seen so near looked funny and rough and enormous; and she laughed. He said:

'The grass is wet. Sit on my chest.'

She sat on his hard chest and moved up and down as he breathed. He said:

'I say, which do you like best of us all?'

'Oh Charlie . . . But I like you, too.'

'But not as much as Charlie?'

'Oh no, not as much as Charlie.'

'Couldn't you like me as much?'

'I don't think so. I like him better than anyone.'

He sighed. She felt a little sorry for him and said:

'But I like you next best,' adding to herself, 'I don't think' – a sop to God, who was always listening. For it was an untruth. Roddy came next, then Julian, and then Martin. He was so boring and faithful, always following her round and smelling slightly of perspiration and dirt, and so entirely under her thumb that he almost had no part in the mysterious thrillingness of the children next door. She had to think of him in his detached aspects, running faster than anyone else, or diving for things at the bottom of the river before he became part of it: or else she had to remember him with Roddy's arm flung over his shoulder. That gave him a glamour. It was thrilling to think of being friends with a person – especially with Roddy – to that extent. It was no use praying that Charlie would be willing to walk about like that with her. He would never dream of it.

Charlie was beautiful as a prince. He was fair and tall with long bright golden hair that he tossed back from his forehead, and a pale clear skin. He had a lovely straight white nose, and a girl's mouth with full lips slightly apart, and a jutting cleft chin. He kept his shirt collar unbuttoned, and the base of his throat showed white as a snowdrop. His knees were very white too. Judith thought of him night and day. At night she pretended he was in bed beside her; she told him stories and sang him to sleep: and he said he liked her better than anyone else and would marry her when they grew up. He went to sleep with a moonbeam across his brow and she watched over him till morning. He fell into awful dangers and she rescued him; he had accidents and she carried him for miles soothing his groans. He was ill and she nursed him, holding his hand through the worst of the delirium.

He called out: 'Judith! Judith! Why don't you come?' and she answered: 'I am here, darling,' and he opened his eyes and recognized her and whispered, 'Stay with me,' and fell into a peaceful refreshing sleep. And the doctor said: 'We had all given him up; but your love has pulled him through.'

13

Then she fell ill herself, worn out with watching and anxiety. Charlie came to her and with tears implored her to live that he might show his gratitude. Sometimes she did; but sometimes she died; and Charlie dedicated his ruined life to her, tending her grave and weeping daily. From the bottom of the grave she looked up and saw him pale and grief-stricken, planting violets.

Nothing in the least like that ever really happened in spite of prayers. He was quite indifferent.

Once she spent the night next door because Mamma and Papa were away and Nurse's mother was going at last. It seemed too exciting to be true, but it happened. The grandmother said she was Mariella's little guest, so Mariella showed her the visitors' lavatory. Charlie met her coming out of it, and passed by politely, pretending not to notice. It was a great pity. She had hoped to appear noble in all her works to him. There was no chance now. It nearly made the visit a failure.

They had a midnight feast of caramels and banana mess which Julian knew how to make because he was at Eton; and next morning Charlie did not come to breakfast and Julian said he had been sick in the night and gone to Grannie. He was always the one to be sick after things. They went up to see him, and he was in bed with a basin beside him, flushed and very cross. He turned to the wall and told them to get out. He spoke to the grandmother in a whining baby voice and would not let her leave him. Julian muttered that he was a spoilt sugar-baby and they all went away again. So the visit was quite a failure. Judith went home pondering.

But next time she saw him he was so beautiful and lordly she had to go on worshipping. Secretly she recognized his faults, but it was no use: she had to worship him.

Once they turned out all the lights and played hide and seek. The darkness in the hall was like crouching enormous black velvet animals. Suddenly Charlie whispered: 'Come on, let's look together;' and his damp hand sought hers and clutched it, and she knew he was afraid of the dark. He pretended he was brave and she the frightened one, but he trembled and would not let go her hand. It was wonderful, touching and protecting him in the dark: it made the blackness lose its terrors. When the lights went on again he was inclined to swagger. But Julian looked at him with his sharp jeering look. He knew.

14

Julian and Charlie had terrible quarrels. Julian was always quite quiet: only his eyes and tongue snapped and bit. He was dreadfully sarcastic. The quiet things he said lashed and tortured Charlie to screaming frenzies; and he would give a little dry bit of laugh now and then as he observed the boiling up of his brother. Once they fought with croquet mallets on the lawn, and even Mariella was alarmed. And once Charlie picked up an open penknife and flung it. Julian held his hand up. The knife was stuck in the palm. He looked at it heavily, and a haggard sick horror crept over his face and he fainted with a bang on the floor. Everybody thought he was dead. But the grandmother said 'Nonsense' when Martin went to her and announced the fatality; and she was right. After she had revived and bandaged him, poor trembling Charlie was sent in to apologize. Later all the others went in, full of awe and reverence, and everybody was rather embarrassed. Charlie was a trifle hysterical and turned somersaults and threw himself about, making noises in his throat. Everybody giggled a lot with the relief, and Julian was very gentle and modest on the sofa. After that Julian and Charlie were better friends and sometimes called each other 'old chap'.

Once at a children's gymkhana that somebody had, Charlie fell down; and when he saw a trickle of blood on his knee he went white and began to whimper. He never could bear blood. Some of the gymkhana children looked mocking and whispered, and Julian came along and told them to shut up, very fiercely. Then he patted Charlie on the back and said: 'Buck up, old chap,' and put an arm round him and took him up to the house to be bandaged. Judith watched them going away, pressed close to each other, the backs of their heads and their thin childish shoulders looking lonely and pathetic. She thought suddenly: 'They've no Mother and Father;' and her throat ached.

Charlie sometimes told you things. Once, after one of the quarrels, chucking pebbles into the river, he said:

'It's pretty rotten Julian and me always quarrelling.'

'But it's his fault, Charlie.'

'Oh, I dare say it's just as much mine.'

Magnanimous Charlie.

'Oh no, he's so beastly to you. I think he's a horrid boy.'

'Rot! What do you know about it?' he said indignantly. 'He's ripping and he's jolly clever too. Much cleverer than me. He thinks I'm an awful ass.'

'Oh, you're not.'

'Well he thinks so,' he said gloomily. 'I expect I am.'

It was terrible to see him so depressed.

'*I* don't think so Charlie.' Then fearfully plunging: 'I wish you were *my* brother.'

He hurled a pebble, watched it strike the water, got up to go and said charmingly:

'Well, I wish you were my sister.'

And at once it was clear he did not really mean it. He did not care. He was used to people adoring him, wanting from him what he never gave but always charmingly pretended to give. It was a deep pang in the heart. She cried out inwardly: 'Ah, you don't mean it! . . .' Yet at the same time there was the melting glow because he had after all said it.

Another time he took a pin out of his coat and said:

'D'you see what this is?'

'A pin.'

'Guess where I found it.'

'In the seat of your chair.'

The flippancy was misplaced. He ignored it and said impressively:

'In my pudding at school.'

'Oh!'

'I nearly swallowed it.'

'*Oh!*'

'If I had I'd 'a' died.'

He stared at her

'Oh, *Charlie!* . . .'

'You can keep it if you like.'

He was so beautiful, so gracious, so munificent that words failed . . .

She put the pin in a sealed envelope and wrote on it, 'The pin that nearly killed C.F.' with the date; and laid it away in the washstand drawer with her will and a bit of uncut turquoise, and some shells, and a piece of bark from the poplar tree that fell down in the garden.

After that she was a good deal encouraged to hope he might marry her.

Sometimes Charlie and Mariella looked alike – clear, bloodlessly cool; and they both adored dogs and talked a special language to them. But Charlie was all nerve, vulnerable, easy to trouble; and Mariella seemed quite impervious. They disliked each other. He thought she despised him, and it made him nag and try to score off her. Yet they had this subtle likeness.

Sometimes Charlie played the piano for hours. He and Julian remembered tunes in their heads and could play them correctly even if they had only heard them whistled once. If one could not remember a bar, the other could: they supplemented each other. It was thrilling to hear them. They were wrapped in shining mists of glory. When Charlie sang Christmas carols his voice was heartbreakingly sweet and he looked like the little choir boy, too saintly, too blue-eyed to live, – which made Judith anxious. The grandmother used to wipe her eyes when he sang, and say to Judith, just as if she had been grown up, that he was the image of his dear father.

The grandmother did not love Julian in the same way, though sometimes in the evening she would stroke his rough stormy-looking head as he lay on the floor, and say very pityingly: 'Poor old boy.' He used to shut his eyes tight when she said it, and let himself be stroked for a minute, then jerk away. He always did things twice as vehemently as other people. He never shut his eyes without screwing them up. At first you thought he was just beastly, but later you found he was pathetic as well and knew why she said: 'Poor old boy' with that particular inflection. Later still you varied hating him with almost loving him.

Judith was the only one he never mocked at. She was quite immune. He did not always take notice of her of course, being at Eton, and she much younger; but when he did, he was always kindly – even interested; so that it seemed unjust to dislike him so much, except for Charlie's sake.

He was an uncomfortable person. If you had been alone with him it was a relief to get back to the others. His senses were too acute, his mind too angular. He would not let anything alone. He was always prying and poking restlessly, testing and examining, and making you do the same, insistently holding your attention as long as he wanted it, so that his company was quite exhausting. He always hoped to find people more intelligent, more interesting than they were, and he would not let them alone till he had discovered their inadequacy and thrown them away.

But the more he poked at a person's mind, the more that person withdrew. He had that knack. He spent his time doing himself no good, repelling where he hoped to attract. He was of a didactical turn of mind. He loved instructing; and he knew so much about his subjects and was so anxious to impart all he knew that he would go on and on and on. It was very tiresome. Judith was too polite to show her boredom, so she got a lot of instruction. Sometimes he tried when they were alone together to make her tell him her thoughts, which would have been terribly embarrassing but that he soon lost interest in them and turned to his own. He himself had a great many thoughts which he threw at her pell mell. He had contemptuous ideas about religion. He had just become an unbeliever, and he said 'God' in quite an ordinary unashamed conversational voice. Sometimes she understood his thoughts, or pretended to, to save the explanation, and sometimes she let him explain, because it made him so pleased and enthusiastic. He would contort himself all over with agony searching for the right, the perfect words in which to express himself, and if he was satisfied at the end he hummed a little tune. He loved words passionately: he invented very good ones. Also he made the most screamingly funny monstrous faces to amuse them all, if he felt cheerful. Generally, however, he was morose when they were all together, and went away alone, looking as if he despised and distrusted them. Judith discovered he did not really prefer to be alone: he liked one other person, a listener. It made him light up impetuously and talk and talk. The others thought him conceited, and he was; yet all the time he was less conceited than self-abasing and sensitive, less overbearing than diffident. He could not laugh at himself, only at others; and he never forgave a person who laughed at him.

He told untruths to a disconcerting extent. Judith told a great many herself, so she was very quick to detect his, and always extremely shocked. Once the grandmother said:

'Who broke the punt pole?'

And they all said:

'I didn't.'

Then she said patiently:

'Well, who went punting yesterday?' And Martin, red and anxious with his desire to conceal nothing, cried joyfully: 'I did' – adding almost with disappointment: 'But I didn't break the pole.' His truthfulness was quite painfully evident. Nobody had broken the pole.

Julian whistled carelessly for a bit after that, so Judith knew.

Sometimes he invented dreams, pretending he had really dreamt them. Judith always guessed when the dreams were untruths, though often they were very clever and absurd, just like real dreams. She made up dreams too, so he could not deceive her. She knew the recipe for the game; and that, try as you would, some betraying touch was bound to creep in.

In the same way he could not deceive her about the adventures he had had, the queer people he had met, plausible as they were. Made-up people were real enough, but only in their own worlds, which were each as different from the world your body lived in as the people who made them were different from each other. The others always believed him when they bothered to listen; they had not the imagination to find him out. Judith as a fellow artist was forced to judge his lies intellectually, in spite of moral indignation.

He was rather mean about sweets. Often he bought a bagful of acid drops, and after handing them round once went away and finished them by himself. Sometimes when Judith was with him he sucked away and never once said: 'Have one.' But another time he bought her eightpence worth all to herself and took her for a beetle walk. He adored beetles. He knew their names in Latin, and exactly how many thousand eggs a minute they laid and what they ate, and where and how long they lived. Coming back he put his arm round her and she was proud, though she wished he were Charlie.

He read a lot and sometimes he was secretive about it. He stayed in the bath room whole afternoons reading dictionaries or the Arabian Nights.

He was the only one who was said to know for certain how babies were born. When the others aired their theories he laughed in a superior way. Then one day after they had all been persuading him

he said, surly and brief: 'Well, haven't you noticed animals, idiots?'
And after they had consulted amongst themselves a bit they all
thought they understood, except Martin, and Mariella had to explain
to him.

Julian played the piano better than Charlie; he played so that it
was impossible not to listen. But he was not, as Charlie was, a pure
vessel for receiving music and pouring it forth again. Judith thought
Charlie undoubtedly lapped up music as a kitten lapped milk.

Julian said privately that he intended to write an opera. It was too
thrilling for words. He had already composed a lovely thing called
'Spring' with trills, and an imitation of a cuckoo recurring in it. It
was wonderful, – exactly like a real cuckoo. Another composition was
called 'The Dance of the Stag-Beetles'. That was very funny. You
simply saw the stag-beetles lumping solemnly round. It made everybody laugh – even the grandmother. Then Roddy invented a dance
for it which was as funny as the music; and it became a regular thing
to be done on rainy days. Julian himself preferred 'Spring'. He said
it was a bigger thing altogether.

Roddy was the queerest little boy. He was the most unreal and
thrilling of all because he was there so rarely. His parents were not
dead like Julian's and Charlie's, or abroad like Martin's or divorced
and disgraced like Mariella's. (Mariella's mother had run away with
a Russian Pole, whatever that was, when Mariella was a baby; and
after that her father ... there Nurse had broken off impressively and
tilted an imaginary bottle to her lips when she was whispering about
it to the housemaid.)

Roddy's parents lived in London and allowed him to come on a
week's visit once every holiday. Roddy scarcely ever spoke. He had
a pale, flat face and yellow-brown eyes with a twinkling light remote
at the back of them. He had a ruffled dark shining head and a queer
smile that you watched for because it was not like anyone else's. His
lip lifted suddenly off his white teeth and then turned down at the
corners in a bitter-sweet way. When you saw it you said 'Ah!' to
yourself, with a little pang, and stared, – it was so queer. He had
a trick of spreading out his hands and looking at them, – brown broad
hands with long crooked fingers that were magical when they held

a pencil and could draw anything. He had another trick of rubbing his eyes with his fist like a baby, and that made you say 'Ah!' too, with a melting, quick sort of pang, wanting to touch him. His eyes fluttered in a strong light: they were weak and set so far apart that, with their upward sweep, they seemed to go round the corners and, seen in profile, to be set in his head like a funny bird's. He reminded you of something fabulous – a Chinese fairy-story. He was thin and odd and graceful; and there was a suggestion about him of secret animals that go about by night.

Once Judith saw a hawthorn hedge in winter, shining darkly with recent rain. Deep in the heart of its strong maze of twigs moved a shadowy bird pecking, darting silently about in its small magically confined loneliness after a glowing berry or two. Suddenly Judith thought of Roddy. It was ridiculous of course, but there it was: the suggestion came of itself with the same queer pull of surprise and tenderness. A noiseless, intent creature moving alone among small brilliancies in a profound maze: there was – oh, what was there that was all of Roddy in that?

He was so elastic, so mercurial in his movements, when he chose, that he did not seem true. He had a way of swinging down from the topmost branch of a tree, dropping lightly, hand below hand, as if he were floating down, and then, long before he reached the usual jumping-place, giving himself easily to the air and landing in a soft relaxed cat-like crouch.

Once they set out to attempt the huge old fir-tree at the edge of the garden. The thing was to get to the top before someone below counted fifty. Julian, Mariella, Martin tried, and failed. Then Roddy. He swung himself up and soon after leapt out from a branch and came down again, pronouncing it too uncomfortable and filthy to be bothered about. Judith looked up and saw the wild swirl of twigs so thick all the way up that no sky showed through. She said to herself: 'I will! I will!' and the Spirit entered into her and she climbed to the top and threw a handkerchief out of it just as Martin said fifty-seven. After that she came down again, and received congratula-tions. Martin gave her his lucky thripenny as a prize, and she was swollen with pride because she, the youngest, had beaten them all; and in her exaltation she thought: 'I can do anything if I say I can,' and tried again that evening to fly through the power of faith but failed.

Afterwards when she was resavouring in secret the sweet applause they had given her she remembered that Roddy had said nothing, – just looked at her with twinkling eyes and a bit of his downward smile; and she thought he had probably been laughing at her for her enthusiasm and her pride. She felt disillusioned, and all at once remembered her bruises and her ruined bloomers.

Roddy had no ambition. He did not feel at all humiliated if he failed to meet a challenge. If he did not want to try he did not try: not because he was afraid of failing, for he knew his power and so did everyone else; and not because he was physically cautious, for fear was unknown to him: it was because of the fundamental apathy in him. He lived in bursts of energy followed by the most lethargic indifference.

When he chose to lead they all followed; but he did not care. He did not care whether he was liked or not. He never sought out Martin, though he accepted his devotion kindly and did not join in the sells arranged for him. But then he never joined in anything: he was not interested in personal relationships.

They were all a little afraid of him, and none of them – except Martin to whom he was as a son – liked him very much.

The things he drew were extremely odd: long dreamlike figures with thin legs trailing after them, giants and pigmies and people having their heads cut off, and ghosts and skeletons rising from graves and flapping after children; and people doing wild dances, their limbs flying about; and amusing monsters and hideous terrifying old women. His caricatures were the best. The grandmother said they were very promising. Julian was always the most successful subject, and he minded dreadfully.

Sometimes Judith sat beside him and watched his quick pencil. It was like magic. But always he soon gave up. He had scarcely any interest in his drawings once they were finished. She collected them in sheaves and took them home to gloat over. That he could execute such things and that she should be privileged to observe and to gather up after him! . . . His drawings were more thrilling even than the music of Julian and Charlie. She could play the piano herself quite nicely, but as for drawing, – there was another clear case of the unreliability of the Bible. However much you cried: 'I can, I can!' and rushed, full of faith, to pencil and paper, nothing whatever happened.

Once she was suddenly emboldened and said out loud the words rehearsed silently for many weeks:

'Now draw something for *me*, Roddy.'

Oh, something designed from its conception for your very own, – something which could be labelled (by yourself, since Roddy would certainly refuse) 'From the artist to Judith Earle,' with the date: a token, a perpetual memorial of his friendship! . . .

'Oh no,' said Roddy, 'I can't.' He threw down his pencil, instantly bored at the suggestion, smiled and presently wandered off.

The smile took the edge off the sting, but there was an old feeling, an oppression, as she watched him going away. It was no use trying to bring Roddy out of his labyrinthine seclusion with personal advances and pretensions to favouritism. Roddy had a power to wound far beyond his years; he seemed grown up sometimes in his crushingness.

Now and again he was very funny and invented dances on the lawn to make them laugh. His imitation of a Russian ballet-dancer was wonderful. Also he could walk on his hands or do backward somersaults into the water. This was very thrilling and made him highly respected.

Once he and Judith were the two hares in a paper chase. Roddy spied an old umbrella in the hedge and picked it up. It was tattered and gaunt and huge; and there was something friendly about it, – a disreputable reckless jollity. He carried it for a long time, swinging it round and round, and sometimes balancing it on his chin or spearing things with it. At the top of the hill they came to the pond covered with green stuff and a white starry froth of flowers. All around grew flags and forget-me-nots, and the hundred other rare enchanting trivialities of water places.

'Well, I don't want this old umbrella,' said Roddy. He considered the water. 'Do you?'

'No. Throw it away.'

He flung it. It alighted in the middle of the pond. It stuck – oh horror! – upright, caught in something, and refused to sink.

'*Oh!*'

It stared at them across the waste of waters, stark, forlorn, reproachful. It said: 'Why did you pick me up, encourage and befriend me when this is what you meant to do?'

'Well, come on,' said Roddy.

They fled from it.

They fled from it, but ah! – it pursued them. From miles away it wailed to Judith in a high thin squeak: 'Save me! Save me!' They made excuses to each other for spoiling the paper chase, and going back the same way. Their feet were compelled, driven.

The pond lay fair and flawless in the evening light. The umbrella was drowned.

Roddy stood at the edge and bit his lip. He said:

'Well, I almost wish I hadn't thrown the poor old chap away.'

She nodded. She could not speak.

The place was haunted for ever.

But what remained more deeply in her memory was the bond with Roddy, the sharing of an emotion, the secret sympathy. Avidly she seized upon it, and with it nourished her immoderate ambitions. One day they would all like her better than anyone else: even Roddy would tell her everything. Their lives, instead of being always remote and mysterious, would revolve intimately round her. She would know all, all about them.

From that far off unsubstantial time Roddy's face was the last, the clearest, the strangest to float up.

There was a field with chalky pits in it and ripening blackberries and wastes of gorse and bracken. The curious smell of the bracken rose faint but penetrating, earthy and disturbing.

She was staring in horror at a dead rabbit lying in the path. It was stretched on its side with its tiny frail-boned paws laid out quiet, and the tender secret white fur of its underneath half revealed. One of them – which? – she could never remember – said:

'Well, I never thought I'd touch it.'

It was like hearing a person speaking in a bad dream.

'How did you do it?' said Roddy's voice.

'Well, it was sitting, and I crept up and chucked a stone to startle it up, not meaning to hurt it. But I must have hit it plumb behind

24

the ear, – I killed it outright anyway. It was an absolute fluke. I couldn't do it again if I tried all my life.'

'Hum,' said Roddy. 'Funny thing.'

He stood with his hands in his pockets looking down at the corpse, making his face a mask. The sun wavered and darkened. The surface of the bracken shone with a metallic light, the grass was lurid, the trees hissed. Judith struggled in a nightmare.

'Well, what shall I do with it?' said someone.

'I'll see to it,' said Roddy.

Then he and she were alone. She bent down and touched the fur. It was dead, it was dead. She fell on her knees beside it and wept.

'I say, *don't*,' said Roddy after a bit. He could not bear tears.

She wept all the more, awful sobs from the pit of the stomach.

'He didn't mean it, it can't be helped,' said Roddy. Then after another interval:

'You know, it didn't feel it. It died at once.'

It died at once. Oh, how pathetic, how unbearable ... Then again, after a long time:

'Look, we'll take it home and give it a funeral.'

He gathered huge fern-leaves and gently wrapped the rabbit in them. She picked it up: she would carry it, though she almost fainted with anguish at the feel of its tender thin body. She thought: 'I am holding something that's dead. It was alive a few minutes ago and now it's – what is it?' – and she felt choked, drowning.

They set off. Weeping, weeping she carried the rabbit down the hill into the garden; and Roddy walked silently beside her. He went away and dug a hole under a laurel bush in the thickest part of the shrubbery. But when it came to the final act, the burying, she could not bear it at all. She was beyond all coherence now, a welter of sobs and tears.

'I say, *don't*,' said Roddy again in a shaking voice.

She was suddenly quiet with shock; for he sounded on the verge of breaking down. He could not endure her grief. Out of the corner of a sodden eye she saw his face start to break up. Quickly she yielded the body, and he took it away.

He was gone a long time. When he came back he took her arm and said:

25

'Come and look.'

Under the laurel bush, at the head of the little mound he had set up a beautiful tablet. It was the top of a cake tin, smooth and clean and shining; and on it he had hammered out with a nail the words: 'In memory of a Rabbit.'

Peace and comfort flowed in upon her ...

The rabbit was under all that quiet and green gloom, under the chill stiff polished moulding of the great laurel leaves, no longer terrible and pathetic, but dignified with its memorial tablet, lapped in the kind protecting earth, out of reach of flies and boys and the mocking stare of the sun. It was all right. There was not any sorrow.

'Thank you!'

He had done it to please her. Charlie would not have done it, Martin could not have. It was a purely Roddy gesture, so unlike him, you would have supposed, and yet, when it was done, so recognizably his gesture and only his. Incalculable Roddy! She remembered how when Martin had sprained his ankle and moaned, he had hovered round him in distress, with a puckered face. He could not stand the unhappiness and pain of people.

She wanted to kiss him, and did not dare. She looked at him, the whole of herself flowing towards him in a warm tumult of gratitude, and quickly touched his arm; and he looked back, withdrawing himself for fear of thanks, smiling his obscure downward smile. She thought: 'Shall I never, never understand him?'

She saw the sky beginning to blossom with evening. The sun came out below flushed clouds and all the treetops were lit up, sombrely floating and rocking in a dark gold wash of light. Across the river the fields looked rich and wistful, brimming with sun, cut with long violet shadows. The river ran a little wildly, scattered over with fierce, fire-opal flakes. But all was softening, flattening. The clouds were drifting away, the wind was quiet now; there would be an evening as still, as carved as death.

She saw it all with the quivering overclear senses of exhaustion. It was too much. Roddy's pale face was all at once significant, and all the others, even Charlie, floated away while she looked at him and loved him. And as she looked she saw the deep light falling on him and he seemed mingled with the whole mysterious goldenness of the evening, to be part of it; and she felt herself lost with him in a sudden dark poignant intimacy and merging, – a lifting flood, all come and gone in a timeless moment.

But afterwards it did not seem true. She only remembered that next time she saw him he had been quite ordinary and indifferent, and she herself, still looking for signs and wonders, chilled with disappointment. Roddy as a child grew dim after that; and the rabbit's grave that she had meant to tend and keep sweet with flowers through the changing seasons, grew dim too. After a while she could not even remember exactly where it was in all that shrubbery. The rabbit lay forgotten.

The others faded too. She could recapture nothing more of them. They were cut off sharp in a final group on the hillside, as if horror had in that instant made a night and blotted them out for good.

Then the grandmother let the house and went away to seek a less damp air for her rheumatism. Being alone came again as the natural stuff of life, and the children next door were gone and lost, as if they had never been.

2

Then they came again – straying so suddenly, strangely, briefly across the timeless confusions of adolescence, that they left behind them an even more disturbing sense of their unreality, – an estrangement profounder than before.

It was winter – the time of the long frost and the ten days' skating, – the time when crossing the river to get to the skating pool was dangerous because of the great blocks of ice coming down with the stream. Those ten days flashed out for ever in life, – a sparkling pure breathless intoxication of movement and light and air that seemed each evening too delightful to be allowed to last; and yet each succeeding morning – she first listening to the day then fearfully peeping at it – had miraculous prolongation. She prayed: *Oh God, let the skating last. Let me skate. Take not my happiness from me and I will love thee as I ought.* And for ten days He hearkened unto her.

Each day she abandoned lessons and, crossing the river, ran across the crunching frost-bound marsh to the edge of the pond. Over and over it the people slipped, glided, swirled with shouts of laughter in the sun. Their lips were parted, their eyes shone, they were beautified.

She wore a white sweater and a crimson muffler. At first people looked at her and then they began smiling at her; and soon she was greeting all those who came regularly and smiling at fresh strangers every day.

There was a girl who came each morning from the London train. She was slender and fair, and she skated with the flying grace of a dream. Her pleated skirt swung out as she moved, her feet in their trim boots were narrow and small, and when she twirled her long slim legs showed to the knee. She appeared like a goddess in the midst of the cheerful sociable incompetent herd. Judith skated to and fro in front of her every day, hoping in vain for a look; for she was proud and absorbed and ardent, holding herself aloof and noticing no one, skating and skating till it got dark. One day she brought a handsome young man with her, and to him was not at all proud and in-different.

They waltzed, they spun, they cut figures, they ran hand in hand, they laughed at each other; and when they rested they sat side by side talking and smoking cigarettes. Unlike his companion, the young man looked at Judith not once but many times: and then he smiled at her; then he whispered something to the goddess, and Judith's heart beat wildly. But the cold scornful creature merely glanced once in a bored way, nodded and went on skating. When evening fell and they were preparing to go he looked up from taking off his boots as Judith passed, and radiantly smiling with white teeth and blue eyes, said 'Good night.' That was, to her regret, the only time she saw this handsome and friendly young man, whose wife she would have been pleased to be.

There was an old gentleman with glasses and a grey moustache who skated very sedately and who took a great deal of trouble to teach her the outside edge. He called her 'my dear', and his eyes gazed at her from behind his glasses with a hungry watery wistfulness. He had little if any conversation, but he would clear his throat and open his mouth as he looked at her as if for ever on the verge of some tremendous confidence. There was also a common but polite boy with pimples who could skate very fast indeed and who for several afternoons raced panting up and down the ice, while she hung on to the belt of his Norfolk jacket, and shrieked.

The tenth morning was Saturday. The London train brought several parties. The goddess had a little girl with her. There were many vulgar shouting groups of incompetents, and one or two quiet and moderately proficient ones. Judith noticed a curious trio of tall slender refined looking people – two boys and a girl. They sat on the bank and slowly ate sandwiches. When they had finished they got up and stood grouped together, making no movement to adjust the skates they carried. As soon as they stood up, Judith recognized them: Mariella, Julian and Charlie.

It had happened.

They had not changed much, but they had grown most alarmingly. Mariella must be close on six foot. Her body had merely been stretched out without much alteration of the long vague curves of childhood. She hardly dared look at the boys: they were enormous.

That was Charlie, really Charlie, that yellow-headed one, a little wild-looking, more beautiful than ever . . . She felt choked.

At that moment Mariella's eyes fell on her. A fearful blush and heart-beating went all through her, and she turned hastily away. But she could feel them observing, questioning, conferring about her. She executed a perfect half-circle on the outside edge, and felt that now, if they did recognize her, she could just bear it.

Somebody was calling from the edge.

'Hey! Hey! Hi!'

She looked round cautiously. There was no doubt about it. Charlie was calling her, and they were all nodding and beckoning. They could, it seemed, easily bear to recognize her, and the sight of her skating towards them caused them no apparent faintness or anguish.

Charlie said rather peevishly:

'I say, how do you *do* it? That turn thing. Who taught you?'

Judith was dumb.

'She doesn't recognize us,' said Mariella with a little giggle. 'You *are* Judith Earle, aren't you?'

'Oh yes. Oh I *do*. Only you've grown so.' She tried to look at them and to her horror felt the tears smart under her eyelids. 'I didn't expect –' Her mouth was trembling, and she stopped in despair, hanging her head.

It was such a shock, such a deep pang of joy and misery ... They would not understand ... After all these years of thinking about them, seeing them so passionately, nursing in her imagination their unreal and dream-like existence, that they should all at once quite casually be there! It was almost as if dead people were to come to life. She prayed to be swallowed up in the ice.

'Well, you're no pigmy,' said Julian.

And they all laughed. Then it was all right. They ceased to swell and waver before her eyes, settled down, began to grow real.

'Well, I don't know how it's done,' said Charlie, still rather angrily looking at the ice. 'Mariella, what on earth did you drag us here for? You don't know any more than I do how it's done. What a stupid waste of a day!' The stress of his petulance made his voice, which was breaking, squeak suddenly now and then, in the funniest way, so that nobody could have taken him seriously.

'Well, you needn't have come.' Mariella's voice was still cool and childish. With her little smile, she turned away from him to watch the skaters.

'And my feet are so cold I can't feel them,' went on Charlie. 'Three great gawps, that's what we are, three great gawps.' He looked at Mariella's back. 'And Mariella's *easily* the gawpest.'

That seemed to unburden him, for he suddenly threw off his bad temper and laughed.

'Put on your skates, chaps,' he said. 'We'll do our damnedest.'

He began to whistle and sat down, struggling with his boots.

'Judith shall show us how it's done. She is so *extremely* able.' He looked at her, giving her his attention for the first time, and charmingly smiled. His eyes were amazing when they looked full at you – brilliant, icy-blue, a little too wide open. His long red girlish lips still parted a trifle in repose; and the whole head had a breath-taking extravagance of beauty.

'How are you, Judith?' he said. 'Do you remember the dear old days?'

'Yes, I do.'

What self-possession he had! She was not up to him. He lost interest in her, and went on with his boots, fiercely whistling.

'Do you really still live here, Judith?' said Mariella.

'Yes, really. Where do you live?'

'Well, we're in London now. Grannie moved there to be near my school. Where do you go to school?'

'I don't. I have classes by myself with a man who coaches boys for Oxford and Cambridge. He's a vicar. And then I have music lessons from a person who comes from London, and Daddy teaches me Greek and Latin. My Mother and Father don't believe in girls' schools.' That sounded rude and priggish. She blushed and added, 'But I do. It's awfully dull by myself.'

'Why don't you get your Mother to send you to my school?' said Mariella. 'It's ripping fun. You could come up to London every day.'

'Mariella *loves* her school,' said Julian. 'It's *topping*. She doesn't learn *anything* and plays hockey *all* day. Judith's parents want her to be *educated*, Mariella. You don't understand. Isn't that so, Judith?'

Judith blushed again and was afraid it was so.

'I believe in female education,' muttered Julian to his boots.

They had become extremely queer creatures as they grew up, thought Judith. The boys especially were very peculiar, with their height and pallor and their trick of over-emphatic speech. Julian was immensely tall and cadaverous, with a stormy, untidy, hideous face, and eloquent eyes that seemed to be changing colour in their deep sockets. He actually had lines in his cheeks, and his nose was becoming hooked, with dilated, backsweeping nostrils.

'Well, I wish you'd come,' said Mariella unruffled, after a silence. 'It's ripping. You'd love it.'

It was nice of Mariella to be so friendly and pressing. Perhaps she had always been very fond of you, had missed you ... Judith's heart warmed.

'I wish *you'd* come back and live here, Mariella. It was so lovely when you did.'

'I'd like to,' said Mariella complacently. 'P'raps we will some day. If Granny's rheumatism would only get better we might come every summer.'

'But it never will get better,' said Julian. 'Not at her age.'

The boots were all on at last, the skates fastened. They got up and wobbled out a few inches on to the ice. There was a chorus of 'Hell!' 'Wow!' 'Goodness!'

Charlie slipped up with a crash, Mariella followed him.

'It's beastly,' he said furiously. 'You can't keep your skates still. I think I've broken my wrist. I shall go home.' The others took no notice. They wobbled further and further out, giggling. They were too tall and thin to balance properly, and their ankles kept on betraying them.

'Come and help us, Judith,' screamed Julian. 'We've never skated before in our *lives*. We can't *stop*. We're too thin to be allowed to fall down.'

They were dragging each other on helplessly.

'Come *here*,' wailed Charlie. 'Judith, come and help me to stand. Shan't we fall in? Are you sure it's safe? My feet are *frozen*.'

Judith giggled as she went from one to the other encouraging, admonishing, supporting. The three ridiculous sillies! They enjoyed their silliness, they enjoyed making her laugh, they were not a bit frightening after all. Never, never since she had bidden them good-bye years ago had been such warm and bubbling happiness. Everything delightful was really starting at last.

As they began to improve they became ambitious. They declared their desire to learn fancy skating, and Charlie swore he would cut a figure of eight before the day was out; and all the time they were simply no good at all. Out of the corner of an eye Judith saw the old gentleman and the boy in the Norfolk jacket wistfully looking on, and she ignored them.

'Now, come along, Mariella,' said Charlie. 'Take hands like this, crossed, and we'll go for a glide.' They sailed rather haltingly away.

Under Mariella's blue wool cap the dark short hair curled softly upwards now, longer than the boyish crop of yore. Her face had preserved its pure and innocent mask. She was laughing, not as other people laughed, unreservedly in the enjoyment of physical pleasures, but rather as if she were making a concession to Charlie's mood, and found the abandonment of laughter alien to her. There was still the curious likeness between the two clear bloodless faces, though Charlie's was forever changing with quick emotions and Mariella's was still, empty almost. They would understand each other, thought Judith. In spite of the friction that used to go on between them, they had always been more obviously, more oppressively blood-relations than any other members of the circle. With years the bond had become even more subtly defined.

Julian was left out. He had never taken any notice of Mariella, yet he had always been the one upon whom her light gaze had dwelt with a faint difference, as if it meant to dwell. In the old days it had sometimes seemed as if she would have been pleased – really pleased, not just indifferently agreeable as she generally was – if Julian had offered to take her for a beetle-walk. She appeared to have a slight respectful interest in him, and a manner which suggested, though only to a remorseless watcher, that she would have valued his good opinion. It still seemed so. When he was teasing her about her school, her eyes, uncertain yet dwelling, had fallen on him a moment; but now, as formerly, you could detect no affection between them.

'We wondered if we should meet you,' said Julian shyly. 'I'm so glad we did.'

Then they had not completely forgotten. She blessed him for the assurance, which only he would have given.

'I couldn't believe it was you,' she said. 'I didn't think I'd ever see you again. I did miss you after you went. I thought perhaps Martin might write to me, but he didn't. How is Martin?'

'He's all right. We don't see him so much now. His people are back from Africa and he spends most of the holidays with them.' He smiled and added: 'I remember Martin was terribly devoted to you. I must tell him I've seen you.'

'And where's Roddy?'

'Oh Roddy . . . He's all right. He's in London. Roddy's very grown up: he's having dancing lessons.' Julian snorted.

'Does he still draw?'

'I don't know. Should think he's too lazy.'

Julian had never liked Roddy.

'Do you still compose, Julian?'

'Oh, do you remember that?' He smiled with pleasure.

'Of course. "The Stag Beetles' Dance". And "Spring with the Cuckoo in it".'

'Oh, that rot. Fancy you remembering!' He looked at her in just the old way, amused but interested, thinking well of her.

'I thought it was beautiful. Have you written anything lately?'

'No. No time. I've given it all up. I've been working like mad for a scholarship. P'raps I'll take to it again a bit at Oxford.'

He seemed to have become enthusiastic about it all at once, encouraged by her interest. He had not changed much.

'And did you get your scholarship?'

'Yes. Balliol. I go up next year.' He was being brief and modest, actually blushing. But Balliol meant nothing to her: she was thinking of his great age.

'You must be eighteen.'

'Yes.'

'D'you know, I remember all your birthdays.'

As she said it she almost cried again, it seemed such a confession of long-cherished vain hope and love. He stared at her, ready to be amused, and then, seeing her face, looked away suddenly, as if he half-understood and were astonished, embarrassed, touched.

'Oh, look at those two,' he said quickly.

Charlie had taken off his coat, and they were holding it up as a sail. With a pang of dismay Judith realized for the first time the ominous strength of the wind. It filled the coat full, and Mariella and Charlie, bearing it high in front of them, went sailing straight across the pond. They could not stop. They shrieked in laughter and agony and went ever faster. They were borne to the pond's edge, stubbed their skates and fell violently in a heap on the grass.

Charlie lay on his back and moaned.

'I've got a pain. I've got a pain. Oh Mariella! Oh God! Oh all you people! The anguish, the *sensation!* – like the Scenic Railway – transports of horror and bliss. I thought: never, *never* shall we stop. We went faster and fas . . . Oh Mariella your *face* . . . I shall *die* . . .'

He writhed with laughter, the tears poured down his face. 'I t-*tried* to say: *drop* the c— I hadn't any *voice* – Oh what a *feeling!* . . . those skimming dreams . . . Oh God!'

He shut his eyes exhausted.

Then soon he had to try again. Then they all tried, and were a nuisance to the other skaters. Everyone looked at Charlie, and nobody was annoyed because of his beauty and radiant spirits, and his charming apologies when he got in the way.

Judith ached with giggling; even Mariella and Julian were wiping their eyes. Charlie was so excited that he looked quite feverish. In his enthusiasm he threw his arms wide and cried:

'Oh darlings!' – and Judith was thrilled because she felt herself included in the endearment.

'You know,' said Julian, 'you'll be sick tonight, Charlie, if you go on like this.'

So he was still the one to be sick.

A small cold mongrel dog came shivering, wriggling across the ice and rolled over before him, waving limp deprecatory paws. Charlie picked it up and wrapped it in his coat, crooning to it and kissing it.

'Oh what sweet paws you have, my chap. Mariella, his paws are particularly heart-breaking. Do look, – all blunt and tufted and uncontrolled. Don't they melt you? Poor chap, – darling chap. You come along with me for a skate.'

He skated away with the dog in his arms, talking his special foolish language to it, and colliding with people at every other step.

Oh, he was strange, thought Judith, looking after him. She had no key to him: she could only dissect him and make notes, learn him by heart and marvel at him, – never hope to meet him some day suddenly, at a chance look, a trifling word, with that secret *Aha!* – that shock of inmost mysterious recognition, as she had once met Roddy.

She thought of Roddy dancing in London, urban and alarming. She saw him distinctly, his dark head, his yellowish pallor, his smile; and wished wildly that he had come instead of Charlie: Charlie who troubled her, made her heavy-hearted with the burden of his lavish indifferent brilliance.

The sharp, blue and white afternoon was paling to sunset. The pond flashed and glittered with empty light. In the middle rose the clump of withered flags, dry starved grasses and marsh plants, berried bushes and little willows, – the whole a blur of pastel shades, purplish-brown, fading green, yellow and russet, with here and there a burning shred of isolated colour, – a splash of crimson, a streak of gold. The whirr and scratch of skates murmured on the air, and the skaters wove without pause, swiftly, lightly, like flies on a ceiling. Beneath the ice the needling grass-blades and the little water-weeds were still, spell-bound; outspread stiffly, delicately in multitudinous and infinitesimal loveliness.

As she stood alone gazing down at them Julian came back to her side and said:

'Do you ever come to London?'

'Hardly ever. If Daddy's at home he generally takes me to a theatre at Christmas; and now and then I go with Mamma for clothes.'

'Well, you'd better come up some time soon and we'll go to a play. Fix it with Mariella.'

'Oh!'

It couldn't be true, – it could never happen.

There was a scratch and stumble of skates, and the other two came to a wavering halt in front of them.

'We must go,' said Mariella.

'Judith's coming to go to a play with us,' said Julian.

'Oh good,' said Mariella, not interested.

'When?' snapped Julian. 'Fix it.'

'I don't know,' she said, with a quick glance at him. 'We must ask Granny. I'll ask Granny, Judith, and let you know tomorrow.'

'Because we're coming back tomorrow,' broke in Charlie. 'Julian, we must, mustn't we? Will you be here, Judith?'

'Oh yes.'

'That's good, because I shall need you. I need thee every hour. I shall have forgotten my breast-stroke by tomorrow. I do believe if we hadn't found you, Judith, we should never have stepped on to the ice at all. We should just have looked at it and faded gracefully back to London. We are so *very* silly.'

He sat down to take off his boots, and began whistling – then burst out singing:

> 'There once were three sillies
> Who stood like lilies –'

A pause –

> 'Refusing to spin –'

36

Another pause –

> 'Crying, Hey, Lackaday!
> The ice will give way,
> And we shall fall in –'

He pulled off his boots; and finished:

> 'If Miss Earle they'd not met
> They'd be standing there yet.'

'Pretty poor,' cried Julian.

'I think it's awfully good,' said Judith.

Charlie bowed, and said:

'I can do more like that.'

'Go on, then.'

'Not now. Pouf! I'm tired.'

He looked it. Save for the bright flush on each cheek his pallor was startling. His eyes looked dark in their shadowy rings, and he leaned back against Mariella while she gravely fastened his shoes and buttoned up his coat. When she put on his muffler he dragged it off again, crying:

'Oh Mariella. *No!* I'm so hot.'

'You're to wear it,' she said quietly. 'You'll catch cold,' and she wound it round his neck again, while he submitted and made faces at her, his eyes laughing into hers, like a child coaxing an elder to smiles.

Watching him, Judith thought:

'Are you conceited and spoilt?'

All that gaiety and proud indifference, all that unconscious-seeming charm, that confident chatter – all might be the product of a complete self-consciousness. Surely he must look in the glass and adore his own reflection. She remembered her old dream of marrying him, and thought with a melancholically prophetic sense of the many people who would yearn to him silently for love, while he went on his way, wanting none of them.

Against the dusk, his head, his face shone as if palely lit.

Narrowly she watched him; but there was no sign for her: all that brilliance of expression glancing and pausing around him, and nothing

37

for her beyond a light smile or two, a casual appreciation of her temporary uses. He and Mariella had scarcely once said: 'Do you remember?' If they still cherished any of the past she was not in it. It was strange to think of such indifference, when they, with the other three, were all the pattern, all the colour and richness that had ever come into life.

In the dying light their mystery fell over them again, and they were as unattainable as ever. If only with the rare quality of their physical appearance they must always enslave her; and she felt worn out with the stress of them.

'Tomorrow,' said Charlie, 'we'll bring Roddy.'

'Yes. Come on,' said Mariella. 'We must hurry for our train.'

They tramped in silence across the cold solitude of the marsh, and the wind came after them, keen and menacing. When they arrived at the river's edge, Charlie stood still, and looked across, saying dreamily:

'There's a light in the old house. I suppose that's the caretaker person. We might look in tomorrow and surprise her. Doesn't it look lonely? ... I wish we would live there again. Where's your house, Judith? I thought it was next door.'

'So it is, but the trees hide it.'

'Oh yes, I'd forgotten.'

Then she ferried them across the river in the punt, and parted from them on the other side, where the lane to the station branched off.

'Well, see you tomorrow.'

Julian looked up at the sky.

'I believe it's thawing,' he said. 'I believe it'll rain in the night.'

'Rot!' said Charlie. 'Why – feel the ground.'

'Yes, but the air's milder. And look at the sky.'

To the east and north the frosty stars pointed their darts; but in the smoky, tumultuous west, black clouds devoured the last of the sun.

Panic seized Judith, and she hated Julian, wanted to strike him.

'Rot! that doesn't mean anything,' said Charlie uneasily.

'And listen to the wind.'

The wind was in the tree-tops, full and relentless, and driving the clouds.

38

'Oh, shut up!' said Charlie. 'Can't there be a wind without a thaw? And come on, can't you, or we'll miss our train.'

'Good night then.'

'G'night Judith. We'll look out for you.'

'I'll be there.'

'Goo'night.'

'Good night.'

Judith ran home, shutting eyes to the clouds, ears to the wind, and, with the slam of the front door behind her, striving to ignore the God of envy, hatred, malice and all uncharitableness whose portents were abroad in the sky.

'Tomorrow they are coming again and bringing Roddy. Tomorrow I shall see Roddy. Oh God, be merciful!'

*

Towards dawn she woke and heard the blind, drearily sighing, futile hurry and hiss of the rain, – and said aloud in the darkness: 'How can I bear it?'

Yet lured by sick fantastic hope she crossed the river that morning and made her way to the pond.

There was nobody there, save one small boy, sliding upon the ice through several inches of water and throwing up before him in his swift career two separate and divided fountains.

Then that was the end. They were lost again. They would not come back, they would not write, she would never go to London to see them. Even Julian would forget about her. They did not care, the rain was glad, there was nothing in the wide world to give her comfort. She turned from the rain-blurred place where their unreal lost images mocked at and confused her, – dreams within the far-off dream of happy yesterday.

3

It was some time in the middle of the war that she knew for certain that Julian was at the front. She heard it from the old next door gardener, who had given her apples and pears long ago, and it was from the grandmother herself that he knew it. She had written to tell him to plant fresh rose-beds and to keep the tennis lawn in perfect order, for very soon, directly the war was over, the grandchildren were to have the house for their own, as a place for week-ends and holidays.

Mr Julian was at the front, safe so far, God be thanked, and Mr Charlie had just been called up; but the fighting, so the grandmother said, would be over before ever he went to France.

Then, nourished afresh on new hopes, desires, and terrors, the children next door came back night after night in dreams.

Julian in uniform came suddenly into the library. He said:

'I've come to say good-bye.'

'Good-bye? Are you going back to the front?'

'Yes. In a minute. Can't you hear my train?'

She listened and heard the train-whistle.

'Charlie's going too – He'll be here in a minute. Good-bye, Judith.'

She put out her hand and he took it and then bent down with a sort of grin and kissed her. He said:

'That's what men do when they're going to the front.'

She thought with pleasure: 'Then Charlie will want to kiss me too'; and she looked out of the window, hoping to see him.

It was impenetrably dark, and she thought anxiously: 'He won't be able to find his way. He always hated the dark.'

'Come on,' said Julian. 'You must come and wave good-bye to me.'

But still she delayed and peered out, looking with growing panic for Charlie.

All at once she saw him in the darkness outside. He was not in uniform, but in grey flannel shorts and a white shirt open at the neck, – the clothes of his childhood. He trailed himself haltingly, as if his feet hurt him.

'Sh!' said Julian in her ear. 'He's disguised himself.'

'Ah, then he won't get killed . . .'

'No.'

She caught sight of his face. It was a terrible disguise, – the shrivelled, yellow mask of an ancient cretin. He looked at her vacantly, and she thought with a pang: 'I must . . . I must pretend I don't know him.'

He passed out of sight with his queer clothes and his limp and his changed face, – all the careful paraphernalia of his travesty. Looking at him, she was seized with sudden terror. There was something wrong: they would see through it.

She tried to reach him, to warn him; but she was voiceless and he had disappeared.

It was Charlie himself, so the old gardener said, who wrote to tell him that he and Mariella were to be married. Master Charles had always been the beloved one, – the one to be ready with a smile and a pleasant word, and never a bit of haughtiness for all his Granny made such a little prince of him.

'And when this old war's over, Lacey,' he says, 'we'll be coming back to live in the dear old house. Granny wants us to,' he says, 'and you may be sure we want to. We were never ones to like London. So look out for us before long.' But ah! he had to come through the fighting first. They were to get married at once, for he was off to the front. Speaking for himself, said the old gardener, he'd have had enough of life if anything happened to Master Charlie.

The next day, the announcement of their marriage at a registry office appeared in *The Times*.

'Why, they can't be more than nineteen,' said Mamma, 'and first cousins, too. A dreadful mistake. However, I suppose the chances are –' and she sighed, settling her V.A.D. cap before the mirror. 'I must write to the old lady. They were good-looking children – one of them especially. Why don't you send a nice little note to the girl, Judith? You used to play together such a lot.'

'Oh, she wouldn't remember me,' said Judith, and went quickly away, sick with shock.

Married, those two. Mariella a wife: Mrs Charles Fyfe.

'I am *young* Mrs Fyfe. This is Charlie, my husband.'

How had it happened?

'Mariella you must marry me, you must, you *must*. Oh Mariella, I *do* want to marry you, and I'm going to the front so I *do* think I might be allowed to have what I want. I may be killed and I shan't have had anything out of life. Oh Mariella, please! You know you're happiest with us, Mariella. You couldn't marry anyone outside and leave us all, could you? Nor could I. I couldn't bear to be *touched* by any other woman. You and I understand each other so well we *couldn't* be unhappy. We are different from other people, you know. Marry me and I'll come back from the war. But if you say no I'll just go out and let myself be killed at once . . .'

And Mariella, pale and childish and not understanding, went away. She went – yes – to Julian, and looking at him full with her dazed look said: 'Charlie has asked me to marry him.' He said not a word, but looked dark and shrugged his shoulders and turned away as who should reply: 'What is that to me?' So Mariella went straight back to Charlie and said:

'All right.'

Her mouth quivered and she nearly cried then, but not quite: neither then nor afterwards. And the grandmother wept bitterly, till in the end Charlie comforted her; and after that, implacably she would give and sacrifice all to Charlie.

No, no, that was too stupid, too abnormal. People only behaved like that in your unbalanced imagination.

Mariella would never have wept, never have gone to Julian, never dreamed of being in love with him, – him or Charlie or anyone else you would have thought, childless, sexless creature that she had always seemed, years behind you in development. How she must have changed to be now liable to passion! All at once she had to be thought of as a woman, the gulf of marriage fixed between you and her.

Had she consented then in her usual placidly agreeable way, just to oblige Charlie, without a notion of what it meant to be in love and marry? Had she gradually fallen in love with him during all the years they were growing up together, or had it been suddenly, with a shock of realization, when he told her he was going to France? Or had he come home one day excited, full of emotion at the thought of what lay ahead for him, and found her looking beautiful, strange, and thrilling to his troubled eyes, and taken her suddenly in his arms, charming her into his own illusion of love?

Or had it been gentle and certain all the time, – an idyll?

'My dear, you know I shall never love anyone but you.'

'Nor I anyone but you.'

'Then let's marry before I go.'

'Oh yes, – at once.'

So they married, with all the others gentle and certain, and acquiescent as a matter of course, saying, whatever their secret thoughts: 'Ah well, it had to be.'

They would spend their few days contentedly together, saying quietly: 'If anything should happen we shall have had this happiness at least:' their few nights ...

When people married they slept in the same room, perhaps in the same bed: they wanted to. Mariella and Charlie would sleep together: that would be the only change for them who had lived in the same house since childhood and knew all about each other. Why had they wanted to make that change – what had impelled them to seek from each other another intimacy? Charlie's beauty belonged to someone now: Mariella of all people had claims upon it. She might have a baby, and Charlie would be its father ...

It was all so queer and unhappy, so like the dreams from whose improbabilities she woke in heaviness of spirit, that it was impossible to realize. This thing had happened and she was further than ever from them, perplexed in the outer darkness, unremembered, unwanted, nothing at all. She might hold on all her life but they would never be drawn back to her.

She was certain now that Charlie was going to be killed. There was that in the fact of his marriage, of his leaping to fulfil the instincts of normal man for life which proclaimed more ominously by contrast the something, – the fatal excess – that foredoomed him; which made darker the shadow falling ever upon the bright thing coming to confusion.

There seemed nothing now in life but a waiting for his death.

They came and went in her dreams – some that caused her to wake with the happiness of a bird, thinking for a moment: 'Then he's safe...', others that made her start into bleak consciousness, heavy with the thought that he was even now dead.

There were dreams of Mariella with a child in her arms; of Mariella and Charlie walking silently up and down, up and down the lawn next door, like lovers, their arms about each other, and kissing as they walked. Then Mariella would turn into Judith, and very soon

43

the whole thing would go wrong: Charlie would cease to walk up and down like a lover, and falter and disappear.

She dreamed of standing in the doorway of the old next door school-room looking out into the hall. Between the inner glass doors and the outer white-painted wooden ones, in the little passage where tubs of hydrangeas and red and white lilies stood upon a mosaic floor, Mariella was talking to one of the boys. She must be saying good-bye to Charlie. The back of her neck was visible, the short curls tilting back as she lifted her head to him. Tall and shadowy, faceless, almost formless, he bent over her, and mysteriously, silently they conferred; and she watched, hidden in the doorway. Suddenly Mariella broke away and ran past through the hall. Her face was white and wild, streaming with tears; she bowed it right forward in her hands and fled up the stairs.

'Oh look! Mariella is crying for the first time in her life . . .'

In the doorway the dark figure still stood. It turned and all at once had a face; and was not Charlie but Julian. She sprang back thinking: 'He mustn't see me here, spying;' and in the agitation of trying to slip away unobserved, the dream broke.

There was a dream of playing some game among them all in the next door garden, and of Charlie stopping suddenly, and crawling away with a weak fumbling step, his hand on his heart.

'He's got a weak heart.'

'Ah, then he won't go to the front.'

'No, he's quite safe.'

She woke up happy.

But sometimes Charlie had been to the front and had come back with that feebleness and sickness upon him. He was going to die of it. He came all pale into the schoolroom and stopped, leaning against the big oak cupboard. He put his hand on his heart, sighing and moaning, looking about him in appalling distress. He said:

'I feel ill. I don't know what it is . . . I'd like to consult my brother.'

He had the face of a stranger, an emaciated and elderly man, – nobody in the least like Charlie; but it was he. He shuffled out again, almost too weak to move, looking for Julian, who would not come.

In horror-struck groups the others watched him. He was dying beyond a doubt. She woke, aghast.

It was at the close of a day in February. Outside, where the gentle dusk glimmered on rain-wet branches, the bird-calls were like sudden pale jets of light, coming achingly to the mind; and all at once the sun, like a bell, struck out a poignant richness, a long dark-golden evening note with tears in it, searching all the land with its fullness and dying slowly into an obscurer twilight. The tree-tops were quiet against the sky. There was no leaf upon them: yet, in that liquid mauve air they stirred in her a sudden soft pang, a beating of the heart, and were, for a moment, the whole of the still hidden spring.

She stood staring through the window; and wars and rumours of wars receded, dwindling into a little shadow beyond the edge of the enchanted world.

She went out into the garden, towards the river. Ah, these shapely boughs, this smell of buds, that tenderly-trailing blue smoke from the rubbish heap, this air like clear greenish water, washing in luminous tides, those few stars cast up and glowing upon translucent strands between the riven pale deeps of clouds! ... Bearing her ecstasy delicately, she came to the bottom of the garden, where the connecting pathway ran towards the house next door. She heard a heavy trailing step she knew, and she waited to bid good night to the old gardener coming home from work.

'Good night, Lacey.'

His mumbling voice said from the shadows:

'Good night, Missie.'

'*Lovely* evening, Lacey.'

'Ah, grand.'

'How does your garden look next door?'

'Ah, a bit forward. There'll be frosts later, you may be bound.'

He sounded tired tonight; he was getting very old. Now for the customary last question.

'When are they coming back, Lacey? It's high time, isn't it?'

He paused; then said:

'You maybe won't have heard, Miss ...'

'What?'

'Master Charlie's been killed ... Yes, Miss. We 'ad word from London this afternoon. Ah, it's cruel. It'll about kill his Granny, that's wot I says first thing – about kill her it will. He was the apple of her eye. That's what we all said – the apple of her eye. She says to me once she says: "Lacey," she says, "Master Charlie'll live 'ere when I'm gorn. I'm keepin' the place on for 'im," she says. "It shall never be let nor nothing. It's 'is, for 'im to bring 'is wife to." Ah, pore little Miss Mariella, pore soul . . .' He broke into feeble weeping. 'Ah, it'll about be the death of 'is Granny. Pore Master Charlie – pore little chap ... everybody's favourite. I remember 'im when 'e was ... Yes, Missie, yes Miss Judith ...'

His voice failed; and with a hand touching his hat over and over again in mechanical apology, confused distress and appeal, he went shuffling away into the shadows.

But of course, of course he was dead; she had expected it all the time. Now it had happened she could turn to other things. She thought: 'It's not bad now; it'll be worse later: then some time it will stop. I must bear it – bear it – bear it!'

That wheezing voice echoed in the solitude and complained: 'Pore Master Charlie, pore little chap,' over and over again through the dark lane among the poplars, above the wall of the garden where the poor little boy had lived long ago.

Had he really lived? Forget him, forget him. He was only a shadow anyway, a romantic illusion, a beautiful plaything of the imagination: nothing of importance. Put him away, be sensible, be indifferent, gather round you once again the imperturbable mysteries of nature, be blinded and made deaf with them for ever. He was much better dead. He was weak and spoilt, selfish; he wouldn't have been any good ... He never could bear blood: he must be thankful to be dead.

Where was he? He seemed to be near, listening to what you had to say of his death.

'Charlie, my darling, if only you'd known how I loved you!'

'I know now. I shall always be watching you.'

Then there is no cause for weeping: he is alive, he is in God's keeping. "Lord into Thy hands I commend his spirit." What did

46

that mean? Pretend, pretend to believe it, cover the blankness with confident assertions.

What had become of that shining head? How did he look now?

At this very moment they were all weeping for Charlie shot dead in France. It was really true: he was dead and in the earth, he had vanished for ever. Her mind wavered and fainted under the burden of their grief: her own she could endure, but theirs was intolerable.

She went back, out of the unregarding night, to the Greek verbs which must be learnt by tomorrow.

A long time after, came the last terrible dream.

They were all bathing together from the next door raft, in a sort of luminous twilight. She saw her own white legs reaching out to touch the water; and she stepped in and swam about. Roddy was there, a dark head bobbing vaguely near her. Sometimes he touched her hand or her shoulder, smiling at her in a friendly way. The others made a dim group on the bank. They were all very happy: she felt ecstasy swelling within her, and passing from her among them all.

Charlie suddenly came into the group. Oh, there was Charlie safe and well and alive after all; and nobody need be unhappy any more!

He did not speak. He emerged swiftly from among them, and they all watched him in silence while he stooped to the dim river and slipped in. He turned his face, his hidden face, downstream, and went floating and swimming gently along. He too was happy.

A dark misty solitude of night and water was ahead of him, and he went into it without pause or backward look, and it folded around him. Horror crept in: for he was disappearing.

A voice broke ringingly, in anguish:

'Come back!'

It shattered itself, aghast, upon emptiness.

Softly he vanished.

She cried aloud and woke into a night streaming, blind with the rain's enormous weeping.

He never came again.

His son was born and his grandmother died; but he was too far, too spent a ghost to raise his head at that.

Part Two

I

THEY were coming back. When she knew this she dared not venture beyond the garden for fear of encountering them unexpectedly. Only the dark was safe; and night after sleepless night she jumped out of the kitchen window into the garden, and crossed the lawn's pattern of long tree-shadows, sharp-cut upon the blank moon-blanched level of the grass. All the colours were drained away; only the white spring flowers in the border shone up with a glimmer as of phosphorus, and the budding tree-tops were picked out, line by cold line, in a thin and silvery wash of light.

She went dancingly down the garden, feeling moon-changed, powerful and elated; and paused at the river's edge. The water shone mildly as it flowed. She scanned it up and down; it was deserted utterly, it was hers alone. She took off her few clothes and stepped in, dipping rapidly; and the water slipped over her breasts, round her shoulders, covering all her body. The chill water wounded her; her breath came shudderingly, in great gasps; but after a moment she started to swim vigorously down-stream. It was exquisite joy to be naked in the water's sharp clasp. In comparison, the happiness of swimming in a bathing suit was vulgar and contemptible. To swim by moonlight alone was a sacred and passionate mystery. The water was in love with her body. She gave herself to it with reluctance and it embraced her bitterly. She endured it, soon she desired it; she was in love with it. Gradually its harshness was appeased, and it held her and caressed her gently in her motion.

Soon next door loomed lightless among its trees. If they were there, they were all sleeping. No eyes would be staring in the darkness, gazing

48

at the enchanted water, wondering at the dark object moving upon its surface.

But no, they had not come yet: the moon came from behind a cloud and illumined the face of the great house; and it was grief-stricken as ever, bowed down with the burden of its emptiness. She turned back and swam home.

The night of full moon came, warm and starry. As she swam towards the willows at the far edge of the next-door garden, – her usual goal – she saw lights in the windows. The long house spread itself peacefully under the moon, throwing out its muffled warmth of lamplight like a quiet smile.

So they had come.

Somebody might be in the garden, – on the river even. She clung close under the bank, by a willow stump, not daring to move, feeling her strength ebb from her.

Then all at once their forms, their voices were near her. Somebody started to play a nocturne of Fauré: Julian. Before her she saw someone tall, in a pale frock, walking along the lawn: Mariella. A moment after a man's figure came from the shadows and joined hers. Which was he? The twin glow of their cigarettes went ahead of them as they paced slowly, arm in arm, across the lawn, just as Charlie and Mariella had often paced in the dreams.

They were so near they must in a moment look down and see her; but they passed on a few steps and then paused, looking out over the river, and up at the resplendent moon. The piano stopped, and soon another figure came and joined them. They were three tall shadows: their faces were indistinguishable.

'Hullo,' said the small clear unchanged voice of Mariella, 'I can't understand your music, Julian. Nor can Martin, can you Martin?'

'Well, it's so damned dull. No tune in it.'

Julian's brief laugh came for answer.

It was like all the dreams to listen to these voices dropping, muted but distinct, from invisible lips close to you in the dark, saying trivial things that seemed important because of the strangeness and surprise of the occasion.

'Why don't you,' said Martin, 'play nice simple wholesome things that we can have on the brain and hum and whistle all day?'

'I'm not simple and wholesome enough to do them justice. I leave them to your masterly right index, Martin.'

'Martin's the world's finest one-finger man, aren't you?' from Mariella, teasing, affectionate.

'Where's Roddy?'

'He went off alone in the canoe.'

'How romantic,' said Mariella.

There was a groan.

'Mariella, why will you –' ·

'What?'

'Quack,' said Julian. 'You *must think* before you speak.'

She laughed.

'Good night,' she said. 'I'm going to bed. When you come upstairs mind and be quiet past the nursery. Remember it's not *your* nursery but Peter's now. Nannie'll warm your jacket if you wake him again, Martin.'

Her cigarette end hit the water a few inches from Judith. Her whitish form grew dim and was gone.

'What a night!' said Julian, after a silence. 'The moon is a most theatrical designer.'

The two strolled on, – none too soon, for the water was glacial to her cramped body, her fingers were rigid upon the willow-roots, and her teeth were rattling in her head.

She heard from Martin:

'When I was in Paris with Roddy –'

And then after a long pause, Julian's voice suddenly raised: 'But what if you bored *yourself* . . . day after day . . . to myself: *Christ!* You *bloody* bore . . .'

The voices sank into confusion and ceased; but in the ensuing silence they seemed to follow her and repeat themselves, charged with the portentous significance of all overheard fragments of speech; so that she felt herself guiltily possessed of the secrets of their hearts.

The moon shone full on the garden bank when she lifted herself out, exhausted, and lay down on the grass.

Around her the shadows stood still. Her body in the moonlight was transfigured into lines of such mysterious purity that it seemed composed less of flesh than of light. She thought: "Even if they had seen me they wouldn't have thought me real." ... Martin would have been astonished if not shocked; he would have turned politely away, but Julian would have appraised her curves, critically and with interest. And Roddy, – Roddy was so long ago he was incalculable. But if that someone dark and curious, with Roddy's face, cherished for years in the part of you which perceived without eyes and knew without reason, – if he had seen, he would have watched closely, and then withdrawn himself from the seduction, from the inconvenience of his own pang; and watched from afar, in silence.

'Oh Roddy, when will you come and reveal yourself?'

The swim home had warmed her, but now, in spite of excited pulses, she felt the cold beginning to strike deeply. She got up and stood still a moment: soon she must hide her silver-white body in the cloak, and then it would cease to be a miracle.

As she stooped for the garment, she heard the long soft ripple and splash of a paddle; a canoe stole into view, floating down full in the middle of the stream. She gathered her dark cape round her and stepped back into the shadows, and as she watched the solitary figure in the stern she forgot to breathe.

'Turn! Oh turn!' she sent after him silently.

But if he did she would dissolve, be swallowed up ...

He did not turn his head; and she watched him go on, past the next-door garden and still onward; – going on all night perhaps ...

If only he had seen her he would have beckoned to her.

'Judith, come with me.'

'I will.'

And all night they would have floated on together.

Someday it would happen: it must. She had always known that the play of Roddy must be written and that she must act in it to the end – the happy end.

'Roddy, I am going to love you.'

The diminishing, unresponsive blot which was he passed out of sight.

Half way back to the house she stopped suddenly, overcome with bewilderment; for that had been Roddy's self, not his shadow made by the imagination. The solitudes of the darkness now held their very

51

forms, were populated with their voices where for so long only
imagined shapes had hovered in the emptiness ... They had slipped
back in that lucid, credulous life between waking and sleep out of
which you start to ponder whether the dream was after all reality
– or whether reality be nothing but a dream.

2

Next day, with unreal ease, she met Mariella in the village. She
came out of the chemist's shop, and they were face to face. There
she was, tall and erect, with her dazed green-blue crystal eyes looking
without shadow or stain upon the world from between dark lashes;
her eyes, that knew neither good nor evil, – the icy eyes of an angel
or a devil. Under her black hat her short hair curled outwards, her
pale smooth face preserved its childish oval, her lips just closed in
their soft faint-coloured bow. The mask was still there, more exquisite
than of old; yet when she smiled in greeting, something strange looked
out for a moment, as if her face in one of its rare breakings-up had
been a little wounded, and still retained the slightest, disturbed
expression.

She seemed pleased.

'Judith! ... isn't it?'

'Mariella!'

'Then you *are* still here. We wondered.'

'Yes. Still here.'

She seemed at a loss for what to say, and looked away, shy and
ill at ease, her eyes glancing about, trying to hide.

'We – we were wondering about you and we thought you must
be away. We remembered you were brainy and Julian said you told
him you were going to college or somewhere, so we thought p'raps
that's where you were. We thought you must be dreadfully frightening
and learned by now. Aren't you?'

'Oh, no!'

What reply was possible to such silliness?

'You were always doing lessons,' she said in a puzzled voice. Then with a smile: 'Do you remember Miss Pim?'

'Yes. Her false teeth.'

'Her *smell*.' She wrinkled her small nose. 'I used to sit and get whiffs of her, and think of tortures for her. No wonder I was backward.' She gave her little giggle and added nervously again: 'Look here, when will you come and see us? We'd like it. This afternoon?'

'Oh Mariella, I'd love to.'

'They're all there. D'you remember everyone? Julian was demobilized a little while ago. He's going back to Oxford in the autumn.'

'And Martin and Roddy?'

'Yes, they're both there. Roddy's just back from Paris. He's supposed to be studying drawing there. Martin ought to be at Cambridge, but he's had appendicitis rather badly so he's missing the term.'

'Are you glad to be back here?'

'Oh yes, we all like it awfully. And it seems to suit the infant.'

'That's good.'

There was a pause. She had thrown off her last remark with careless haste, defying you not to know about the infant; and her eyes had escaped again, as if in dread. In the pause the gulf of things never to be said yawned for a moment beneath their feet; and it was clear that Mariella at least would never breathe her husband's name.

'I – I was just buying some things for him,' she said. 'Some things Nanny wanted. But you can't get much here.' ... Her voice trailed off nervously. Then:

'This afternoon,' she said. 'Good-bye till then. Don't come too early because the boys are always dreadfully lazy after lunch.'

She smiled and went on.

3

At five o'clock Judith surprised the parlourmaid by taking off her hat in the hall, wiped her perspiring hands and announced herself.

At the threshold of the sitting room she paused and gasped. The room, magnified by fear, seemed full of giants in grey flannels. Mariella detached herself from a vast crowd and floated towards her.

'Hullo!' she said. 'Do you want tea? I forgot about it. We never have tea. I needn't introduce, need I? You know everyone.' She put a light hand for a moment on Judith's arm, and the room began to sink and settle; but the faces of the boys-next-door were nothing but a blur before her eyes as she shook hands.

'D'you remember which is which?' said Mariella.

Now she would have to look up and answer, control this trembling, arrest this devouring blush.

'Of course I do.'

She lifted her eyes, and saw them standing before her, smiling a trifle self-consciously. That gave her courage to smile back.

'You're Martin – you're Roddy – you're –' she hesitated. Julian stood aloof, looking unyouthful and haughty. She finished lamely – 'Mr F-Fyfe.'

There was a roar of laughter, a chorus of teasing voices to which, plunged once more in a welter of blushes and confusion, she could pay no heed.

'I thought you mightn't like – might think me – I didn't know if – you looked as if you –' she stammered.

'I'm sorry, I'm sure, that you should feel the need of any such formality,' said Julian stiffly. He too was blushing.

'It was only his shyness,' mocked a voice.

Judith thought: 'After all, he was always the friendly one.' That he too should be shy restored her self-confidence, and she said looking full at him and smiling:

'I'm sorry. Julian then.'

'That's better,' he said, still stiffly; but he smiled.

Their faces had become clear to her now; but there was still a point of trouble and strangeness in the room, – the queer-looking sallow young man Roddy. Her eyes fluttered over him and went on to Martin. He smiled at her, and she took a step nearer to him.

'Are you at Cambridge?' she said.

'I am.'

'That's where I'm going.'

'Are you really?'

'For what purpose?' said Roddy softly.

'Well, I want to learn everything about literature – English literature anyway, from the very beginning,' she said earnestly.

'That's precisely what Martin's aiming at. Isn't it, Martin, you bookworm?'

'I don't get on much,' said Martin with a swift confiding smile. 'I'm such an idle devil. And so slow.'

She pondered.

'I don't think I'm particularly clever,' she said. 'Do you suppose most girls who go to College are?'

'Martin and I think they must be,' said Roddy, twinkling. 'They look it, I will say.'

'I saw some when I went for my examination. They were very plain.' There was laughter; and she added in strict fairness: 'There were two pretty ones, – two or three.'

'Then you intend to become a young woman with *really* intellectual interests?' said Roddy.

'Well, yes. I think so.'

'That's rather serious.'

She became suddenly aware that they were all laughing at her and stopped, overcome with shame and dismay.

'Never mind.' Roddy was twinkling at her with irresistible gaiety, and his voice was full of caressing inflections. 'Martin will be delighted to see you. But don't go to Newnham or Girton. Awful places – Martin is terrified of them. Go to Trinity. He'll chaperone you.'

'Oh give over, Roddy,' said Martin, indulgently smiling. 'You're too funny.'

'I hope your appendicitis is better?' asked Judith politely.

'Much better, thank you.' He made a little bow.

Nobody had anything more to say. They were not very good hosts. They stood around, making no effort, idly fingering and dropping the tags of conversation she offered them, as if she were the hostess and they most difficult guests. As in the old days, they formed their oppressive self-sufficient circle of blood-intimacy with its core of indifference if not hostility to the stranger. Charlie was dead, but now when they were all gathered together she felt him weighing, drawing them further aloof; and she wished miserably that she had not come.

They were all casually engaged by themselves. Roddy was cleaning his pipe, Martin and Mariella playing with a spaniel puppy. It floundered on to Martin's lap, and a moment after:

'Oh again!' came Mariella's clear little pipe. 'What an uncontrolled chap he is! I'm sorry, Martin.'

'It'll dry,' said Martin equably surveying his trousers. 'It's nothing.'

Julian had sat down to the piano and was strumming *pianissimo*. Roddy took up the tune and whistled it.

'What shall we do?' said Mariella. She went on rolling the puppy.

Julian turned round in his playing and looked at Judith. Gratefully she went over and stood beside him. By the piano, watching Julian's hands, she was isolated with him and need not be afraid.

'Go on playing. Something of your own.'

He shook his head and said:

'Oh, that's all gone.'

What lines, what harshness the war had given his always furrowed face!

'But it'll come back.'

'No. It was a feeble spark; and the God of battle has seen fit to snuff it. The war made some chaps poets – of sorts; but I never heard of it making anyone a musician.'

'Well, you can still play.'

'Oh, I strum. I strum.' He sounded weary and disgusted. Was he saying to himself: '*Christ!* You *bloody* bore?'

'I'd always feel –' she struggled '– compensated if I could strum as you do. Ever since I was little I've envied you to distraction.'

He cheered up a little and smiled, looking interested in the old way.

'Play what you were playing last night.'

'How do you know what I was playing last night?'

'I was on the river and I heard you.'

'Did you?' He was flattered. It touched his imagination to think of himself playing out into the night to invisible listeners.

'All alone, were you?' He looked her over with alert interest.

'Oh yes. I said to myself: that must be Mr Fyfe playing.'

He laughed.

'You know, you were monstrous.'

'Not at all. It was you. You defied me to pretend I'd ever known you.'

'Nonsense. I was looking forward to you. Last time was – When? Centuries ago.'

'Yes. That skating time.'

'Lord yes. Another world.'

Abruptly he stopped his soft playing; and Charlie came pressing upon them, making himself remembered above all else on that day.

'Why stuff indoors?' said Mariella. 'Come out, Judith.'

She followed Mariella almost light-heartedly. After all, she was the sort of girl who could talk to people, even amuse them. She had proved it with Julian; and success with the others might reasonably be expected to follow.

A child was playing on a rug under the cedar tree, and his nurse sat sewing beside him. Judith recognized her as a figure out of the old days, a dragon called Pinkie, Mariella's nurse who had become her maid. Wrinkled, stern, with the fresh cheeks and clear innocent expression of an old nurse, she sat guarding Mariella's son.

'May I please take him, Pinkie?' said Mariella. 'Pinkie won't let me touch him as a rule.'

'You're so careless,' she said severely; then recognized Judith and beamed.

Mariella lifted the child easily and carried him under one arm to where the group of young men had formed by the river's edge.

Judith watched him with a painful interest and wonder. Here in front of her was Charlie's child: she must believe it.

He was a tall child of slight build and oddly mature looks for his two years. He had frail-looking temples and a neck far too slender, it seemed, to support the large head covered with a shock of fine straight brown hair, he had Mariella's dark lashes framing brilliant

57

deep-set eyes, and nothing else of his parents save his pallor and a certain fine-boned distinction which no Fyfe could lack.

The circle was a barren thing; it could not stretch to enclose new life. Mariella's child was outside and irrelevant. Sometimes a cousin put out a large hand to steady him, or whistled to him or made a grimace, squeaked his teddy-bear or shouted at him encouragingly when he fell down. They looked at him with tolerant amused faces like big dogs, mildly gratified when he paused, steadying himself for a moment with a hand on their knees; but they soon forgot about him. Julian alone appeared to have an interest in him: he watched him; and Mariella herself now and then for a moment watched Julian watching him.

It was absurd, incongruous, incredible that this should belong to Mariella, should have been begotten by Charlie, carried in her body for nine months, as any woman carries her child, born of her in the ordinary way with agony and joy, growing up to love and be loved by her, and to call her mother.

But anybody could have a child; even mysterious childish widows like Mariella, tragic dead young husbands like Charlie; the simple proof was there before her eyes. Yet Mariella was such a childless person by nature. It was as if her body had played a trick on her and conceived; but to the creature it had brought forth her unmaternal spirit bore no relationship. So it seemed; but you could never tell with Mariella.

'Come here,' said Judith, and held out her hand.

He stared, then edged away nervously.

'Do you like children?' asked Mariella politely.

'I love them,' said Judith, and then blushed, detecting a fatuous fervour in her voice. But, thank heaven, Roddy had strolled away with Martin and was out of hearing.

'Do you?' Mariella glanced at her and seemed to find nothing more to say. She pulled the puppy to her.

'Good chap, go and play with Peter. Go on.'

'Then Peter is his name.'

'*Michael* Peter,' emphasized Julian mockingly. 'Mariella had the highest motives; but I fear she has done for him. Michael alone or Peter alone he *might* have stood up against – but the combination!

I tremble for his adolescence. However he ought to have a spurious charm, at any rate until he leaves the university. The only hope is that he himself may find the double burden excessive, and cancel himself out to a healthy James or Henry. We could do with a Henry or so in our family. Perhaps after all we should commend your far-sightedness, Mariella?'

'I don't know what you're talking about,' she said in her little cheerful voice. 'I think Michael Peter is a very nice name. And he's quite a nice boy, isn't he?'

He was running up and down the lawn with the puppy in pursuit, pawing at him, nipping his calves, tripping him up. At first he bore it equably, but after a while stopped in distress, pushing at the dog with impotent delicate hands, nervously exclaiming and as if expostulating with him in a language of his own, but not once looking towards any of them for assistance. The puppy crouched before him, and all at once let out a sharp yelp of excitement. He put his hands up to his ears. His lip shook.

'Damn that puppy!' said Julian furiously. He strode over to his nephew and lifted him in his arms.

'The boy's tired, Mariella, and you know it, and there you sit, calmly, *calmly*, – and let that damn fool noisy puppy bully him and pester him and smash his nerves . . .'

He was white. He stared with naked antagonism at Mariella, and the air seemed to quiver and grow taut between them. She got up swiftly to catch the puppy and touched her son's head in passing.

'Poor Peter-boy,' she said quietly. 'Silly boy! It's all right.'

'I must go,' murmured Judith.

It was unbearable. She must slip away and hide from the shame and shock of her own perception of the suppressed hysteria.

'Must you go?' Mariella smiled at her with a sort of sweet blankness 'Well – you must come again soon. Come often.'

'I'll see you to the door,' said Julian. 'I'm taking the boy in.'

Without another word or look Mariella went away; and he marched off into the house, carrying the child; and Judith followed him, sick at heart.

Everything had gone wrong. Martin and Roddy had not returned and she dared not seek them to say good night. Alas, they would not

59

care whether she did so or not since they had not been sufficiently interested in her to stay beside her. Even Martin did not want her, preferred Roddy. She had hoped to gain assurance enough to look at Roddy, once, calmly, and see him as he was; but in the few glances they had exchanged she had seen nothing but an unreality so poignant, so burning that it blurred her whole mind and forced her eyes to escape, helpless. Tonight when she was in bed they would all come before her, haunting and tormenting, trebly indifferent and unpossessed now that this longed-for meeting was accomplished, a bitter and fruitless fact. Imagination at least had been fecund, it had fed itself: – but the reality was as sterile as stone. What might she have done, she wondered, that she had not done, how should she have looked in order to please them? Was it her clothes or her looks or her idiotic seriousness about College that had condemned her to them? Bleakly pondering, she followed Julian into the sitting room.

He sat down at the piano with the boy on his knee, and began softly playing. Judith stood beside him.

After a little the child flung his head back against Julian's shoulder, raptly listening. When he did this Julian's face smoothed itself out and all but smiled. He continued to play, then stopped and said:

'Sit down. You needn't go yet,' – and continued his quiet music.

To free his arms she gently took the child from him and set him on her own lap, where he sat motionless and as if unconscious of the change.

Gradually as she watched the crooked fingers sliding along the keys from chord to chord, and saw around her the familiar room, the past stole over her. He was the boy Julian and she the half-dreaming privileged listener; and as if there had been no gap in their knowledge of each other they sat side by side in unselfconscious intimacy. What had there been to fear? She saw now that she would always be able to pick him up just where she had left him, and find him unchanged to her; she could say anything to him without danger of mockery or rebuff. But he had always been the easiest: the sense of blood-relationship was tempered in him by his critical intelligence; and he was always prepared at least to sharpen his wits against the stranger, if not to befriend him.

He paused and she said:

'Nothing has changed here. I remember every single thing in the room and it's all the same, – even to the inkstains on those boards. It's like a dream to be back here talking to you – one of those dreams of remembered places where everything is so familiar it seems ominous. I've often had a dream like this –'

She stopped, wishing her last words unsaid; but he took her remark to be general and nodded, and leaned forward to look at Peter, lying wan and sleepy in her lap. He was very tired; but not fretful: only silent and languid. Julian touched his cheek.

'And is Peter part of the dream too?' he asked softly.

'Yes. Isn't he?'

He was the passive, waiting core of the ominousness, the unexpected thing you shrank from yet knew you had to come back to find. In the dream, it was quite natural to sit there with Julian, holding Charlie's child.

'Isn't it strange,' he said musingly, 'that this is the only proof – the *only* proof that Charlie ever lived? A child! Not another whisper from him ... I haven't even a letter. I suppose *she* has.' An utter misery showed for a moment in his face, and he paused before adding: 'And no portrait. Do you remember him?'

'Of course.' Her throat ached with tears. 'He was the most beautiful person –'

'Yes he was. A *spring* of beauty. He didn't care about that, you know, in spite of what people said. His physical brilliance somehow obscured his character, I think, made it difficult to judge. But he had a very simple heart.'

Was it true? Who had ever known Charlie's heart? Was not Julian speaking as it were in epitaphs, as if his brother had become unreal to him, – a symbol for grief, – the individual ghost forgotten? Perhaps Mariella alone of all people had known his heart – strange thought! – and still had him quick within her; but she would never tell.

'It's not often I speak of him to anyone,' said Julian; and his usually narrow swift-glancing eyes suddenly opened wide and held hers as if he had some unendurable thought. They were pits of misery. What was he remembering?

After a long silence he took the boy on his lap again and said softly:

'Peter shall play.'

Peter put out both his hands, and carefully, delicately dropped them on the keys, listening and smiling.

'Is he musical?'

Julian nodded.

'Oh yes. He's that — more or less. I seem to detect all the symptoms.'

He looked down at the leaning head on his shoulder with a sort of harsh tenderness; and after a while he spoke again as if out of a deep musing.

'What, one asks oneself, is she going to do about him?'

'Mariella?'

'Yes.'

'Well — it's more or less mechanical, with a boy, isn't it? School and university, — and in his case, musical instruments?'

'How *wretched* he's going to be,' he said fiercely. 'Can't you *see*?'

'She wouldn't let him be wretched,' she said, startled.

'She? — she won't know it! And if she did, she'd be helpless.'

'Well, he's got you.'

'Me!' He gave his bark of laughter.

'I mean — you like him,' she ventured timidly.

'I can't stand brats. And they can't stand me.'

'I'm not talking about brats. I'm talking about Peter. I thought you liked him.'

He laughed.

'You look so shocked. Do *you* like brats then?'

'Yes.'

'Hmm - Well, I dare say Mariella says the same. In fact, I've heard her. She's very correct, poor darling, in all her little contributions.' He looked at the clock. 'It's time I took him up. Wait for me.'

When he came back he laughed again.

'You still look shocked. I'm not a nice man, am I?'

'I'm not thinking about you.'

After a pause he said:

'It's all right, Judy. You're right. I do like him. But because I'm bound to feel, must I refuse to think?'

'Think what?'

'That he ought never to have been born.'

'Oh!' she blushed, horrified.

He flung at her:

'What do you wish for the people you love? Life?'

'Of course. Don't you?' She was confused, out of her depth.

'No – God, no!'

'Then what?'

'Unconsciousness. Heavenly, *heavenly* annihilation.'

'Then why don't you kill him?' She was shocked at the sound of her own words.

'Because I don't love him enough.' He laughed. 'Luckily I don't love anyone enough – never shall. Not even myself.' He turned to the window and said, speaking low, with strained composure: 'Sometimes – in moments of clear vision – I see it all, the whole futile sickening farce. But it gets obscured. So my friends are safe. Besides, I'm so damned emotional: if they implored me to save them I shouldn't have the heart to argue how much wiser they'd be to die.'

She wondered with alarm if he were mad and sat silent, waiting in vain for an intelligent counter-argument to present itself. Finally she stammered:

'But it's not a futile sickening farce to normal people.'

'Oh, normal people! they're the whole trouble. They don't *think*. They don't see that you can't miss anything of which you've never been conscious. All the things for which they value life – their food, their loves and lusts and little schemes and athletic exercises, all the little excitements – what are they but a desperate questioning: "What shall I do to be happy, to fill up the emptiness, leaven the dreariness? How can I best cheat myself and God?" And, strange to say, they don't think what a lot of trouble would have been saved if they'd never been – never had to go hunting for their pleasures or flying from their pains. A trivial agitation that should never have begun; and back into nothing again. How silly! ... As you may have guessed, I am not altogether convinced of the One Increasing Purpose. I have the misfortune to be doubtful of the objective value of life, and especially of its pains. Neither do my own griefs either interest or purify me. So you see –'

He turned from the window and smiled at her.

63

'Yes, even I have my compensations: music, food, beautiful people, conversation – or should I say monologue? – especially this sort of bogus philosophy to which you have been so patiently listening. Do you agree with me, by the way?'

'No. Do you?'

He laughed and shrugged.

'Still,' she added, 'it's a point of view. I'll think about it. I can't think quickly. But oh! –' She stopped.

'What?'

'I'm so thankful I've been born.' She blushed. 'Even if I *knew* you were right I wouldn't feel it.'

'Ah, you've never bored yourself. Perhaps you never will. I hope and believe it's unlikely.'

She looked at him with distress. Poor Julian! He had to be theatrical, but his unhappiness was sincere enough. His jesting was so humourless, so affected that it crushed the spirit; and all his talking seemed less a normal exercise than a forced hysterical activity assumed to ease sharp wretchedness. It was not fair to judge and dislike him: he was a sick man.

He sat down again at the piano, and she rose on an impulse and went and stood beside him.

'Some chaps dance,' he said. 'They haven't stopped dancing since they've been back. I play –' He plunged into a medley of ragtime – 'and play – and play – and play. Syncopation – gets you – right on the nerves – like cocaine – No wonder it's popular.'

'Do you like it?'

'Intellectually,' he said, 'I adore it. It's *so* clever.'

He played on loudly, rapidly, with pyrotechnical brilliance, then stopped. 'My passions, however, are too debile to be stirred.'

He flung round on the piano stool and dropped his face into his hands, rubbing his eyes wearily.

'Julian – I wish you weren't – I wish you could –'

He looked up, startled, saw her expression, looked quickly away again and gave an embarrassed laugh like a boy.

'It's all right,' he said. 'You needn't take any notice of me. I'm being a bore. I'm sorry.' The last words were faintly husky.

'Oh, you're *not* a bore, you're not! Only – *don't* be so miserable.'

In the awkward silence that followed she said:

'I must go.'

'No, you're not to go,' he said gently. 'Stay and talk to me.' He paused. 'The trouble is, I can't sleep, you know, and it makes me a bit jumpy. I don't like my thoughts, and they *will* they *will* be thought about. But I shall get better in time.'

'Poor Julian!'

He allowed his face to relax, and his manner was suddenly quiet and simple, almost happy: the unexpected sympathy had made him cheerful.

'You mustn't go, Judith, you must stay to supper.'

'I can't. What will Mariella say?'

'Mariella doesn't say. Whether she *thinks* is the problem, – or even *feels*. Is she a *very* remarkable person? Or is it *simply* arrested development?'

'No. I don't think so.'

'Not?'

She smiled to herself, struck with a fancy.

'Perhaps she's bewitched, Julian.'

As she said it she grew suddenly thoughtful; for it had flashed upon her that perhaps that was the explanation of Roddy; perhaps he was the same, and in that case it was not use – he would never ...

'Bewitched. I never thought of that.' He mused, pleased with the idea. 'You know it must mean something, that nobody's *ever* suggested giving her a *petit nom*, or curtailing the mouthful; she's always been Mariella.'

He began humming a little tune in his contentment. Quickly she said:

'Just to go back to Peter. You don't mean it, do you? Why should he be wretched? Think of the things you can teach him. You know you'll love that.'

He looked a trifle dashed; but after a moment his face cleared again, and his eyes smiled kindly at her.

'Don't worry. At all events, I'll see he's not ill-treated – except in my own way. That is, if she'll let me. She will. She's very good-tempered, I must say. She's never allowed me to quarrel with her. She well might have.'

He looked like brooding again; but seeing her gazing at him anxiously, added:

'It's odd how natural it seems to be talking to you alone like this. You haven't changed a bit. I always remember you listening so solemnly and staring at me. I'm so glad I've found you again. I could always talk to you.'

'At me,' she corrected.

He made a face at her, but looked cheerful. She had always known how near the edge to venture without upsetting him. He hummed his little tune again, then played it on the piano.

'I think I made that up ... It's rather a nice little tune. Perhaps I'll take up my music seriously again.'

'Oh, you must, Julian. It is so well worth it: such a special talent.'

He looked at her with sudden attention.

'How old are you Judith?'

'Seventeen. Nearly eighteen.'

He studied her.

'You must put your hair up.'

'Must I?'

'Yes, because then you'll be beautiful.'

She was still speechless when Mariella, Martin, two Great Danes and the puppy came in.

*

'Hullo!' said Mariella. 'Still here?'

'I'm afraid so. But I'm just going.'

'She's not. She's staying to supper,' said Julian.

'Oh good,' said Martin surprisingly; and his shy red face smiled at her.

'Of course you must,' said Mariella cheerfully. 'We're just going to eat now. Where's Roddy?'

'He stayed down at the boat house. He said he'd come soon.'

'He'd better,' said Julian, and turning to Judith explained politely: 'What with poor Martin having to build himself up so, experience has proved it's wiser to be punctual.'

'I'll go and fetch him,' said Judith, to her own surprise.

She left them amicably wrestling, and escaped light-heartedly into the garden. The cool air refreshed her brain, shaken and excited from its contact with Julian; and she walked slowly to the boat house by the shrubbery path, sniffing as she went at wild cherry, japonica, almond and plum. It was joy to look for and recognize afresh the beauties of the garden; its unforgotten corners, – places of childish enchantment. Somewhere near, under the laurel, was the rabbit's grave. She remembered that evening, how she had been shaken with revelation. This was just such another mysterious and poignant fall of the light: anything might happen. Her senses were so overstrung that the slightest physical impression hit her sharply, with a shock.

There on the raft was the curious young man Roddy. He raised his head from the examination of an old red-painted canoe, and smiled when he saw her.

'I'm sent to say supper's ready.'

'Thank you very much. I'll come.'

'I'm staying to supper.' She smiled radiantly at him, sure of herself and full of an immense amusement.

'I'm delighted.'

His golden-brown eyes sent her their clear and shallow light.

'What are you doing?'

'Seeing if this old canoe is sea-worthy. You see, there's a leak, but I don't *think* it's anything much. I'll leave her in the water over-night. I want to rig her up with a sail.' He stroked the canoe lovingly.

'You like going in boats, don't you?'

'I suppose I do rather.'

'I like it too. Especially at night.'

But he would not give himself away. She saw him slipping down the stream, alone in his canoe, the night before, but she was not to know it, she could not say: 'I saw you.'

He bent over his canoe, fingering the wood, then straightened himself and stood looking down the long willow-bordered stretch of water. The sun had gone out of it and it was a quiet grey limpid solitude. A white owl flew over, swooping suddenly low.

'There he goes,' said Roddy softly. 'He goes every evening.'

'Yes I know.'

She smiled still in her immense mysterious amusement. She saw him look up at the poplar from whence the owl had come, and as he did so his whole image was flung imperishably on her mind. She saw the portrait of a young man, with features a trifle blurred and indeterminate, as if he had just waked up; the dark hair faintly ruffled and shining, the expression secret-looking, with something proud and sensual and cynical, far older than his years, in the short full curve of his lips and the heaviness of his under-lids. She saw all the strange blend of likeness and unlikeness to the boy Roddy which he presented without a clue.

He caught her smile and smiled back, all his odd face breaking up in intimate twinklings, and the mouth parting and going downward in its bitter-sweet way. They smiled into each other's eyes; and all at once the light in his seemed to gather to a point and become fixed, dwelling on her for a moment.

'Well?' he said at last; for they still lingered uncertainly, as if aware of something between them that kept them hesitating, watching, listening subconsciously, each waiting on the other for a decisive action.

He spread out his hands and looked down at them; a nervous gesture and look she remembered with a pang.

'Yes, we must go,' she said softly.

At supper he sat opposite her, and twinkled at her incessantly, as if encouraging her to continue to share with him a secret joke. But, confused amongst them all, she had lost her sense of vast amusement and assurance; she was unhappy because he was a stranger laughing at her and she could not laugh back.

Beside him was the face of Martin, staring solemnly, with absorption, watching her mouth when she spoke, her eyes when she glanced at him.

Thank God the meal was soon over.

A gay clipped exhilarating dance tune sounded from the drawing-room. Roddy had turned on the gramophone. He came and took Mariella without a word and they glided off together. Judith stayed with Julian and Martin in the verandah, looking in at them. She was frightened; she could not dance, so she would be no use to Roddy.

'Do you dance, Julian?'

68

'No. At least only with two people.'

Alas, – wounding reminder of his elegant unknown world where she had no place! . . . She blushed in the dusk.

'Julian's very lordly about his dancing,' said Martin. 'I expect he's rotten really.'

'It may be,' said Julian, stung and irritable. 'It may be that I therefore bestow the burden of my gyrations on the only two creatures of my acquaintance whose rottenness equals mine. It may be that I derive more satisfaction from the idea of this artistic whole of rottenness than from the physical delights of promiscuous contact.'

'It may be,' said Martin pleasantly, unperturbed.

Julian hunched his shoulders and went away, clouded by a dreadful mood.

'Poor old Ju,' said Martin softly.

'Yes, poor thing.' Her voice implied how well she understood, and he looked grateful.

In the drawing-room, Roddy and Mariella moved like a dream, smoothly turning, pausing and swaying, quite silent.

'Well, shall we?' Martin smiled down at her.

Now she must confess.

'I can't Martin, I don't know how. I've never learnt. I haven't ever –' Shame and despair flooded her.

'Oh you'll soon learn,' he said cheerfully. 'Come and try.'

'Oh, I couldn't.'

She glanced at the competent interweaving feet of Mariella and Roddy, at Mariella's slender back pivoting gracefully from the hips, at Roddy's composed dancing-face and shoulders. She could not let them see her stumbling and struggling.

'Well, come and practise in the hall. Here now. Can you hear the music? Follow me. This is a fox-trot. Look, your feet between my feet. Now just go backwards, following my movements. Don't think about it. If you step on my feet it's my fault and *vice versa*. Now – short, *long* short, two short. Don't keep your back so stiff, – quite free and supple but quite upright.'

'Do it by yourself,' said Judith perspiring with anxiety. 'Then I can see.'

He chasséed solemnly round the hall, pausing now and then to show her how he brought his feet together; then, with a firm hand on her shoulder-blades he made her follow him.

'That's good. It's coming. Oh good! Sorry, that was my fault. You've got the trick now.'

All at once the music had got into her limbs; it seemed impossible not to move to it.

'But you can!' said Martin, letting her go and beaming at her in joyful surprise.

'Come back into the drawing-room,' said Judith, exalted.

They went.

'Now,' she said trembling.

Martin put his arm round her and they glided off. It was easier than walking, it was more delicious than swimming or climbing; her body had always known how it was done. Martin looked down at her with eloquent eyes and said:

'You know, you're marvellous. I didn't know anyone could learn so quickly.'

'It's because I've had such a good teacher,' she said sweetly.

They went on dancing, and every now and then she looked up and smiled at him and his eyes shone and smiled in answer, happy because of her pleasure. He really was a dear. In his looks he had improved beyond expectation. He was still a little red, a little coltish and untidy, but his figure was impressive, with powerful heavy shoulders and narrow hips; and the muscles of his thigh and calf bulged beneath his trousers. His head with the brown wings of hair brushed flat and straight on it, was finely set, his eyes were dark and warm, kindly rather than intelligent; his nose was biggish and thick, his mouth long, thin and rather ineffectual, with a faint twitch at one corner, – the corner that lifted first, swiftly, when he smiled his frequent shy smile. His teeth were magnificent; and he smelt a little of Virginian cigarettes.

'You must dance with Roddy,' said Martin. 'He's ever so much better than I am.'

Roddy and Mariella were dancing in the porch now, not speaking or looking about them. The record came to an end, but they went on whirling while Martin sought a new tune and set it going; then they glided forward again.

Roddy had forgotten her: she was not up to his dancing.

At last Mariella stopped and disengaged herself.

'I want to dance with Martin now, she said.

Roddy left her and strolled over to Judith.

'Been giving Martin a dancing-lesson?' he said.

'Goodness no! He's been teaching me. I didn't know how.'

'Oh? – How did you get on?'

'Quite well, thank you. It's easy. I *think* I can dance now.'

'Good!'

It was plain he was not interested; or else was incredulous. He thought she was just a stumbling novice; he was not going to dance with her or even offer to go on teaching her. Roddy would never have bothered to give her hints or be patient while she was awkward. He was so good himself that he could not condescend to incompetence. But Judith, still, though more doubtfully, exalted, said:

'Shall we dance?'

He looked surprised.

'All right. Certainly. Just let me cool down a bit.'

He was not in any hurry. He sat on a table and watched Mariella's neatly moving feet.

'She's good at her stuff,' he said.

'Do you adore dancing?'

'Well, I don't know that I adore it. It's fun once in a way.'

'It seems funny not to be mad about a thing if you can do it so beautifully.'

He looked at her with amusement.

She must remember not to ask Roddy if he adored things. His secret life went on in a place where such states of feeling were unknown.

'Shall we?' he said at last.

She was not going to be able to do it; the rhythm had gone out of her limbs. He was going to be too good for her and she would stumble and he would get disgusted and not dance with her any more . . .

After a few moments of anguish, suddenly she could, after all. Long light movements flowed from her body.

Roddy looked down.

'But you can dance,' he said.

'I told you I could. You didn't believe me.'

71

He laughed.

'You don't mean to tell me you've never danced before?'

'Never.'

'Swear?'

'Cross my heart.'

'But of course,' said Roddy, 'you couldn't help dancing, such a beautiful mover as you.'

He had really said that! She lifted her face and glowed at him: life was too, too rich.

The music came to an end. Roddy stood still with his arm round her waist and called imperiously to Martin for another tune.

'Come on,' he said, and tightened his arm round her. You might almost dare to suppose he was a little, a very little exalted too.

'But you do love it, Roddy!'

He looked down at her and smiled.

'Sometimes.'

'Do you now?'

'Yes.'

'Good!'

She was silenced by happiness.

They were alone now. Martin and Mariella were on the verandah, and she heard Mariella say:

'Darlin' Martin, fetch me my coat.'

'Mariella's very fond of Martin, isn't she?'

'I don't know. I suppose she is. What makes you think so?'

'I heard her call him darling just now.'

He laughed.

'Oh yes. She does that now and again.'

'She doesn't call you darling,' said Judith twinkling.

'No. Nobody ever does.'

'Not anybody, – ever?'

'Not *any*body – *ever*.'

'What a pity! And it *is* so enjoyable to be called Darling.'

'I've no doubt it is. I tell you I've no experience.' He peered into her face, and repeated piteously: 'Nobody *ever* does.'

Judith laughed aloud.

'I will,' she heard her own voice saying.

'You really will?'

She waited.

'Go on,' he urged.

The word would not come.

'Go on, go on!' he shouted triumphantly.

'Oh, be quiet!'

'Please! ...'

'No ...'

She hid her face away from him and blushed. Laughing silently he gathered her up and started whirling, whirling. A deeper dream started. The room was a blur, flying, sinking away; only Roddy's dark red tie and the line of his cheek and chin above it were real.

She laughed and gasped, clinging to him.

'Giddy?'

'Yes. No. I don't know.'

He stopped and looked at her amusedly.

'Oh, I *am*.'

She threw out an arm blindly and he caught it and supported her.

'Come out on the verandah and get sober,' he said.

The spring night greeted them with a chill fragrance. Roddy's eyes were so bright that she could see them shining, brimming with amusement in the dim light.

'What are you looking at, Roddy?'

'You.'

'I can see your eyes. Can you see mine?'

He bent his head over hers.

'Yes, of course. They're like stars. Lovely dark eyes.'

'*Are* they? ... Roddy paying compliments, – how funny! Roddy, I remember you. Do you remember yourself when we were children?'

'Not much. I never remember the past. I suppose I'm not interested enough, – or interesting enough.'

She felt checked, and dared not ask the 'What do you remember about me?' which should have opened the warm little paths of childish reminiscence. Roddy had no desire to recall the uninteresting figures of himself and the little girl Judith: that trifling relationship had been

73

brushed away as soon as it had ceased. She must realize that, for him, no long threads came dragging from the web of the past, tangling the present.

She stared into the dark garden, wondering what safe topic to propose.

'When do you go back to Paris, Roddy?'

'Oh, – soon, I suppose.'

'Do you work very hard there?'

'Terribly hard.'

'Drawing or painting?'

'Some of both. Nothing of either.'

'I suppose you wouldn't show me some of your things?'

'Couldn't. I've nothing here. I'm having a rest.' He twinkled at her.

'What a pity! I should so have loved ... Which are you best at, drawing or painting?'

'Oh, I don't know. Drawing, I think. But I'm not any good. I just waste time.'

'Why do you?'

'Why indeed?'

'How funny! If I could draw I'd draw all day. I'd be so excited at being able to, I'd go on and on. I'd be so horrid and enthusiastic. I wouldn't have any sense of humour about it. You'd think me *nauseating*, wouldn't you?'

He nodded, smiling.

'But I'd *draw*. I'd be the best drawer in the world. Oh, you are lucky! I do envy people with a speciality, and I do love them. Isn't it funny how fingers take naturally to one form of activity and not to another? Mine – mine –' she spread them out and looked at them – 'mine wouldn't draw if I spent all my life trying to make them; but – they know how to touch a piano – only a little of course; but they *understand* that without having it explained. And some fingers can make lovely things with a needle and thread and a bit of stuff. There's another mystery! Then there are the machine makers, and the ones that can use knives like artists to take away bits of people or put bits in, – and the ones that can remove pain just by touching .. Some people *are* their hands, aren't they? They understand

74

with them. But most people have idiot hands, – destroyers. Roddy, why are some of our senses always idiots? All my senses are semi-imbecile, and I'm better off than lots of people, I suppose. Seems to me, what they call the norm is practically idiot, and any departure is just a little more or less so. Yet one has this *idea* of perfection –'

She stopped abruptly. He was not interested, and his face in the wan light was a blank which might be hiding mockery or distrust of a girl who affected vaporous philosophizings, trying, no doubt, to appear clever. She flushed. Such stuff had been her food for years, chewed over secretly, or confided to the one friend, the Roddy of her imagination; and here she was in the foolishness of her elation pouring it out to this unmoved young man who thought – she *must* remember this – that he was meeting her for the first time. It was plain, it must be plain to him, that she was a person with no notion of the rules of behaviour.

'Come back and dance,' suggested Roddy at last.

It was curious how much easier it was to get on with Roddy if he had an arm round you. His mind, the whole of him, came freely to meet you then; there was entire happiness, entire peace and harmony. It was far more difficult to find him on the plane where only minds, not senses, had contact, – the plane on which a Julian, one whose physical touch could never be desirable, was reached without any groping. Roddy put something in the way. He guarded himself almost as if he suspected you of trying to catch him out; or of taking an impertinent interest in him. His mind would be thrilling if you could dig it out: all hidden and withheld things were.

'I don't want ever to stop,' she said suddenly.

'We won't,' he promised and held her closer, as if he were as much caught away and dazed as she.

He bent his head and whispered laughingly:

'Just say it.'

'Say what?'

'That word you like – in your delicious voice – just as a kindness.'

'No, I won't – now.'

'When will you?'

'You are naughty, Roddy ... Perhaps when I know you better.'

'You'll never know me better than you do now '

'Don't say that. Why do you?'

'There's nothing more to know.'

'Oh, if there's nothing more to know, then you are –'

'What?'

'More or less – as far as I can tell –'

'What?'

She whispered:

'A darling.'

'Ah, thank you.' He added rapidly, in the full soft voice of laughter: 'Thank you, darling.'

'Now we've both said it. Aren't we absurd?'

'No, very sensible.'

'Did you like it?'

'I adored it.'

'Roddy, are we flirting?'

'Are we?'

'If we are, it's your fault. You make me feel sort of stimulated. I didn't flirt with Martin.'

'I'm very glad to hear it. Martin wouldn't have liked it at all.'

They laughed and danced on. He held her very close, the cold rim of his ear touching her forehead.

'To think I've never danced before!'

'Why haven't you?'

'Nobody to dance with.'

'Nobody?'

'Nobody at all.'

'Have you been living on your little lone since I went away?'

'Ever since then.'

'Well, now I've come back we'll dance a lot, won't we?'

'Oh yes. But you'll disappear again, I know you will.'

'Not yet. And not for long.'

She could have cried, he was so comforting.

He spun, holding her tightly, stopped, held her a moment more, and let her go as the record came to an end. She watched him as he went, with that secret of idle grace in his movements, to switch off the gramophone. He looked pale and composed as ever, while she was flushed, throbbing and exhausted with excitement. She stood at the open French windows and leaned towards the cool night air; and he found her silent when he came back.

'A penny for them, Judith.'

'I was thinking – what extraordinary things one says. I suppose it's the dancing. It seems so incredibly easy to behave as one naturally wouldn't –'

'I find that myself,' he said solemnly.

'The – the unsuitable things that generally stay inside one's head, – they spring to one's lips, don't they?'

'They do.'

'Values are quite changed. Don't you think so?'

She must make him realize that she was not really a cheap flirtatious creature: re-establish her dignity in his eyes. She had behaved so lightly he might be led to think of her and treat her without respect, and laugh at her behind her back after she had ceased to divert him. It was very worrying.

'Quite, quite changed,' he said.

'Isn't it queer? I suppose – it doesn't do much harm? One oughtn't to think worse of a person for –'

He threw back his head to laugh at his ease, silently, as always, as if his joke were too deep down and individual for audible laughter.

'Are you laughing at me, Roddy?'

'I can't help it. You're so terribly funny. You're the funniest person I've ever met.'

'Why am I?'

'You're so incredibly serious.'

'I'm not – not always.'

'I'm afraid you are. I'm afraid you're terribly introspective.'

'Am I? Is that wrong? Roddy, please don't laugh at me. It leaves me out if you laugh by yourself like that. I could laugh *with* you at anything, if you'd let me –' she pleaded.

'Anything – even yourself?'

She pondered.

'I don't know. Perhaps not. That's a weakness, isn't it?'

'There you go again! Never mind about your weaknesses. I was only teasing you. Let me see you smile.'

To obey him her lips went upwards sorrowfully; but when she saw his laughing, coaxing face, her heart had to lift too.

'Well you're very nice anyway,' he said, 'serious or no. Have you forgiven me?'

'Oh yes. Yes, Roddy.'

As she said it she realized with a passing prophetic sense of helplessness and joy and fear that whatever he did she would always inevitably forgive him. But she must not tell him that, yet.

Martin and Mariella came strolling back from the garden, the spark of their cigarettes going before them. She heard Mariella's little laugh bubbling out contentedly, her childish voice answering his in an easy chatter. Yes, Mariella was happy with Martin. He was polite and kind to her, and she was equal to him without effort. As she came into the light Judith was struck afresh by the lack of all emphasis, the careful absence of any one memorable feature in the memorable whole of her beauty. Her lovely athletic body effaced itself in simple clothes of no particular fashion or cut, subdued in colour, moderately long, moderately low in their necks and short in their sleeves, – negative clothes that nevertheless were distinguished, and said 'Mariella' and nothing else in the world.

It was time to go.

'Oh must you?' said Mariella.

Roddy said not a word. He had detached himself as soon as the others came in, and was idly busy in a corner, tuning a guitar. Either he had not heard or was not interested. It seemed impossible that his face had been off its guard a few minutes ago, warming and lighting in swift response.

Julian lounged in again silently, a book in his hand. He looked tired and fierce, as if daring her to remember his recent lapse into friendliness. The strange disheartening people . . .

She stammered: 'Well, good night everybody. Thank you so much.'

'One of the boys will see you home,' said Mariella dubiously.

'Oh no. It isn't necessary. I'll just climb over the wall if the gate's locked. I shall be quite all right, honestly . . .'

There was no need to protest. They dismissed the matter in silence.

'Well, come in any time,' said Mariella.

But any time was no good. She had dreaded just such a noncommittal invitation. Any time probably meant never. Despondently she looked back to smile her thanks; and as her eyes took in the group of them standing there looking at her, she felt suddenly startled.

But they were all alike!

So strange, so diverse in feature and colour, they yet had grown up with this overpowering likeness; as if one mind had thought them all out and set upon them, in spite of variations, the unmistakable stamp of itself. Alone among all the tall distinguished creatures Roddy made sharp departure, and preserved, though not wholly intact, the profounder individuality of his unimportant features.

4

It was some weeks later. The day had been long and fruitless. She had idled through the hours, playing the piano, reading *Pêcheurs d'Islande* with voluptuous sorrow, doing nothing. A letter from her mother in Paris had arrived in the afternoon. They were not coming home just yet. Father had caught another of his colds and seemed so exhausted by it. He was in bed and she was nursing him, and it had meant cancelling this party, that party. Why should not Judith come out and join them, now that her examinations were over? It would amuse her; and Father would be glad to have her. They would expect her in a few days; she was old enough now to make the journey by herself.

Her heart was heavy. She could not leave the house, the spring garden, this delicious solitude, these torturing and exquisite hopes. How could she drag herself to Paris when she dared not even venture beyond the garden for fear of missing them if they came for her? If she went now, the great opportunity would be gone irrevocably; they would slip from her again just as life was beginning to tremble on the verge of revelation. She must devise an excuse; but it was difficult. She swallowed a few mouthfuls of supper and wandered back into the library.

The last of the sun lay in the great room like blond water, lightly clouded, still, mysterious. The brown and gold and red ranks of the dear books shone mellow through it, all round the room from the floor three quarters way to the ceiling; the Persian rugs, the Greek bronzes on the mantelpiece, the bronze lamps with their red shades, the tapestry curtains, the heavy oak chairs and tables, all the dim richnesses, were lit and caressed by it into a single harmony. The portrait of her father as a dark-eyed, dark-browed young man of romantic beauty was above the level of the sun, staring sombrely down at his possessions. She could sit in this room, especially now with hair brushed smooth and coiled low across the nape, defining the lines of head and neck and the clear curve of the jaw, – she could sit alone here in her wine-red frock and feel part of the room in darkness and richness and simplicity of line; decorating it so naturally that, if he saw, his uncommunicating eyes would surely dwell and approve.

She and the young man of the portrait recognized each other as of the same blood, springing with kindred thoughts and dreams from a common root of being, and with the same physical likeness at the source of their unlikeness which she had noticed in the cousins next-door. She was knit by a heart-pulling bond to the portrait; through it, she knew she loved the elderly man whose silent, occasional presence embarrassed her.

There was sadness in everything, – in the room, in the ringing bird-calls from the garden, in the lit, golden lawn beyond the window, with its single miraculous cherry-tree breaking in immaculate blossom and tossing long foamy sprays against the sky. She was sad to the verge of tears, and yet the sorrow was rich, – a suffocating joy.

The evening held Roddy clasped within its beauty and mystery: he was identified with its secret.

'Roddy, I love you! I've always loved you.'

Oh, the torment of loving!

But soon the way would open without check and lead to the happy ending. Surely it had started to open already.

The pictures came before her.

Roddy playing tennis, – playing a characteristic twisty game that irritated his opponents, and made him laugh to himself as he ran and leapt. His eyes forgot to guard themselves and be secret: they were clear yellow-brown jewels. She was his partner, and with solemn fervour she had tried to play as she had never played before, for his sake, to win his admiration. But he was not the sort of partner who said: 'Well played!' or 'Hard lines'. He watched her strokes and looked amused, but was silent even when she earned him victory after victory

Afterwards she said:

'I do love tennis. Don't you?'

He answered indifferently:

'Sometimes, – when they let me do as I like; when I'm not expected to play what they call properly. One of my lady opponents once told me I played a most unsporting game. "My intelligence, however corrupt, is worth all your muscle" – was what I did not just then think of saying to her. She was in a temper, that lady.'

She smiled at him, thinking how she loved the feel of her own body moving obediently, the satisfaction of achieving a perfect stroke, the look of young bodies in play and in repose, – especially his; and she hazarded:

'I love it just for the movement. I love movement, – the look of people in motion and the thought and feel of my own movements. I suppose I am too solemn over it. I want so much to do it as well as I can. I'm solemn because I'm excited. I sometimes think I would like above all things to be the best dancer in the world, – or the best acrobat; or failing that, to watch dancers and acrobats for ever.'

Looking back on their few but significant conversations, she decided that there was something about him which invited confidences while seeming to repel them. Though his response – if it came at all or came save in silent laughter – was uncoloured by enthusiasm and unsweetened by sympathy, he made her feel that he understood and even pondered in secret over her remarks.

'There are some things I tell you, Roddy, that I tell no one else. They make themselves be told. Often I haven't known they were inside me.' She rehearsed this silently. One day she would say it aloud to him.

Then she had added:

'Do you still caricature, Roddy?'

'Now and then, – when I feel like it.'

'It is funny how a caricature impresses a likeness on you far quicker and more lastingly than a good portrait. Do you remember you once did one of me when we were little and I cried?'

'I'd forgotten that.'

'Do you see everybody with their imperfections exaggerated – always?'

'Only with one eye. That's my defence. The other has so frequently to be shut – or wounded. But there's a great deal of aesthetic pleasure to be had from the contemplation of monsters.'

'I suppose the temptation is to shut the normal one more and more until finally it ceases to work; especially if the other one has a greater facility. And it has, hasn't it, Roddy?'

'Perhaps. You must stay by me and counteract it.'

'Which is it?' she looked at him laughing.

He shut one eye.

'I shut it entirely to look at you,' he said.

Afterwards when she played again, a single with Martin, he lay on the bank, indolent after his burst of energy, watching her long after the others had lost interest and gone indoors. Passing him once, she had closed one eye and looked at him inquiringly; and all his face had broken up in warm delighted twinklings. He did welcome the most trivial jokes from her; and they were always trivial, and not nearly frequent enough.

Next time had been the time of Julian's extremely bad temper. He had played tennis with malice and vicious cuts and nasty exclamations of triumph. Over Roddy's face slid down the mask of deadly obstinacy which was his anger.

He came from the game and flung himself on the bank without a word, while Julian remained on the court, peevishly patting balls about.

'He annoys me,' said Roddy after a bit, watching him under heavy lids. Presently he took a piece of paper from his pocket and worked in silence.

'Roddy, may I see it?'

He made no reply; but after a few more minutes he flung it over to her.

It was a terrible success (Julian had always been the most successful subject); and it was devilish as well as funny.

'Oh Roddy!' She began to giggle.

'Sh! Look out! He's coming back.'

He snatched the paper from her and crushed it up.

'Let me keep it.'

'Well, don't let him see it. He hates it.'

He flung it hurriedly into her lap as Julian came up; and as she stuffed it into her pocket with studied carelessness, his lips suddenly relinquished the last of his obstinacy, and he flashed her a look suffused with laughter and the sense of shared guilt. Surely he had never looked at anyone before with such irresistible intimacy and appeal. The less assured face of the child Roddy peered for a moment in that look; but the dark and laughing fascination was new and belonged to the young man; and she melted inwardly at the remembrance of it.

Then there had been the time Martin and Roddy had come to tea – so exciting a little time that she still dwelt on it with beating heart.

She felt again her delighted astonishment at sight of the pair of them coming up the garden. She had washed her hair and was drying it in the sun when they appeared; it was spread in a mass round her shoulders and down to her waist, and she was brushing the last of the damp out of it.

'Hullo!' said Martin.

'Hullo!'

They came smiling up to her.

'Are you busy?' said Martin.

'No, only washing my hair. Please excuse it.'

'We like it,' said Roddy. He watched her brushing, combing it and shaking it back over her shoulders as if fascinated.

'Are you doing anything this afternoon?' said Martin.

'Oh no!' – eagerly.

'Shall we be in the way?'

'Of course not.'

'Then may we come to tea?'

'Will you really?'

'Julian has got some tiresome people we don't like, so we escaped, and Roddy suggested coming to find you.'

Roddy raised his eyebrows, smiling faintly.

'Well, we both suggested it,' continued Martin with a blush. 'May we really stay?'

Which, oh which of them had suggested it? . . .

'Will you wait here while I go and put my hair right?'

'It's not dry yet,' said Roddy. 'Let me brush it at the back for you.'

She stood still in embarrassed pleasure while he brushed and combed her hair.

'You do it beautifully. You don't pull a bit.'

'I'm a good hair dresser. I brush my mother's when her maid's out.'

'Has she got lovely hair?'

'Goodish. Very long. Not such lumps of it as this though.' He took up a handful and weighed it. 'Extraordinary stuff.'

It was the first time that she had ever heard him mention his mother. Why, Roddy must have a home life, a whole background of influences and associations of which she knew nothing ... She felt startled and anxious; and the old ache at being left out, failing to possess, stirred in her.

She saw him brushing his mother's hair with careful hands. His mother had long dark hair perfumed deliciously. She had a pale society face, and she sat before her brilliantly lit dressing table wearing a rich wrap and pearls, and put red on her lips, and made Roddy fetch and carry for her about the bedroom. They talked and laughed together. She had never heard of Judith.

Judith dismissed the picture.

Roddy went on brushing, while Martin stared and smiled at her. They made a most intimate-looking little group. She thought of herself for a moment as their sister. Roddy would often brush her hair for her if she was his sister, or if ...

'There!' said Roddy. '*Je vous félicite, Mademoiselle.*' He adjusted her tortoiseshell slide and bowed to her with the hairbrush over his heart.

'I love your garden,' said Martin.

She showed them the garden and then the house. They asked questions and admired the furniture and the rare books she picked out for them in the library.

'When Daddy comes back you must meet him,' she said. 'He'd love to show you his books.'

She was sure he would like such appreciative young men.

'I'd like to meet him awfully,' said Martin. 'I've often heard about him.'

She glowed.

'No wonder you're a bookworm, Judy,' said Roddy, searching the shelves with absorbed eyes. 'I'd be myself if I had this always round me.'

He could hardly tear himself away from browsing and gazing.

In the hall hung a water-colour portrait of Judith at the age of six.

'Ah!' said Roddy. 'I remember you like this.'

He looked from her to the portrait, and then at her again, as if remembering and comparing, and dwelling on the face she smilingly lifted to him until she had to drop her eyes.

They had tea in the drawing-room, — exquisite China tea in the precious Nankin cups which always appeared for visitors. Everything in the house was precious and exquisite: she had never realized it before; and she thought:

'Now that they have seen me in my beautiful home, against my own background, the only daughter of such richness, they will think more of me.'

It certainly seemed so. Conversation flowed happily about nothing. She was, for the first time, completely at her ease; and they listened with interest, — even with a sort of deference, as if they thought her rather a special person.

After tea they went down to the river. The westering sun spread on the water as far as eye could see in a full embrace of shining light.

'Let's bathe,' said Martin.

They ran next door for their bathing suits while she undressed in the boat-house. Then they returned and undressed behind the boat-house; and they all plunged into the water together.

Judith and Roddy stood on the raft, watching Martin diving sideways, and backwards and forwards, always perfectly, his magnificent muscle swelling and rippling as he moved. He swam and dived with a faultless ease of technique, as if he could never tire.

But Roddy would not exert himself. After two swift arrow-like dives he stood on the raft looking funny and boyish, with his hair plastered close over his head and his too-slender body shivering slightly. She noticed how delicately he was made in spite of his height. He had the look of a cat, graceful, narrow and lazy; and his skin was almost as smooth as her own.

When she dived he watched her body and all her movements closely; and she wondered whether his artist's eye were detecting the faults and virtues of her form and if she compared at all favourably with his models in Paris.

She swam a little and talked to Martin, and came back to the raft.

'Have you had enough, Roddy?'

'Soon.'

'Do you prefer watching?'

'I always prefer watching.'

It was true. He would watch with deep concentration while others moved and took exercise, as if he were drawing them in his mind or getting them by heart; but his own impulses towards physical activity were rare and of brief duration.

'I like swimming,' said Judith; careful not to say she adored it.

'You do it very nicely.'

'But this is dull compared with swimming at night.'

'Ah!'

'Have you ever done that?'

'No, never.'

'You don't need to wear a bathing-suit then. It's far more delicious with nothing on.'

'I suppose it is.'

'I do it quite often.'

Now she was going to tell him something she had never meant to tell him. She could not stop herself. As if he were expecting it, he turned his face to hers, and waited.

'I saw you once when I was bathing. It was before we met again. You were in a canoe, alone, and I knew it was you. I watched you go past.'

'I know you did.'

'You –'

'I saw you,' he said.

86

She was paralysed; and of the questions which flooded her mind not one could be spoken.

She lifted her eyes and saw his weighing on her, making her answer him, with something heavy and fixed, dazed almost, at the back of their clear shining. She gazed back; and in a moment was lost, sinking in timeless soundless darkness and clinging to his eyes while she drowned.

It was all over in the duration of two or three heavy heart beats: and then they were standing together aimlessly, shivering in wet bathing-suits and Martin came all streaming and fresh from the water and broke in upon them with cheerful upbraidings.

They parted from her with happy thanks and friendly looks, and Roddy said that some day he would come and spend a whole afternoon in the library if he might; and then instead of the casual: 'See you again soon' which she dreaded, they gave her a specific invitation to a picnic in two days' time.

That had been the last time.

It was a day without sun. The muffled light fell all day across the countryside as if through faintly shining bluish glass; and beneath it the spring held itself withdrawn and still, as unchanging as a picture. Around the gentle green of the picnic meadow was the wild and ardent green of the little hedge; and here and there across the hedge, the blackthorn flung great scatters of frail-spun snow. Beyond the meadow the larch copse was lit all over with plumes of green fire; and upon its fringes, pure against the dim purple-brown of its tangled trunks, a stripling tree or so sprinkled its fresh leaves out upon the darkness like a swarm of green moths arrested in flight. Everywhere was the lavish, pouring green, smouldering and weighed-down with the ache of life, and quiet, quiet, turned inward upon itself and consuming its own heart. Everywhere the white blossom, as it rose, freed itself lightly from its roots in earth's pangs of passion and contemplation, and, floating upon the air, kept but one secret, which was beauty, paid no heed, gave no sign.

Roddy lay with his head in the moss, sniffing at primroses, nibbling grasses, teasing Martin under his breath, watching them all with half-closed eyes.

Everyone was quiet and happy; all the peevishness was gone, all the tension smoothed out. The cigarette smoke curled in patterns into the still air; and now and again the spring stirred, shook out a long breath of blossom and leaf and wet earth; and then was tranced again.

They made a wood fire and watched it sink to crumbling feathery ash round a glowing core; and they ate oranges and tomatoes and very young small lettuces stolen from the garden by Martin who was still, so Roddy said, a tiger for raw vegetables. But there were no onions: he declared he had given them up.

Nothing memorable was said or done, yet all seemed significant, and her happiness grew to such a poignant ecstasy that her lips trembled. She rolled over and hid her face in her hands for fear it should betray her by indecent radiance; but nobody noticed. Their eyes looked calm and dreaming: even Mariella's had a less blind stare, a depth of meditation.

If only the moment could stay fixed, if their strange and thoughtful faces could enclose her safely for ever in their trance of contentment, if she could be able to want nothing from them beyond a share of their unimpassioned peace: if only these things could be, they would be best. For a moment they seemed possible; for a moment she achieved a summit and clung briefly to it, tasting the cool taste of no desire. But it would not do: it was the taste of being old and past wanting people, – past wanting Roddy who already tasted so sharply and sweetly that she must have more of him and more of him; and whose presence in the circle made collective indifference a pretence too bleak to strive for.

The sun flooded the meadow all at once in a tide of pallid light; and the earth ceased to struggle and brood in the dark coil of itself, and spread itself smiling and released. The spell within the clouded crystal of the afternoon broke; they stretched and stirred. Judith looked up at the big elm.

'Who can climb this?' she said.

'Up with you,' said Martin.

She climbed as she had not climbed since childhood, lifting herself lightly, unhesitatingly from branch to branch. At the top she looked down and saw them all small beneath her, looking up. Boldly from her eminence she called to the little creatures to come up; but not one of them would.

She descended again, feeling young and silly in the face of their lack of physical ambition. But they were all smiling upwards to receive her. Martin held his hands up to her and she took them and jumped from the bottom bough.

'You haven't forgotten your stuff,' he said, and his eyes dwelt on her with their faithful brown look.

'I wish I could do that,' said Mariella. 'I never could.'

'And now,' said Julian, 'divert us with a hand spring or so,' – and his harsh face looked half-amused, half-clouded with an odd look, – almost like jealousy.

He had never been really pleased with the spectacle of other people's successes: He found it too bitter not to be himself the one to excel. But he could not trouble her today or make her doubtful.

Roddy said nothing, – only looked at her out of glinting, twinkling eyes.

It was time to go home.

She parted from them gaily, taking her immense happiness with her unbroken, for once stepping clear out of the day into sleep with it wrapped round her.

But now, when she looked back for that day, it was a million miles behind her, floating insubstantially like a wisp of shining mist: and all that returned to her out of it, clear and whole, were two detached impressions which, at the time, had barely brushed her consciousness: the look of young lilac-leaves with the sun on them, glittering above the garden-gate where she had bidden them good-bye; and the expression she had surprised on Mariella's face some time in that day, – but when, she had forgotten.

Whatever had disturbed Mariella's face then, it had not been happiness. The other faces, even Roddy's, had unaccountably become blurred in the mist; but Mariella's came back again and again, as if to stress the significance of its momentary defencelessness; as if, could it only be solved, there, in a flash, would be the whole clue to Mariella.

She got up and studied her hair in the mirror above the mantelpiece.

While she stared there came a tap on the window behind her. She turned and there was Roddy peering through the pane and laughing at her. She ran to the window and opened it.

'Roddy!'

It did not seem possible that he should have come when she wanted him so badly.

'I've knocked twice. You were too busy to hear me.'

'I've put my hair up.'

'It's ravishing. Will you please come in it to a fireworks party which Martin is giving in about an hour's time?'

'Fireworks! of all heavenly things! Hurrah for Martin!'

'He only thought of it this afternoon, and he dashed into the town and bought up the whole stock. He sent me to fetch you. He says he must have you. Julian's terrified of the big rocket and he wants you to persuade him to light it. And you're to stay to supper afterwards. Mariella's away for the night. Can you face it?'

'Oh, how glorious!'

He gave her a hand and she jumped out of the window.

Roddy was in his best mood. He was friendly and talkative; his face was almost wide awake; his very hair looked alert, ruffled about his forehead; and he was sunburnt and clear-eyed, at his ease in grey flannels and yellow shirt and an ancient navy-blue jacket.

The river had an enchanted beauty and stillness in the half-light. It was moon-coloured, with a dying flush in it; faint opal flickers lit the ripples that broke away on either side of the canoe.

'It won't be dark enough for a while, yet,' said Roddy. 'They'll wonder where I am.'

'Why? Didn't you tell them?'

'They didn't know I'd slip off so soon.'

She blushed. It really looked as if Roddy had come early in order to have a little time alone with her. He would not say so; but he twinkled and smiled so gaily that she smiled back at him, as if giving him secret for delightful secret.

'They'll tease me,' he declared.

'No. Will they?'

'Yes, I assure you –'

'How silly!'

'Isn't it? Do you know, they'll suspect us of the most desperate flirtation on this exquisite secluded river.'

'*Will* they?' She was troubled.

'What common minds! As if a man couldn't be alone with a girl without making love to her.'

'Oh, I do agree, Roddy.'

He threw back his head and laughed silently: he had been laughing all the time. And it had seemed for a moment that Roddy was prepared for the first time in her memory to have a little serious conversation.

'Oh Roddy, how you do laugh at me!'

'I can't help it Judy. You are so incredibly solemn. You don't mind, do you? Please don't mind. I adore people who make me laugh.'

It was that his laughter left her out, making her feel heavy and unhumorous. If only he would teach her to play with him, how quick and apt he would find her!

'I don't mind,' she said. 'Only I do wish I could be ready for you.'

Being himself, was Roddy more likely or less likely to fall in love with a person he never took seriously?

'You'd forgive anybody, however badly they treated you, wouldn't you, Judy?'

'Forgiving or not forgiving doesn't mean much to me. I never could feel wronged. I might not be able to help feeling hurt, but *forgiveness* wouldn't come into it.'

'Hmm!' said Roddy. 'Are you sure you're so civilized? Personally I never forgive anybody anything. I'm like God. I love my grievances, and want people to feel them.'

'I know you're laughing really. I know it isn't true, what you say.'

He said quickly, quite seriously:

'I never would forgive a person who made a fool of me.'

'I wouldn't *like* it; but if it only affected myself, it wouldn't be important. A thing that happens to yourself alone doesn't *matter*.' She stopped and blushed painfully, thinking: 'How he'll mock'; but instead he looked at her gravely and nodded, saying:

'I dare say you're right.'

It was beginning to get dark.

He steered the canoe under the willows into narrow shadinesses, lit a cigarette and lay back watching her.

'And what will they teach you at college, Judy?'

No one but he knew how to say 'Judy.'

'I don't know, Roddy. I'm rather frightened, – not about the reading, – about the girls, all the people. I don't understand a bit how to live with lots of people. I never have. I shall make such mistakes. It oppresses me, such a weight of lives crammed together in one building, such a terrifying press of faces. I prefer living alone.'

'Don't get standardized, or I shan't come and visit you.'

'Will you come and visit me?'

'If I ever find myself not too desperately busy,' he said twinkling.

'I shall look forward to that. Perhaps I'll see Martin sometimes too. Perhaps it won't be so bad ... Roddy, do you realize I've never known anyone of my own age except the gardener's little girl and one or two local children – and all of you? After you left, when we were little, I was so lonely I ... You don't know. Daddy would never let me be sent to school. Now you're back, I expect every day to wake up and find you all vanished again.'

'We shan't vanish again.'

'If only I were sure!'

'I'm sure.'

'Oh you! You're the most vanishing of all. You slip through my fingers.'

'Not I. It's you who do that.'

'I?'

'Yes. You elude ....' He made a gesture with his hand. 'I don't understand how you work. You're an enigma. You intrigue me.'

'I'm very glad.'

'And I'm afraid of you.'

'You're not. You're only amused at me.'

'No. You're wrong.'

He fell silent, smoking and watching her; all his attention fixed in his eyes. It was as if he could not look away. Her head swam, and she stammered:

'What are you thinking?'

'That it's a good thing we – agree so – completely about the standards of conduct proper between the sexes; otherwise it might be a good thing you're so exceptionally forgiving.' His voice had an edge of question.

'Roddy, what are you talking about?'

'Nothing. A slight emotional conflict, – now resolved.'

He sat up suddenly, brushing some mood all in a minute from his mind and his eyes and his voice. He lit another cigarette and started paddling.

Supposing Roddy had been going to say: 'Kiss me?' ... Better not to think about it.

The stars were bright now: it must be dark enough for Martin's fireworks. Things were happening next door: Martin was preparing to celebrate in earnest. He had hung a row of fairy lanterns all along the eaves of the verandah, and the lights glowed rose, blue, green and white among the leaves of the vine. His shadowy figure was moving on the lawn, and another moved beside it: that was Tony Baring, Roddy explained, his friend and Martin's, staying for the night. Julian was playing the piano; he was visible in profile against the window.

'What a party, Roddy! And I the only lady. Please protect me.'

'Oh yes, we all will. We'll each protect you against all the others, so you're fairly safe.'

A sudden light flared up in the garden.

'Hey!' said Martin's voice. 'Hi! Here everybody! My fireworks have started. Where the hell has Roddy got to? I wanted –'

'Here we are!' shouted Judith. 'Hullo, Martin! Martin! We're here, we're watching. Hurrah for you, Martin!'

'Oh good! Is that you, Judy? I've got some pretty hot stuff here. Watch!'

He spoke in the anxious excited voice of a small boy displaying the charms of his hobby to some indulgently attentive adult.

'Oh Martin, that's splendid. Oooh, what a beauty! How I adore fireworks!'

It was essential that dear Martin should be made to feel his fireworks a success. They had behind them so eager a purpose of giving amusement to others that they deserved tremendous encouragement. You felt he had spent every penny of his pocket-money on them.

There was a shout of laughter and screams from Julian. He had left the piano and was joining the others on the lawn; and the Catherine

93

Wheel had broken loose and was after him, snapping and leaping at his heels.

A shower of golden sparks went up in a fountain and poured down over the tulips and wall-flowers. Another followed; but this time the shower was rainbow-coloured. The deep talk and laughter of Martin, Julian and Tony was a strange not quite human chorus in the moonless dark.

'Oh Roddy, isn't it exciting?'

'It is indeed.'

The fireworks became more and more splendid. Long crystal-white cascades broke and streamed down to the grass. Things went off in the air with a soft delicious explosion and blossomed in great blazing coloured drops that lingered downwards like a drift of slow petals.

'Oh Roddy, if only –! They're so brief. I wish they were never quenched but went on falling and falling, so lovely, for ever. Would you be content to burst into life and be a ten seconds marvel and then vanish?'

But Roddy only smiled. On his face was the mask behind which he guarded his personal pleasures and savoured them in secret.

Suddenly the willow-trees were revealed cloudily in a crude red light, – and an aching green one, – then one like the concentrated essence of a hundred moonlights. The three men on the lawn were outlined in its glare, motionless, with their heads up. She heard Martin cursing. Something was a complete failure: it spat twice, threw a thin spark or so and went out. Then the big rocket took wings with a swift warning hiss, left in its wake a thick firefly trail and broke at a great height with a velvety choke of fulfilment and relief, bloomed rapidly in perfect symmetry, a huge inverted gold lily, – then started dropping slowly, flower unfurling wide from the heart of coloured flower all the way down.

'Roddy, look at that! Honestly, you feel anything so lovely must be made by enchantment and thrown into the air with no cause behind it except the – the stress of its own beauty. I can't connect it with Bryant and May, can you?'

Then all was gone. There was a splash. A swan drifting near the canoe shook itself and swirled sharply, with puffed wings, into the shadows. Roddy picked a charred stick out of the water and held it up.

94

'Signs and wonders!' he said. 'The swan had a revelation too. Here's a remedy against fancy, Judy. Wouldn't you like to keep it?'

'Throw it away at once.'

He flipped it over his shoulder, laughing.

The fireworks were over, and the three men were coming down towards the water's edge.

Roddy whispered:

'Shall we escape?'

'Oh ...'

It was too late.

'Hullo! Hullo!' called the cheerful voice of Martin. 'Did you enjoy my fireworks?'

All at once there was much laughter and talk and greeting, and she was drawn out of their exquisite aloofness into the voluble every-day circle. Martin stretched an eager hand and out she stepped from the canoe among them all. Half-dazed, she saw shadows of men standing round, appearing and fading as in a dream, felt dream-like touches of men's hands; heard unreal voices bidding good-evening to Judith; was conscious of dim confusion of movement towards the house. Did her own face rise so wanly against the darkness, deep-shadowed under the features, a firm-cut austere mask? Beneath the masks the hidden eyes held now and then a straying gleam from the fairy-lanterns. It was all so nearly a sleeper's dream that to speak audibly seemed a vast effort.

Roddy strolled up from the river's edge, having made fast the boat. He came close and stood behind her shoulder, just touching it; and at once the dream broke and every pulse was alert.

They went into the house for supper.

Tomato-sandwiches and cake, fruit-salad and bananas and cream, lemonade and cider-cup loaded the table. Martin had prepared the whole thing himself with a passion of judicious greed.

Tony Baring sat opposite and stared with liquid expressive blue eyes. He had a sensitive face, changing all the time, a wide mouth with beautiful sensuous lips, thick black hair and a broad white fore-head with the eyebrows meeting above the nose, strongly marked and mobile. When he spoke he moved them, singly or together. His voice was soft and precious, and he had a slight lisp. He looked like a young poet. Suddenly she noticed his hands, – thin unmasculine hands, – queer hands – making nervous appealing ineffectual gestures that contradicted the nobility of his head. She heard him call Roddy 'my dear'; and once 'darling'; and had a passing shock.

There was a submerged excitement in the room. Mariella's absence had noticeable effect: there was a lightness of wit, an ebullience of talk and laughter; gay quick voices answering each other.

The polished table was blotted over with pools of red candleshade, and pale pools from the white tulips picked in honour of the guest. The great mirror opposite reflected the table with all its muted colours; reflected too the back of Tony's broad head and a bit of Roddy in curious profile, and her own face, lustrous-eyed, dark-lipped, long of neck and mysterious. When she looked at it she thought it was transfigured; and she knew who made the electric feeling.

It was time to go home.

But Roddy got up and started the gramophone; then caught her by the hand and led her out on the verandah.

'One dance,' he said.

'And then I must go.'

'You dance better than ever tonight.'

'It's because I'm so enjoying myself.'

He laughed and tightened his arm round her.

'Judy –'

'Yes? Oh Roddy, I do love it when you say "Judy." Nobody else says it like you.'

He bent his face to look into her lifted one with a soft hidden smile.

'What were you going to say?' she asked.

'I forget. When you look at me with your enormous eyes I forget everything I mean to say.'

The gramophone stopped abruptly, with a hideous snarl; and the form of Julian darted forth like a serpent upon them.

'You've waked the boy with that damned noise,' he said. 'I knew you would.'

He was gone; and in the succeeding shock of quiet the wail of Peter floated down to them. Quick footsteps sounded in the room above; and suddenly there was silence.

'He was cross.'

'Yes,' said Roddy indifferently. 'He's fussier than twenty old Nannies. The brat's nurse has gone to see her sister buried, so he's looking after him.'

'It's funny how Julian seems to take charge of him, rather than Mariella.'

'Oh, Julian's always got to know best. I expect he told her she couldn't be trusted with him. I believe they had words, – I don't know. Anyway she went off to London this afternoon to a dog show or something, and left Julian triumphant.' Roddy chuckled. 'God, he's a peculiar man.'

'I never can believe that baby belongs to Mariella – and Charlie.'

But he gave her no response to that; although, as she spoke the name, with stars, lights, voices, music, his shadowed face, all that was lovely life around her, the pathos of that death struck her so wildly it seemed he must feel it too and draw closer to her.

How he watched her!

'Roddy, what are you thinking about?'

She pleaded silently, suffocated with strange excitement: 'Let us be frank. There'll never be another night like this and soon we'll be dead too. On such a night let us not miss one delight, let us speak the truth and not be afraid. Tell me you love me and I will tell you. You know it's true tonight. Never mind tomorrow.'

But he shook his head slowly, smiling.

'I never tell.'

She turned to go into the house.

'Nor I. But I think one day I will, – tell somebody, one person, something – the truth, just once, – just to see how it feels.'

He followed her in silence into the house.

Martin and Tony were lying in arm-chairs, looking sleepy.

'Poor things – longing to go to bed. It's all right, I'm going now. I want to say good night to Julian.'

On such a night Julian must not be left angry, alone. There must be no failure on her part at least.

'He's with Peter.'

'In his old room?'

'Yes.'

'I know. I'll be back in a minute.'

She ran up the stairs. Dimmed light streamed through a door ajar in front of her. It was the room where Julian and Charlie had slept years ago. Softly she pushed the door open.

Julian sat by the window with the child on his knees. He had thrown a shawl over his head and out of its folds the pale face peeped, owl-like and still. In his little night-suit he looked absurd and touching.

Julian raised a face so haggard and suffering that she paused, half-ashamed, uncertain what to say or do.

'Come in, Judith,' he said.

'Only for a minute . . . Won't he sleep?'

'No. I think he's feverish. He got a fright, waking up alone. He's very nervous.'

He bent over the child, rocking him, patting his shoulder.

'I expect he's just playing up. You ought to put him back in his cot.'

'No. He'd cry. I couldn't *endure* it if he cried any more. I'll keep him till he's asleep.'

Solemn in his shawl, Peter bent his too-brilliant gaze upon her as she stooped to touch his cheek. He never smiled for her; but then neither did he greet her as he greeted most people with a clear: 'Go 'way.' He accepted her with grave politeness.

'Do you like holding him?'

'Yes,' he said simply.

He was holding the child to comfort himself.

'He's very nice,' she said. 'What a different sort of childhood he'll have from yours, with the others always round you! He's likely to be the eldest of the next generation by a good deal, isn't he?'

'I should say so,' he said bitterly. 'I don't mind betting not one of us provides a little cousin for him. I don't see us breeding somehow. Unless possibly Martin . . .'

Not Roddy. No . . .

'Well, you mustn't let him be lonely.'

'That's her affair.'

'Is it? She seems to let you take charge. Julian, does she love him?'

He was silent for a moment before answering: 'I think she does.' He put his hand to his head and said suddenly, very low: 'Oh God, it's awful! You know I quarrelled with him – Charlie – over that marriage. I never saw him after it – we were never reconciled. But after the child was born, she wrote and told me he had said in his last letter to her that if anything happened to him he would like me to be the child's guardian ... So I suppose he forgave me.'

'Of course, of course, Julian,' she said, half-weeping at the look of his bowed head.

Was this the canker that gnawed Julian, – interminable thought of Charlie dead like that, without a reconciling word?

'I blame only myself,' he said, still in the low voice. '*She* has been very good. Never a word of – anything. Always that sweet empty unresentful way, – like a child. Sometimes I think she never knew – or never understood, anyway. I think she can't understand that sort of thing. It's a sort of insensitiveness. She might hate me over Peter, but she doesn't seem to. Why doesn't she?'

The expression she had surprised on Mariella's face came back to her, still undecipherable.

'I almost wish she would,' he went on. 'I wish I was certain she was jealous or even critical of me. I haven't the least idea where I am.' He rubbed his eyes and forehead wearily. 'It's odd how her presence affects me. She gets on my nerves to a degree! Nothing but this sweet blank passivity ... You know I like people with spikes and facets, people who thrust back when I thrust, brilliant, quick glittering people. And I like people who are slow and deep and warm; and I think you're one of that sort, Judy. But what is she? Sometimes I think she's watching me intently but I don't know where from, and it makes me irritable. She's got quality, you know, – incredible physical and moral courage. I think that must have been what Charlie loved in her. But cold, cold and flat – to me.'

He sighed and shivered.

'Oh Julian, you're very tired, aren't you? There's nothing to worry about. You've got things on your mind because you're so tired. Does your head ache?'

'Yes. No ... I'm in a bad mood, Judith. You'd better leave me.' But he spoke gently and raised his face to smile at her. It was then she saw that he had been crying.

'I will leave you, Julian. I only came to say good night. And to say I was sorry I made you angry. I wouldn't have waked him for the world.'

'It's all right. I'm sorry I was angry. Don't worry.'

'Good night, Julian.'

'Good night, Judith . . . You look so lovely –'

She thought: 'I shall never see him like this again. I must remember . . .'

They looked at each other deeply, and when she turned silently away she had in imagination stooped and kissed his cheek.

As she opened the door, laughter and talk came suddenly to her from below, – a faint roar of male voices that struck her with strange alarm, and seemed to threaten her. She took a step back into the room again, listened and whispered:

'Julian, who is that, Tony?'

He shrugged.

'I don't know. He doesn't talk to me. He writes verse I believe. He's just bringing out a book. I gather from his conversation he is *quite* the thing at Cambridge – in certain circles.'

'Is Roddy very fond of him?'

'Oh Roddy! *Fond* of him! I don't know.'

'He seems to be very fond of Roddy.'

'Yes, it looks like it.' He glanced at her sharply.

She knew then she had dreaded that he would answer in that way, give her just such a look. She remembered that Tony had been suddenly hostile; his eyes, stony and watchful, had fastened on her when she came in from the verandah with Roddy.

The voices came up to her again, like a reiterated warning. 'Keep away. You are not wanted here. We are all friends, men content together. We want no female to trouble us.'

Better not to go down among them all, safer to stay here in the quiet with Julian She lingered, looking back in doubt and loneliness; but this time he did not tell her to stay. The muffled shining of the lamp filled the room, flowed over his form, his forehead bowed, drowsy and meditative, one great shoulder curving forward to support the white bundle lying against it. His pose suggested the something in him which it was hard to name, – a kind of beauty and nobility a little twisted. Close beside his narrow bed stood Peter's cot, and Peter's two plush animals lay upon the pillow.

Softly she closed the door upon that strange pair. If Mariella had seen them, would her face have changed?

Downstairs again.

It would not be Roddy who would offer to take her home. She saw in one glance that he had finished with her for tonight: he leaned against the mantelpiece, and Tony, beside him, had an arm about his shoulders; and Tony's eyes, coldly upon her, said he was not for her. Something licked sickeningly at her heart: it was necessary to be jealous of the young poet Tony; for he was jealous of her. To her good night Roddy replied with chilling mock-formal politeness, bowing his head, laughing at her. Martin put her cloak about her shoulders with reverent hands, and they went out.

The night was dark. All the blossoming things of earth were hidden, and the fragrances abroad seemed shaken from the stars that flowered and clustered profusely in the arching boughs of the sky. They were back at her garden-gate. Above it rose a faint broken shadow where, by day, lilac and laburnum poured over in a wild maze to the lane. But when they came to the cherry tree they found it still glimmering faintly, – a cloud, a ghost.

Judith stretched up a hand and picked a scrap of cherry and held it out to Martin.

'That's the secret of it all, I do think. Cherry blossom grows from the seeds of enchantment. Keep it and wish and you'll have your heart's desire. Wish, Martin.'

He snatched it and her hand with it. They waited. He held the spray and clutched her hand, sighed and said nothing. Their forms were shadows just outlined against the luminous tree.

'What were you going to say?' she whispered.

'I – don't know.'

'No wishes?'

'Too many.'

He was lost, – caught away, spell-bound, lost.

'What a night! Isn't it Martin?'

'It's the very devil.'

'I don't feel a bit like myself, do you? There's some sort of strange-ness about, – magic. Or is it just being young, do you think?'

'Perhaps.'

'Don't let's ever be old Could you bear it?'

'I shouldn't like it.'

'Well wish that. Wish never to be old.'

Silence.

'No,' he said at last. He held her hand still and bent his head, twisting his bit of cherry. His voice came huskily: 'I've wished something else.'

Gently she drew her hand away. She must run away quickly from whatever was happening: no emotional conflict with Martin must thrust across and confuse the path where all was prepared for one alone.

'Don't go in,' implored Martin. 'Can't we walk?'

'Oh I must – I must go in.'

'Oh Judith!'

'I must, Martin. Thank you for bringing me home. I must fly now. It's so late –' she said in panic.

'When shall I see you again?'

'Soon – soon.'

He was speechless. She called a soft good night and left him and the darkness swallowed him up.

As she went towards the solitary light burning for her in the hall she thought with a sudden fear that he had implored her for assurance just as she mutely implored Roddy every time he left her; and she had answered – not, surely not, as Roddy would have answered?

'Roddy, come out of your dark maze and make me certain!'

She must warm herself with the remembrance of the first part of the evening, ignore the little chill of those few last minutes. What were his eyes telling her when he bade her good night? Surely they were whispering: 'Take no notice. We know what has passed between us, we know what must come. Though we must keep our secret before others, we do not deceive each other.'

Yes, that was it.

She started running; and wondered why; and ran as hard as she could.

As she opened the front door, she stopped, aghast. The telephone bell was screaming, screaming, screaming.

Telegram for Judith Earle. From Paris.

'Father died this evening. Come tomorrow. Mother.'

As she hung up the receiver silence in a vast tide flowed in and drowned the house, his house, as if for ever.

He had been deep in the business of dying while she, his daughter – No. She must not think that way; she must just think of him dead. What an extraordinary thing ... Last time she had seen him had he looked as if he were going to die? There came a doubtful indistinct picture of him – yes – going upstairs to bed, early, not later than ten o'clock. She had looked up the staircase and seen him near the top, mounting with a hand on the bannister; going to bed so early, looking – yes – a little feeble; the bowed back and slow yielding step, the slightly laborious stair-mounting of a man getting old – yes – a delicate elderly man, a little frightening, a little pathetic to see unexpectedly: for could youth then really depart? He had been young and he had come upon old age. Some day she too – she too ... yes, for a moment she had thought that. And now he was dead.

She crept to the library and switched on all the lights and stared at the portrait of a young man. That handsome youth had lived, grown old and died. He had begotten a daughter who was looking at him and thinking these things. But the cold portraits of people held them bound for ever in unreality; they could not die: they had not lived.

She sank into a chair, burying her face in her hands, seeking for a memory that would make her know that he had lived and died.

She was very small and he, very kind and noble, was taking her to hear the child-genius play. Her excitement was too great to bear: she too would be a child-genius; and when the violin came it wrought on her so violently that she was sick where she sat. He had been deeply disappointed in her, his kindness and nobility turned to disgust.

At night, every night for a long time, with the night light burning, he had sat on her bed and sung softly to her. He sang 'Uncle Tom Cobley'.

'All along out along down along lea ...'

Ah the haunting echo, the loneliness of that! Over and over he sang the names of the mysterious company of men, but so softly that the slipping syllables wove round her hazily and fled before she caught them.

Then he sang of a golden apple.

'Evoe, evoe, wonderful way
For subduing – subduing the hearts of men ...'

Evoe, evoe ... The sound started a pang, a question, a stir of rich sadness that went aching on, through the twice-sung whisper of the sibilants, right on after the fall, the lingering soft pause and fall of the last words.

At the end he sang 'Good night ladies'. When he had finished she said 'Again'; and he sang it again and yet again, always more low, till finally it was nothing but a plaintive sigh. She lay listening with eyes shut, weeping with sorrow and delight.

'Good night ladies, we're going to leave you now –'

That was so sad, so sad!

'Merrily we'll roll along, roll along, roll along,
Merrily we'll roll along on the deep – blue – sea.'

She saw a dim swaying far-stretching line of lovely ladies all in white, waving good-bye upon a dark sea-shore. The great ship faded away over the waves, bearing further and further the deep-throated chorus of singers. The long line swayed, reached vainly forward. Their white hands glimmered. She saw them fade, alas! fade, vanish out of sight.

Oh, he had known how to stir mystery in a child. He had turned sound inside out for her, making undreamed-of music, – and pictures besides, and light and colour. He had seemed to forget her for weeks at a time, but when he had remembered, what a more than compensating richness had come into life! She had planned to grow so beautiful and accomplished that he would be proud of her and want her with him always. They were to have travelled together, famous father and not unworthy daughter, and they were to have discussed very intellectual topics and she was to have looked after him when the steps, going upstairs, started, really started, to have that feebleness ... He was to have lived to be very old and go upstairs on her arm, cherished by her.

No more lessons in Greek: no more hearing him softly open his door to listen to her playing, – (though he never praised her, what praise that had been!) No more talk – now and then, when he remembered her, when his eyes dwelt on her with interest – of books and pictures and music and famous people he knew. No second proud visit to Cambridge with him, no seeing him sigh, smile, dream from an old don's window over Trinity Great Court in the sun, after the lunch-party The three elderly bachelors had smiled at her, embarrassed by her presence, doubtful as regards the attentions due to a young lady. They had been shy with her, courteous, careful and elegant of speech, a little dusty altogether, but gentle like their rooms, like the old gold light falling outside on ancient buildings. She had listened to them all savouring and playing with words, quoting Greek, saying 'Do you remember?' He had seemed so distinguished, so brilliant, a man ripe and calm with knowledge. And afterwards he had shown her the colleges and the Backs and promised to come often to see her when she came up. He had talked of his youth and for a moment they had trembled on the verge of shared emotions: no more of that, no hope of future rich Cambridge occasions.

No more watching his intent and noble profile in the lamp light, stooped hour after hour over his writing, opposite the bust of Homer. Once or twice he had looked up and smiled at her as though vaguely content to have her with him. His desk was empty for ever. That was pathetic; it would bring tears if dwelt on; it made him so human.

Did it hurt to die?

Now in a flash she remembered the question:

'Daddy, does it hurt to die?'

Years ago. Grandmamma had just died. When he came to say good night to her in bed, she had asked him that:

He had remained silent and brooding. His silence filled her with terror: her heart beat and, red and panic-stricken, she stared at him. He was going to tell her something dreadful, he knew something so terrible about Grandmamma, about death and the way it hurt that he could not speak ... He was going to die ... *She* was ... Oh God! Oh Jesus!

At last he had sighed and said.

'No, no. It doesn't hurt at all to die.'

She had flung herself weeping into his arms, and he had clasped her in silence; and from his quiet, pressing shoulder, comfort had poured in upon her.

It did not hurt at all to die, it was quite all right, he had said. He had just died.

She looked about her, at the brooding room. Nothing but loneliness, helplessness, appalling silence. She was cold too, shivering.

A little while ago she had been next door. Now the house would all be dark, shut to her. Supposing she were to run back to them with her tidings, surely they would help, advise, console: for they were her friends.

'Roddy, Roddy, my father's dead.'

He was standing with Tony's arm around his shoulders, remote, indifferently smiling. He did not like grief, and Tony kept him from her. Her time was far away and long ago.

'Julian, my father's dead.'

He was bowed over the child; and he raised his head to listen, but made no answer. He had plenty of his own sorrows; and he feared she would wake the child.

But Martin might be told, Martin would listen and comfort with large and inarticulate tenderness. He would be standing under the cherry tree, waiting, just as she had left him. She ran to the window.

There was nobody in the garden. A faint light was abroad, – it might be the small rising moon or the dawn – making the cherry tree pale and clear. It seemed to float towards her, to swell and tower into the sky, a shining vision.

Then death, lovely death, lay at the heart of enchantment. It was the core of the mystery and beauty. Tomorrow she would not know it, but tonight no knowledge was surer. And he whom they were to mourn was – in one minute she would know where he was, – one minute.

She leaned out of the window.

Now! Now!

But the cherry tree was nothing but a small flowering cherry tree. Before her straining eyes it had veiled itself and withheld the sign.

Part Three

I

JUDITH, looking dazed, shut the door of the Mistress's room behind her, and after a quarter of an hour's wandering, found her way back to her own room. She sat on a hard chair and said to herself: Independence at last. This is Life. Life at last is beginning; but rather because it seemed so much more like a painful death than because she believed it.

She surveyed the four walls in which her independence was to flower. They were papered in sage green with perpendicular garlands of white and yellow rosebuds. There was a desk, a kitchen chair, a cane table, a narrow iron bedstead behind a faded buff curtain; and a distinctive carpet. It was of a greenish-brown shade, striped round the edge with yellow and tomato-colour, and patterned over with black liquorice-like wriggles.

'But I can't *live* in ugliness . . .'

A clamorous bell roused her from a state of apathetic despair; and she opened her door and crept along in the wake of the click of heels and the laughter of many voices.

This was Hall – huge, bare, full of echoes and hard light, whiteness and cold blue curtains . . . blue and high like twilight above ice and snow when the full moon is rising.

'I can always think of that and not mind if nobody talks to me . . .'

Down one wall, a row of black frocks and white aprons at attention; at the top of the room, High Table beginning to fill up: black garments, grey, close-brushed intellectual heads, serious thin faces looking down the room, one young one, drooping a little: piles of chestnut hair and a white Peter Pan collar. Crowds of dresses of all colours, shapes and sizes, all running about briskly, knowing where to go; a sea of faces bobbing and turning, chattering, bright-eyed, nodding and laughing to other faces, sure of themselves.

'Margaret, come and sit here ... here ... here! Next to me! Sylvia, next to me ... Is there a place for Sylvia? ...'

'I am lost, lost, abandoned, alone, lost,' thought Judith wildly and pounced for the nearest chair and clung to it. She was between two girls who stared at her, then looked away again. She bowed her head: the old terror of faces engulfed her.

There fell a silence. A voice like a bell went through the room, calling: *Benedictus benedicat*. And then came a roar, – a scraping, an immense yelling that rose to the ceiling and there rolled, broke, swelled again without pause. Beneath its volumes she felt herself lost again; but nobody else appeared to have noticed it.

'Can I pass you the salt?' said her neighbour.

'After you,' said Judith earnestly.

'Thanks.'

The conversation swirled on around her.

'Who d'you think's engaged? Three guesses ... Let's look at the tombstone. Soup ...... how classically simple ... just soup ... Take a hundred dirty dishcloths, soak them in hot water, add a few onions ... Dorothy's bobbed her hair. It suits her. It doesn't suit her ... My dear, who *is* that girl next to you? ... I've done six hours every day this vac ... May you be forgiven ... Well anyway, four regularly ... I'm going to *work* this term, seven hours solid, no dances ... I've got to ... you should have heard the jawing I got from Miss Marsh because I only got a third in Part I ... Well I think that was jolly good: I shall think myself jolly lucky if I get the same ... Old Marsh has lost every human instinct ... D'you know Sibyl Jones has done ten hours every day for two months? ... She's *bound* to collapse ... Third years ought to be more sensible at their age ... I *say*, I *do* believe Miss Ingram's dyed her hair. I'm *sure* it's a different colour ... D'you suppose she's in *love*? ... I knew a girl at Oxford who over-worked most fearfully, and she woke up one morning and every hair on her head had come off and was lying on the pillow beside her, looking like a nasty practical joke. Rather a jar, wasn't it? But she took to a wig, my dears, a flaxen waved wig and it was such an improvement that she left off her glasses and became quite flighty and took to powdering her nose as well, so it was a blessing in disguise; and then her Maths coach proposed to her and they got married, and all I wonder is whether he got a shock or whether she'd warned him, because I s'pose she takes it off at night and she's as bald as an egg without it; but I suppose anyway baldness doesn't matter in true love ... It's a warning isn't it?'

'Pleasant idiocy,' said Judith very quietly in the yell of laughter that followed. 'Idiotic pleasantry.'

'Did you speak?' said the girl on her other side.

'N-no.'

'I suppose you've come up for a little visit? I wonder whose guest? ...'

'No, no. I've come up for good – I've just arrived. I came up a day late. I –'

'You mean you're a fresher?'

'Yes.'

'But you're at the wrong table!' said the girl, horrified. 'There's your table at the other end of the room. This is a second year table.'

'Oh dear! How awful! Does it matter? I couldn't recognize anybody and nobody told me anything ... I don't know a soul ...' She felt the shameful tears coming. Such a bad beginning ...

'Never mind,' said the girl almost kindly. 'It doesn't matter for once. And you'll soon get to know people. Isn't there anyone here from your school?'

'I've never been to school. This is the first time I've ever been away from home ...' Stupid weakening thing to say, inducing self-pity, bringing more tears.

'Oh really?' said the girl, and added politely after a pause:

'Do you know Cambridge?'

'A bit. I came once with Da— my father. He simply adored it. He was always coming back. That's why he wanted me to –'

'Oh really? How naice. I expect he'll often be running up to see you then, won't he?'

She turned her head away in silence. Never, never would he be running up to see her, to rescue her. Why had she mentioned him? He had vanished and left her stranded among creatures who dared to assume he was still alive . . .

Trips. Labs. Lectures. Dons. Vacs. Chaperons. The voices gabbled on. The forks clattered. The roof echoed.

'Ugly and noisy,' muttered Judith. 'Ugly and noisy and crude and smelly . . .' You could go on for ever.

There were eyes staring from everywhere, necks craning to look at her . . .

'But I can abstract myself. I can ignore their rudeness . . .'

It was the moonlight filling the blue that made it so cold and pure. Above the icefields and the snow lay the cold translucent pastures of the air . . .

She studied the row of faces opposite her, and then more rows, and more, of faces. Nearly all plain, nearly all with a touch of beauty: here and there well-cut heads, broad white placid brows; young necks; white teeth set in pleasant smiles; innocent intelligent lovely eyes. Accepting, revealing faces they were, with no reserves in them, looking at each other, at things – not inward at themselves. But just a herd, when all was said: immature, untidy, all dull, and all alike, commonplace female creatures in the mass. How boring it was! If you could see Mariella's clear thorough-bred face among them, – would that too get merged?

That was where she should be humbly sitting, among those quieter heads, right at the end. There was a light there, flashing about: the tail of her eye had already caught it several times. She looked more closely. It was somebody's fair head, so fiercely alive that it seemed delicately to light the air around it: a vivacious emphatic head, turning and nodding; below it a white neck and shoulder, generously modelled, leaned across the table. Then the face came round suddenly, all curves, the wide mouth laughing, warm-coloured . . . It made you think of warm fruit, – peaches and nectarines mellowed in the sun. It seemed to look at Judith with sudden eager attention and then to smile. The eyes were meeting her own, inquiring deeply.

'Who's that?' said Judith excitedly, forgetful of her position.

'Oh, one of the freshers. I don't know her name.'

Her name, her very name would be sure to have the sun on it.

All at once Judith found courage to eat her pudding.

Another scraping of chairs, and they were all on their feet. Someone, highly flushed, flew to the door at the edge of the dais and wrenched it open, holding it back while the Mighty streamed slowly out. They were gone. The girl returned, even more highly flushed.

'My dears! *Do* you think they saw me giggling? Bunny, you *were* a beast to make me giggle! Did I do it all right? I thought I'd never get it open in time. Miss Thompson looked *so* severe: but did you see what a sweet smile I got from Miss Ingram? Oh what an experience! Hold me up someone.'

Willing hands supported her limp form. The roar broke out again, pouring out of Hall along the corridors.

Judith went back to her room and sat by the window. Outside, the dusk was chill and deep. The treetops were all round her window. It was like being in a nest, to sit here with all the highest boughs swirling round the pane. If only the corridors did not echo with high voices and strange feet, if only you could forget the carpet, if only you could turn round and see Martin – (not Roddy – he was too unreal a memory to bring consolation) it might be possible to be comforted.

The feet were less frequent now, the voices quieter. What were the mysterious animals doing? The vast building was full of them, streaming in and out of their burrows, busy with their strange separate affairs.

Night, dropping across the flat fields of Cambridgeshire had blotted out a dim west slashed with fire. The tree trunks threw up their branches in a stiff black net and caught a few stars.

Now shut your eyes and see the garden at home, the summer sun wildly rich on the lawn, hear the hot whirr and pause of the mowing machine; smell the mown grass mixed with the smell of roses and pinks and lavender; see the white butterflies dancing above the herbaceous border; see Mamma, going slowly up the steps with a basket of sweet peas, pause and draw up the striped Venetian blind; because now it is evening; the sun is behind the massed, toppling dark-green luxuriance of the unmoving chestnut trees, has drained its last ray out of the rooms and left them warm, throbbing and wan. Now it is night. Go down to the river: they are all there, waiting in the dark for you ... Now there is only Roddy, coming close, just touching your shoulder, his head bent to look into your lifted one. Listen and hear him say: 'Darling' ... of course it had been in fun. But his rich voice goes on whispering and repeating it .. His eyes drown again and again with yours ...

Then all at once a far train-whistle roused her, cutting across this immense strangeness with a suggestion of ordinary familiar things; and Judith, faint with home-sickness, sent towards it the desire of all her being to fly in its wake back to the life she knew ...

Impossible to stay in this room. She opened the door and wandered down the corridor. At the far end was a great chatter of voices through a half-open door. Peering in she saw a cloud of cigarette smoke and a room full of girls sprawling in chairs and on the floor.

'Who's captain of hockey? Jane of course you're going to play hockey? And lacrosse ... Jane I must say it's topping to see you again ... Jane, your year looks a dull lot ... Who's the one who planted herself at our table? ... Oh d'you think so? She's got such a haughty expression ... sort of superior ... Perhaps she's shy ...' A clear voice, high and extraordinarily resonant cut in. 'She's the most beautiful person I ever saw. I adore her ... Have some toffee someone.'

Judith half-saw half-imagined the flash of a head under the lamp as she fled past. If that voice ... ? that voice had the sun in it.

She went on downstairs, looked for the fifth time in the box labelled E for letters addressed to herself, knew for the fifth time there could be none, and went on again, wandering among the ground-floor corridors; desired in sudden panic to get back to her room and found she had lost her way.

A girl came out of a door carrying a hot water can. She wore a pink flannel dressing-gown.

'Could you tell me,' asked Judith, 'how to get to a corridor called C?'

The girl looked at her closely and then beamed behind her glasses.

'Oh Miss Earle! Of course! We were up together for Scholarship Exams. Come in.'

Judith, helplessly conscious that this unpleasant dream was becoming a definite nightmare, followed her.

'Sit down,' said the girl. 'I'm so glad you came to find me. You remember my name – Mabel Fuller.'

Oh God! The creature thought she had been singled out for the purpose of soliciting friendship . . .

'I am so very glad you came to see me. I dare say you feel very strange?'

'A little. But I'm quite all right, thank you.'

'One feels very lonely at first. Never mind. Do you know anyone else? No, nor do I.' Her eyes glinted. 'We must stick together till we've got out bearings. It's a great thing to – I had a friend here once. She said the life was very jarring – such a whirl. We must try to make our little rooms as restful as possible. Do come to my room and work whenever you like. I always think it helps, don't you, to have somebody else in the room concentrating.'

Earnestly her eyes beamed and glinted behind their glasses. Presumably she was kind and well-meaning, but her skin was greasy and pink was not her colour; and her lank hair smelt; and when she talked she spat. The colourless face had nothing of youth in it. Perhaps this was what really clever girls looked like.

'I've spent today putting my room to rights,' said Mabel, looking happily round her. 'I do enjoy having a little corner of my own, my own things round me and . . . Tomorrow I must start work in earnest. How do you feel about your work? You're bound to waste time at first unless you plan out your day methodically. You must come and work in here. I won't disturb you. I'm a very hard worker myself. I shan't mix much with the other students.' She flushed. 'I shan't have time. And then of course there's getting into Cambridge for lectures and . . . Do you ride a bicycle? I find since I had pneumonia it tires me so . . . We must go to lectures together at first – keep each other company . . .'

'Are you reading English too?' said Judith with sinking heart.

'Oh yes.' Mabel bit her finger nervously. 'I didn't manage to get a scholarship, you know. It was a disappointment. I was feeling very poorly and altogether . . . I didn't do myself justice, Miss Fisher said. She wrote such a nice letter and . . . I was so set on coming here, it meant so much to me, I want to teach you know – if my health permits ... I haven't very good health ... so with what I'd managed to save and a little help from my mother ... she couldn't afford it really but when she saw what it meant to me ... so I must do well ... I can't disappoint her ... Are you preparing to earn your living?'

'I don't know,' said Judith blankly.

'You don't look like it,' said the other hurriedly with a furtive half-hostile glance at Judith's clothes. 'Most girls who come here have got to depend on their brains for a livelihood, so of course no one's got a right to come here just to amuse themselves, have they? But I dare say you're going to do very well. Miss Fisher told me this morning you'd done very good work for the scholarship. Oh yes. She quite praised you. I thought perhaps ... some of my notes and essays might be of use to you ... I take very full notes – my memory rather fails me sometimes and then ... I thought perhaps if we worked together we might – you know – help each other ... Another mind coming fresh to a subject ... We might ...'

Her eyes betrayed her: brain-sucker, probing for new full-blooded life. Judith thanked her politely and rose to go.

'Don't hurry,' said Mabel. 'I'll make you a cup of cocoa. I always think cocoa's so nourishing.'

She busied herself with a saucepan over the fire and breathed stertorously through her nose. Her skin glistened unhealthily in the firelight. The room was very close, full of pink casement cloth, and china ornaments. She had not minded the carpet: she had decorated the room to suit it. On the mantelpiece stood many photographs of creatures stoutly whaleboned about the throat or heavily whiskered and collared according to sex; and alone on top of the book-case was set the incongruous lovely photograph of a girl with curly bobbed hair. The large eyes laughed at you mischievously: the face insisted on being looked at – a soft face, sensuous and wilful, with a wide bow of a mouth; the smile a trifle consciously sweet, but irresistible.

'Oh, how pretty!' said Judith.

'My sister Freda,' said Mabel. 'Yes, she's generally admired.' She glanced suspiciously at Judith, as if to intercept the look of one saying incredulously: 'Your sister?' But Judith only looked dreamy.

For which minded most: Mabel because Freda was so pretty, or Freda because Mabel was so repulsive? Or were they fond of each other, sharing confidences and joking about Freda's lovers? . . . And was Freda vain and heartless or . . .

'Here's your cocoa,' said Mabel. 'Drink it hot.'

It was thick and syrupy, and Judith gave up after a few sips; but Mabel drank hers with obvious relish and ate doughnuts greedily out of a bag.

And did Mabel's mother console her by saying she was proud to have a clever daughter at College? – because she couldn't say, for instance, with any truth: 'Your hair, Mabel, is of a much finer quality than Freda's' – there was nothing of that sort to be said. Or did she pet Freda and neglect Mabel? . . .

'I really must go now,' said Judith. 'Thank you so very much. Good night.'

'Would you like to go for a walk with me on Sunday after church? We might go and hunt for pretty autumn leaves and berries. I always think they make a room look so bright . . .'

'Thank you very much.'

College leaves, college berries, picked with Mabel . . . Supposing you looked like Mabel, would you love beauty even more passionately, or be so jealous of it that you hated it?

Her eyes yearned at Judith. It was curious: they had in them a sort of avid glint – almost like the eyes of old men in railway-carriages . . . And did Freda maliciously encourage her to wear pink flannel? And . . .

'One thing more,' she said. 'I do hope you won't allow yourself . . . I mean we mustn't allow ourselves to – to get into a foolish set. It's so difficult to know at first . . . There's a set here, I'm told' – she paused, flushing unbecomingly to her forehead – 'there's a set here that thinks a great deal too much about – about going out, and dancing, and – men – all that sort of silliness . . . There, I'm sure you don't mind my telling you. You can always come to me for advice . . . I'm told the Mistress judges us by the people we go about with . . .

'Good night, Miss Earle,' she finished earnestly. 'There's your way: up the stairs and turn to the right. I'll look out for you at breakfast tomorrow.'

Black Mabel-haunted days and nights stretched out. No hope. No escape. Three years of Mabel settling down like a nightmare-bat, blotting out the light. Nobody but Mabel was going to speak to you for three years.

She passed two maids, flaxen-haired, red-cheeked, thick-featured Cambridgeshire types. They were turning out the lights in the corridors; and they smiled broadly at her. Maids were always nice, anyway.

'Good night,' she said shyly.

'Good night, Miss.'

At the corner of the corridor she heard one remark to the other: 'There's a sweet faice.'

A little comforted, she came to her own room, undressed and dropped a few tears.

If he could have known how very unlike his Cambridge this place was! Too late now ... There was not a spire, not a light of Cambridge to be seen, not a whisper to be heard. Almost she could believe something Childe Rolandish had happened to it and it was gone; so that even its unseen nearness was no comfort.

'Come in,' she said in startled response to a tap at her door. Someone stood there in a dressing-gown, with bright hair rolling over her shoulders.

'Oh!' cried Judith in uncontrollable rapture. 'I did hope ...'

They gazed at each other, blushing and radiant.

'I saw you at Hall.'

'Yes. I saw you.'

'I sat at the wrong table. It was awful.'

'I wish you'd been sitting beside me ... What's your name?'

'Judith Earle. What's yours?'

'Jennifer Baird.'

Yes. Jennifer was the right name.

'That's a nice name.'

'Why didn't you come yesterday?'

'I just forgot. I muddled the date ... Wasn't it an awful beginning?' They laughed.

'I always make muddles, don't you? I never remember dates and things.'

'Nor do I.'

They laughed again.

'I am thankful to find you, I can tell you,' said Jennifer. 'I was thinking I should be obliged to leave.'

'So was I.'

They beamed at each other.

'This is the third time I've come to find you. Where on earth have you been? I was afraid you'd locked yourself into the lavatory to cry or something.'

'I've been . . .' Judith laughed happily. 'I've been with something awful.'

'What?'

'It's called Mabel Fuller.'

'My God! Fuller. Has she pounced on you already? She tried me this morning. It's a funny thing, – she makes straight for the pretty ones. That sounds as if I meant I was pretty.'

'So you are.'

'I only meant I wasn't so hideous as her and you're lovely. She's a vampire-bat. D'you know, I found out something: she's twenty-seven at least. Think of it! I was rude to her. I suppose you weren't. I should say you were much more well-bred than me.'

'I wondered if she wasn't a *tiny* bit pathetic?'

'God no! What an idea! She hasn't a notion how revolting she is. She actually prattled about dress to me, – wondering how she'd look in a jumper like mine. As if anything but an Invisible Cloak would improve her. I can't stand people who spit when they talk.'

'I do wonder,' pondered Judith, 'how people like that get produced from quite normal parents. It must be the working-out of some ancient and fearful curse.'

'She's an ancient and fearful curse anyway,' said Jennifer gloomily. 'I'll tell you another thing. I believe she's got sex-repression.' She stared impressively at Judith; then broke into loud whistling. 'Have you got a cigarette? Never mind . . . I've just learnt to blow smoke-rings. I'll teach you.' More whistling. 'It's terrible to be so swayed by appearances. I'm afraid it's a sign of a weak character. Ugly people rouse all Hell's devils in me. And beautiful ones make me feel like the morning stars singing together. I want beauty, beauty, beauty . . . Don't you? Lovely people round me, lovely stuffs, lovely colours –

lashions and lashions of gorgeous things to touch and taste and look at and smell.' She flung her head back on its round white throat and took a deep sighing breath. 'O colours! . . . I could eat them. I'm awfully sensuous – I look it, don't you think? Or do I mean sensual? I always get them muddled; but I know it's unladylike to be one of them. I say – why didn't you speak to me after Hall?'

'Oh, how could I? You had people all round you. I passed your room, and there were dozens of girls in it.'

'Oh yes! Creatures I was at school with. I had a year in Paris after I left school. I think it developed me. I feel so much more mature than my contemporaries. I used to hunt at Chantilly. Have you ever done that? . . . They were all talking about you.'

'I heard them say I had such a haughty expression. I haven't have I?'

'Of course not. That's women all over. I wonder if men are really nicer? I suppose you're not engaged?'

'Oh no!'

'Nor am I. I don't suppose I shall ever marry. I'm too tall, – six foot in my stockings. It's awful, because I'm sure I shall always be falling in love myself – and I'm terrified of getting repressions. Are you in love?'

Judith thought of Roddy, blushed and said no.

'Oh well, you're too young I suppose. I'm twenty and two months – God! . . . Perhaps we shall both get engaged while we're here. Me first, I hope.' She chuckled deeply.

'But we shan't have time for anything except work,' said Judith. 'Mabel says we're expected to do at least eight hours a day.'

'Christ! Does she though! Just the sort of miserable immorality she would feed you up with. We're in the world to enjoy ourselves, not to pass exams, aren't we? Well then . . . I have a prejudice against intellectualism. It leads to all sorts of menaces. Perhaps you don't know . . . I dare say you were brought up in blackest ignorance, – like me. But I've managed to overcome all obstacles in the way of enlightenment. Do you call innocence a virtue? I don't. I call it stupidity.' She talked on so rapidly that her words ran into each other and got blurred. Leaning heavily on the mantelpiece she continued. 'Are these photographs your people? They look divinely aristocratic.

You're not an Honourable are you? You look as if you might be. Come and see my room. I say, let's make our rooms absolutely divine, shall we?'

'Mother told me to get whatever furniture and things I wanted,' said Judith. 'But what's the good with that carpet?'

'I've turned mine upside down,' said Jennifer. 'It's an artistic buff now. Come and look.'

She led the way back to her room and opened the door upon a scene of chaos. Her clothes had been half-unpacked and left about in heaps. The room was full of smoke and reeked of stale Gold Flakes Gramophone records, biscuits, apples, cake-knives, spoons, glasses and cups smeared with cocoa-sediment were strewn about the floor.

'It isn't as nice as I thought,' said Jennifer. 'The swine have feasted and rioted; *and* left me to clear up after them. Christ! What a spectacle! Have an apple.'

She sat down in her trunk and looked discouraged.

'I say, Judith Earle, do you think you're going to enjoy College?'

'Not much. It's so ugly and vulgar.'

'It is. And the students are such very jolly girls.'

'Yes. And I'm frightened of them. I don't know a soul. I've never in my life been with a lot of people and I don't feel I shall ever get used even to the smell of them. It's different for you. You've heaps of friends already.'

'Nonsense. There's no one. I've been screeching like a parrot all the evening, pretending to be awfully jolly too; but it strikes me as pretty grim ...' She brooded and whistled. 'More than a little grim ...' She drooped, flickered out completely.

'We'd – we'd better stick it out together,' said Judith with a blush, fearful lest her suggestion should condemn her to Jennifer – for Mabel had said it and she had felt sick.

'I should say we will. A thing's much less bloody if you can talk about its bloodiness to someone else. Do you mind the word bloody? I noticed you flinched. It's all a question of habit.' She revived – 'Christ! To think only a few days ago I was stalking in Scotland with my angel cousins! It's a very broadening thing for a young girl to have boy-cousins of her own age. I'm indebted to them for a lot of useful information – about sex and one thing and another. One of them gave me a bottle of champagne as a parting present. We've been drinking it – out of tooth glasses. Ugh! I dare say I'm a little tight. Don't you think so? One's got to do something . . . I'd offer you some, but I'm afraid the swine finished it. The bottle's in the cupboard.' She climbed over a trunk, opened the cupboard door and looked in. 'As I thought. Not a drop . . .'

There was a silence. She lit a cigarette, formed her full and vivid lips into an O and struggled painstakingly with smoke-rings.

The suddenness, thought Judith – the sureness, the excitement! . . . glorious, glorious creature of warmth and colour! Her blue eyes had a wild brilliance between their thick lashes: they flew and paused, stared, flew again . . .

'Isn't it awful,' said Jennifer, 'to have enlightened parents? They never ask you whether you care to be enlightened too, but offer you up from the age of ten onwards as a living sacrifice to examiners. And *then* they expect you to be grateful. Hmm!' She glowered at the photographs of a pleasant-looking couple on the mantelpiece. 'God! I'm tired. Give me a hand out of this trunk, and I'll get to bed.'

She struggled up, slipped off her dressing gown and stood revealed in striped silk pyjamas.

'Too late for my exercises tonight,' she said. 'Are you keen on muscle? It's more womanly not to be. I've over-developed mine. I can lend you a book called "How to Keep Fit" with pictures of young men in loin-cloths. You look wiry. Can you run?'

'Yes – and climb –' said Judith excitedly.

'Oh! . . . I can't imagine you doing anything except wander about looking innocent and bewildered. We might have some tests tomorrow!'

She went to the window, opened it wide and leaned out. Judith came and stood beside her. The night was still, dark and starry.

'The grounds are beautiful,' murmured Judith.

'Yes – great trees –' she murmured softly back. 'And nightingales, I believe, in spring.'

'Nightingales . . .'

'Oh, there's lots of things to look forward to,' said Jennifer, turning round and smiling full at Judith. Their eyes sparkled and flashed: sympathy flowed like an electric current between them. She went on:

'Oh Lord! Look at my bedroom. I'll just clear a space and sleep among the wreckage. Won't my gyp be pleased? It's best to begin as I shall certainly go on, so I'll leave it to her. She'll like it as soon as I've won her heart … Good night, Judith. I must tell you most people call me Jane.'

'I shall call you Jennifer. It's delicious, – different from anyone else. It's like you.'

From the pillow Jennifer's face broke into shy smiles, like a gratified child's.

Judith busied herself quietly in the sitting-room, tidying the cups and knives – enjoying the novel sensation of rendering service. After a few moments she called:

'You wouldn't suppose from their conversation that these girls are intellectual – would you?'

There was no reply. After a few more minutes she peeped into the bedroom. Jennifer's peaceful flushed countenance and regular breathing greeted her astonished senses.

She was sleeping the sleep of the slightly intoxicated just.

2

The Indian summer stretched out through October that year. The closing harmonies were so complete that the gardens of the earth seemed but to repeat and enrich the gardens of the sky; and a day like a sunflower broadened to a sunset full of dahlias and late roses; with clouds above them massed, burnished and edged with bloom like the foliage of the trees of earth. Slowly at night the chill mists, bitter-sweet in smell, luminous beneath the moon, crept over and blotted all out.

The weeks drifted on. College became a pleasant habit. Lecturers ceased to be oracles. Work ceased to be important. Young men stared in lecture rooms and streets. There grew the consciousness of fundamental masculine apartness: of the other sex mysteriously calling to and avoiding it across an impassable gulf. Bookshops became places in which to wander and browse whole mornings. Towards the town, back from the town, the long road stretched out daily between the flat ploughed fields: the immense and crushing arc of the sky was swept forever with rich changes.

And the buildings, – the fall of sunlight and shadow on grey stone, red stone, the unblurred design of roofs and walls at dusk, – the buildings lifted their bulk, unfolded their pattern, glowed upon the mind by day and by night, breaking in upon essays, disturbing time-papers.

Jennifer's shining head, curved cheek, lifted white throat lay against the blue curtain, just beyond the lamplight. Very late she sat there and said nothing, did nothing; made you lift eyes from the page, watch her, dream, wait for her smile to answer yours.

The garden, the river, the children next door were far away. Sometimes when you listened, there was nothing to be heard, not even Roddy; sometimes the bird-calls, the wet green scatters of buds, the flowering cherry tree; sometimes the sunny mown lawn in stripes, the red rambler clouds heavy on the hot wall; sometimes the mists, the bloom on the clouds, the fallen yellow leaves in the dew; sometimes the rooks rocking in the blown treetops, the strong dark bewildering pattern of bare branches swirling across the sky, the tragic light crying out for a moment at sunset, haggard through torn clouds, then drowned again: sometimes these moved in their seasons through the garden so faintly behind your shut eyes they stirred no pang. Sometimes the silent group waiting in the darkness by the river had vanished as if they had been childish things put away.

Time flowed imperceptibly, casting up trifles here and there upon its banks.

3

King's Chapel at Evensong. The coloured windows faded gradually out: only a twilight blue was left beneath the roof: and that died too. Then, only the double rows of candle-flames gave light, pointing and floating above the immemorial shadows of the floor and the shadows of benches and the shadowed faces of the old men and youths. Hushed prayer echoed; and the long rolling organ-waves rose and fell half-drowning the singing and setting it free again. All was muffled, flickering, submerged deep under cloudy water. Jennifer sat there motionless, wistful-eyed and unconscious, neither kneeling nor standing with others, but leaning rigidly back with eyes fixed and brilliant.

And afterwards came the emerging into a strange town swallowed up in mist. White surprising faces glimmered and vanished under the lamps. The buildings loomed formlessly in the dense sky, picked out by dimly-lit windows, and forlorn lanterns in the gateways. The life of Cambridge was thickly enshrouded; but under the folds you felt it stir more buoyantly than ever, with sudden laughter and talk dropping from the windows, weighing oddly in the air: as if the town were encouraging her children to sleep by drawing the curtain; while they, very lively at bedtime, went on playing behind it.

4

The lecture room window-pane was full of treetops – a whirl and sweep of black twigs on the sky. The room swam and shone in a faint translucent flood; and a bird called on three wild inquiring notes. These skies of February twilights had primroses in them, and floods; and with the primroses, a thought of green.

The small creakings, breathings and shufflings of the lecture room went on. The men: rows of heads of young looking hair; bored restless shoulders hunched beneath their gowns; sprawling grey flannel legs. The women: attentive rather anxious faces under their injudicious hats; well-behaved backs; hands writing, writing. Clods, all of them, stones, worse than senseless things.

The lecturer thought smoothly aloud, not caring who besides himself listened to him.

It was a situation meet for one of those paragraphic poems beginning

'The solemn greybeard lecturer drones on';

and after a few more lines of subtly satirical description some dots and a fresh start:

'Sudden a blackbird calls ... Ah sweet! Who heeds?'

No one heeds. Attention to greybeards has made everyone insensible to blackbirds. The conclusion would develop neatly along those lines.

A year or two ago, how fervently you would have written, how complacently desired to publish that sort of thing! No regret could be quite so sickly as that with which one wished out of existence the published record of last year's errors of taste.

'My dear he's the sort of person who'd *make arrangements* to have his juvenilia published after his death.'

That was the sort of condemnatory label Tony and his friends would attach, spreading their hands, leaving it at that.

'Roddy, where are you? Why do you never come?'

He flashed into mind, – leaning idly against the mantelpiece, listening with an obscure smile to Tony's conversation.

It was the sort of evening on which anything might happen. Excitement took her suddenly by the throat and made her feeble and tingling to her finger-tips.

The last of the light fell lingeringly on the grey stone window-frame. If the gold bloom lasted till you counted fifty, it would be a good omen. One, two, three, four and so on to twenty, thirty, forty ... crushing the temptation to count faster than her own heartbeats ... forty-five ... fifty.

It was still there, vanishing softly, but with a margin of at least another twenty to spare.

The ecstasy grew, making her stomach feel drained and helpless and beating in odd pulses all over her.

She bent over the desk, pretending to write, and making shaky pencil marks.

Somebody got up and switched on the light; and all at once darkness had fallen outside, and the window-pane was a purple-blue blank.

Roddy was in Tony's room, leaning against the mantelpiece, quite near. She would pass Tony's staircase on her way out: it was the one in the corner, facing the Chapel. She had seen his name every time she went by. Once she had met him coming out of the doorway, and he had looked through her; and once as she passed, someone in the court had shouted 'Tony'! and he had leaned from his high window to reply.

Oh this intolerable lecture!

Suddenly it was over. She came out and saw the bulk of King's Chapel in the deep twilight with its row of buttresses rising up pale, like giant ghosts.

'I've left my essay behind in the lecture room. I must go back. Don't wait for me.'

She went back a few steps until the gloom had swallowed them, and waited alone in the dark court. There was a light in Tony's window. Lingeringly she crept towards it and paused beneath it, stroking the wall. She lifted her head and cried speechlessly: 'Oh come! Come!'

Nobody came and looked out through the uncurtained pane. Nobody came running down the stairs.

And if she did not go on quickly the 'bus would start without her.

Let it start and then walk up and knock on Tony's door and say quite simply:

'I've missed my 'bus, so I've come to see Roddy.'

Roddy would spring forward to greet her. All would be made right with Tony.

For a moment that seemed the clear, delightful inevitable solution.

But what would their faces hide from her or betray? What unbearable amusement, suspicion, astonishment, contempt?

And what was there to do on such a night save to say to Roddy: 'I love you,' and then go away again? To dare everything, run to him and cry:

> I am Lazarus come from the dead,
> Come back to tell you all, I will tell you all.

But what if he should answer with that disastrous answer

> That is not what I meant at all,
> That is not it, at all.

If he were to stare and coldly reply, with real speech:
'Are you mad?'

Oh, but it should be risked! ...

She stood still, hesitating, her hand pressing the wall, power and intoxication dying out of her. She felt the night cold and damp, and heard approaching footsteps, a torn fragment of laughter, a male voice raised for a moment in the distance.

She looked up once more at Tony's window and saw that the curtains had been drawn; and she sprang away from the wall and ran towards the street in her urgent flight from wound, from the deliberate-seeming insult, the cruelty of drawn curtains.

The college 'bus was packed with girls. Heads were craning out in search of her.

'Oh Judy! There you are! We've been keeping the 'bus and keeping it. What on earth happened to you?'

'I couldn't get in. The room was locked. And then – Oh dear, I've run so! Is there room for me?'

'Yes, here. Come on, Judy. Here. Come and sit down. You're all out of breath. Come in.'

They welcomed her. Their little voices and gestures seemed to stroke and pat. They were so glad she had come in time, so considerate and kindly, so safe.

The 'bus rolled through the streets, past where the solemn lamps and the buildings ended, out on to the road where was only the enveloping night wind. The 'bus swayed and the rows of bodies swayed and the faces smiled faintly across at each other, amused at their own shaking and jerking; but all half-dreaming, half-hypnotized by the noise and the motion; all warm, languid, silent.

The noise and the motion and the swaying faces seemed eternal. Nothing else had ever been, would ever be. Of course Roddy had not been there: he had never been there at all.

5

Martin was a great athlete. He was always rowing, always training; but once or twice he borrowed a motor-bicycle and came out to tea, when Judith and Jennifer gave combined tea-parties to young men.

On these occasions his face was very red and he looked too big for the room. He was quite silent and stared with concentration at Judith and Jennifer alternately; and seemed not to take to his fellow guests. He was undoubtedly a heavy young man to have at a tea-party – a bad mixer. Jennifer's jokes, oaths, and sallies brought no gleam to his countenance, and Jennifer was bored with him. Impossible to convince her that Martin was not a dull young man.

Martin dull? . . .

God-like in form he dived from the raft and swam over the river, swiftly, with laughter, water and sun upon his face. He sat among them all and smoked his pipe, looking kindly and comforting. You could depend on his eyes solicitously watching, his smile inviting you to come in, when all the others, neither kindly nor comforting, had shut the door and gone away. He was the one to whom Mariella chattered at her ease and made little childish jokes, calling him 'darlin',' looking at him with candour and affection, sometimes even with a glint of mischief, as if she were a girl like any other girl; as if that something never fell across her clear face and obscured it. He shared a bedroom with Roddy; had a little screen at home, so he said, which Roddy had decorated, and given to him; he came walking up garden-paths with Roddy laughing and talking at his side.

In the darkness under the cherry tree he bent his head and tried to speak, twisting his scrap of cherry, trembling with enchantment. He had been a thing to fly from, surprised, with beating heart.

But when Jennifer said he was a dull young man, it was very difficult to argue with her; for it seemed almost as if, transplanted alone to this new world, he were indeed quite dull, rather ordinary.

He came to tea three times. The last time Judith went with him down the stairs – his deliberate, assured masculine tread sounding significant, almost alarming in that house of flustered uneven foolish-sounding steps – and said good night to him at the front door.

Fumbling with the lamps of his motor-bicycle he said:

'Why can't one ever see you alone?'

'It's not allowed, Martin. I can't ask you to tea alone. And I can't come to your rooms without a chaperon.'

'Oh damn the chaperon. I shan't ask you to tea at all. Can't you break a footling rule for anybody you know as well as me?'

She said deprecatingly that it was impossible.

'You mean you won't.'

That was what she meant. It was not worth while to break rules for dull Martin.

'Who's that Jennifer person you're always with?'

'A person I'm very fond of –' She flared at his tone.

'Never see you anywhere without her,' he muttered.

'Well you needn't come to tea with me.'

'Oh I shan't come again.'

'I shan't ask you.'

Silence fell. She looked up at the dark and starless sky; then at him still adjusting lamps, his head averted.

What were they about, parting in anger? How far indeed they were from the other world to mistrust and misunderstand so obstinately they had to quarrel!

Her heart misgave her suddenly at sight of the great building looming above her: there was no security in it, no kindness. Supposing when she went back Jennifer's room were empty, and Jennifer, utterly weary of her, had taken the chance to escape, and were even now knocking at strangers' doors, sure of her welcome? ... How quickly without that form, that voice, all would crumble and dissolve and be but a lightless confusion! She should never have left the places where Martin stood by her side, listening, watching, waiting everywhere to wrap her in safety.

She said softly:

'Martin, when is Roddy coming to see you?'

'He was here,' said Martin, 'a week or two ago. Staying with Tony Baring,' he added. And then again: 'Only for a night or two.'

Then finally trying in great embarrassment to soothe the pain which, even to his ears, cried out terribly in the silence and could not find words to cover it.

'I scarcely saw him myself. He was very busy – so many people to see. He'll be up again soon, I expect, and then we must have a party.'

'Oh yes, Martin ... You know, it's very naughty of him. He said he'd come and see me.'

Her voice was thin and cheerful.

'He's very forgetful,' said Martin helplessly.

'I suppose,' she suggested lightly, 'he forgot even to ask after me.'

'Oh no, he asked after you. I'm sure he did.'

She laughed.

'Well I must go in ... Tell him when you write to him ... No, don't tell him anything. But Martin, you must come and see me sometimes, please, *please*, – in this hateful place. I feel I shall lose you all again. You know Mother's going to live abroad for a year or two? So I shan't be there in the summer, next door. It's awful. She let the house without telling me. What shall I do without it? Please come and see me. Or listen, I tell you what: it doesn't seem to work somehow, your coming here. I can't talk to you and I feel I don't know you; but when the days get longer we'll go for a long walk together, miles and miles. Shall we? Remember!'

'Rather!'

He was happy again.

She called after him:

'And Martin, I'm sorry I was cross.'

'My fault,' came his ringing cheerful voice; and his engine started and he departed with a roar and a rush.

Alone in the dark she stood still and contemplated the appalling image of Roddy risen up again, mockingly asserting that only he was real; that his power to give himself or withhold himself was as the power of life and death.

It was urgent, now, to find Jennifer quickly. She was in her room, lying on the floor, staring at the flicker of firelight over her yellow velvet frock.

'Oh Jennifer!'

Judith sank down beside her, burying her face in her lap.

'Darling.'

'I'm not very happy tonight. It's a mood. I think I don't feel very well. And the night seems so sad and uneasy, with this wind. Don't you feel it?'

Jennifer put out her hands and clasped them round Judith's face, gazing at her sombrely.

'What has he said to you?' she whispered.

'Who?'

'That Martin.'

'Nothing. It's nothing to do with him.'

'You love somebody, I think. Who is it you love?'

'I love nobody.'

Jennifer must never never know, suspect, dream for a moment . . .

'You mustn't love anybody,' said Jennifer. 'I should want to kill him. I should be jealous.' Her brooding eyes fell heavily on Judith's lifted face. 'I love you.'

And at those words, that look, Roddy faded again harmlessly: Jennifer blinded and enfolded her senses once more, and only Jennifer had power.

When the longer days came and Martin wrote to ask her to come for a walk one Sunday, she had another engagement and regretfully refused; and after that he wrote to tell her to bring a friend to a river picnic with him and another young man. She brought Jennifer; and Jennifer flirted broadly with the other young man; and the picnic was not a success.

After that the year closed without sight or sign of him; and she forgot to care.

6

Gradually Judith and Jennifer drew around them an outer circle of about half a dozen; and these gathered for conversation in Jennifer's room every evening. That untidy luxuriant room, flickering with fire-light, smelling of oranges and chrysanthemums, was always tacitly chosen as a meeting-place; for something of the magnetism of its owner seemed to be diffused in it, spreading a glow, drawing tired heads and bodies there to be refreshed.

Late into the night they sat about or lay on the floor, smoked, drank cocoa, ate buns, discussed – earnestly, muddle-headedly – sex, philosophy, religion, sociology, people and politics; then people and sex again. Judith sat in a corner and watched the firelight caress and beautify their peaceful serious faces; talked a great deal suddenly now and then, and then was silent again, dreaming and wondering.

Even the most placid and commonplace faces looked tragic, staring into the fire, lit by its light alone. They were all unconscious; and she herself could never be unconscious. Around her were these faces, far away and lost from themselves, brooding on nothing; and there was she, as usual, spectator and commentator, watching them over-curiously, ready to pounce on a passing light, a flitting shade of expression, to ponder and compare and surmise; whispering to herself: 'Here am I watching, listening. Here are faces, forms, rooms with their own life, noise of wind and footsteps, light and shadow. What is this mystery? ...' And even in her futile thoughts never quite stepping over the edge and staring mindlessly and being wholly unaware.

They broke up at last with sighs and yawns, lingered, drifted away little by little. Judith was left alone with Jennifer.

'One more cigarette,' she suggested.

'Well, just one.'

Jennifer let down her hair and brushed it out, holding it along her arm, watching it shimmer in the firelight with an engrossed stare, as if she never could believe it was part of her.

Always Jennifer. It was impossible to drink up enough of her; and a day without her was a day with the light gone.

Jennifer coming into a room and pausing on the threshold, head up, eyes wide open, darting round, dissatisfied until they found you. That was an ever fresh spring of secret happiness. Jennifer lifting you in her arms and carrying you upstairs, because she said you looked tired and were such a baby and too lovely anyway to walk upstairs like other people.

Jennifer basking in popularity, drawing them all to her with a smile and a turn of the head, doing no work, breaking every rule, threatened with disgrace, plunged in despair; emerging the next moment new-bathed in radiance, oblivious of storm and stress.

Jennifer dispensing her hospitality with prodigal and careless ease, recklessly generous in public and in secret, flashing the glow of her magnetism suddenly into unlit and neglected lives, allowing them to get warm for a little, and then light-heartedly forgetting them. But never forgetting Judith – or not for long; and coming back always to sit with her alone, and drop all masks and love her silently, watch-fully with her eyes.

Jennifer singing Neapolitan folk-songs to a be-ribboned guitar. Where she had picked up the airs, the language, the grace and fascination of her manner, no one knew. But when she sat by the window with bright streamers falling over her lap, singing low to her soft accompaniment, then, each time, everyone fell madly in love with her.

Jennifer chattering most when she was tired, or depressed, her words tripping over each other, her absurd wit sparkling, her laugh frequent and excited: so silent, so still when she was happy that she seemed hypnotized, her whole consciousness suspended to allow the happiness to flow in.

Jennifer looking shattered, tortured after a few hours spent by mistake over coachings and time-papers in stuffy rooms; starting up in the end with a muttered: 'Oh God, this place! . . .' wrenching open the door and rushing downstairs, oblivious of all but the urgency of her mood. From the window you could see her in the grounds, running, running. Soon the trees hid her. She was tramping over the ploughed fields, her cheeks glowing, her hair like a light against the dark hedges. She was going, alone, tensely, over the long fields. What was she thinking of? She had her evasions. No good to ask her: her eyes would fly off, hiding from you. She would not let herself be known entirely.

By Judith's shadowy side ran the hurrying flame of Jennifer; and from all that might give her pause, or cloud her for a moment Jennifer fled as if she were afraid.

The lonely midnight clouded her. Jennifer was afraid of the dark.

Was it that people had the day and the night in them, mixed in varying quantities? Jennifer had the strength of day, and you the strength of night. By day, your little glow was merged in her radiance; but the night was stronger, and overcame her. You were stronger than Jennifer in spite of the burning life in her. The light hid the things for which you searched, but the darkness and the silence revealed them. All your significant experiences had been of the night. And there, it was suddenly clear, was the secret of the bond with Roddy. He too had more shadow in him than sun. *Chevalier de la lune*, that was he – '*Que la lumière importune*' – ah! yes! '*Qui cherche le coin noir*' – yes, yes – '*Qui cherche le coin noir.*' Some time – it did not matter when, for it was bound to happen – he would say in the dark 'I love you.'

Meanwhile there was Jennifer to be loved with a bitter maternal love, because she was afraid. And because, some day, she might be gone. For Jennifer said 'I love you' and fled away. You cried 'Come back!' and she heard and returned in anguish, clasping you close but dreading your dependence. One day when you most needed her, she might run away out of earshot, and never come back.

But there was value in impermanence, in insecurity; it meant an ache and quickening, a perpetual birth; it meant you could never drift into complacence and acceptance and grow old.

There was Mabel, drifting into Judith's life when conscience pricked and being joyfully dismissed again when the exigencies of duty seemed satisfied. There were little notes from Mabel found, with a sinking feeling, among her letters.

Dear J.,

Would you care to come to church with me on Sunday? I shall be ready at 10.15. I do hope you will come this week.

Yrs.
M.F.

Dear Judith,

I thought you did not look quite yourself at lunch today. If there is anything worrying you, perhaps I might help you? Or if you are tired, come and rest in my armchair. I shall be working and will not disturb you.

Yours Mabel.

P.S. It's all *this rushing* about that *wears you out* and makes you *unfit* for work.

M.F.

Mabel wrote her advice now, more often than she dared speak it.

Mabel, always pathetic, so that you could never entirely disregard her; always grotesque and untouched by charm so that it was impossible to think of her or look at her without revulsion; so that the whole thing was a tedious and barren self-discipline.

Mabel little by little relinquishing the effort to draw Judith into her life and desperately endeavouring to fit herself into Judith's: chattering to other girls, trying to be amused by their jokes, to share their enthusiasms and illusions; pretending to have a gay home-life, full of interesting friends and fun; pretending to laugh at the thought of work and to treat lightly that nightmare of the Tripos which crushed her to the earth.

Once or twice Judith tried to draw her into the evening circle, explaining her loneliness, appealing beforehand for her pathos ... But it was no good. She was of another order of beings, – dreary and unadaptable. And Jennifer, with a wicked light in her eye, spoke loudly and with malicious irreverence of dons, the clergy and the Bible; and mentioned the body with light-hearted frankness; and Judith felt ashamed of herself for thinking Jennifer funny.

Mabel striving doggedly to believe that Jennifer was in the nature of an illness from which Judith would recover by careful treatment, then striving to ignore the importance of the relationship – staking out an exclusive claim in Judith by references suggestive of a protective intimacy.

'Now, now! Pale cheeks! What will your mother say, I'd like to know, if I let you go home looking like this? I shall have to come and put you to bed myself.'

And there followed the flush and the hungry gleam while awkwardly she touched Judith's cheek.

Mabel at long last voluntarily dropping out of all the places into which she had tried to force herself, going back without a word to her solitary room and her doughnuts. There were no more little notes rearing unwelcome heads in the letter-box. She asked nothing.

From the window late at night Judith could see her lamp staring with a tense wan hopeless eye across the court. In the midst of talk and laughter with Jennifer, she saw it suddenly and knew that Mabel was sitting alone, hunched over note-books and dictionaries, breathing stertorously through her nose hour after hour, dimly hoping that her uncurtained window might attract Judith's attention, persuade her to look in and say good night.

'Jennifer, I won't be five minutes. I must just go and see Mabel. It's awful. You don't know. She expects me; and she'll sit up all night working if I don't go.'

'Tell her about the young lady of Bute with my love and a kiss,' said Jennifer in the loud voice edged with brutality which she reserved for Mabel. 'And say the mistress is very disappointed in her because she's discovered she doesn't wear corsets. She's going to speak about it publicly tomorrow night because it's very immoral. And ask her what *will* her mother say if you let her go home with all those spots on her face.'

Judith escaped, laughing, ran down the dark stairs to Mabel's room and tapped.

'Come in.'

It was clear from her voice she had been alert at the sound of the known footsteps. She raised a pallid face that tried for a moment to begrudge its gladness and preserve a stiffness.

'Now, Mabel, I'm come to put you to bed. I like all your talk of looking after *me*. It's you who need it. What do you suppose you'll feel like tomorrow if you work any more? Come on now.'

That was the way she loved to be talked to. Judith filled her hot-water bottle and made cocoa, while with laborious modesty she donned her flannel nightdress with its feather-stitched collar; and pouted coyly and happily, like any other girl, because Judith was such a dragon.

Then she leaned back in her chair with the work-lines in her face smoothing out, and yawned contentedly and talked of little intimate things, giving them to Judith without reserve, as Judith gave hers to Jennifer – suddenly, pitifully like any other girl.

These were her happy compensating moments: they made her think for a while that the friendship was rare and firm.

How easy it was, thought Judith, to permit her to enjoy your incongruous presence; to step right into her world and close the gates on your own so fast that no chill air from it might breathe against her security! Alone with her like this, no lapse of taste on her part ruffled the nerves. You accepted her and let her reveal herself; and she was, after all, interesting, human, gentle, and simple. There was nothing – this time you must remember – nothing grotesque or ridiculous to report to Jennifer afterwards, hatefully betraying and mocking ...

She spoke of her life in the narrow church-bound village home; her future: she would teach, and so have her own little independent place in the world. She didn't think she was the marrying sort; but you never knew. Independence was what she craved: to support herself and be beholden to no one. Only she must pass well: (and her eyes would wander haggardly to the books) – it all depended on her health – she'd never enjoyed very good health. She always thought if she felt better she wouldn't forget so. It made work very hard. Freda had always been the strong one. Everything came easy to Freda. Everyone admired and petted her: she was getting so spoilt, and extravagant too. She wouldn't go so far as to say she and Freda had much in common, but you couldn't help but love her in spite of all her naughtiness. And the quick way she had of answering back! She recited some of Freda's quick answers, giggling like any other girl.

There was a curate who had coached her in Greek and Latin. He was a wonderful man, a real saint: not like anyone else at all, young, a beautiful face and such eyes. Once he had come to tea with her, and they had had a wonderful talk, just the two of them. Freda had been out. It really seemed as if he looked on her as a friend. She hoped so ... He had helped her.

Judith listened, asked questions, sympathized, cheered her with offers of notes and essays; tucked her into bed with an effort at motherliness; and flew with a light heart back to Jennifer.

The curate ... at all costs, she must *not* tell Jennifer about the curate.

7

The long days of May stretched out before Judith and Jennifer. Each day was a fresh adventure in the open air, and work an unimportant and neglected nuisance. For weeks the weather remained flawless. Life narrowed to a wandering in a green canoe up small river-channels far from the town, with Jennifer paddling in wild bursts between long periods of inaction. To all Judith's offers of help she answered firmly that a woman should never depart from her type.

They landed finally and made ready to bathe.

'Off, off, you lendings!' cried Jennifer. 'Do you know, darling, that comes home to me more than anything else in all Shakespeare? I swear, Judith, it seems much more natural to me to wear no clothes.'

She stood up, stretching white arms above her head. Her cloud of hair was vivid in the blue air. Her back was slender and strong and faultlessly moulded.

'Glorious, glorious pagan that I adore!' whispered the voice in Judith that could never speak out.

Beside Jennifer she felt herself too slim, too flexible, almost attenuated.

'You are so lovely,' Jennifer said watching her.

They swam in cool water in a deep circular pool swept round with willow, and dried themselves in the sun.

They spent the afternoon in the shade of a blossoming may bush. All round them the new green of the fields was matted over with a rich and solid layer of buttercup yellow. Jennifer lay flat on her back with the utter relaxed immobility of an animal, replenishing her vitality through every nerve.

Slowly they opened books, dreamed through a page, forgot it at once, laid books aside; turned to smile at each other, to talk as if there could never be enough of talking; with excitement, with anxiety, as if tomorrow might part them and leave them for ever burdened with the weight of all they had had to tell each other.

Judith crept closer, warming every sense at her, silent and entirely peaceful. She was the part of you which you never had been able to untie and set free, the part that wanted to dance and run and sing, taking strong draughts of wind and sunlight; and was, instead, done up in intricate knots and overcast with shadows; the part that longed to look outward and laugh, accepting life as an easy exciting thing; and yet was checked by a voice that said doubtfully that there were dark ideas behind it all, tangling the web; and turned you inward to grope among the roots of thought and feeling for the threads.

You could not do without Jennifer now.

The sun sank, and the level light flooded the fields and the river

Now the landscape lost its bright pure definitions of outline, its look as of a picture embroidered in brilliant silks, and veiled its colours with a uniform pearl-like glow. A chill fell and the scent of may grew troubling in the stillness. They turned the canoe towards home.

Nearer the town, boats became more frequent. Gramophones clamoured from the bowels of most of them; and they were heavily charged with grey-flannelled youth. Jennifer, observing them with frank interest, pointed out the good-looking ones in a loud whisper; and all of them stared, stared as they passed.

Above the quiet secretly-stirring town, roofs, towers and spires floated in a pale gold wash of light. What was the mystery of Cambridge in the evening? Footfalls struck with a pang on the heart, faces startled with strange beauty, and every far appearing or disappearing form seemed significant.

And when they got back to College, even that solid red-brick barrack was touched with mystery. The corridors were long patterns of unreal light and shadow. Girls' voices sounded remote as in a dream, with a murmuring rise and fall and light laughter behind closed doors. The thrilling smell of cowslips and wall-flowers was everywhere, like a cloud of enchantment.

In Jennifer's room, someone had let down the sun-blind, and all was in throbbing shadow. Her great copper bowl was piled, as usual, with fruit, and they ate from it idly, without hunger.

'Now a little work,' said Judith firmly. 'Think! only three weeks till Mays . . .'

But it was impossible to feel moved.

Jennifer, looking childish and despondent, sat down silently by the window with a book.

Judith wrote on a sheet of paper:

Tall oaks branch-charmèd by the earnest stars; and studied it. That *was* a starry night: the sound of the syllables made stars prick out in dark treetops.

Under it she wrote:

> . . . the foam
Of perilous seas in faery lands forlorn.

What a lot there were for the sea and the seashore! ... The page
became fuller.

> Upon the desolate verge of light
> Yearned loud the iron-bosomed sea.

> The unplumbed salt estranging sea.

> From the lone sheiling of the misty island
> Mountains divide us and a world of seas:
> But still the blood is strong, the heart is Highland;
> And we in dreams behold the Hebrides.

Ah, that said it all ...
The lines came flocking at random.

> But the majestic river floated on,
> Out of the mist and hum of that low land
> Into the frosty starlight, and there flowed
> Rejoicing through the hushed Chorasmian waste
> Under the solitary moon ...

> Ah sunflower weary of time
> That countest the steps of the sun ...

Ah sunflower! ... Where were they – the old gardens of the sun
where my sunflower wished to go? They half unfolded themselves
at the words ...

> Nous n'irons plus aux bois
> Les lauriers sont coupés.

O mors quam amara est memoria tua homini pacem habenti in
substantiis suis ...

How with one tongue those both cried alas!
And then in the end, sleep and a timeless peace

> Nox est perpetua una dormienda.

There were so many tumbling and leaping about in your head you
could go on for ever ...

Now to study them. What did it all mean? Was there any thread running through them with which to make a theory? Anybody could write down strings of quotations, – but a student of English literature was expected to deal in theories. It was something to do with the sound ... the way sound made images, shell within shell of them softly unclosing ... the way words became colours and scents ... and the surprise when it happened, the ache of desire, the surge of excitement, the sense of fulfilment, the momentary perception of something unknowable ... Some sort of truth, some answer to the question: What is poetry? ... No it was no good. But it had been very enjoyable, writing things down like that and repeating them to yourself.

Jennifer was half asleep with her head upon the window-sill. The bowl of fruit burned in the dimness. How like Jennifer was her room! Yellow painted chairs, a red and blue rug on the hearth, cowslips in coloured bowls and jars, one branch of white lilac in a tall blue vase; the guitar with its many ribbons lying on the table; a silken Italian shawl, embroidered with great rose and blue and yellow flowers flung over the screen: wherever you looked colour leapt up at you; she threw colour about in profuse disorder and left it. Her hat of pale green straw with its little wreath of clover lay on the floor. Nobody else had attractive childish hats like hers. A wide green straw would remind you of Jennifer to the end of your life; and beneath it you would see the full delicious curve of her cheek and chin, her deep-shadowed eyes, her lips that seemed to hold all life in their ardent lines.

She turned her head and smiled sleepily.

'Hullo!' said Judith. 'Haven't we been quiet? I've done such a lot of work.'

'I've done none. I couldn't remember the difference between ethics and aesthetics. What rot it all is! ... Now listen and we'll hear a nightingale. He's tuning up.'

They leaned out of the window.

The icy aching flute in the cedar called and called on two or three notes, uncertain, dissatisfied; then all at once found itself and bubbled over in rich and complicated rapture.

Jennifer was listening, tranced in her strange immobility, as if every other sense were suspended to allow her to hear aright.

She roused herself at last as Judith bent to kiss her good night.

'Good night my – darling – darling –' she said.

They stared at each other with tragic faces. It was too much, this happiness and beauty.

The end of the first year.

8

The next moment so it seemed, the soft and coloured autumn days were there again; the corridors, the echoing steps, the vast female yell of voices in Hall, the sense of teeming life in all the little rooms, behind the little closed doors – all these started again to weave their strange timeless dream; and the second year had begun.

Midway through the term came Martin's letter.

Dear Judith,

Roddy is in Cambridge for two nights, staying with Tony. He wants to see you. Will you come to tea with me tomorrow at 4.30? I am to tell you he will never forgive you (a) if you don't come (b) if you come with a chaperon. He says that chance alone prevented him from being your bachelor uncle; and that I myself was a maiden aunt from the cradle. So please come.

Martin.

Dear Martin

Bachelor uncles are notorious; and curious things are apt to happen to strictly maiden aunts as all we enlightened moderns know. But an aunt and uncle bound by holy matrimony are considered safe (as safety goes in this world) and I have notified the authorities of their brief presence in the university and am cordially permitted to wait on them at tea tomorrow at 4.30.

Judith.

Judith looked around Martin's room. It was untidy and rather dirty, with something forlorn and pathetic and faintly animal about it, like all masculine rooms. It made you want to look after him. Men were helpless children; it was quite true. You might have known Martin's room would give you a ridiculous pull at the heart.

'I'm afraid things are in a bit of a mess,' said Martin, blowing cigarette ash off the mantelpiece into the fire.

He was smoking an enormous pipe. His face was red. His great form looked lumbering and shapeless in an ancient tweed coat and a pair of voluminous grey flannel trousers.

'How are you, Judith?' His brown eye fixed itself on her. He was very shy.

'I've been ill, Martin.'

'Oh! . . .' He looked troubled and embarrassed. 'Did you – did you have a decent doctor?'

'Oh yes. It was almost pneumonia, but not quite.'

'I didn't know you'd been ill . . .'

'You haven't been to see me for ages, Martin.'

'I know. I've been so busy.' Violently he blew the ash about. What a shame to pretend to reproach him. He was obviously overcome . . . 'And I didn't think you wanted . . . I suppose you're all right again now?'

Footsteps sounded outside on the stair. Judith collected herself and sat rigid. The door opened and Roddy, smiling, eager, debonair, came into the room.

'Hullo Judy! Marvellous to see you.'

'Roddy!'

He stood before her and looked down into her face.

'I thought I was never going to see you again, Judy. You're looking marvellous.'

He was going to be irresistible. Already something in her was starting to leap up in response to him; and watching his face, she saw with a terrible pang that it was true, unarguable, proved over again more clearly than ever, that he had some quality which separated him from everybody else in the whole world, startled the imagination and made him of appalling significance to her.

'I'm cold. Thank God for a good fire. It's starting to snow.' He flung himself down on the hearth-rug. 'Trust Martin to make a good thick atmosphere with no beastly fresh air about it. Tea! Tea! Tea! Let me make you some toast, Judy. I make it so well.'

While he toasted great hunks of bread, Martin buttered scones and cut the cake, and Judith poured out tea.

They chattered, joked, teased each other. They played absurd drawing and rhyming games. Judith made them laugh with malicious stories of dons and students. Roddy threw back his head, his whole face wrinkled and flattened with silent laughter, his eyes gleaming with amusement under their lids. Martin stared, laughed, Ha! Ha! – stared again. They encouraged her, listened to her, were delighted with her; and the old sense of abnormal self-assurance grew within her taut mind.

At last she made herself look at the clock. So late! There would barely be time to get back before Hall.

'I've got a car outside,' said Roddy carelessly, 'I can run you out in no time.'

He added, interrupting her thanks:

'It isn't mine, it's got no hood, it always breaks down and it's hellishly uncomfortable, so I don't advise it really.'

It sounded as if he were suddenly regretting his offer, trying to withdraw it. She looked at him, all her confidence collapsing in a moment. His face had become a mask.

She said swiftly.

'If you would take me I should be very grateful.' Her voice sounded to herself strained, beseeching, horrible.

He bowed.

It took ten minutes to get the car started, with Martin and Roddy madly swinging her by turns.

'Good night, Martin. Thank you for my lovely tea party. I'll see you again soon, won't I?'

He nodded, looking gravely down at her in the lamp-light.

'Don't catch cold,' he said. There was something dejected about his attitude, a flatness in his voice ... Things had gone wrong for him ... Ever since that panic-stricken voice had broken in on the laughter and talk, the game for three, with its vibrating cry: 'If you would take me home ...' from that moment all had been faintly blown upon by a ruffle of uneasy wind. They were no longer three persons, but two men and one woman.

She knew it and loathed herself because Martin knew it too.

'I'm due to dine with Tony in twenty minutes,' said Roddy. 'You'd better come along too. I'll call for you on my way back. I shan't be long.'

Roddy's voice had forced a note of carelessness ... as if he were trying to pretend to Martin that nothing had happened; that the female had not suddenly singled him out and stretched an inviting hand to him as he stood beside his friend.

Even Roddy was aware of it.

'No,' said Martin, 'I won't dine with Tony. I'll see you tomorrow perhaps.'

He waved his hand and turned away. The car started. She was alone with a strange man.

The night was dark, with a piercing wind and a faint flurry of snow in the air. Roddy drove at a great pace, and she sat beside him in silence, her shoulder touching his.

'Cold?' he said suddenly.

'No, I don't feel – anything.'

All of life was concentrating in her dark beating mind: her body was insensible to the weather. She saw the gates of College fly past. its lights gleamed and were gone; and she could not speak. On they went, the long straight empty road flung before them in small lengths by the headlights and rolled up into nothingness behind them, cast away for ever.

He stopped the car suddenly.

'Where's this place?'

'I think we've passed it long ago.'

The wind took her small voice away from him. He leaned towards her.

'What?'

She turned to him.

'I think we've passed it long ago.'

'I think we have.'

Silence. The great wind blowing through illimitable deeps of night lifted and whirled her beyond time and space. She saw his hand lying on the wheel – a pale blur; and her own crept out and lay beside it; and she stared at them both. He watched her hand fall beside his and did not move a hair's breadth nearer to touch it. He and she were alone together. No need for speech or movement. Their hands would lie motionless, side by side, for ever and ever.

She heard him laugh softly; and as he laughed her hand came quickly to her lap.

'Well, what d'you want to do?' he said very low.

'I don't want to go back.'

'Do you want to go on?'

'Yes.'

The car went forward again. Once she leaned towards him and said in his ear:

'Roddy!'

'Yes?'

'*You* didn't want to go back, did you?'

'No.'

She lay back again, mindlessly at peace in the midst of the roaring of the wind, and the road's monotonous unfolding.

Once he burst out laughing, patted her knee and cried:

'*Aren't we mad?*'

His voice rang boyishly, happily.

Now came the snow, thinly at first, but soon in wild drifting clouds, blotting out the road, settling thick and fast over all, sifting and piling on the wind-screen.

'Oh Lord, we must turn,' said Roddy. 'This is frightful.'

He turned the car and then stopped her to light a cigarette. She saw his face, lit by the flare of the match, glow suddenly, warmly out of the darkness with unknown curves and strange planes of light and shadow, and narrowed eyes, eyes not human, never-to-be-forgotten.

He waved the dwindling flame in her face.

'Solemn face! What are you staring at? Smile – quick, quick, before the match goes out!'

The match went out.

'I am smiling, Roddy.'

'That's right. Poor Judy covered with snow! There you sit, so modest and unassuming. Shall I get you home alive?

'I don't care.'

She slipped her arm through his, and he gave it a quick friendly pressure and drove on.

Now they were before the gates of College. After all they had not driven very far. Time started again with a reluctant painful beat as the car crept in under the archway, and she realized that it was little more than an hour since they had left Martin. It seemed so short now – less than a moment; a pause between a breath and another breath.

They sat side by side in the car without moving.

'I suppose I must go in now,' she said at last. 'They'll still be at Hall.'

He shivered and beat his hands together. She took one and felt it, and it was icy.

'Your hands. Oh Roddy! Will you come in and get warm by my fire?'

He seemed to be considering and then said in a stilted way:

'If I may – just for a minute – I've got rather chilled driving without gloves.'

She could find nothing to say. A cold shy politeness had descended on them both. She led the way into the hall and up the stairs. At every step snow fell off them: their shoulders and arms were covered in it. The corridors were silent and deserted, echoing only her light footsteps, and his heavier ones. She heard her tread, and his following after it, marching, marching towards her far-off door. Judith was bringing Roddy, Judith was, in sober truth, bringing Roddy to her room. If anyone saw her there would be trouble.

Somebody – Jennifer perhaps – must have drawn the curtains and heaped the fire in the little room. The warmth drew out the smell of the chrysanthemums; and their heavy golden heads, massed in a blue jar, held mysterious intensity of life in the firelight. She switched on the reading lamp, and all the colours in the room leapt up dimly, secretly: purple, blue and rose-colour glowed around them, half-lit, half-obscured.

'This is rather seductive,' he said. He sank on his knees by the fire and held out his hands to the blaze, looking about him with a faint smile. She came and knelt beside him; and his eyes fastened narrowly on her face.

146

'It's like you: seductive,' he said softly.

'Oh Roddy! Seductive. That's all it is. I see it now. I hate it. Am *I* nothing more than that?'

'You ... I don't know what you are. I can't make you out. You *never* behave as I think you probably will.'

'I'm glad of that.'

'Why are you glad?'

'Because I believe you ascribe to me the worst motives, – the most ambiguous. You suspect me – you guard yourself against me.'

'I don't, Judy.'

'Ah you do. But you needn't. I won't do you any harm. Unless being – very fond of you can do you harm. But I don't think I'm a *femme fatale*.'

'I don't know what you are. You disturb me very much. You seem to me completely incalculable. Your eyes watch me and watch me. Such marvellous eyes.'

She lifted them to his in a long steady look and remained silent.

'You're very nice,' he said. 'Rather a dear. I believe you're quite without guile really. Why do you trust people so? It's very foolish of you.'

'Is it foolish of me to trust you?'

'Incredibly foolish.' He added, raising his voice and speaking slowly: 'It's no good trying to make me – adequate.'

'Ah you like to destroy yourself to me.'

'But don't you see? I go through the days in a sort of apathy; blind and deaf; blinder and deafer every day. I never think, I never care. I'd much better be dead, only I'm too lazy to shoot myself.'

'Oh Roddy, don't.'

She covered her ears with her hands. He had never spoken at such length, or with such obvious intent to convince.

'I'm only trying to warn you,' he said, rather defiantly, 'I'm not worth saving. Nobody must *ever* take me seriously. I'm not worth wasting a moment over. Nobody can do anything with me.'

His mood was verging towards laughter. His face broke up teasingly as he finished speaking and turned to look at her. But she averted her face, drearily pondering.

Why had he spoken like that? A self-contempt so settled, so hopeless ... He had seemed to be warning her to keep away from him for her own sake.

'It's no good,' she said suddenly, involuntarily.

'What's no good?'

'You're what I choose to think you are. There's no point in heaping yourself with abuse. You can't make me dislike you; you can only make me sad. But I suppose that gives you pleasure.'

He was silent. She went on tremulously:

'And when you – when people say they don't feel or care – that they're no good – it only makes me think – I could shew them how to feel and care. I could make them happy. I could look after them. I dare say you know that's – the effect it has on me. That's why you say it.'

He was still silent. She leaned her head forward against the wall and felt tears smart under her lids.

He seemed to be musing, his eyes fixed on the fire, his hands held out to it.

'Are your hands still cold?' she said wearily. 'Get them warm before you go.'

Suddenly he held them out to her.

It was a gesture so impulsive, so uncharacteristic, it seemed of startling significance; and she could not answer it.

'Yes, they are cold,' he said. 'Let me feel yours. Yours are cold too. What funny hands – so thin and narrow, such delicate bones. Rather lovely.' He clasped them hard in his own. 'When I do that they seem to go to nothing.'

She smiled at him dimly, half-tranced, feeling her eyelids droop over her eyes, giving him, with her helpless hands, all of herself; as if, through her finger-tips, he drew her in to himself in a dark stemlessly flowing tide. He stroked her palms, her whole hand, over and over with a lingering careful touch, as if learning the outline by heart.

'They feel so kind,' he said musingly. 'They are, aren't they, Judy? Dear little kind things – like the rest of you. Are you always kind, Judy?'

'Always to you, Roddy, I shouldn't wonder.'

He relinquished his clasp suddenly, saying with a shake of the head:

'You shouldn't be ... However, I've warned you '

'Yes, you've warned me.'

She smiled at him sadly.

In a minute she must tell him to go. They would be coming out of Hall, bursting into the room to discover the cause of her absence.

'Are you tired?' he said.

She nodded, realizing suddenly the collapsed forward droop of her body, the whole pose of deadly fatigue.

'I've been very ill, you know.'

'Oh dear! You never told me. You let me take you for that bloody cold drive. You'll be ill again.'

'It's all right. I shan't be ill again.'

'You *are* naughty,' he said, looking at her anxiously.

He never could bear people to be ill or in pain.

'Come and lie down at once on the sofa,' he said.

She obeyed him, and let him arrange the cushions beneath her shoulders, with a delicious sense of dependence.

'The drive won't have hurt me,' she said, 'because I enjoyed it so much.'

He stood looking down at her.

'Did you enjoy it?' he said softly.

'Yes, didn't you?'

'Yes.'

'Wasn't it a queer unreal drive?'

'Quite unreal, I suppose.'

'I wish it had never stopped.'

He made no answer to this but still stood watching her.

'You'll have to go, Roddy. They mustn't find you. Besides you'll be missing your dinner.'

'I've missed that long ago, I should think.'

'Oh Roddy, how awful! I've made you miss your dinner.'

'I know. It's monstrous of you. And I'm so hungry.'

'I've missed mine too but I'm not hungry ... Roddy what will Tony say to you?'

'He'll be very much annoyed.'

'Shall you say you were with me? He wouldn't like that, would he?'

'No.'

'Tony is jealous of me. Once he looked at me with pure hatred. I've never forgotten it. Does he love you?'

'I think he does.'

'I think he does too. Do you love him? You needn't answer. I know I mustn't ask you that.'

'You can ask me anything you like.'

But he did not answer.

'It is so terrible to be hated. Tell him I won't do you any harm.'

But perhaps that was not true. Perhaps she meant endless mischief. Supposing she were to take Roddy from Tony, from all his friends and lovers, from all his idle Parisian and English life, and attach him to herself, tie him and possess him: that would mean giving him cares, responsibilities, it might mean changing him from his free and secret self into something ordinary, domesticated, resentful. Perhaps his lovers and friends would be well advised to gather round him jealously and guard him from the female. She saw herself for one moment as a creature of evil design, dangerous to him, and took her hand away from his that held it lightly.

'I'll tell him you won't do me any harm,' he repeated absently. He was staring into her face.

'You're going away now,' she said, 'and I don't know when I shall see you again.'

'I don't know either,' he said smiling.

'Tomorrow you'll have forgotten. But I shan't forget this evening.'

'Nor shall I. I don't forget you, Judy. I sometimes wish I could. I'm a little afraid of you.'

'Afraid of me?'

'Afraid of you – and me.'

Later on when he was gone she must make herself think of that. It might have power to hurt: she could not tell now, with his unmasked, disturbed face watching her. Now there was nothing but depth under depth of welling happiness.

'You know, Roddy,' she said after a silence, 'the awful thing about you is that I can never pick up again where we left off. Tonight you've talked to me as I've always longed for you to talk to me, as if we could trust each other, as if we were two creatures of the same sort alone together. Don't you feel we know each other better after tonight Roddy?'

He was silent for a moment, his eyes twinkling; then he said:

'I feel you've made me say a great many indiscreet things.'

'Poor Roddy! You'd better go, before I wring something out of you you'll regret to your life's end,' she said bitterly. 'You know I shan't rest until I've forced you to tell me all your secrets. And when you have, I'll go and tell them to everybody else.'

She shut her eyes and turned her face from him. There was a long silence.

'Don't be cross with me,' he said in the end.

'I'm not.'

'Didn't I tell you I was inadequate?'

'Yes you told me.'

'Well now you believe it, don't you?'

'No. No. No '

'Ah – you're incorrigible . . . Good-bye, Judy.'

She turned towards him again, took his hand in both hers and clung to it.

'Roddy, you *have* – quite liked – being with me .. haven't you?'

His face softened.

'I've adored it,' he said gently.

'And when shall I see you again?'

He shook his head.

'Roddy, when?'

He stooped swiftly until his face almost touched hers, and murmured, watching her:

'Whenever you like.'

His lips closed on hers very lightly. She put her arms round his neck and kissed his cheek and forehead. When after a moment or two he raised himself she thought he was smiling again.

She lay perfectly still, watching him while he lit a cigarette, smoothed his hair, put on his coat and went to open the door. Then he turned, still smiling, and nodding as if encouraging her to smile back. But she continued to lie and stare up at him as if from the bottom of a well; as if all of her were dead except the eyes which just moved, following him.

The door closed after him. Soon the sound of his footsteps faded along the corridor.

She raised her hand slowly and with difficulty, as if a weight were holding it to her side, and pulled the lamp's green shade down; and the whole room sank softly into semi-obscurity.

Some trick of green light brought suddenly to mind the look of early spring woods at twilight: fresh buds and little leaves dashed with rain, an air like dark clear water lighting the branches with a wan glimmer.

She looked at her body lying long, slender and still on the couch; she saw her breast rise and fall faintly with her breathing; and she had a sense of watching herself return from a long swoon, bathed in crystalline new life, transformed and beautified.

The trivial femininities of the room had made, she thought, an inept background for his elegance. But now there seemed something graceful, foreign, curious in the lights and shades, in the forms of flowers, books, furniture; as if he had left his impress upon them.

She heard the footsteps of Jennifer coming swiftly towards her door ... Not a word, not a whisper to Jennifer. She and he could never meet, even in mind. The profoundest instinct forbade it.

Jennifer came gaily in.

'Tired, darling?' she said. 'You were quite right not to come to Hall. It was bloodier than ever. Come darling, let me put you to bed – you're so tired. I'll look after you. I'll make you some scrambled eggs after you're in bed.'

Then Jennifer suspected nothing. She did not see that all was changed. She was deep in the mood of tender solicitude which came upon her now and then since the illness, when she remembered to think Judith fragile. She lifted her in her arms, and carried her into the bedroom ...

Nothing had changed after all. There was Jennifer laughing, talking, letting the eggs get burnt while she did her hair; bending down finally to kiss you a tender good night. Judith tried to think of Roddy. A little while ago he had been stooping over her as Jennifer stooped now, with eyes that were different and yet the same. But he had disappeared; she could not now remember what he looked like.

Nothing was altered then, no order was reversed or even shaken. There were these moments; but all around and about the extravagant incongruous brilliances, the divine crudities, the breath-taking magnificences of their pattern, life went on weaving uninterruptedly: weaving uncoloured trivial things into secure fabric.

9

Then, almost it seemed, while she still told herself these things: while the memory of Roddy's brief presence still surged up bewilderingly to drown her a hundred times a day, and then slipped away again, lost in the mysterious and doubtful darkness cast by his ensuing silence; while Jennifer remained the unquenched spring of all gaiety and reassurance, all delight: while the whole ordered dream went on as if it could never break; even then, with the third year, the shadow of change began to fall.

It was a look, a turn of the head, a new trick of speech, a nothing in Jennifer which struck at her heart in a moment; and then all had started to fall to pieces. Jennifer was no longer the same. Somewhere she had turned aside without a word, and set her face to a new road. She did not want to be followed. She had given Judith the slip, in the dark; and now, when she still pretended to be there, her voice had the false shrillness of a voice coming from far away.

She remembered Jennifer saying once, suddenly: 'There's one thing certain in my life: that is, that I shall always love you.' And afterwards her eyes had shone as if with tears and laughter. She remembered the surprise and joy, the flooding confidence of that moment; for it had been said so quietly, as if the realization of that 'always' held for her something sorrowful, a sobering sense of fate. Her manner had had a simplicity far removed from the usual effervescence and extravagance: she had seemed to state a fact to be believed in forever, without question. In her life where all else was uncertain, fluid and undirected, where all turned in mazes of heat and sound, that only was the deep unshaken foundation, the changeless thing ... She had seemed to mean that, sitting back in her chair, her arms laid along her lap, her hands folded together, everything about her quiet and tender, her eyes resting on Judith as they never had before or since, long and full, with a depth of untroubled love.

That had been on a day in late April, at the beginning of the last summer term. The happiness of reunion had never before seemed so complete. She had been in Scotland, Judith in Paris with Mamma, living resentfully in a reflection of Mamma's alien existence. And then they were together again, and the summer term had opened with its unfailing week or so of exquisite weather.

They had taken the green canoe one morning and wandered up the river to Grantchester. There was no one at all in the Orchard when they reached it.

'Thank God I see no grey flannels,' said Jennifer. 'I suppose the grass is still too wet for undergraduates to sit out.'

A light breeze was blowing through the orchard, ruffling long grass, dandelions, buttercups, and daisies. Under the trees, the little white tables, set in the green silken brilliance, were dappled with running light and shadow, and the apple branches, clotted with full blossom, gleamed against the sky in a tender childish contrast of simple colours, – pale pink upon pale blue. The air was dazed with a bewilderment of bird-song.

A rough brown terrier with golden eyes came prancing out on them, making known their presence with barkings half-ferocious, half-friendly. The dark waitress came lazily from the house, reluctant to serve them.

'Is the Orchard open?'

'Oh yes, it's open.'

'Can you let us have lunch?'

'Oh I dare say.'

'What can you let us have?'

'You can have a cheese omelette and some fruit-salad.'

'Divine,' said Jennifer, and leapt for joy.

'You better have it in the shelter. The grass is wet.'

She wandered away, smoothing her black untidy hair. She would not smile. There was something arresting and romantic in the thin sallow dark-browed young woman, preserving her ugliness, her faint unrelaxing bitterness among all the laughing renewals of her surroundings.

'I'd like to pick her up and shake her into life. Make her smile and be young. Make her cheeks pink and her eyes bright,' said Jennifer. 'If I were a man I'd fall bang in love with her. What is her name do you think? Jessica? Anne? Rosa?'

'Miriam.'

'Yes, Miriam.'

How the remembered insignificant words brought flooding back the irrecoverable quality of that day!

Tits and robins, perching all around them, and the golden-eyed dog, had helped them to finish their meal.

Then they had lain back in their chairs, staring and saying nothing. And then it was that Jennifer had turned and broken the silence with her quiet, inevitable-seeming declaration; and after it Judith had reached out to touch her hand for a moment; and continued to sit beside her and dream.

Later in the afternoon they had seen grey-flannelled legs approaching and risen to go.

They met the dark girl walking down the gravel path towards the orchard, carrying a trayful of crockery.

'We've come to pay you,' said Jennifer radiantly smiling.

She gave the price without a flicker.

'Judith, have you that much on you, darling?' said Jennifer, and added, turning again to the girl: 'We *have* so enjoyed ourselves.'

There was no response save a quick suspicious glance.

Currant bushes, wallflowers, narcissi, pansies, yellow daisies and tulips blossomed richly on each side of the path.

'What a delicious garden!' said Jennifer. 'It's at its very best, isn't it?'

'It's looking nice,' she admitted.

Jennifer pointed to a clump of stiff, purple-black tulips.

'Those tulips are like you,' she said, her eyes and mouth, all her glowing face, coaxing and appealing.

And suddenly the girl gave a little laugh, looking with soft eyes

155

first at Jennifer, then away, shyly and deprecatingly, as who should say: 'The idea! Me like a tulip! Well, you *are* a one – Daft ...' but gratified and amused all the same.

'I shall always think of you when I see tulips like that,' said Jennifer. 'Good-bye!'

'Good-bye, Miss ...' She smiled, almost mischievously this time, and hurried on with her tray.

'She was quite human,' said Jennifer. 'I wonder if she's got a lover or if she's longing for one, or if she's been jilted, or what ... What makes her all shadowy and tight inside herself?'

She stood looking after the girl, as if meditating going back to ask her.

How Jennifer struck sparks with ordinary people! She knew how to live. To be with her was to meet adventure; to see, round every corner, the bush become the burning bush.

In a little while she would have forgotten the girl whose problem was now so urgent and exciting; but you yourself would always remember, – seeing it all dramatically, seeing it as a quiet story, hearing it as an unknown tune: making of it a water colour painting in gay foolish colours, or an intricate pencil pattern of light and shadow.

They left the Orchard.

'I think,' said Jennifer, 'we will never come here again.'

They had not come again. That time had remained unblurred by any subsequent return in a different mood, with more companions, in another weather or season.

But Judith had thought, whilst she nodded agreement: 'Some day, when I'm much older, I'll come back alone and think of her; and then perhaps write and say: do you remember? Or perhaps not, in case she has forgotten.'

And now, it seemed, far sooner even than Judith had feared, Jennifer was forgetting everything. They had meant to go away together during the summer vacation; go to Brittany, and bathe and walk and read: but in the end Jennifer's don had said cold things regarding Jennifer's progress, and requested her to attend college during the Long. Judith had gone on a reading party with three of the circle, and written Jennifer long letters which were answered briefly and at rare intervals.

But that was not surprising. Jennifer's letters had always been spasmodic, if passionately affectionate. Then the letters had ceased altogether. Judith had written asking if they could not spend September together, and Jennifer had answered in five lines, excusing herself. She was going to shoot in Scotland in September.

And then the third year had started, with everything as it had always been, or seeming so, for a few moments; and then in one more moment shivered to pieces.

She would not stay behind alone, after the others had gone, to say good night. She ceased to talk with abandonment and excitement, her eyes shining to see you listening, to feel you understanding. There seemed nothing to say now. In particular, she would not speak of the Long.

It was, of course, Mabel who was the first to hint of ill-tidings. Eating doughnuts out of a bag, late one night, during one of Judith's charity visits, she said:

'Has that Miss Manners been up lately?'

'Who's Miss Manners?'

'Why – that Miss Manners, Jennifer's friend, who stayed with her so much during the Long.'

'Oh yes –'

'I was sure you must have heard about her, because they seemed such very great friends. They were always about together and always up to some lark.' She gave a snigger. 'We used to wonder, we really did, how long it would be before Jennifer got sent down, the way they used to go on, coming in so late and all. But somehow Jennifer never gets found out, does she?' Another snigger. 'What a striking-looking girl she is.'

'Who?'

'Miss Manners.'

'Oh yes ... I've never seen her. Only photographs.'

'Everybody said what a striking pair they made ... I expect she'll be up soon again, don't you?'

'I don't know at all,' said Judith. 'I expect so.' Mabel looked solemn.

'The wrestling matches they used to have out there on the lawn! I used to watch them from my window. I wonder they didn't ...

157

I really wonder ... any of the dons ... It looked so ... throwing each other about like that ... It's not the sort of thing you expect – quite, is it? I mean ...'

'Oh, wrestling's glorious,' said Judith. 'I love it. Jennifer's tried to teach me. But I'm not strong enough for her; the – the – Manners girl is much more of a match for her.'

Mabel pursed up her mouth and was silent.

It was necessary to leave her quickly for fear of striking her; because her deliberate intent was obvious; because she knew quite well now that you had never before heard of Miss Manners; because you were seeing that girl plainly, tall, dark and splendid, striding on the lawn with Jennifer, vying with her in feats of strength, a match for her in all magnificent unfeminine physical ways, as you had never been. Her image was all at once there, ineffaceably presenting itself as the embodiment of all hitherto unco-ordinated and formless fears, the symbol for change, and dark alarms and confusions. And the unbearable image of Mabel was there too, watching by herself, gloating down from the window with glistening eyes that said:

'At last!'

She stopped short in the corridor, and moaned aloud, aghast at the crowding panic of her thoughts.

Judith, returning from her bath, heard voices and laughter late at night behind Jennifer's door. Should she stop? All the circle must be there as usual, laughing and talking as if nothing were amiss. She alone had excluded herself, sitting with a pile of books in her room, pretending to have important work. It was her own fault. She had said she was busy, and they had believed her and not invited her to join their gathering. She would go in, and sit among them and smoke, and tell them things, – tell them something to make them laugh; and all would be as before. They would drift away in the end and leave her behind; she would turn and look at Jennifer in the firelight, put out a hand and say: 'Jennifer ...'

She opened the door and looked in.

The voices stopped, cut off sharply.

In the strange, charged, ensuing silence, she saw that the curtains were flung back. Purple-black night pressed up against the windows, and one pane framed the blank white globe of the full moon. They were all lying on the floor. Dark forms, pallid, moon-touched faces and hands were dimly distinguishable; a few cigarette points burned in the faint hanging cloud of smoke across the room. The fire was almost out. Where was Jennifer?

'Hullo, there's Judith,' said one.

'Is there room for me?' said Judith in a small voice. She came in softly among them all, and went directly over to the window and sat on the floor, with the moon behind her head. She was conscious of her own unnatural precision and economy of movement; of her long slender body wrapped in its kimono crossing the room in three light steps, sinking noiselessly down in its place and at once remaining motionless, expectant.

Where was Jennifer?

'All in the dark,' she said, in the same soft voice. And then: 'What a moon! Don't you know it's very dangerous to let it shine on you like this? It will make you mad.'

One or two of them laughed. She could now recognize the three faces in front of her. Jennifer must be somewhere by the fireplace. There was constraint in the room. She thought with awful jealousy; 'Ah, they hate my coming. They thought they were getting rid of me at last. They come here secretly without me, to insinuate themselves. They all want her. They have all hated me always.' She said:

'Give me a cigarette someone.'

Jennifer's voice broke in suddenly with a sort of harsh clangour. From her voice, Judith knew how wild her eyes must be.

'Here, here's a cigarette, Judith . . . Have something to eat. Or some cocoa. Oh – there was a bottle of cherry-brandy, but I believe we've finished it.'

Horrible confusion in her voice, a stumbling hurry of noise . . .

'I have just licked up the last dregs,' said a deep voice.

'Who's that who spoke then?' said Judith softly and sweetly.

'Oh . . .' cried Jennifer shrilly, 'Geraldine, you haven't met Judith yet.'

What was she saying? Geraldine Manners was staying the week-end, no, was walking on the lawn with her; had just arrived, no, had been in the room for months, since the summer, for they were such very great friends . . .

'How do you do. I'm guessing what you are like from the way you speak,' said Judith softly, laughingly.

'Oh, I'm no good at that.'

How bored, how careless a voice!

'Shall I switch on the light?' said someone.

'No!' said Judith loudly.

She lifted up her arm against the window. The kimono sleeve fell back from it, and it gleamed cold and frail in the moonlight, like a snake. She spread out her long fingers and stared at them.

'I would like to be blind,' she said. 'I really wish I were blind. Then I might learn to see with my fingers. I might learn to hear properly too.'

And learn to be indifferent to Jennifer; never to be enslaved again by the lines and colours of her physical appearance, the ever new surprise and delight of them; learn, in calm perpetual darkness, how the eyes' tyrannical compulsions had obscured and distorted all true values. To be struck blind now this moment, so that the dreaded face of the voice by the fireplace remained for ever unknown! . . . Soon the light would go on, and painfully, hungrily, with awful haste and reluctance, the eyes would begin their work again, fly to their target.

'Don't be absurd, Judith,' said someone. 'You don't know what you're talking about'; and went on to talk of work among the blind, of blinded soldiers, of St Dunstan's.

The conversation became general and followed the usual lines: it was better to be deaf than blind, blind than deaf. Jennifer and Geraldine were silent.

'It's time we went to bed,' said someone. 'Jennifer, I must go to bed. I'm almost asleep. What's the time?'

Now the light would go on.

It went on. The room suddenly revealed its confusion of girls, cushions, chairs, cups, plates and cigarette-ends. Everybody was getting up, standing about and talking. Jennifer was on her feet, voluble, calling loud good nights. They made a group round her and round somebody still sitting on the floor beside her. Judith caught a glimpse of a dark head leaning motionless against the mantelpiece. Now they were all going away. Judith followed them slowly to the door and there paused, looking over her shoulder towards the fireplace.

'Stay,' said Jennifer shrilly. She was standing and staring at Judith with wild eyes; pale, with a deep patch of colour in each cheek, and lips parted.

'No, I must go. I've got some work,' said Judith, smiling over her shoulder. She let her eyes drop from Jennifer's face to the other one.

At last it confronted her, the silent-looking face, watching behind its narrowed eyes. The hair was black, short, brushed straight back from the forehead, leaving small beautiful ears exposed. The heavy eyebrows came low and level on the low broad brow; the eyes were long slits, dark-circled, the cheeks were pale, the jaw heavy and masculine. All the meaning of the face was concentrated in the mouth, the strange wide lips laid rather flat on the face, sulky, passionate, weary, eager. She was not a young girl. It was the face of a woman of thirty or more; but in years she might have been younger. She was tall, deep-breasted, with long, heavy but shapely limbs. She wore a black frock and a pearl necklace, and large pearl earrings.

Judith said politely:

'Is this the first time you have been here?'

'No.' She laughed. Her voice was an insolent voice.

'I'm tired,' said Jennifer suddenly, like a child.

'You look it,' said Judith. 'Go to bed.'

'I'll get undressed.' Jennifer passed a hand across her forehead and sighed.

The woman by the fireplace fitted a cigarette into an amber holder slowly, and lit it.

'I'm not sleepy yet,' she said. 'I'll wait till you're in bed and come and tuck you up.'

'This room feels –' cried Jennifer staring around her in horror. She dashed to the window and flung it wide open; then disappeared into her bedroom; and there was not another sound from her.

The woman started singing to herself very low, as if forgetful of Judith's presence; then broke off to say:

'I like your kimono.'

Judith wrapped the long red and blue silk garment more closely round her hips.

'Yes. It was brought me from Japan. I gave Jennifer one. A purple one.'

'Oh, that one. She's lent it to me. I forgot to bring a dressing-gown.'

She turned her head away, as if to intimate that so far as she was concerned conversation was neither interesting nor necessary.

Judith bit back the 'Good night Jennifer' which she was about to call; for she was never going to care any more what happened to Jennifer; never again soothe her when she was weary and excited, comfort her when she was unhappy. She would look at Jennifer coldly, observe her vagaries and entanglements with a shrug, comment upon them with detached and cynical amusement: hurt her, if possible, oh, hurt her, hurt her.

Now she would leave her with Geraldine and not trouble to ask herself once what profound and secret intimacies would be restored by her withdrawal.

She smiled over her shoulder and left the room.

10

A week later, Geraldine was still there. She and Judith had not met again; when she and Jennifer, arm in arm, were seen approaching, Judith avoided them; and changing her place at Hall – her place which had been beside Jennifer for two years – went and sat where she could not see the sleek dark head next to the fair one, turning and nodding in response.

All day they were invisible. Geraldine had a car, and they must go miles and miles into the country in the soft late autumn weather.

It seemed to Judith that life had ceased to bear her along upon its tide. It flowed past her, away from her; and she must stay behind, passive and of no account, while the current of Jennifer met and gaily mingled with a fresh current and fled on. It seemed as if even the opportunity for the gesture of relinquishment was to be denied her. And then, wearily returning from lectures one morning she found upon her table a torn scrap of paper scrawled over violently in an unknown hand.

Please be in your room at six o'clock this evening. I want to see you.

Geraldine Manners.

It was an insolent note. She would ignore such a command. She would put a notice up on her door: *Engaged* – and turn the key; and when the woman came she would just have to go away again.

But at six o'clock, Geraldine knocked loudly and she cried: 'Come in.' They stood facing each other.

'Sit down,' said Judith. But neither of them made any movement.

'I wanted to see you.' Her voice was low and emotional – angry perhaps; and Judith had a moment's fainting sense of impotence. The woman was so magnificent, so mature and well-dressed; if there was to be a fight, what chance was there for a thin young student in a woollen jumper?

She leaned against the mantelpiece and, staring at Judith, flung at her:

'What's all this about?'

Judith sat down again, without a word, and waited, steadily holding the green eyes with her own. She heard the blood beat deafeningly in her ears.

Geraldine went on:

'I think it's the damnedest bit of impertinence I ever heard. School-girls! My God!' She flung her head back theatrically.

Judith thought, with a shudder of excitement and anguish: 'Wait. Wait. It is because you are unused to it that it seems like physical blows. Soon you will be able to collect yourself. This is anger and you are the cause. You are being insulted and called to account for the first time in your life. Carry it off. Carry it off.'

And her blood went on repeating 'Jennifer' in her ears.

Geraldine took a gold cigarette case and the amber holder from a gold chain bag with a sapphire clasp

163

'It's pretty awful, isn't it, to be so mean and petty? I'm sorry for you, I must say.'

'Please don't be sorry for me.' She noted her own voice, icy and polite.

Geraldine had inserted a thin, yellow cigarette in the holder and was searching for a match.

'Here,' said Judith. She got up, took the matchbox from the mantelpiece and struck a light. Geraldine stooped her head down over the little flare. White lids, black curling lashes, broad cheek-bones, Egyptian lips – the heaviness, the thick waxen texture of the whole face: Judith saw them all with an aching and terrible intensity, her eyes clinging to the head bowed above her hand. She should have smelt like a gardenia.

'Thank you,' said Geraldine. She lifted her head, narrowed her eyes and puffed out smoke, moving and stretching her mouth faintly round the amber. She smoked like a man.

Judith sat down again.

Geraldine seemed now very much at her ease. She leaned against the mantelpiece, dominating the room: and she seemed of gigantic height and significance.

'Are you a friend of Jennifer's?' she said.

'Jennifer – is a person I know well.'

She looked at Judith as if in surprise at her tone and manner.

'I had no idea of that. She never mentioned you.'

For a moment that dealt a blinding blow, with its instantaneous implications of dishonesty and indifference. But she repeated:

'I've known her well for two years. You can ask her. She *might* admit it.' And as she spoke the last words she thought with sudden excitement: 'Just as I never mentioned Roddy . . .'

'Oh, I can't get anything out of her,' said Geraldine and added truculently: 'You might as well tell me what it's all about.'

'I have nothing whatever to tell you. I don't know why you've come. I'd like *you* to tell me what it's all about – or else go away, please.' She was conscious all at once of a terrible inward trembling, and got up again. The other watched her in silence, and she added: 'I haven't been near her – since that night in her room. I've kept away – you know that night . . .'

'What night?'

Judith broke into a sort of laugh; and then checked herself with a vast effort: for the suppressed hysteria of weeks was climbing upwards within her and if it broke loose, it might never, never cease.

'Well – one night,' she said, 'I thought perhaps you remembered.'

There was not a flicker on Geraldine's face. She must be very stupid or very cruel.

'What beats me,' said Geraldine, 'is why this dead set against me? – against her and me. What do you want to interfere with us for? It's not your business, any of you. I thought I'd come and tell you so.'

There was a curious coarseness about her: almost a vulgarity. It was difficult to combat.

Judith lifted her eyes and looked at her in silence.

'So you've all sent Jennifer to Coventry.' She laughed. 'It's marvellous. A female institution is really marvellous. At least it would be if it weren't so nauseating.' Still Judith was silent, and she added contemptuously:

'I should have thought a bit better of you if you'd come yourself. Do you generally get other people to do your dirty work for you?'

Judith got up and went towards the door.

'Where are you going?' said Geraldine sharply.

'To Jennifer, to ask her to explain.'

'You can't do that.' The change in her voice and manner was noticeable. 'Jennifer's lying down. I left her trying to sleep. She mustn't be disturbed.'

'I can go to Jennifer whenever I like. I can always go to Jennifer. I don't ask you whether I am to or not.'

At last this was anger, anger! At last she was able to want to wound, to cry: 'I! I! I!' brutally, aggressively, triumphantly in the face of her enemy. Pure anger for the first time in life.

'*Please!* Listen.' Geraldine took a few steps towards her. 'Please don't go now. She's very much upset. I left her crying.'

Crying – crying? Oh, that was a good thing. It was splendid that Jennifer should have been made to cry ... And yet ... if this woman had made her cry – poor Jennifer, darling Jennifer – you would –

The situation seemed to have become reversed. Judith felt herself momentarily strong in self-assurance; and Geraldine was hesitating, as if doubtful what to say.

'What's she crying about? It takes a good deal to make Jennifer cry.'

Geraldine shot her a glance and said venomously:

'Yes. As far as I can make out, one of your charming friends must have taken a good deal of trouble to make her cry this morning. Anyway she seemed to have got it into her head that she's treated somebody, or one of you, very badly – and that somebody was hurt – *you* were hurt – because she'd been neglecting you for me.'

'How do you know she meant me?'

She was silent, and then said:

'She was crying a good deal and thoroughly upset and I heard her say your name. So I went and asked someone where your room was and came straight. But you were out.'

'Did she tell you to come?'

'She didn't tell me not to.'

'Then she told you where my room was. She knows you're here.'

'I didn't ask her where your room was. I – found out.'

'And does she know you're here?'

'No.' She added after a silence. 'I didn't come here to be cross-questioned.'

'What did you come here for?'

'Just to tell you we care *that*' – she snapped her fingers – 'for your mean little jealousies.'

'Oh, it seems scarcely worth coming, just for that. It wasn't worth losing your temper over, was it? Little jealousies are so common – in a female institution. I do think you over-estimate their importance. It isn't as if you cared what we said, because you've just told me you don't – either of you.'

'And,' she said, raising her voice angrily; '*and* to tell you I consider you owe me an apology – me and Jennifer.'

'Oh!' Judith buried her face in her hands and laughed. 'Oh! that's very funny.'

She looked up at Geraldine with a sudden fantastic hope that she would see her laughing too; but the face presented to her was hostile and heavy. At sight of it she felt the laughter begin to shake her terrifyingly; and checked it with a gasp.

Geraldine said:

'I suppose you will deny having anything to do with this?'

'Oh deny it – of course I do,' said Judith with weary contempt.

'Deny having insinuated – suggested –' she began loudly.

'I have never bothered to mention your name to anyone. Why should I? It's nothing to do with me.'

'No,' she said, her face and voice rousing a little from their heavy deliberate monotony. 'It's nothing to do with you.' She thought a moment and added slowly: 'Then there's some misunderstanding.'

'Yes, some misunderstanding. Why go on treating it as if it were important?'

After a silence she said:

'Anything, however slight, that comes between me and Jennifer is important.'

Judith felt herself start to tremble again. Those slow words rang a doom for her; and her spurious advantage was at an end.

'I'm sorry,' she said uncertainly, 'If I have come between you and Jennifer.'

'Not *you*,' she said. (Yes, she was a stupid or a cruel woman.) 'But I know what people's mischievous tongues can do, and I wanted to get to the bottom of it before I go away. Just to assure myself that I'm not leaving her to face anything – unpleasant or distressing.'

'Ah, so you realize how easily she's influenced.'

That was it then: the woman was afraid. She had given herself away at last: she knew the terrible insecurity of loving Jennifer. Judith felt a quiver of new emotion dart through her: it seemed like a faint pity.

'I don't want her bothered,' said Geraldine aggressively. 'I loathe this interfering.'

'You don't quite understand,' said Judith in a voice of calm explanation, 'how much Jennifer means to some people – a lot of people here. They love her. Naturally they resent it a little when somebody else comes in and claims all her attention. They miss her. Isn't it natural? And then you see, since you've been here I believe she's been getting into awful trouble for neglecting her work. I heard one of them say so a day or two ago – and another one said it was time someone spoke to her or she'd be sent down. So I dare say that's what happened: somebody tried to give her a sort of warning. Of course it was silly: but then, as you say, girls are silly. It was meant kindly.' She paused, feeling a kind of faintness, took a deep sighing breath and continued:

'If my name was brought into it, it was because I have had – I think – a certain amount of influence with Jennifer. She and I were a good deal together at one time. But lately I have been working very hard. They had no business at all . . .'

She felt her voice dwindling and stopped, trembling now un-controllably.

Geraldine lit another cigarette and leaned back against the mantel-piece. Oh, she was going to lean there for ever! If only she would allow you to soften her into some emotion of pity and understanding so that you might fling yourself down and weep, crying: 'Now you must understand. Now I have told you all. Leave me.' But there was no hope of that. Her hostility was hardening. She was more alert now; and she seemed to be taking note for the first time since her sweeping entrance of Judith's person. Her eyes went attentively over face, hands, feet, hair, clothes, and over the whole room. Something alive was rear-ing itself from the stony envelope. She was silent for a long time, and then said uncertainly:

'I hope you won't – mention all this to her.' Judith laughed.

'I can't quite promise that,' she said. 'You see, we've been used to telling each other most things. There's no reason to make a mystery of it. Is there?'

She was silent again; and then said:

'I think it would be best not to say anything to her. I don't want you to think there's been any fuss. I don't think she'll care to hear any more about it. She was very unwilling to – to dwell –'

That brought home Jennifer's attitude with painful clarity. She was, of course, flying to escape. Why should she go free always, always? This time it would be easy to make her uncomfortable, if not to hurt her. And yet, it could not be done. Once more she felt the faintest stir of sympathy with Geraldine. She said with a shrug:

'Very well, I won't refer to it.'

'We'll agree,' said Geraldine, 'to keep it to ourselves.'

Judith nodded.

Geraldine threw away her cigarette, smoothed her sleek hair, stood upright as if preparing to go and said with brisk indifference:

'Well, I'm sorry if I've been a nuisance.'

'Oh, you haven't been a nuisance.'

Judith crushed her cold hands into her lap. Now it was almost over: soon she could let herself collapse. But Geraldine still lingered, looking about her.

'You've got nice things,' she said. 'Most of the rooms I've seen are too frightful.'

'I'm luckier than most girls here. I have more money.'

'Do you like being here?'

'I have liked it – and disliked it.'

'Hmm. Jennifer hates it. I don't wonder. I think I've persuaded her to leave and come abroad with me.'

Defeat at last. She had no answer to that, not one weapon left. She stared before her, paralysed.

'I can't think,' added Geraldine, 'how she's stuck it so long.'

Judith heard herself say slowly, softly:

'As I told you, there are a great many people here who love her. That makes a difference, doesn't it? People have to love Jennifer.' She buried her face in her hands, and thought aloud, in a sort of whisper: 'People have to love her and then she seems cruel. But she doesn't mean to be. There's something about her – people don't seem to be able to love her clearly and serenely: they have to love her too much. Everything gets dark and confused and aching, and they want to – touch her and be the only one near her; they want to look after her and give her everything she wants. It's tiring. And then when they're tired she gives them back life. She pours life into them from herself.'

She stopped short, seeing in a flash how it had always been between herself and Jennifer. Tired, you had come again and again to her, pressing close to be replenished from her vitality. But Jennifer had not drunk life from you in return: quietness and tenderness and understanding, but not life. And the quietness had passed into sadness –

yes, you knew now you had seen it happening sometimes, – sadness, flatness: the virtue had gone out of her in the incessant giving of herself, the incessant taking on of an alien quietness. You had wanted too much, you had worn her out. Perhaps after all you had been unlucky to Jennifer, committed that crime of trying to possess her separateness,– craved more than even she could give without destroying herself. So in the end she had gone to someone more wholesome for her nature. Perhaps after all the balance had been sorely ill-adjusted: she your creator, you her destroyer. Perhaps she should be surrendered to Geraldine now, ungrudgingly. She said, looking up at Geraldine:

'I dare say you make her very happy.'

Geraldine said, answering Judith's gaze unwaveringly:

'Yes, we are very happy together. Absolutely happy.'

'She is a good companion, isn't she?'

'Oh yes,' she said, her heavy lips lifting in a faint curious smile.

What was in her voice? – insolence? – triumph? – malice? an obscure challenge? She seemed to be implying that she knew things about Jennifer of which you had no knowledge. She was a terrible woman.

Judith could find no words, and the other continued:

'She's starting to find herself. It's very interesting. Of course nobody's understood her here.'

'And you think you do?'

'I do, yes.'

'Oh, but I'd never dare say that about a person I loved! You might seem to touch everywhere and all the time be strangers.' Judith clasped her hands and spoke urgently:

'Don't you feel how you might long to say to someone you love: I give you all myself, all myself – and all the time be sad because with all your efforts and longing you *know* you never could – that the core can't ever be stirred at all? It seems such dreadful arrogance to say –' she stopped short, pressing her hand to her lips, shutting her eyes. After a pause she added quickly: 'But I don't doubt you love her ...' she sighed. 'Thank God this term is nearly over. This is a terrible place for getting overwrought.'

Geraldine seemed to be thinking deeply. Her face was awake and preoccupied behind its heavy mask.

'It's very odd,' said Judith, 'how she doesn't value her brains in the very least – isn't interested in them – can't be bothered. I suppose you know she's the most brilliant history student of her year. Easily. Of course she's never worked, but she could have done anything she liked. In spite of all her idleness and irresponsibility they were still excited about her – they thought she'd do something in the end. And I was going to make her pull it off. I could have – in one term. I mean I could have once. Not now of course.'

Her voice ceased drearily. As if it would matter to Geraldine how much Jennifer wasted brains, or academic opportunities ... as if it would move her!

The bell started to ring for Hall.

'There!' said Judith, 'I must brush my hair I suppose, and go down. Are you coming to Hall?'

'No. I'm going to dine in Cambridge.'

Judith rose and stood before her, looking full at her for the last time. She thought suddenly: 'But she's not beautiful! She's hideously ugly, repulsive.'

That broad heavy face and thick neck, those coarse and masculine features, that hothouse skin: What taste Jennifer must have to find her attractive! ...

Oh, no, it was no good saying that. In spite of all, she was beautiful: her person held an appalling fascination. She was beautiful, beautiful. You would never be able to forget her face, her form. You would see it and dream of it with desire: as if she could satisfy something, some hunger, if she would. But she was not for you. The secret of her magnetism, her rareness must be for ever beyond reach; but not beyond imagination.

Judith cried out inwardly: 'Tell me all your life!' All about herself, where she had come from, why she was alone and equivocal, why she wore such clothes, such pearls, how she and Jennifer had met, what knowledge her expression half-hid, half-revealed. Time had swept her down one moment out of space, portentously, and now was sweeping her away again, unknown. And now, in the end, you wanted to implore her to stay, to let herself be known, to let you love her. Yes, to let you love her. It was not true that you must hate your enemies. What was all this hatred and jealousy? Something so terrifyingly near to love, you dared not contemplate it. You could love

171

her in a moment, passionately, for her voice, her eyes, her remarkably white hands, for loving Jennifer – anything.

The bell stopped ringing.

'Good-bye,' said Judith. 'I'm late.' She held out her hand.

Geraldine took it. Her hand was cool, smooth and firm.

'Good-bye.'

'Are you – staying much longer?'

'I'm going away tomorrow.'

'I'd like to have known you better,' said Judith, very low, and she lifted her eyes to the long, hidden eyes of Geraldine. 'I hope you and she will be happy when you go abroad.' She opened the door politely, and then said, smiling: 'We won't forget each other, will we?'

'No,' said Geraldine, still watching her. But she did not smile.

They went their different ways along the corridor.

Now to go down to the dull food and clamour, to sit among them all and torture herself with fancying intercepted glances which might have pity in them; to hear, perhaps, her name and Jennifer's in a whispered aside; to try with anguish to guess which of them it was who had dared to drag her pain from its hiding-place and proclaim it aloud.

I I

Jennifer lay in bed; and on her door was pinned a notice signed by the matron: *No visitors allowed*.

Her friends were disconsolate, and the evening gatherings were leaden-spirited. It was certain there had not been so much evening work done before in the whole two years. There was nothing better to do now: no excitement, no laughter or colour. They went on tiptoe past the shut door and the notice: for Jennifer, so it was said, was threatened with nervous collapse, and her only chance lay in sleep and quiet. But in all the rumours, discussions and communications which went on over Jennifer's case, Judith took no part.

Once indeed when they were all at Hall and the corridor was empty of echoes, Judith had crept up to the door, lingered hesitating, then noiselessly turned the handle and looked in.

The electric lamp shone beside the bed and Jennifer lay with her face turned to the wall. All that was visible was her hair, tossed in a rough mass over the pillow and palely burning where the dim light struck it. Her death-like unconsciousness was intolerable pain. She should have stirred at least, feeling a presence through all the seals of sleep ... But she did not move; and night after night the sight of that unstirring hair upon the pillow returned, mocking her longing to reach to Jennifer with a picture that seemed the symbol for all that was eternally uncommunicating and imperturbable.

They said she was to be sent home before the end of term; then that her mother had arrived, was to take her away on the morrow.

That night the message came: Jennifer wanted to say good-bye to Judith.

Jennifer's boxes stood packed and strapped in a corner. Her personality had already, terrifyingly, been drained from her two rooms. There was now only a melancholy whisper of that which, during the two years of her tenancy, had filled the little space between her walls with a warm mystery. She had become identified with the quickening of imagination, the lyrical impulse. Oh how ridiculous, how sad, to have made one person into all poetry! Tomorrow it would all be finished.

Judith went softly from the sitting-room into the bedroom: and there was Jennifer lying back on her pillow and waiting.

'Hullo, darling,' she said. Her voice was low and mournful.

'Jennifer!'

She put out her hand and Judith took it, clung to it, while Jennifer drew her down beside her on the bed.

'Jennifer, darling, how are you?'

'I'm better, I've slept. I was so tired. But I'm going away.'

'I know.'

'Don't tell anyone, Judith, but I'm not coming back.'

'Oh Jennifer, what shall I do without you?'

'Darling I *can't* come back,' she said in an urgent, painful whisper.

'I know. I know. And I must come back, I suppose. I'm like that:

173

I can't uproot. You're wise, you never grow roots. So you can go away when you want to without making a wound in yourself. It's no good my pretending I could do the same. I must wait; though goodness knows for what: the examinations I suppose. This place without you ... *Oh!*'

She pressed her forehead against the hand that still held hers, abandoning, with her last words, the effort to speak lightly.

'Darling,' said Jennifer. 'It is making a wound – you ought to know. You're making a wound.'

'Then why do you go away from me?'

'Judith, I've got to go!' She sighed wearily. 'What I really wanted to say to you was: please forgive me for everything.'

'Forgive ... Oh Jennifer ...'

'Don't say there's nothing to forgive. Say I forgive you.'

'I forgive you then.'

'Because I have hurt you, haven't I?'

'It wasn't your fault. Nothing's been your fault.'

'I've been unhappy too. I thought I was going off my head a little while ago.' She sighed again. 'It's all such a muddle. I do get into such muddles. I'm so used to flying to you to be got out of them, I can't think how I shall manage without you.'

Judith was silent, her throat aching with tears. Never to hear Jennifer's step hurrying along the corridor, never again to see her burst flushed and desperate into the room crying: 'Oh darling, I'm in such a muddle ...' That had been such a thing to look forward to: it had been such pleasure to comfort, advise, explain, even though the muddles had generally been found to be laughable trifles.

'I wanted to say some more things, but it's so difficult,' Jennifer went on. 'Now you're here I can't say anything.'

'Don't try, darling. I'm quite happy.'

Her face had got thinner, thought Judith, her expression had little if anything of the child left in it, and her lips which had always been slightly parted in repose were now folded together in an unnatural line.

'Mother's come to fetch me.' She laughed. 'She is being extremely dutiful and chilling and grieved at me. I hope you haven't come across her. She's not a bit nice. I'm going to Scotland. Oh the

moors! I'll soon get better there. Then I'll go abroad or something.'
She laughed again. 'I suppose Mother'll try to send me back here
next term. I shall have some glorious wrangling. Perhaps they'll wash
their hands of me for ever. If only they would! Oh, if I could be
on my own! – no ties!'

Her eyes sparkled at the thought of breaking her fetters. Already,
in spite of her sorrow, she was thinking with excitement: *What next?*
She was ready to contemplate a fresh start. Soon her indomitable
vitality would light upon and kindle fresh objects; and all around her
would live, as once you had lived, in her glow. She would have no
time, no room, to remember what had once absorbed her. Judith
turned her head away, tasting despair; for it seemed that the zest for
life they had both shared burned in Jennifer undiminished now that
the time of sharing was over; while for her it had gone out, like a
snuffed candle.

Jennifer fastened her great eyes upon her, whispering: 'You don't
know how I shall miss you.'

Ah, she saw she had wounded, – was trying, too late, to make
amends. Judith answered, making her voice harsh and scornful:

'Oh no you won't. You'll find heaps of new thrilling people and
you'll soon forget me.'

'Oh –' was all Jennifer said, beneath her breath. She shut her eyes,
and Judith saw her mouth alter and quiver. 'You don't understand,'
she whispered after a long time. 'No, you don't understand. God, I'm
in such a muddle.'

It was no use trying to find comfort from hurting Jennifer. There
was nothing but pain to be had from the spectacle of that beloved
face shrinking and helpless. Whatever it cost all must be made easy
for her.

'I'm sorry, Jennifer, I'm sorry, my darling. There! don't worry.
I understand. Don't cry. Listen: it's like this, isn't it? You're not happy
here any more. You're restless. And you've been – been living too
hard and you're worn out. So you want to get away from all the people
you've been with – all the ones you associate with feeling ill and awful
– you want to start afresh, somewhere quite new. Isn't that it?'

'Partly,' whispered Jennifer.

'Things have all gone wrong lately. And I'm involved, aren't I?

It's really about me that things have gone wrong. I don't know why – but I know it is so. So you really can't bear to see me any more.

'Oh Judith!' She hid her face. 'It sounds so terrible when you say it like that: "Can't bear to see me any more" ... Oh!'

'But I'm right, aren't I, Jennifer?'

'It sounds as if it were your fault, as if you thought it was something you'd done –'

'Then it's not – something I've done?'

'God, no!'

The relief of that fierce denial brought a momentary illusion of happiness, for she had painfully persisted in trying to fasten the chief blame on herself.

'I'm glad ... But it is true, isn't it, that I'm involved in all that's gone wrong; and that you must get away from me?'

'Oh yes, oh yes, because I can't *bear* myself – because I must forget – because the thought of you is such a reproach ... the way I've treated you –' her voice was almost inaudible.

'Don't Jennifer, don't. You've nothing to blame yourself for. It's just the way things happen. That's how I look at it. As long as it's not anything I've done, as long as you tell me I haven't – disappointed you somehow, I don't mind – much not understanding –'

'Oh, you're so good to me, you're so kind. And there's nothing I can do except hurt you. I've never done anything for you.'

'You've been all my happiness for two years.'

'It was very silly of you to be made happy by a person like me. You might have known I'd let you down in the end.'

'You haven't let me down.'

'Yes. I've made you unhappy.'

It was not much use denying that.

Geraldine seemed to be in the room, watching and listening. Judith felt her head droop as if beneath a tangible weight, and a most dreary sense of impotence fastened upon her. What was the use of talking, when all the time Geraldine, absent and untalked-of, controlled their secret decisions? To ignore her made a mockery of all attempted solutions and consolations, and yet to speak of her seemed impossible.

'Well, you've been unhappy too.'

'Yes. Oh yes. Oh Judith! There's something I must ask you.'

She put her face against Judith's arm, and the desperate pressure of her eyes, nose, lips upon the bare flesh was strange and breath-taking. Her lips searched blindly over wrist and forearm into the hollow of the elbow where they paused and parted; and Judith felt the faint and quivering touch of her teeth . . .

But then Jennifer flung her arm away and said in a dry and careful voice,

'I wanted to know: did you cry in your room night after night because I – because of the way I was behaving?'

'I've never cried, Jennifer.'

That was true enough. There were no tears to soften such arid and infecund griefs.

'Ah!' she said. 'You say that as if –'

'Why did you think I'd cried?'

'It was just an idea I got. Something somebody said put it into my head and I couldn't get rid of it. But now – I don't know. The way you spoke makes me almost wish you had cried: because you seemed to mean you hadn't been able to.'

She shut her eyes and lay still.

'Jennifer, don't. Don't let's go on. What's the use? You know we're not putting anything right or doing each other any good. It's getting late – so I'd better go. You'll be so tired tomorrow and it'll be my fault. I ought never to have come.'

'Don't go yet!' she besought. 'Look. We won't talk any more. There's some things I must say, but perhaps I'll be able to say them later.' She sat up in bed. 'I've been feeling so gloomy! Let's try to be cheerful for a change. Really, my gloom has been beyond a joke. I've wanted to hide in a dark hole. Imagine! I think my hair must look awful. Fetch me my brush, darling. I simply haven't had the heart to give it a good brushing for ages.'

Her spirits were rising: the tone of her voice had changed, and the peculiar individuality of her manner of speech had returned with surprising suddenness.

'Would you like me to brush it?' asked Judith.

'Oh yes, darling. You've a lovely hand with the hair brush. Geraldine would brush my hair for me every night, and my God, the agony!'

The brush wavered and stopped for a moment in Judith's hand. But Jennifer seemed unaware of any cause for embarrassment. It was as if she had cast from her the self whose lips were sealed upon that name. It was of no more account to her in her present mood to announce that Geraldine had brushed her hair than to declare, as she did in the next breath, that her hair needed washing. Geraldine no longer existed for her as a person of dark significance. She had become dissolved like all other grave perplexities into a uniform light ebullience and froth; and her name had been thrown off unconcernedly and forgotten on the instant.

Amazing, terrifying, admirable creature – thought Judith – who, when life pressed too heavily upon her, could resolve life into airy meaninglessness; could pause, as it were deliberately, and re-charge herself with vitality.

Judith brushed out the strange, springy electric stuff, and then buried her face in it a moment. Surely Jennifer's secret lay in her hair: perhaps, if it were cut off, the virtue would go out of her.

'I'm hungry,' said Jennifer. 'Darling, there's some cake in the cupboard. Mother brought it. She does know how to minister to the flesh I will say. She's that sort of woman you know: holds you with hotwater bottles and pudding and destroys you spiritually. And would you like to make some chocolate, darling? Let's feel bilious together for the last time.' She laughed cheerfully.

They ate and drank, and then Judith came and lay on the bed beside her, and she slipped her arm beneath Judith's thin shoulder, patting it as she talked.

'I forgive all my enemies,' said Jennifer. 'Tell Mabel I forgive her and I hope God will cure her spots in time. She has been an enemy hasn't she? She'd like to knife me. Give all my history and economics books to Dorothy. She can't afford to buy any. I shan't ever look at them again, thank God. If I have to earn my living I shall direct my talents towards something more flashy. Where shall I be, I wonder, by the summer? When you're all sweating over your exams. I shall laugh to think of you.

'Darling, I've left you my copper bowl. You always said it had nice lights in it. If I go to Italy I'll send you a crate of oranges for it. It looks its best with oranges. It's the nicest thing I've ever had, so of course it's for you. Take it and don't forget me.' She lay back looking white and tired.

'Jennifer –' Judith clutched her hand and was speechless. After a while she added: 'I shall feel I haven't quite lost you. Your lovely bowl. It's always seemed such a part of you.'

'It's all of me,' whispered Jennifer. 'I leave it to you.'

The momentary lightness was now past, vanishing as swiftly as it had come. There was now such a sense of approaching desolation as had never been before in life. This was the end.

'Then I must say good-bye,' said Judith.

'Draw back the curtain.'

Judith obeyed. As she went to the window she felt Jennifer's eyes upon her.

The night was frosty, dark and still, and the midnight stars glittered in trembling cold multitudes over the arch of the sky. Below the window the unmoving trees made a blot of yet profounder darkness. Across the court, the opposite wing of the building was just distinguishable, a mass impenetrably deep; but there were no lights in the windows: not even in Mabel's. Everybody in College was asleep.

'Oh!' sighed Jennifer. 'The smell of the limes, and the nightingales! I'd like to have had them once again.'

Judith let the curtain drop and came quickly and sank on her knees by the bed.

'Then come back, Jennifer, and have them with me. Why not, why not? You'll be well by next term. Everything will be forgotten. Our last term ... Jennifer!'

'No!' she covered her face with her hands. 'No, Judith, I could never come back here. Everything's gone all wrong. Everything's as if – as if it had been poisoned. I must go away and get it straight. Listen.' She put both arms around Judith's neck and held her in a hard painful embrace. 'The things I meant to say, – I don't think I can say them. I thought I could before I saw you, but now you're here it doesn't seem clear any more. I don't really know what I think – what I mean, and if I tried to explain you might – might not understand. Oh Judith!'

She began to cry, and stopped herself. 'There are things in life you've no idea about. I can't explain. You're such a baby really, aren't you? I always think of you as the most innocent thing in the world.'

'Jennifer, you know you can tell me anything.'

Yet she knew, while she pleaded, that she shrank from knowing.

'Oh yes, it's true, you understand everything.' Jennifer tightened her arms desperately and seemed to be hesitating, then said at last: 'No, I'm in a muddle. I'm afraid. I should explain all wrong, as I always do. But I'll write to you, darling. I may not write to you for some time: or it may be tomorrow. But I swear I'll write. And then I'll explain everything.'

'And we'll see each other again, Jennifer? We'll meet often?'

'Perhaps. I don't know. It depends,' she whispered.

Her face was still hidden, her arms firm in their strangling grip.

'Oh yes, yes, Jennifer! Please! Why these mysteries? Jennifer – if – if there's somebody else you're fond of I don't mind. Why should it make any difference to you and me? I'm not jealous.'

'I'll write to you,' repeated Jennifer, very wearily whispering.

'Soon then, soon, Jennifer. Tell me how you are, what you're going to do. Tell me if you go abroad, who – who you go with. Tell me everything. Because I shall wonder and wonder. I shall imagine all sorts of things ... Jennifer ...'

'Hush darling. I'll be all right. I swear. And I swear that *directly* everything gets clear I'll write to you. And then we'll see. You do trust me don't you?'

'Yes.'

'And you must promise me to answer.'

'Yes.'

'But don't write before I write to you.'

'No.'

'Good-bye, my darling.' She let her arms fall to her sides.

At the door Judith turned, forcing her mouth into a smile, but Jennifer was not looking at her. Once again, only the tangle of her hair was visible, burning in the lamplight.

The end of the term.

There had been no word from Jennifer. She had vanished. But she was to be trusted: you had only to wait and she would write. Or was she not to be trusted?

Her copper bowl stood on the table, and there seemed no other rumour of her left in the whole place, save on the tongues of people; and even they were sparing of her name, spoke it with doubt and hesitation.

On the last day of term, Judith, peering a moment into the aching emptiness of Jennifer's room, saw the cord of her old manly Jaeger dressing-gown lying in the grate.

12

Then, for months, there was nothing in life save work: a careful planning out of day and night in order that sleeping and eating and exercise might encroach as little as possible on the working hours.

Soon, midsummer term was back with unprecedented profusion of blossom on the fruit trees, buttercups in the meadows, nightingale choruses in the cedars and limes. But now it seemed neither exciting nor delightful to be kept awake till dawn by nightingales; for sleepless nights lowered your examination value. By day the two thrilling and unearthly pipe-notes of the cuckoo seemed a mechanical instrument of torture: you found yourself desperately counting the calls, waiting between each, with a shrinking of all the nerves, for the next to strike. Almost you resented the flowery orchards and meadows with their pagan-like riot of renewal. You noted them with a dull eye from behind the stiff ponderous academic entrenchments of your mind. But sometimes in the night, in dreams, the orchards would not be denied: they descended upon you and shook out fragrance like a blessing; they shone in pale drifts, in clouds, in seas, – all the orchards of England came before you, luminous and stirring beneath the moon.

From early morning till late at night the desperate meek untidy heads of girls were bowed over tables in the library, their faces when they lifted them were feverish and blurred with work.

Pages rustled; pencils whispered; squeaking shoes tiptoed in and out. Somebody tapped out a dreary tune on her teeth; somebody had a running cold; somebody giggled beneath her breath; somebody sighed and sighed.

Outside, in the sunshine, tennis racquets struck vibrantly. Long ago, you also had played tennis in May.

Mabel had a fortification of dictionaries around her corner; whenever you looked up she caught your eye and smiled weakly from a hollow and twisted face. Mabel had wished evil to Jennifer. But that was so long ago it had ceased to matter.

'Mabel, you've worked four hours on end. Come to lunch now.'

'No thank you, Judith. I feel I don't want any lunch. I'd rather go straight on and perhaps have a cup of tea later.'

'Mabel, you're to come with me.'

She came. But as often as not she laid down her fork after one mouthful and sat and stared in front of her; then crept back to the library.

The copper bowl was filled this term with golden tulips or with dark brown wallflowers.

Where was Jennifer?

Examination week. The sky was fiercely blue all day; the air breathless, heavy. To walk into the town was to walk into a steam bath, where footsteps moved ever more languidly, and the dogs lay panting on the pavement, and the clocks seemed to collect themselves with a vast effort for their chiming.

This week there was nothing in your mind save the machine which obeyed you smoothly, turning out dates and biographies, contrasting, discussing, theorizing.

Judith walked in a dream among the pale examination faces that flowed to their doom. Already at nine o'clock the heat struck up from the streets, rolled downwards from the roofs. By midday it would be extremely unpleasant in Cambridge.

This was the great examination hall. Girls were filing in, each carrying a glass of water, and searching in a sort of panic for her place. Here was a white ticket labelled Earle, J. So Judith Earle really was expected, an integral part of this grotesque organized unreality. No hope now.

The bench was hard. Beside her sat a kind broad cow-like creature with sandy hair and lashes. Her ruminative and prominent eyes shed pity and encouragement. She was a good omen.

All over the room girls' heads turned, nodding and winking at friends, whispering, giggling and grimacing with desperate bravery. One simulated suicide by leaning her bosom on her fountain pen.

Just behind sat Mabel. Her face was glistening and ghastly, and she sniffed at a bottle of smelling salts.

'Mabel, are you going to faint?'

'No, I don't think so. I generally feel faint-like first thing in the morning. I'll get better later.'

'Mabel you're not fit – you mustn't –'

'Sh! I'm all right. Only it makes my head feel stupid.' She stared aghast. 'I don't seem to be able to remember a thing.'

'Don't worry, Mabel. It'll all come back when you settle down to it. I'll look round now and then and see if you're all right.'

'Thanks, Judith.'

'Poor Mabel! Good luck. Wait for me afterwards and I'll take you to have a cup of coffee. That'll do you good.'

'I shall enjoy that. Good luck, Judith.'

She summoned a smile, even flushed faintly with pleasure.

Then panic descended suddenly upon Judith. Her head was like a floating bubble; there was nothing in it at all. She caught at threads of knowledge and they broke, withered and dissolved like cobwebs in the hand. She struggled to throw off a crowding confusion of half remembered words.

Unarm Eros, the long day's task is done. And we must sleep . . . Peace! Peace! Dost thou not see my baby at my breast That sucks the nurse asleep? . . . Who said that? Who could have said such a thing? *I am Duchess of Malfi still . . . Cover her face. Mine eyes dazzle. She died young.* Beatrice died young too. *Here Mother . . . bind up this hair in any simple knot . . . ay that does well . . . Prithee undo this button . . . Thank you, Sir . . . Cordelia! Cordelia!* So many of them died young. There were those two, you had forgotten their names now, and Cordelia, and Desdemona too. *O, thou weed! . . .* It might be useful to remember them . . . But they had already slipped away. *This was the parting that they had Beside the haystack in the floods.* William Morris. *Speak but one word to me over the corn. Over the tender bowed locks of the corn.* Gold cornfield like Jennifer. *A bracelet of bright hair about the bone.* That had always been Jennifer's bright hair. *Only a*

183

woman's hair ... *Calm hair, meandering in pellucid gold.* But Jennifer's hair had never been calm ... *Speak but one word to me.* Roddy, one whisper from you!

It was Tennyson who said: *The wrinkled sea beneath him crawls* ... And Browning who said: *The old June weather Blue above lane and wall.* Keats, Coleridge, Wordsworth, and Shelley ... What had they said? and Blake:

Bring me my bow of burning gold; Bring me my arrows of desire ... Once you had composed a tune for that. *Bring me my bow of burning gold* ... Oh, stop saying that now. Think about the origins of drama, the rise of the universities, the development of the guilds, the order of Shakespeare's plays ...

A headful of useless scraps rattling about in emptiness –

The clock struck nine.

'You can begin now,' said a thin voice from the dais.

There was an enormous sigh, a rustling of paper, then silence.

The questions had, nearly all, at first glance a familiar reassuring look. It was all right. Panic vanished, the mind assembled its energies coolly, precisely, the pen flew.

After an hour the first pause to cool her forehead with a stick of frozen Eau de Cologne and to sip some water. Behind, poor Mabel's dry little cough and sniff went on. The head bowed low over her writing looked as if it could never raise itself again.

Girls were wriggling and biting their pens. Somewhere the tooth-tapper was playing her dreary tune. The Cow looked up, shed a peaceful smile around her and continued to write, with deliberation, a little impeded by her bosom.

Another hour fled. The trouble was having too much to say, rather than too little. The room was rigid, dark with concentration now. There came an appalling confusion of haste and noise, and a girl rose and ran from the room, supported by the invigilator. The handkerchief she held to her nose was stained sickeningly with scarlet. She returned in a little while, pallid and tearful, resumed her seat, bowed herself once more over the paper.

Three hours. It was over. You could not remember what you had written; but you had never felt more firm and sure of mind. Three hours nearer to life.

Into the street once more, beneath the noon sun's merciless down-beating. But now its rays seemed feeble: their warmth scarcely penetrated chilled hands and feet, or shivering, aching back.

A troop of undergraduates passed on the way from their examination room. They looked amused and exhilarated. They stuffed their papers into their pockets, lit pipes, straightened their shoulders and went cheerfully to lunch.

The girls crept out in twos and threes, earnestly talking, comparing the white slips they carried.

'Did you do this one?'

'What did you put for that?'

'Oh, I say! Will they take off marks do you think?'

'It was a beast.'

'Oh, it might have been worse.'

Girls really should be trained to be less obviously female students. It only needed a little discipline.

There was Mabel to be looked after. She was grateful, passive: she drank much coffee but refused food. She broke the heavy silence once to say with a quiet smile: 'Of course I see now I shan't pass – It seems a pity, after all that work – My memory is practically gone –'

Back to the vault now for another three hours.

Suddenly round the corner came a slender, dark, sallow boy. He walked with an idle grace, leaning slightly forward. His faint likeness to Roddy made the heart leap; and his expression was dejected and obstinate, just as Roddy's would be if he were forced to spend an afternoon scribbling infernal rubbish.

Judith paused at the entrance of the vault and looked back. His eyes were eagerly fixed on her: and she smiled at him.

He was delighted. His funny boy face lost its heaviness and broke up with intimate twinklings; and flashed a shyly daring inquiry at her before he vanished round the corner.

It was like a message from Roddy, sent forward to meet her from the new life, to say: 'Remember I am coming.'

That day passed smoothly; and the next. The days sinking to evenings drenched with the smell of honeysuckle and draining to phantasmal and luminous twilights of blossom and tree-tops and starry skies, flowed imperceptibly to their end.

Suddenly there were no answers to be written from nine till twelve, from two till five – no lectures, no coachings, no notes, no fixed working hours. Instead, a great idleness under whose burden you felt lost and oppressed. The academic years were gone for ever.

13

The evening before the end of term.

Judith walked with the rest of the circle arm in arm across the grass, down the wooded path, past the honeysuckle for the last time.

The garden spread out all her beauties that were hers alone, over-burdening the watchers, insisting:

'See what you are leaving. Look at what you will never have again.'

The whole shrine lay wide open for the last time, baring its mysteries of cedar and limes and nightingales, of lawns and mown hay, of blossoming shrubs and wild flowers growing beneath them, of copper beeches and all the high enclosing tree-tops, serenely swimming like clouds in the last of the light.

They chose careers for each other, light-heartedly discussing the future, and making plans for regular reunions.

'But what's the good?' said one. 'We shall all be scattered really. We can't come back year after year as if things would all be the same. There's nothing more awful than those gatherings of elderly people trying to be girls together again. The ghastliness of pretending to get back to where one was! If we meet again, let it be in the big world. I shall never come back here.'

'Oh, but I shan't have the strength to resist it,' said another. 'You see I more or less know I shall never be so happy again. I've got to teach brats algebra. I shall be *pulled* back to indulge in vain regrets.'

'Does it mean so much to you?' murmured Judith. 'You talk as if your life was over.'

'Something that matters – terribly to me is over,' she said, almost fiercely.

'Oh!' Judith sighed.

'Doesn't it mean anything to you then?'

Judith was silent, thinking how it had all meant the single tremendous calamitous significance of Jennifer; how since her going it had been like the muddy bed of a lake whose waters have been sapped day after day in a long drought; like a tasteless meal to be swallowed without appetite; like a grey drizzling unwholesome weather. Nothing had brought even a momentary illusion of restored contentment: nothing save her copper bowl glowing for her sake with flowers or fruit. Not one of those to whom she had turned had been able to soothe the gnawing perpetual sore, or bury for a single day that one face. And they knew it. The three years' absorption in Jennifer had separated her irrevocably from them, and, though they had kindly welcomed her, it had been with the tacit assumption that she was not of them.

They were so charming, so gentle, so sensitive and intelligent: fascinating creatures: how fascinating she had never troubled to realize and would never know now. To all, save Jennifer, that had offered itself, she had turned an unheeding ear, a blind eye. And so much that might have been of enduring value had offered itself: so many possible interests and opportunities had been neglected.

There had been that girl the first year who, from the pinnacle of her third-year eminence, had stooped, blushing and timid, with her invitation to an evening alone. Frail temples, narrow exquisite bone of cheek and jaw, clear little face with lips whose composure seemed the result of a vast nervous effort, so still were they, so nearly quivering, so vulnerable; eyes with a sad liquid brilliance in their steadfast gaze; small head with smooth brown hair parted in the middle; narrow hands folded in her lap; she had sat, the most important scholar in the College, like a shadow, a moth, a bird, listening, questioning, listening again.

She was a poet. She never shewed her verses, but to you she promised to shew them. She had a mind of such immaculate clarity that you feared to touch it: yet she was offering it to you, all that evening.

It had come to nothing after all. She had retired very soon, shrinking from Jennifer as if she were afraid.

There had been the girl with the torturing love affair that had gone wrong. One night she had suddenly spoken of it, telling you all. You had lingered by her with a little tenderness and pity and then passed on. She had said 'You won't tell Jennifer, will you?'

There had been the girl who drew portraits and who had wanted you for a model. There had been the silent girl who read 'The Book of the Dead' night after night in her room, who was studying, so it was whispered, to raise the devil and who looked at you with a secret smile, half malice, half something else; there had been that most beautiful young girl in the first year, with her cold angelic face and shining silver-fair hair; all those and countless others had offered themselves. There had been Martin ignored and neglected because he disliked Jennifer. And there had been books, far more books in far more libraries: and new poetry, new music, new plays, – a hundred intellectual diversions which you had but brushed against or missed altogether by secluding yourself within the limits of an unprofitable dream.

She said at last:

'Oh yes. It means something. I don't know yet how much. I'm afraid now I've missed a lot.'

They were all silent, and she thought with nervous dread that they were all thinking of Jennifer.

'Isn't it extraordinary,' said another, 'how time seems to have stood still in this place? Nothing's moved since we've been here. Even though I suppose it's all been advancing towards the Tripos, I don't *feel* as if there'd been any step forward. Everything – what's the word? – static. Or else just making circles. I feel I've been sitting in a quiet safe pool for three years.'

'And now we're going to be emptied out.'

And swept into new life, thought Judith longingly. Yet her heart misgave her. The building, caressed with sunset, looked motherly and benign, spreading its sheltering breast for the last time above its midgets. New life might find nothing so secure and tranquil as its dispassionate protection.

The clock struck the hour pensively.

'Well, I think it's beastly,' said one. 'I'm going in to finish packing.'

Where, on this calm lime-scented last evening, was Jennifer?

14

In the end there was no time to say good-bye to anyone. Girls were scattering, flying about with labels and suitcases, or with flat-irons to press the frocks they were to wear in May Week.

May Week had been fun last year: five nights' dancing on end, with Jennifer and a young cousin of hers at Trinity, and a boy in the Navy. This year it had not seemed worth while to accept invitations.

While Judith was engaged in strapping her boxes and throwing the accumulated rubbish of three years out of drawers and cupboards into a heap on the floor, a maid came smiling and said a gentleman was waiting downstairs.

It was Martin.

'Martin! Oh, my dear!'

'I came on the chance, Judith. I motored up to see a man who's going abroad. Are you – are you staying up for May Week?'

'No, Martin. I'm catching a train in about two hours and going straight home.'

'*Really* home, do you mean? next door to us?'

'Yes. Thank Heaven. It's not let any more. Mother and I will be there part of the summer anyway. Will you – will any of you be there?'

'Mariella's down there now, with the boy. And Roddy and I are going for a bit. In fact I'm going today – motoring. That's what I came for – to see if you'd care to motor back with me.'

'Drive home? Oh, how marvellous! You are an angel, Martin, to think of me.'

He was as shy as ever, bending his head as he talked to her. Observing him she thought that she herself had grown up. The loss of Jennifer had given her a kind of self-assurance and maturity of manner, a staidness. For the first time she was seeing Martin from an entirely detached and unromantic angle, and she thought: 'Then this is how I shall see Roddy. He won't confuse and entangle me any more. All that sort of thing is over for me.'

'It's very nice to see you again, Judith. It's ages since – You look a bit thin, don't you?'

'It's those miserable exams., Martin. I did work so hard ... I don't know why.'

'Oh! You shouldn't have.'

He seemed quite overcome.

Dear Martin! ... In some corner of her heart a weight was lifting ... Jennifer was suddenly remote.

'Wait for me, Martin ... I'll be ready in a quarter of an hour.'

She had not said good-bye to Mabel. She had been dreading that last duty ... No time now, thank heaven, for anything prolonged ... Simplest to write a little note and tell someone to stick it in her door

She wrote.

Dear Mabel,

I have been called for unexpectedly in a car. I have only ten minutes to finish packing and do all the last things. I knocked on your door a little while ago but got no answer.

She hesitated. Was it too gross? It was; but it must stand now; it could not be crossed out.

And now I'm afraid I haven't a minute to try and find you. I'm *dreadfully* sorry not to see you to say good-bye, Mabel. Won't it be sad when next October comes to think we shan't all be meeting again? You must write and tell me what happens to you, and I will write to you. I dare say we shall see each other again. You must let me know if you ever come my way –

That must stand too ... What else? ... Results would be out tomorrow – Better not to refer to them; for Mabel had certainly failed. She had not been able to remember anything in the end. The last three days she had given in one or two sheets of paper blank save for a few uncertain lines.

She finished:

I do hope you are going to get a good long rest. You do need it. You worked so marvellously. Nobody ever could have worked harder We've all been so sorry for you feeling so ill during Tripos week It was terribly hard luck.

Good-bye and love from

Judith.

Nothing could be added. There was nothing more to be said. Mabel's face this last week came before her, blank, haggard, still watching her from moribund eyes, and she dismissed it. She had thought she would have to kiss Mabel good-bye: and now she would not have to.

She must be quick now, for Martin.

The car turned out of the drive and took the dusty road.

Almost she forgot to look back to see the last of those red walls.

'I'm saying good-bye to it, Martin. Ugh! I hate it. I love it.'

The poplars seemed to grow all in a moment and hide it. It was gone.

'Well Martin, how are you? What's been happening to everybody? How are they all?'

She was slipping back, she was slipping back.

They left Cambridge behind them, and she tried to recall it, to make it come before her eyes, and could not. The dream of wake, the dream of sleep – which had it been?

She wondered if she would ever remember it again.

Yesterday Martin had been standing with her under the cherry tree.

Now he was telling her about his home in Hampshire. He acted as estate agent for his mother now that his father was dead. She must really come and stay with them and meet his mother. He was perfectly happy farming his own land: he never wanted to do anything else. He was improving the fishing and shooting: they had just bought a bit of land they had been after for two years: half a mile more river and a biggish wood. Forestry was the most fascinating subject: he was going to take it up more seriously. Martin's life seemed very happy, very ordered, very clear and useful. He knew what he wanted.

The cousins had all been scattered this last year or so. Mariella had been working with a woman vet in London. She had spent most of last summer at his home because she had been hard up and obliged to let the house on the river. Peter had been there too. He seemed a nice enough little chap, but nervy. He had a nursery governess now, and Mariella seemed to think more about her dogs than him. At least that was the impression she gave. Mariella, so Martin said, had not changed at all.

Julian he had scarcely seen. He thought he wrote about music for one or two weeklies, but he didn't know which. Also he had heard that he was writing a ballet, or an opera or something; but he did not suppose it was serious. He had developed asthma since the war, poor chap, and he spent all the winter abroad and sometimes the summer too.

And Roddy. Oh, Roddy seemed to be messing about in Paris or in London nearly always, doing a bit of drawing and modelling. Nobody could get him to do any work: though last year he had done some sort of theatrical work in Paris – designing some scenery or something – which had been very successful. He was saying now that he would like to go on the stage. Martin laughingly said he was afraid Roddy was a bit of a waster. Anyway he was coming for a week or so, and Judith would see him for herself.

At six o'clock in the evening they stopped before the front door of her home. There, waiting to enfold her again, was the garden. The air was sweet with the smell of roses and syringa, the sun-flooded lawn stretched away towards the river, and the herbaceous border was burning miraculously with blue delphinium spires, white and yellow lilies, and great poppies.

'Good-bye Martin. It's been lovely. We'll meet soon, won't we? Come and fetch me.'

She went into the cool and shadowed hall. There was the old butler hastening forward to receive her; and her mother's voice came from the drawing-room saying softly:

'Is that my girl?'

Part Four

I

SHE was ready for the picnic. She wore a yellow linen frock and a hat of brown straw, shaped like a poke bonnet and trimmed with a beautiful yellow ribbon. It was Mamma who tied the ribbon in a great bow: the loops fell in the nape of her neck and the ends ran down between her shoulder blades.

'Lovely young creature,' said Mamma dispassionately observing her.

Judith had been home more than a week, and Mamma was being charming. She had taken her to London to buy frocks. They had stayed at Jules for a couple of nights, and Mamma had ordered pretty clothes generously from her own dressmaker. She had said at last in her curious, harsh yet beautiful voice, with a shrug of her shoulders, as Judith paraded before her in the fifteenth model:

'As you see, everything suits that child.'

And the dressmaker had solemnly agreed.

They had been together to a play, and to the opera; and every morning and every night Judith sat on Mamma's bed and they chatted together with friendly politeness, almost with ease.

She was a woman exquisitely dressed, manicured, powdered and scented. Her face did not age, though the colourless cheeks were now a little hollowed, and the eyes sharper. Her eyes were like blue diamonds, and she had an unkind reddened mouth with long pointed corners. The bones of her face were strong and sharp and delicate, and something in the triangular outline, in the set of the eyes, the expression of the lips, made you think of a cat.

She was elegant in mind as well as in person, capable, quick-witted. Her conversation was acute and well-informed over a wide field, – and men admired and delighted in her. She had always, thought Judith, seemed to move surrounded by men who paid her compliments. She had no woman friends that you could remember. She remarked, now and then, how much she disliked women; and Judith had felt herself included in the condemnation. She had never been pleased to have a daughter: only a handsome son would have been any good to her. Her daughter had discerned that far back in a childhood made vulnerable by adoration of her.

There was scarcely anything about Mamma to remember: nothing but a vague awestruck worshipful identification of her with angels and the Snow Queen.

There was one night when she had come in, dressed for a dinner party, all in white, with something floating rosy and iridescent about her. The dress had geraniums on it, at breast, waist and hem, a bunch on one shoulder, and flowing geranium-coloured ribbons. There were diamonds in her fair cloud of hair. She bent over the cot, smiling secretly with eyes and lips as if she were very pleased; and Judith hid her face from that angelic presence; and neither of them spoke a word. A man's voice called: 'Mildred!' from the door: not Papa.

'Come in,' she said, 'here's the child.'

Somebody tall and moustached came and stood beside Mamma and looked down, making jokes and asking silly questions, and laughing because she would neither answer nor look at him.

'Don't be silly, Judith,' said Mamma.

'She hasn't a look of you,' said the man.

'No, nothing of me at all.' Her voice sounded bored.

'Are you sorry?'

'Fred isn't.'

They both laughed a little.

They stood leaning on the cot-rail in silence side by side, and Judith's hand stole out unnoticed and touched a geranium. She gave it a little pull and it slipped out of the bunch into her hand.

'Come then,' said Mamma; and then over her shoulder, 'Go to sleep, Judith.'

She would have been annoyed if she had noticed the geranium. It was not real after all: it was made of pink velvet. Judith hid it under her pillow

Mamma slipped her hand into the man's arm and floated away.

That was the only vivid recollection of her left. The children next door came close on the heels of the geranium-frock in memory; and after that they, and not Mamma, absorbed her passion. Mamma was more and more away, or busy; and more and more obviously not interested in her daughter. All life that was not playing next door, or alone in the garden, was lessons and governesses. Mamma and Papa were relentless about education.

They had dual personalities in Judith's mind. There were Mamma and Papa who loved each other, of course, and loved their only daughter; and sometimes took her to the seaside, and now and then to London for the pantomime. Once or twice she went abroad with them; but on the many occasions when they left her behind, they wrote her affectionate letters which she dutifully replied to in French, so that they might see how her French was progressing; and they brought her back beautiful presents. Often when they were at home they read aloud to her in the evenings.

The three were blent in a relationship of a romantic and consoling sort, – an ideal relationship; but then Fred and Mildred would take the place of Mamma and Papa, and shatter the illusion. For they, alas, seemed made of stronger and more enduring fibre: they were real: and they were not often together: and when they were, there was often coldness and now and then quarrelling. Life with Fred and Mildred was neither comforting nor secure. Fred was quite an elderly man, and terrifyingly silent and preoccupied. He read and wrote books, and had a few elderly friends. Sometimes these would pause for a moment between their long spaces of ignoring her; and, searching her face, would tell her she was growing up like her father. And, each time, their voices, their faces, their words made an unknown past spring up in her for a moment, rich with undreamed-of vanished graces – and she would go away with an ache of sadness. People loved Fred; Mildred they admired and deferred to, but did not love. That was clear at an early age, when Judith went walking with one or other of them past the row of cottages at the top of the garden, and they stopped to speak to the cottage people over the fences. The cottage people had one sort of voice, look, reply for Fred; and quite another for Mildred.

Judith grew up with a faint obscure resentment against Mildred for the way she treated Fred, for her competence – her dry, unmerciful, cynical success in dealing with the world. Fred was not at home in the world: even less at home, thought Judith, than she herself; but Mildred was steeped in its wise unkindnesses. She did not seem to realize that Fred needed to be looked after.

Then he died; and they became Mamma and Papa again. Mamma had been gentle, tired-looking, and pale in her black clothes, and dependent for a little while on Judith. She had not spoken much of Papa; but she seemed engrossed in sad contemplations, and her replies to letters spoke of him with tenderness and pride.

But all that had not lasted long. After the first six months she had not appeared to want Judith much during vacations. She was always visiting, always travelling, always surrounded by flattering talkative men and bridge-playing scented women; and she came only once for a few hours to College during the whole three years. She had a flat in Paris, with a little room for Judith; but she expected Judith to lead her own life and to stay with her own friends, or with the one aunt, Papa's sister, for a part, at least, of every vacation. Reading-parties, short visits to friends' homes, long visits to the old literary maiden aunt in Yorkshire, had absorbed the time. There had been one rapturous summer month alone with Jennifer in a cottage in Corn-wall; but there had never been a visit to Jennifer's home. Her parents, she said, were too unpleasant to be inflicted upon anybody except herself; and then only for brief spaces and at rare intervals. Like Roddy, she appeared and vanished again, without a background, blazing mysteriously into and out of ordinary life.

The hoped-for letter from Mariella, asking her to stay, had never come. She had not seen Mariella since the summer of Papa's death; and had had no sign from her save one little ill-expressed conventional letter of sympathy, sent, so the writer said, from them all 'to tell you how dreadfully we simpathise.' (But Martin had written a note on his own account.)

The wandering vacations abroad and in England had become a habit; and now, all at once, there was home again. Mamma had come home, out of pure kindness and consideration for Judith; for she did not love it, did not want to live there, found it a heavy expense;

and had, so she said, several magnificent opportunities of selling it.

'But it seemed only fair you should have it, this summer at any rate,' she said. 'I know you feel romantic about it.' She added, 'I see no reason why we shouldn't spend a very pleasant summer together. You are very companionable – quite well-read now and quite intelligent; and extremely presentable, I will say. I do not intend you to stay with me permanently. I should find it extremely tiresome to be always dragging you about with me; and I dare say you'd dislike it too. We are quite unsuited to being together for long; we should only irritate each other. I thought you might have made up your mind what you wanted to do by now –' (Mamma's remarks had generally a faint sting in their tails) –, 'however, since you haven't, I look forward to having you with me, till the winter at least. You can decide then what you will do, and I will help you if I can. Does this arrangement suit you?'

The arrangement promised to work admirably. It was a step of considerable importance, thought Judith, that Mamma should want her at all. And even though they never spoke intimately, they were never at a loss for topics: there were books, people, plays, and clothes to discuss. And Mamma seemed happy in the garden, reading or wandering about; she admitted that she loved going out with a basket and a pair of scissors to cut flowers for all the rooms.

Surely it was going to be possible at last to establish a satisfactory relationship; to feel deep affection as well as interest, admiration, and that curious pang and thrill of the senses which her scent, her clothes, the texture of her skin and hair gave you and had given you from babyhood.

Mamma finished tying the bow, remarked: 'Well – enjoy yourself,' in a half-amused, half-mocking voice; and dismissed her to her picnic.

2

They were all collected at the front door as she came down the drive: all except Roddy. They had ceased to hold terror for her now, or anguish: she had grown up. She could observe the tall group they made without a tremor. What a way they had of all standing together, as if to prevent a stranger from breaking in among them! But that did not matter now. Since she had met them again, there had been no approach to intimacy on either side, no significant interchanges; and she had not minded, had not lain awake feverish with doubt and longing. She was equal to them now. Her heart was in a stupor or dead; and it seemed as if they were never going to disturb her any more.

Mariella, Julian, Martin; but no Roddy . . .

Julian had come down for the day. He was more cadaverous than ever. His face was composed of furrows, projections, and hollows, with eyes blazing far back in his head. A lock of his thick brown hair had turned white. He wore elegant white flannel trousers and an apricot-coloured shirt of softest silk; and he made Martin, in blue cotton shirt and old grey flannels, look rustic and unkempt.

'Pile in,' said Martin. 'Mariella, I *can't* let you drive my new car You do understand, don't you, angel?'

'I'm not at all a good driver,' said Mariella, smiling vaguely round upon them all. 'I smashed Martin's car to pieces last year, didn't I, Martin? I ran it into a wall. He was awfully nice about it.'

'He's an awfully nice man,' said Julian, putting his hand on Martin's shoulder.

Martin was the only one who ever received obvious marks of affection from the rest. They all treated him in the same way – with a sort of teasing tenderness.

'Judith will you come in front with me? And Mariella and Julian, you go there . . . Yes, that's right. Will you be comfortable? Are you all quite happy?' Martin was terribly anxious lest there should be a hitch. Everyone had got to enjoy the picnic.

'Is the food in? *And* the drink? Who's got the opener? Oh, I have. Mariella, remember that this is Julian's Day in the Country and don't sit there and never open your mouth, but point out objects of interest as we go along, and any country sight or sound you happen to notice. Are we ready then? To Monk's Water, isn't it?'

The car swooped up the drive.

'Is Martin safe?' cried Julian clinging to Mariella. 'I don't believe he's safe. If he goes fast I shall jump out. Oh let's stay at home and have a picnic in the garden. Don't let's go away from this nice house and see objects of interest. I didn't mean it when I suggested it. I never wanted to. Oh why can't you ever see a joke any of you? Oh! ...'

He subsided with a groan and shut his eyes as Martin swung round the corner and out on to the road. Mariella was giggling like a little girl, Martin was grinning, everybody was in the proper picnic mood. But where was Roddy?

'Martin, what's happened to Roddy?'

'Oh, Roddy,' said Martin. 'Poor old Roddy's got a headache.'

'A headache?' Something leapt painfully in her.

'Yes. We left him lying down. The idiot would play tennis all yesterday in the broiling sun without a hat, and the consequence is a touch of the sun I suppose. He kept me awake most of the night shivering and warning me he was going to be sick. He looked awful at breakfast I must say, – bright yellow; so we gave him an aspirin and put him on the sofa and left him.'

'Left him, Martin? But oughtn't someone to have stayed with him?'

'Oh Lord no. He'll sleep it off and be all right tomorrow. His temper was his worst trouble, so we thought we'd keep away.'

Martin laughed cheerfully, as if he were amused about Roddy's headache. How cruel, how callous people were! They called themselves his friends and they left him ill and alone, and went off to enjoy themselves. He might get worse during the day: he might be sickening for a serious illness.

Roddy's absence and his headache mattered terribly. She realized suddenly that it was chiefly because of seeing him that she had looked forward to the picnic; that she had hoped to watch him, to talk to him; that she had had a pang of dismay at his absence from the group by the door; that she had been secretly alert for his coming, in a fever for some mention of him until the very moment of starting; and that then a weight had descended; and that now the day was utterly ruined.

After all, was she going to be obliged to live, to feel, to want again?

Roddy was lying in the deserted house, on the red sitting-room sofa, with the blinds down. His forehead and closed eyes were contracted with his headache. He tossed his head and buried it in the cushions; and his hair got ruffled, and the cushions became more and more uncomfortable. He swore. You came in on tip-toe and knelt down beside him.

'Roddy, I've come to see you,' you whispered.

'Oh, Judy, I've got such a headache and nobody cares.'

'Darling, I care. I'm so terribly sorry. I've come to make it better.'

You stroked his forehead with cool fingers, smoothed his pillows, gave him a drink and told him to lie still.

'That's better. Thank you, Judy. Do stay with me.'

It was bliss looking after him. He had ceased to withdraw himself and be proud: he was utterly dependent. You bent and kissed his forehead ...

Martin broke in upon her dream, saying: 'Quite comfortable, Judith?'

And after he had adjusted the wind-screen, explained to her some of the devices on the dash-board, looked round to see that the others were all right, he addressed himself with satisfaction to his driving again, resuming his one-sided muttered conversations with his car and with passers-by.

'Now, now, come along old lady ... that's right ... What's the matter with you? Got a pain? ... Well done old girl.' ... 'Now my dear sir, what are you up to? ... Put out your hand Madam before you turn corners like that ... Look out, you little brutes, spinning tops in the road. Lucky for you I didn't run you clean over ... Oh, so you think you can race me, do you? Well, try, that's all.'

As a variant he read the signposts aloud.

Judith watched the deep-golden, dark-shadowed country slip by: its woods and fields wore a sullen empty look.

They reached their destination at tea-time, and walked down the steep slope to the edge of Monk's Water.

Bracken and long grass came pouring from the top of the hill to the very bank of the stream; and the beech-trunks rose up from that soft, swirling blue-green cascade, up and up, as far as eye could see. They sprang up clear from their lovely symmetrical pattern of naked roots and climbed the air in one long pure lift and flow, or in a lightly twisting spiral. Ardently they soared, column after smooth grey-green column, lightly balancing on their roots, gathering their power, sweeping it upwards for the final high breaking of the boughs. The strong outflung whirl of the snaky boughs was lost at last in a fountain of foliage. The bright spray wove closely and shut out the sky; but the sun pierced it and lay beneath it in pools of dappled green light.

The smell of bracken was on the air, and the little Monk's Water slipped past in front of them, brown and clear, singing over its shallows, hiding beneath its over-hanging greenery.

'This is where I once found a new kind of beetle,' said Julian, looking round him with pleasure.

'I shall bathe after tea,' said Mariella. 'Boys, we must all bathe. I rather wish I'd brought Peter now. Don't you, Julian?' She looked at him uncertainly.

'Well I told you to, didn't I? You said he'd got to stay with his governess,' he said, in an unkind voice.

'Never mind, Mariella,' said Martin quickly. 'I think you were right not to bring him. He'd probably have found it very tiring, a long expedition like this.'

'That's what I thought,' she said, agreeing with a sort of pathetic childish complacence.

Judith remembered once again, with a pang of amazement, that Mariella was a mother.

'What about tea?' said Martin. 'God, I do hope nothing's been forgotten.'

He opened the picnic basket and searched eagerly among its contents until he found a napkinful of raw tomatoes and lettuce.

Judith smiled at him suddenly. Whoever changed, Martin remained unchanged. He had always been, was now, and would be till he died, kindly, greedy and comforting. He would always eat raw vegetables and smell very faintly of healthy sweat, and ask nothing much of life save that the people he was fond of should be cheerful.

He caught the smile and answered it swiftly, radiantly.

They ate sandwiches, fruit and cake; and the flies, gnats, mosquitoes and midges came in murmurous clouds around them; and Julian started to lose his temper.

'Smoke, all of you, smoke! Don't stop for a moment!' he shouted. 'My God, we shall all be devoured. *Now* you know what the Insect Age will be like. Now you see to what end you've been helping to produce the next generation, Mariella: to battle with insects and to be defeated.'

They lit cigarettes and frenziedly puffed smoke into the air until the main body of the cloud died away.

'Now please may we go home?' he said plaintively. And all at once Judith was reminded of Charlie as a small boy, difficult, petulant, imperious, and yet all the time half laughing at himself in a way that disarmed rebuke: as who should say: 'I know I'm being a beast and I *will* be a beast, as long as I like; but you mustn't mind and you mustn't take me seriously.'

Julian went on:

'Let's all go home and have a nice quiet game of something in the billiard room. Oh I do hate outdoors so. I do hate the country.'

Martin looked distressed.

'You're very ungrateful,' said Mariella. 'It was Martin's treat for you.' She took Martin's hand and patted it.

'Because you said you remembered coming here once when you were a boy and finding a new insect, and how you'd always wanted to come back,' explained Martin.

'Oh my accursed sentimentality! I wanted to bring back the days when I was a carefree beetle-hunter. *Weren't* there any flies then? Or didn't one notice them?'

'I remember one of the beetle walks when I went with you,' said Judith. 'We came back with our legs and arms swollen up like balloons.'

'Do you remember that?' He sat up and smiled at her. 'Did we go on beetle walks together?'

'Yes.' She blushed. 'Sometimes. I was very proud when you took me.'

He laughed delightedly.

'I believe I remember. You *were* a peculiar child. What else did we do when we were young? Can you remember?'

'I remember a lot.'

'Oh do tell us.'

She shook her head.

'What were we like? Who was the nicest? Martin of course: you needn't answer that. But who was the most attractive? Which did you like best?'

'If you can't remember I shan't remind you.'

'Oh I believe it was me!' cried Julian; 'I'm almost sure it was. Haven't I always been your favourite?'

She laughed teasingly in his face.

'Well, I'm sure I deserved to be,' he said. 'You were *my* favourite anyway. Absolutely my favourite woman. You always have been ... Have we changed very much?'

'No. Very little.'

'Which of us has changed most?'

Judith paused a moment and then answered: 'Mariella.'

And directly she had said it she realized afresh how true it was: too true to have been so lightly spoken. Mariella had changed indeed.

Her smile, and Julian's, faded abruptly.

'Oh, have I?' she said, looking away embarrassed.

'I don't think Mariella's changed a bit,' said Martin with surprise.

'Ah well,' said Julian coming out of a deep musing, 'I *feel* changed, Heaven knows ... Now I shall have a short sleep, my children, and then I am at your disposal for a jolly game of tag. Judith has, as usual, cured me of most of my bad temper, and slumber will complete the process. Judith, angel, you'll stay by me won't you, and wave cigarettes? ... Go away chaps. Judith and I are going to converse until I fall asleep. Remember I haven't seen her for three years.'

'I'm going to look for a place to bathe,' said Martin. 'Mariella, will you come?'

'Yes.' She held out her hands to him, giving him her sweet, small smile of the lips. He pulled her up on to her feet and they started to walk away.

'I'll come and find you,' called Judith. 'I want to bathe too.'

Martin turned eagerly.

'There are one or two pools somewhere down this way,' he said. 'Will you follow us?'

'Yes.'

'Good.'

He waved and she waved back; and they were lost round the corner.

Julian lay down in the shade of an elder bush, lit another cigarette, and looked at Judith with bright appraising eyes.

'Well, Judith?' he said, and smiled. And as of old the smile trans-figured the whole harsh face with beauty.

'Well, Julian? What have you been doing with yourself?'

'Nothing, nothing.'

'You're happier than you were last time I saw you.'

'What makes you say that?'

She hesitated.

'Your – acting is much more natural.'

He laughed and made a face at her.

'Doesn't my elegant and elaborate window-dressing dazzle you? Well, never mind. It never did, did it? And I never minded. You're the only woman I've never been able to deceive to whom I have re-mained consistently attached.'

'Are there many you've been able to deceive, Julian?'

He paused.

'There are some who have loved me,' he said. 'So they must have been deceived.'

'You think if they hadn't been they couldn't have loved you?'

He nodded.

'Ah, I don't believe that. Nor do you.' She sighed, 'It's a thing I never would have believed ... how one can go on loving a person one knows to be – cruel and selfish and indifferent.'

Whom did she have in mind, – she wondered as she said it. That was not Jennifer, surely: surely not Roddy?

'Not,' she added quickly, 'that you're any of those things. I can't allow you the satisfaction of thinking so.'

'I'm all of them,' he said:

> '... bloody,
> Luxurious, avaricious, false, deceitful,
> Sudden, malicious, smacking of every sin
> That has a name ...

And that reminds me Judy, I hear you acquitted yourself with supreme distinction in your tripos. I'm very glad – very proud to know you.'

'It hasn't given me much satisfaction.'

'Now, now! Less of that.'

'It's true. I'm not being modest.' She turned away from him and said: 'I worked very very hard. I thought of nothing but work, because I didn't have anything else – particularly pleasant – to think about. One doesn't much value that sort of success.'

There was a silence.

'And I suppose,' said Julian, 'that's all I'm to be told about it.'

She shrugged her shoulders.

'There's nothing,' she said. 'Just that.'

'Nobody ever will confide in me,' he complained. 'I don't know why. I'm quite madly interested – especially in love affairs. I suppose my face puts them off.'

She laughed ... No, nobody would confide in Julian. He would be too clear-sighted, too scientifically interested, too cold and reasonable. He would give such good advice and so much of it. People only wanted a muddle-headed outpouring of sympathy.

He went on:

'It's far too long since I last saw you. Why didn't I come to see you at Cambridge? Or write to you? I meant to.'

'Why not indeed? ... Because you forgot about me.'

'I never forgot about you, Judy. You were always in the back of my mind. But life was very full ... And I wanted to wait.'

He gave her a quick glance, whose meaning she did not pause to interpret. She said hurriedly:

'I am glad life was full. You have been happy, haven't you? Tell me about these three years.'

'They haven't been – outwardly – dramatic,' he said with a smile. 'It's been ill-health, and again ill-health for me.'

'Poor Julian!' She took up his hand and pressed it for a moment; and her eyes started with tears. She had forgotten the asthma which had hollowed his always hollow cheeks, ploughed deeper the lines about the mouth, lifted and bowed the always high stooping shoulders.

'It's all right,' he said rather awkwardly. 'It's given me a good excuse for never doing anything I didn't want to do. These years since the war have been an uninterrupted succession of self-indulgences. I was happy in a way at Oxford. But I only stayed a year. It didn't do really. The locust-eaten years behind me were too strong. I couldn't work, I couldn't play. I was too old altogether. But the gentleness of people, the peace, the beauty! – all that was very comforting. I took to my music again, a little. ... But, as I say, it wasn't any good trying to recapture what I had once found there. And then of course the climate did me in. So I came down, – a physical wreck, but more or less sane again. Since then I have been in France, Switzerland, Austria – all over Europe. I have composed a ballet which will never be performed. I have written three songs. I have contributed pseudo-highbrow criticism of modern music to several periodicals. I have listened – oh listened very happily to a great deal of music in a great many countries. I have had a Russian mistress, and a French and an Austrian. I think that was all.' He gave her a quick look as if to see what effect this announcement had upon her; but her face remained unmoved. Julian's passions had always been an uninteresting if not distasteful subject for speculation. 'And I got tired of them all and treated them monstrously and left them. They seemed to me quite insupportable after a bit – so stupid. I have tried in vain to be cured of asthma at the inept hands of countless doctors. I have read a lot – and talked more, as you may guess. I have spent and still spend much time looking for someone to whom I might attach myself permanently. But that of course is the most tiresome romantic folly. Nobody could love me for long: I know that well. And I dare say I myself am incapable of anything except a little passing lust. In short, Judy, you see in me what is known as a waster. It's in the family, I'm afraid. Roddy's another. Charlie was designed for one from birth ... But he'd have been a happy one, poor boy ... Whereas my conscience pricks.' He rolled over on the grass to look at Judith, lazily, laughingly. 'That's all,' he said. 'Now it's your turn.'

'No, no. Go to sleep. I've nothing to tell you.'

'The mosquitoes have all disappeared,' he said. 'Why? Perhaps I'd better take the opportunity – I shall be so charming when I wake up again. Thank you, Judith. You've done me good.' He shut his eyes; and re-opened them to say: 'I told you you were always in the back of my mind. It's true. Always.' He took her hand. 'Judith, am I going to be allowed to know you at last?'

'Oh yes Julian, of course.'

'Hmm – I wonder.'

He was staring at her with intense inquiry and concentration; but she turned her eyes away. She could not feel that the matter was of much importance.

'We're going to see each other a lot?'

'As much as you like.'

'What are your plans?'

'I'm here till the end of July. Then I go abroad with Mamma. To France. To Vichy part of the time. She will believe the cure does her good.'

'I shall come and find you in France. I shall come to Vichy and take you away from Mamma. I do better in France. You might find me quite a pleasant companion. There's so much I should like to shew you, – do with you. Shall I come?'

'Yes, Julian. Do.'

'And you'd talk to me?'

She nodded.

'In the end,' he said, watching her intently, 'I believe you will ... I told you I could wait.'

He relinquished her hand, and shut his eyes.

She got up and sprang away from him down the bank.

The afternoon was breathless with a thundery heat. The fern-clad slopes were sculptured and glittering cascades. Monk's Water hid between its shady banks. She followed its twisting course, looking ahead of her for the blue of Martin's shirt, the white of Mariella's linen frock.

Roddy was a waster ... It was in the family ... Roddy was no good, he was a waster. Perhaps, like Julian, he had mistresses: a French, an Austrian, a Russian – countless mistresses. Perhaps that was an integral part of being a waster ...

She came round a sharp corner, and saw, through the elder bushes, a whitish form in the water. It straightened itself swiftly, alert at the sound of her footsteps.

'Judy?' called a voice uncertainly – Mariella's voice.

Judith parted the elder bushes and looked through: and there was Mariella standing naked in midstream with clear brown water up to her knees.

'Goodness, I'm glad it's you!' she cried happily. 'I thought it might be someone else. Come on in, Judy. It's so lovely.'

She stood in the full sunlight, her arms lifted and laid across her forehead to shade her eyes, her lips laughing. Her tall body glowed in the glowing air, narrow of hip, breastless almost, with faint, long, young-looking curves; the whole outline smooth and very firm in spite of its slenderness. Her voice vibrated gaily, excitedly. She was happy.

'We took off our shoes and stockings,' she called, 'and waded down till we found this pool. Martin said he thought he remembered a place where it got deeper, and he was right, wasn't he? It's not *very* deep, but still you can swim round. The water's full of tiny trout. I've been watching them. Martin's bathing a little further down in another pool. I've left my clothes under that bush. You leave yours there too and come on in.'

Judith stripped and waded out to join her.

'This is the sort of bathing I love,' she went on. 'Nothing on and not very much water. You know, it's funny, I never could learn to swim properly; I don't know why. The boys used to laugh at me so because I always sank and had to be rescued. I gave it up in the end.'

It was the first time since childhood, thought Judith, that they two had been alone together. How deep was the difference in them? Mariella, naked, with her childish curly head and her unselfconscious body looked much the same now as she had looked that evening long ago when Judith had stayed the night with her, and they had had their evening bath together. And yet, a little while ago, it had seemed so certain that Mariella was profoundly changed: in the set of her face especially, – in the grown-up expression of reserve and sadness, – the whole look of a woman whose countenance has started to assume the cast it will wear in middle age. But now, alight and laughing in sun and water, it had once more the blank clearness and candour of her childhood.

Mariella splashed the water, hummed a little tuneless tune, laughed when a stone gave way beneath her foot and threw her headlong into the stream; and the bathing days with Jennifer returned to Judith with a pang. The body beside her now was like Jennifer's in height, strength, firmness of mould: and yet how unlike! This body seemed as unimpassioned as the water which held it; and Jennifer's had held in every curve a mystery which compelled the eyes and the imagination.

'I really wish I'd brought Peter,' said Mariella, stooping down to peer into the water. 'He'd have been so excited about these little fishes. Martin and I have just made him a little aquarium and he's so thrilled with it.'

'What fun, Mariella! It must be fun having him to play with. He's such a good age now.'

'Well, he really likes playing by himself best,' she said, looking faintly troubled. 'He's such a queer quiet little boy.'

'Well that's much better for him than always having to be amused, isn't it?'

'Of course it is!' She cheered up. 'He – I s'pose it's him being an only child and me being fairly busy – and then I do think it's much better for a child to learn to play by himself, don't you?' She echoed Judith's words complacently, as if they sprang from her own original and profound conviction.

After a pause she went on reflectively:

'That governess of his is a very strict person. She says she must have entire charge of him.'

'She's new, isn't she?'

'Quite new.' Then gravely, like a child pretending to be grown up: 'I thought perhaps I might sack her. I'm not altogether satisfied with her.'

She seemed to be waiting to be encouraged in her desperate plan.

'But why, Mariella?'

She hesitated, flushing.

'Well, she's so *frightfully* superior,' she said at last, looking apologetic, a little sheepish. 'I do hate bossy people, do you?' Her eyes sought Judith's with a flicker of appeal.

'I should think I do.'

'Well that's what it is,' she said with relief.

Judith took her arm and patted it, saying laughingly: 'Mariella, you're afraid of her, I do believe! You know you'd never *dare* sack her. Shall I come and do it for you?'

'Well' – Mariella dropped her voice and said in an embarrassed confiding way, 'She simply doesn't take any notice of me – absolutely none. His own mother! I really sometimes wonder if ... Do you suppose –' She stopped, and a faint flush suffused her whole face.

'What, Mariella?' said Judith softly.

'Well, I sometimes wonder if Julian could possibly have told her I – I don't know how to look after him.'

She stooped again over the water, and her curls fell forward, hiding her face.

'Oh no, Mariella! He couldn't ... He'd never do a thing like that.'

But was it not more than possible?

'Well p'raps not ... But he might, you know ...' She picked pebbles out of the water, her face still hidden. 'He never did think I was much good at looking after Peter. You see, the thing is I ought to be very grateful to him really ...'

'Why, Mariella?' asked Judith. To herself she said: 'In another minute I shall get to know Mariella': and she almost held her breath to listen, waiting for the moment of revelation, and fearful lest a word or movement of hers should alarm the speaker, close her lips suddenly, and for ever.

'Well, he's very helpful about Peter.' Still she picked pebbles from the stream and threw them away again. She went on as if with an effort: 'The thing is, you see, he got that governess for Peter, interviewed her and everything. Isn't he funny? He said poor old Pinkey – you remember her – wasn't good for him and he must have somebody more suitable for his nervous temperament. I'm afraid he *has* got a very nervous temperament. I s'pose it's being musical ... He took simply terrific trouble to find that governess. I daresay she does manage nervous children well. Peter seems very cheerful with her I must say ... And he doesn't wake up with one of his screaming fits nearly so often ... So I can't say anything, can I? Julian always will think he knows best. He always was an awful boss, wasn't he?' She raised her face to smile with a suspicion of roguishness.

'Yes, always.' Judith smiled back, eager to encourage Mariella with a sense of shared amusement.

The stratagem was successful. Mariella swam a few strokes to the bank, sat down there, splashing the water with her feet, and said, more cheerfully: 'Of course it's very nice he takes such an interest.'

Judith came and sat beside her on the bank, and continued: 'Where shall you send Peter to school?'

Her face clouded over again, troubled and alarmed.

'I don't know,' she said. 'I haven't thought. I'm not very good at that sort of thing. He's so delicate and ... I suppose Julian will see about it ... I think he's got some plans ... Of course Peter isn't quite like other children because he's so musical, Julian says ...'

There was a long silence. The sun had dried their wet bodies, and they leisurely dressed again and continued to sit on the bank side by side, watching the flow of the water. The faintest ruffle of breeze had sprung up, and the sculptured fern cascades were coming to life, stirring now and then. The golden light on the beeches had become richer and more tender.

'It must be very interesting to have a child,' said Judith at last.

'Oh, do you think so? Do you want one?'

Judith nodded.

'I never wanted one.' She smiled faintly. 'I always thought puppies so much nicer than babies.'

'But what did you feel when your baby was born, Mariella?'

She shook her head.

'I can't remember.' Her lip quivered. 'I didn't feel much. I was awfully ill and – there seemed so many bothers going on. I didn't see him for quite a long time and then – Oh, I don't know! He was such an ugly miserable little baby and I simply couldn't believe he was mine. It didn't seem as if it could possibly be true that I had a baby. I just kept on thinking: What on earth am I to do with him? Then the doctor told me he might not live. And then I s'pose I suddenly wanted him to live.'

'Yes. You loved him.'

'I s'pose so ... I began to think of names for him ... And I thought after all it might be nice if he grew up and – and stopped being pale and thin. But he never has. Still we're all more or less pasty-faced, aren't we? Then there was Julian ... and I thought – Oh I don't know ... Poor Granny was dying and I took him to see her. She was so happy because he'd been born; because you know she absolutely adored –' She stopped, her high unnatural little narrative voice failing abruptly.

The simplicity, the pathos, the unreality of her life! ... Judith felt the tears burn her lids as she remembered that strange marriage, the deaths of Charlie and of the grandmother – the only woman who had ever in all her life protected, cared for and advised her – and realized in what child-like bewilderment and dismay she had borne her child.

She had never talked at such length or with so obvious a satisfaction in talking. For once, Mariella had things she needed to say.

Judith put a hand tightly on hers as it lay on the grass. It quivered a moment, startled, then lay still, and Mariella turned her amazing eyes full on Judith. Sun and sky were mirrored in them so that they swam with more than their usual blind radiance, but the expression of her lips was tremulously pleased and grateful. Soon she sighed and said:

'I s'pose *he*'d have adored Peter too. He and Julian were like that about children. I s'pose he'd have done everything for him. He was looking forward awfully ... It's a pity really Peter's not more like him – in looks I mean – not in –' She checked herself.

Mariella was talking of Charlie: in a small, shy but unreluctant voice, she was talking of him: she was preparing to say the things which it had seemed never could be said. In another few moments it would be possible to say gently: 'Mariella, why did you marry him?'

She leaned her cheek on her elbow and continued:

'I don't really understand children.'

'But later on, Mariella, when he's older you'll be so happy with him, – doing things together. You'll be such a marvellously young mother for him.'

'Oh, later on!' was all she said; and added: 'I don't believe boys care much anyway about their mothers being young.'

If Julian had heard her say that, so shrewdly, would he not have been disconcerted?

Judith turned to her, opened her mouth to speak.

But then, as on another occasion, Martin burst in upon the pregnant moment – coming round the corner with a loud 'Hullo!' – fresh, pink and cheerful from his bathe; and Mariella rose from Judith's side, her lips lifted lightly to smile him an agreeable welcome, her whole customary manner enfolding her in one instant.

'Hullo!' she called back. 'Did you have a nice bathe? We did, didn't we, Judy?' Empty little voice, with perhaps a trace of relief in it ... It was all over.

They went back to find Julian.

They slipped back towards home along the chalky roads in an evening heavy with dark shadows.

Martin drove in silence, and Judith sat beside him. Perhaps she would tell him to drive straight home without bothering to drop her; and then they might invite her to come in for a moment, and she would see Roddy – see for herself how ill he was.

Martin turned and looked at her suddenly, and said with a nervous twitch of his mouth:

'It is such fun seeing you again.'

'Such fun, Martin.'

'At Cambridge –' He stopped.

'Yes Martin?'

'It was ghastly not seeing you oftener at Cambridge.'

'I know, Martin. It seemed so difficult with those disgusting rules. It was hopeless trying to see one's friends.'

'It wasn't my fault we didn't meet oftener,' he stammered out. 'I wanted to. I thought you were fed up with me, so I kept away.'

'What made you think such a silly thing, Martin?'

He hesitated, and flushed.

'Because I – didn't get on – with your friends.'

She sighed.

'You mean Jennifer?'

'Well – yes.'

'You didn't like her, did you?'

Jennifer had always been at her worst when Martin was there.

'I – I couldn't hit it off ... I – of course I could see she was – very nice ... I could understand why you – were so fond of her ...' He floundered on, his eyes fixed on the road in front of him, his foot gradually forgetting to press the accelerator. 'But you seemed – quite different when she was there ... at least you were different to me. It felt as if we were strangers.'

She sighed again, and said patiently:

'I'm sorry, Martin.'

Impossible to try to explain to him. What he said was all so true. Let him think what he liked: she was not responsible to him for her behaviour, not obliged, as he seemed to think, to treat him with consideration. Dull, dull, tiresome Martin. No wonder he had roused a devil in Jennifer.

'Oh!' he said, overcome, 'Good heavens, there's nothing for you to be sorry about. I wasn't meaning to accuse you.'

'It sounded as if you were,' she said in an aggrieved voice. It was an easy game, upsetting Martin.

'Oh Judy, you *know* I wasn't,' he said unhappily; and in his agitation he completely forgot to accelerate, and the car slowed down till she scarcely crawled.

'Hey sir!' shouted Julian from the back. 'May I ask what you are up to, sir? Does the road belong to you, sir, or does it not?'

Martin made a grimace over his shoulder and drove on.

'All I meant,' he said presently, very quietly, 'was that I'd missed you awfully, and that I'm terribly glad I've – I've met you again.'

'So am I, Martin. Honestly I am.'

She was remorseful.

'I'm going away tomorrow – must get back to the farm.' He swallowed hard. 'I wonder if – I'd awfully like you to meet my mother. Would it bore you frightfully to come and stay?'

'It wouldn't bore me one little bit. I'd love to meet your mother.'

'Oh good!' He beamed. 'I'd love to show you my home. It's rather nice.'

Mariella leaned over his shoulder to say:

'Drive straight to the station, Martin. Julian will miss his train if we don't hurry.'

In another ten minutes they were at the station.

'We'll come and see you off, Julian,' said Mariella.

'I mustn't wait,' said Judith. 'Mamma's having supper early. I promised I'd be back. Good-bye and thank you all very very much. Good-bye Julian.'

She held out her hand to him. He took it and elegantly kissed it.

'*Au revoir, mademoiselle,*' he said. '*Nous nous reverrons au mois d'août. Sans faute, n'est ce pas?*'

She nodded.

'*Alors au plaisir ...*'

He gave her one searching look, waved his hand and disappeared into the booking-office.

Mariella, following him, turned back for a moment to say in a small voice:

'Good-bye, Judith. I'll see you again, shan't I?'

Her face was for once without its little smile. It was composed and – yes – quite grown up: yes, it had turned into one of those un-numbered women's faces, masked with a faint fixed perplexity and sadness: and, behind the mask, not alive at all.

She turned to Martin who still lingered beside her.

'Then – if my mother writes to you? –' he said.

'Yes, Martin. I'll come.'

'You must come.'

'I'd love to.'

To see one of the circle detached and against a separate back-ground of home and parents would be interesting: though, alas, Martin's father had died. It was he who had been brother to Mariella's mother, and to the father of Julian and Charlie, and of Roddy. Martin's mother was quite external ... Still, there might be portraits, photo-graphs, all sorts of family things ...

She detached her hand from his, and started to run.

The train was not even signalled yet. In five minutes she could be with Roddy. She would make some excuse – say she had left some-thing. She could reckon on a clear quarter of an hour at least in which to see him, tell him she was sorry, tell him ... and quickly go away again.

She knocked on the sitting-room door.

'Come in,' said a cross voice.

'Roddy,' she said timidly, standing at the door. 'I've come to see you. Just to ask how you are. Only for a minute. Am I disturbing you?'

'Oh, come in, Judy.' His voice was polite and surprised.

He was sitting at the writing-table. He wore no tie, and his shirt was open at the neck; his sleeves were rolled up and his hair was standing on end. He looked tired: his face was more sallow than usual, and his lips drooped. The sunlight came into the room through the lowered red blinds, heavy and dark, and as if with a sinister watchfulness. Values were not normal in this queer house light. It altered the character of the friendly and familiar room, and gave to the lonely-looking figure of Roddy an unreal significance and remoteness; gave it terror, almost, and strangeness. The living light seemed to make the blood beat in time with its own dark-blooded feverish pulse.

'Nice of you to come, Judy.' His voice made him utterly unapproachable. 'How cool you look. Did you enjoy your picnic? I should have thought it was much too hot to be comfortable anywhere.'

'It was horrid without you, Roddy.'

'Nonsense. You didn't miss me at all.' His smile was bland and cold.

'Didn't I? Didn't I? Roddy – it was all spoilt for me when they told me you weren't well. I couldn't bear to think of you alone with a headache on a day like this.'

'Oh, the headache's gone. It wasn't much. My own stupid fault.'

'Are you sure it's gone? You don't look very well.'

He laughed.

'I'm all right. I can't think why you should be so concerned about me.'

He was not going to allow you the satisfaction of sympathizing with him.

'Then there's nothing I can do for you?'

'Nothing at all, thank you Judith.'

He still sat in front of the writing-table, leaning his head on his hand and looking at her with a curious hard expression. Presently he rubbed his eyes with an impatient gesture, as if they hurt him; bent his head rather drearily and started to draw figures on the blotter.

'You oughtn't to try to write if your eyes hurt you. You ought to rest.'

'I have been resting.' He jerked his head in the direction of the old capacious nursery sofa, whose tumbled cushions still bore the impress of his body. 'I got sick of it. I had some letters to write, so I thought I'd better get them done. I'm going away tomorrow or the day after.'

'Back to Paris?'

'No. To Scotland with my mother.' His eyes twinkled for a minute. 'She thinks I need a holiday.'

To Scotland with his mother. Why did not he say, like Martin: 'I want you to meet her?'

She came and stood beside him.

'Well I must go now.' She could not keep the utter wretchedness out of her voice. 'I only came to see how you were.'

'It was very sweet of you, Judy.'

His voice was all at once gentle and caressing. He took her hand up lightly, and played with the fingers; and she felt the old helplessness start to drown her.

'Well, it's good-bye, I suppose, Roddy,' she said very low.

'It looks like it, Judy.'

'Always, always going away. Aren't you?'

He smiled at her.

'I'm sorry I haven't seen more of you, Judy. We haven't had any of our serious conversations this time, have we?'

Oh the charming mockery and indifference! . . . She took her hand away and said briefly:

'No, we haven't.'

This time there would be nothing new and delightful to remember. Save for this present vain exchange of words, they had scarcely spoken to one another. The evening when they had all bathed together, the afternoon she had played tennis with them, neither eyes nor voices had encountered each other secretly, alone together. She had seen him watching her now and then: that was all.

'Last time we met,' he said, his eyes on her, 'we had a *very* serious conversation.'

'Ah, I thought you'd forgotten that.'

She felt herself tremble slightly.

'No. No.' His fixed gaze never wavered from her face; and she could not move. She looked down and saw, on the writing-table, a white square and the name Anthony Baring Esq. on it. Roddy had a delicate and graceful handwriting.

'There's the car,' he whispered.

'I must go.'

'Come this way, through the garden door.'

He got up and put his arm round her and led her towards the door, clasping her close to him. The reddish light pressed, whispering and furtive.

'You kissed me last time,' he murmured. 'Will you kiss me again?'

She swiftly kissed his cheek.

He laughed; then drew his breath in suddenly and stopped laughing. Down came his stranger's face to her. She felt his mouth hard, and her own terribly soft and yielding. The pressure of his lips was painful, alarming, – a contact never dreamed of. She drew back and saw, in the mirror opposite, her own white-faced reflection, one hand to its mouth.

'Tonight,' he said very low, 'shall I come and fetch you in the canoe? We'll go down, down, – to the islands. Just us two. Shall I come?'

She nodded, speechless.

'Late. Be waiting for me about eleven.' He added, in his usual, careless voice: 'Not unless it's fine, of course. There may be a thunderstorm.'

She went out of the room, into gold deeps of light and the evening shadows.

She came back into her own garden. The sinking sun flooded the lawn. Its radiance was slit with long narrow shades, and the great chestnut trees piled themselves above it in massed somnolence. The roses were open to the very heart, fainting in their own fragrance; and around them the dim lavender-hedges still bore white butterflies upon their spear-tips. The weeping beech flowed downwards, a full green fountain, whispering silkily. Forms, lights, colours vibrated, burned, ached, leapt with excess of life. The house was wide open at every door and window; and Mamma, going up the steps with a basket of flowers, paused and drew up the striped Venetian blind.

3

For hours, it seemed, they had not spoken a word. The paddle fell now and again upon the water with a light musical clash, like the sound of the shattering of thinnest crystal. Now and again the moving blade woke the water to a rich and secret murmur; as if a voice half woke out of sleep to speak a tender word; then swooned into sleep again.

She saw his arm move and glimmer; his form was just discernible in the stern of the boat, shoulders bowed forward, head motionless. Once or twice he started to whistle a fragment of tune, and then was silent again.

She lay among cushions in the bows, and watched the dark yellow moon rise, bare of clouds, behind the poplar trees. The night was heavy and still.

The canoe slipped down towards the islands. Then she would move, if her limbs still remembered how to move: he would give her a hand to help her out and they would stand among the little willows and whisper together.

Mamma was fast asleep at home, her alien spirit lapped in unconsciousness. Her dreams would not divine that her daughter had stolen out to meet a lover.

And next door also they slept unawares, while one of them broke from the circle and came alone to clasp a stranger.

The boat hissed suddenly among willows, and came to rest against a shallow bank. The clustering thin light blades of the willow-leaves fell over them as they stepped out, bit them with infinitesimal teeth.

She followed him without will, or conscious movement, through nettles and long grass, to a clearing among the bushes, in the middle of the leafy little mound which was the island. In the old days they had often picnicked here, and thought the minute patch of earth a whole world and made themselves kings and queens of it. They had gathered blackberries from these low bushes in the hot sun; and come home again with purple mouths and fingers.

Now the little boy Roddy was this tall man whose shoulder touching hers was more bewildering than the moonrise; whose head above hers was a barrier blocking out the world.

They stood side by side. He turned to her and whispered:

'Well, Judy?'

'Well, Roddy! . . .'

'Judy, I'm going to say good-bye to you here.' His voice was low, grave, distinct.

'For a long time, Roddy?'

She saw him nod his head; and she bowed her own and began to sob, but without tears.

He murmured some low inarticulate exclamation, and took her gently in his arms.

'Don't cry, Judy. Don't cry . . . Darling, don't.'

The tenderness of his voice checked her in an instant. His hand moved up and down her bare arm, lingering over its curves, tracing the outline with a touch that made her shiver.

'Lovely smooth arm,' he whispered. 'You are so lovely.'

'No.'

'Yes. I think so. I've always thought so.'

'As long as you think so, then – that's all I care about. You – can have it all.'

Now the moon rose, clear at last above the tree tops, and gleamed strangely into the eyes bent upon her face. His lips were smiling a faint fixed smile. His teeth glinted. The two faces gazed at one another, floating wan upon darkness.

The web had broken. Roddy had shaken himself free and come close at last. The whole of their past lives had led them inevitably to this hour.

'Roddy, I love your hair . . .' Her hand went up and stroked it; and he shut his eyes. 'I love your eyes.'

'I love you all – every bit of you.'

Breathless, sure of him at last, with a delicious last-minute post-ponement of his embrace she moved away, softly laughing.

'Roddy, how much do you like me? This much?'

She held out her hands, parting them slowly.

'More than that.'

'This much?'

He copied her, laughing eagerly but silently.

'This much?'

He held his arms out wide. She hesitated a moment and then came into them; and he was not laughing any more, but covering her face and neck with kisses.

It was a quivering darkness of all the senses, warm, melting, relentless, tender. This stranger was draining her of power; but underneath, the springs of life welled up and up with a strong new beat. He clung to her with all his force as if he could never let her go. He was a stranger, but she knew him and had known him always. She took his caressing hands and held them on her breast. In that moment he was her child; and she longed to lay his head where his hands quietly lay. He drew deep breaths, and now and then his rich voice murmured a broken word or two.

She raised her head from his shoulder and gazed in passionate detail at his face.

'Speak, Roddy, speak.'

He shook his head and smiled – a ghost of his former smile, flickering on his lips alone. His half-shut eyes glittered as if with tears. In the moonlight she worshipped his dark head and moon-blanched features. Gradually he loosened his hold, threw his head back, and stood motionless, arms hanging at his sides, his face an unconscious, sleeping mask. If Roddy were to die young, this was how he would look.

'Roddy – Roddy – Roddy – I love you – I love you – I love you.'

No answer. He stooped his head and fell to closer kissing.

'Roddy – say –'

'What do you want me to say?' he whispered. Again the flickering smile.

'I love you, Roddy.'

If he would whisper back those few words, there would be peace for ever.

She laid her cheek against his, murmuring endearments.

'My dear, my darling, my little one, I love you. My dear, I've always loved you. Did you know it?'

He shook his head faintly.

'I love you too much, I'm afraid.'

Far too much, if she was to wait in vain for any response save kisses . . .

'No, Judy, no.' The words broke from him painfully. 'You must forget about me now. Kiss me and say good-bye.'

'Why, oh why?' She clutched him desperately.

'I'm going away,' he whispered.

'But you'll come back? You'll come back, Roddy?'

He was silent, utterly silent.

'I can't. I can't,' he said at last.

'I'll wait, Roddy. I don't care how long I wait. I shall never want anyone else. I'll wait years.' There was no answer; and after a while she added in a small laboured whisper: 'If you love me a little.'

'Oh!' He threw up his head with a sort of groan. 'Yes. Yes. Yes.'

'You love me?'

He must, he *must* say it.

'Yes, I love you.' The words came out on a groaning breath. She put her lips on his, and stood silent, drinking in her bliss.

He tossed his head suddenly, as if waking up.

'Judy, we must go back, we must go back.'

He sighed and sighed.

'No. A little longer. We'll talk a little before we go. We must talk.'

He laughed – a normal teasing laugh.

'A little conversation,' he said. 'You're a tiger for conversation, aren't you?'

'I don't mind your laughing at me.'

They were going to laugh gaily at each other, with each other, for ever.

He put his hand beneath her chin and turned her face up to his.

'Lovely Judy. Lovely dark eyes . . . Oh your mouth. I've wanted to kiss it for years.'

'You can kiss it whenever you want to. I love you to kiss me. All of me belongs to you.'

He muttered a brief 'Oh!' beneath his breath, and seized her, clasped her wildly. She could neither move nor breathe; her long hair broke from its last pins and fell down her back, and he lifted her up and carried her beneath the unstirring willow-trees.

He had brought her back home. Languorous and bemused she stepped out upon the bank in the breaking dawn, and turned to look at him beneath her heavy lids. She could not see him clearly: he seemed blurred, far away.

'Good-bye,' he said briefly.

'I'll see you before you go,' she said mechanically.

Not that it really mattered now. Time was not any more and he would be with her for ever.

He nodded; and then abruptly turned the canoe down stream again: looked at her once, faintly smiled, waved his hand an instant and went on.

She walked through the waiting, clear pale-coloured garden, into the house, up to her bedroom; stared in the dim glass at her strange face; sank into bed at last.

4

It was on the next evening that she awoke to the realization that Roddy had not come – might not – certainly would not now. He was going away. He, who always found self-expression, explanations, so difficult, would be at a loss to know what to say when he too woke up. He who never made plans would be helpless when it came to making any which should include her too in the future. Last night he had been dumb, he had sighed and sighed, whispered inarticulately: he would find it hard to be the first to break silence, to endeavour to re-establish the balance of real life between them. She would write him a letter, tell him all; yes, she would tell him all. Her love for him need no longer be like a half-shameful secret. If she posted a letter tonight, he would get it tomorrow morning, just before he left.

She wrote:

Roddy, this is to say good-bye once more and to send you all my love till we meet again. I do love you, indeed, in every sort of way, and to any degree you can possibly imagine; and beyond that more, more, more, unimaginably. The more my love for you annihilates me, the more it becomes a sense of inexhaustible power.

Do you love me, Roddy? Tell me again that you do; and don't think me importunate.

I am so wrapped round and rich in my thoughts of you that at the moment I feel I can endure your absence. I almost welcome it because it will give me time to sit alone, and begin to realize my happiness. So that when you come back – Oh Roddy, come back soon!

I have loved you ever since I first saw you when we were little, I suppose, – only you, always you. I'm not likely ever to stop loving you. Thank God I can tell you so at last. Will you go on loving me? Am I to go on loving you? Oh but you won't say no, after last night. If you don't want to be tied quite yet, I shall understand. I can wait years quite happily, if you love me. Roddy I am yours. Last night I gave you what has always belonged to you. But I can't think about last night yet. It is too close and tremendous and shattering. I gasp and nearly faint when I try to recall it. I dissolve.

When I came back to my room in the dawn I stared and stared at my face in the glass, wondering how it was I could recognize it. How is it I look the same, and move, eat, speak, much as usual?

Ought I to have been more coy, more reluctant last night? Would it have been more fitting – would you have respected me more? Was I too bold? Oh, that is foolishness: I had no will but yours.

But because I love you so much I am a little fearful. So write to me quickly and tell me what to think, feel, do. I shall dream till then.

There is so much more to tell you, and yet it is all the same really. My darling, I love you!

Judy.

She posted it. Next morning she hurriedly dressed and ran downstairs in the sudden expectation of finding a letter from him; but there was none.

Now he would have got hers ... Now he would have read it ... Now he would be walking to the station ...

She heard the train steam out; and doubt and sorrow came like a cloud upon her; but only for a little while.

In the cool of the evening she wandered down to the river and sat beside it dreaming. She dreamt happily of Jennifer. She would be able to love Jennifer peacefully now, think of her without that ache, see her again, perhaps, with all the old restlessness assuaged. Jennifer's letter would surely come soon now . . .

If Roddy were to ask her to come away with him at once, for ever, she would take just the copper bowl from her table and spring to him, and leave all the rest of the past without a pang.

Perhaps Roddy had written her a letter just before he had gone away; and if so it might have come by the evening post. She left the river and went to seek it.

Who could it be coming towards her down the little pathway which led from the station to the bottom of the garden and then on to the blue gate in the wall of the garden next door? She stood still under the overhanging lilacs and may-trees, her heart pounding, her limbs melting. It was Roddy, in a white shirt and white flannels, – coming from the station. He caught sight of her, seemed to hesitate, came on till he was close to her; and she had the strangest feeling that he intended to pass right by her as if he did not see her . . . What was the word for his face? Smooth: yes, smooth as a stone. She had never before noticed what a smooth face he had; but she could not see him clearly because of the beating of her pulses.

'Roddy!'

He lifted his eyebrows.

'Oh, hullo, Judith.'

'I thought you'd gone away.'

'I'm going tomorrow. A girl I know rang up this morning to suggest coming down for the day, so I waited. I've just seen her off.'

A girl he knew . . . Roddy had always had this curious facility in the dealing of verbal wounds.

'I see . . . How nice.'

A face smooth and cold as a stone. Not the faintest expression in it. Had he bidden the girl he knew good-bye with a face like this? No, it had certainly been twinkling and teasing then.

'Well I must get on.' He looked up the path as if meditating immediate escape; then said, without looking at her, and in a frozen voice: 'I got a letter from you this morning.'

'Oh you did get it?'

There could never have been a more foolish-sounding bleat. In the ensuing silence she added feebly: 'Shall you – answer it – some time?'

'I thought the best thing I could do was to leave it unanswered.'

'Oh . . .'

Because of course it had been so improper, so altogether monstrous to write like that . . .

'Well,' she said. 'I thought . . . I'm sorry.'

She ought to apologize to him, because he had meant to go away without saying anything, and she had come on him unawares and spoilt his escape.

'I was very much surprised at the way you wrote,' he said.

'How do you mean, surprised, Roddy?' she said timidly.

She had known all along in the deepest layer of her consciousness that something like this would happen. Permanent happiness had never been for her.

It was not much of a shock. In a moment that night was a far, unreal memory.

'Well' – he hesitated. 'If a man wants to ask a girl to – marry him he generally asks her himself – do you see?'

'You mean – it was outrageous of me not to wait – to write like that?'

'I thought it a little odd.'

'Oh, but Roddy, surely – surely that's one of those worn-out conventions . . . Surely a woman has a perfect right to say she – loves a man – if she wants to – it's simply a question of having the courage . . . I can't see why not . . . I've always believed one should . . .'

It was no good trying to expostulate, to bluff like that, with his dead face confronting her. He would not be taken in by any such lying gallantries. How did one combat people whose features never gave way by so much as a quiver? She leaned against the wooden fence and tried to fix her eyes upon the may-tree opposite. Very far, but clear, she heard her mother at the other end of the garden, calling her name: but that was another Judith.

'I'm afraid you've misunderstood me,' he said.

'Yes. I've misunderstood you. You see – this sort of thing has never happened to me before and I thought . . . when a person said . . . Why did you say . . . I didn't know people said that without meaning it . . . I suppose we must mean different things by it. That's what it is. Well . . .' Her voice was terrible: a little panting whine.

'I don't know what you mean.'

Probably that was true: he had forgotten he had ever said: 'I love you.' She could not remind him; for in any case he would not be affected. What were three little words? . . . And after all, she had probably more or less forced him to say them: she had wanted to hear them so much, she had driven him to say them. Yes, he had groaned, and quickly repeated them to keep her quiet, stop her mouth so that he could go on kissing her. She said:

'But why, Roddy, *why* did you take me out . . . behave as you did . . . kiss me so – so . . . I don't understand why you bothered . . . why you seemed . . .'

He was silent. Oh God! If only he would wound and wound with clean thrusts of truth, instead of standing there mute, deaf.

'Roddy, after all these years, these *years* we've known each other can't you tell me the truth? We were good friends once, weren't we?'

'Yes, I think so.'

'Oh, I see! I see! And you could never feel like being – more than that.'

He shook his head.

'I see! I see! And you could never feel like being – more than see. And you thought there had better be an end . . . because you were never going to love me: and I obviously – was it obviously? – was becoming more and more – foolish – and tiresome. So you thought – you'd say good-bye – like that – and then go away for good. Was that it!'

He passed a hand across his forehead: his first gesture. Then he too was feeling, however slightly.

'I thought that was what you wanted: what you were asking for,' he said.

'So you thought you'd oblige –' No, no, not sarcasm. She waited a moment and added: 'I see. You misunderstood me. I dare say it

227

was quite natural. You thought I wanted what you wanted – just a little – a little passion – to round off a flirtation – and be done with it. Well . . .'

The lane was so still that she could hear the dull beat of oars in passing boats on the other side of the fence. The evening had become very cold.

She gave a little laugh and said:

'I really am very sorry to make this fuss. It's too laughable that I should – *I!* . . . I suppose you never dreamed I – wasn't used to this sort of thing – from men?'

'I thought you knew pretty well what you were about.'

'And I didn't! I didn't! I was being *deceived* – like any . . . Oh, it's so *vulgar!*' She shut her eyes, laughing weakly. 'That's why you didn't make your meaning plainer, I suppose. You thought I was quite used to – that sort of thing – kissing – just for a lark. Just for a lark, Roddy – that was it, wasn't it? And I got serious, and tried to – to let you in for more . . . I tried to *catch* you. Poor Roddy! But you'd never get let in, would you? You know your own mind. You're cautious. You'll see –,' she waved her hand slightly, 'I'm not dangerous. I'll never bother you any more. And I'm very *very* sorry.' She broke down with a gasp, but did not weep.

'I'm sorry, Judith. I apologize. I –' His voice had now the faintest trace of emotion.

'*Oh!*' She controlled herself. 'Apologize! Have *I* accused you? This is just another damned muddle. I'm only trying to understand it.'

'I really think I had better go,' he said.

'No!' She put out a hand and clutched his arm in desperate protest. 'Not yet, Roddy. Not for a moment. Can't we – Oh God! I wish I'd never written that letter. Then there'd have been no need for all this . . . You'd have gone away and said nothing – and gradually I'd have understood. I should have seen it all in its proper light. Things would have somehow come right again, perhaps. And now I suppose they never can . . . Can they, Roddy, can they? Oh, if they could!'

How he was hating this scene! It was a shame to prolong it. He swallowed hard and said, rather nervously:

'Do you suppose you really meant – all you said in your letter?'

It was her chance. She must say it was all nonsense, that letter, that it was written in a moment of madness; that she did not mean it now. Then they might somehow manage to laugh together and part friends. He was such a good laugher! She could go away and bury her disappointment; and next time they met, be to him what he wanted: a light flame of passion, blown out, relit again. He had given her the taste for his kisses. She would miss them, and desire them painfully. If she could act her part skilfully now, she need not be for ever without them.

But it was no good: the thing would not be lied about.

She nodded, gazing at him in utter despair. She went on nodding and nodding, asserting the truth in silence and with all her force, compelling him to believe it. She saw him flush faintly beneath his sallow skin.

'I'm very sorry then,' he said, in his frozen voice.

She cried out:

'Oh *Roddy*! Did you never like me? Didn't you even *like* me? All these years! It seemed as if you did ... I couldn't have grown to – like you so much if you hadn't given me a little – a little return ...'

'Of course I liked you very much,' he said. 'I always thought you were extremely attractive.'

'Attractive!' She bowed her face in her hands. 'Yes. I was attractive to you. And so ... That you should have treated me so lightly, Roddy! Did I really, really deserve that?'

He was silent.

'If you'd warned me, Roddy ... given me some hint. I was so romantic and idealistic about you – you've no idea ... I thought you *must* think of me in the same sort of way I thought about you ... Couldn't you have warned me?'

He said in a voice choked with exasperation:

'I did try to shew you, I tell you. I should have thought I'd shewn you often enough. Didn't I say I was never to be taken seriously?'

She sighed and nodded her head slowly. She was beaten.

'Yes. Yes you did. I wouldn't be warned. I was such a fool. Oh it's all my fault. A good sell for me.'

'Well, I'd better go now,' he said after a pause.

He took a step or two and then turned back. She still leaned against the wall, and something in her attitude or expression seemed suddenly to move him. He lingered, hesitated. His face shewed a little trouble and confusion.

'I suppose you're all right?' he said.

'Oh, I shall be quite all right.'

'Please forget all about me.'

'I shan't forget about you. But I shall forget all this – if you will do the same. We will meet in the future, Roddy, won't we? – just as usual, – with all the others?'

'I think it would be better not to. I think we'd better not write to each other or ever meet again.'

'Not ever meet again, Roddy?' How did he come to be master of such cold decisions? She felt like a child in futile conflict with the fixed and unalterable will of a grown-up person. 'Why? Why? Why? Please do let me. Please do. I won't ever be a nuisance again, I promise. You've said you liked me. I must see you! If I can't see you, I can't ever see any of them again. Don't you see? And then I'd have *nothing* ... You wouldn't tell them, would you, Roddy? Please let me see you again.'

It had lasted too long. In another moment she would be on her knees to him, hysterical, loathsome.

A nervous quiver of his lips checked her suddenly and made her quiet. In some obscure way he was suffering too. He looked like the little boy whose face had implored her not to cry that time of the rabbit's death. Yes, the spectacle of other people's pain had always affected him unpleasantly.

'It's all right, Roddy,' she said. 'Don't worry about me. I'll get on without you.'

'I'm not worth wasting one moment's regret on,' he said, almost earnestly. 'Believe me, Judith. It's true.' He looked at her for the last time. 'I can only say again I'm very sorry and ask you to forget all about it.'

She took a deep breath.

'One thing more,' she said. 'I'm not ashamed of anything I've done. There's nothing to be ashamed of in loving a person and saying so.'

It was not true. The shame of her surrender, her letter, her un-requited love would go on gnawing, burning, till the end of her life.

He left her, walking away from her with a graceful and noiseless tread.

After all, it did not seem to hurt much: certainly not more than could be borne in secret, without a sign.

It had all been experience, and that was a salutary thing.

You might write a book now, and make him one of the characters; or take up music seriously; or kill yourself.

It was all so extraordinary ... That night had seemed to Roddy so insignificant that instead of hurrying away quickly when he got that letter, he had had a girl he knew down for the day: and that was how he had spoilt his own escape.

Shut the door on Roddy and turn the key and never open that room again. Surely it would be quite easy. She saw herself as a tiny person walking firmly away and not once looking back. There were plenty of other things to think about ... What was there, safe and simple, to think about?

Strawberries and cream for supper. Good. Two new frocks: but he was to have admired her in them ... A visit to London next week, and a play.

She noticed suddenly that her hands were bleeding from slight abrasions. How had that happened? Best to go in now and arrange her face a little. This shivering had been going on for a long time.

5

Three weeks later she stepped out of the train at a little country station in Hampshire; and was there met by a beaming Martin, and conveyed swiftly in his car to his home.

The long drive wound through shrubbery and great beech trees, and opened in a wide sweep before the long low many-windowed house-front. It was an old manor, built of exquisitely time-tempered brick. The great porch was covered with clematis and jasmine; and here and there climbing bushes of yellow or white roses wove their way up the walls and coiled around the window-frames. Beyond it and on each side of it she caught or imagined glimpses of a rich old garden, lawns and a herbaceous border, cedar trees, yew hedges, and an espalier of peach-trees along a high wall.

A manservant appeared, took her suitcase and slid away again.

Martin led the way through the oak-panelled hall into a large bright flowery chintz drawing-room. All the colours were blue and pink and white; and there were photographs everywhere, and vases full of delphiniums, roses and lilies. The French windows opened on to the sunny lawn, and, set in front of them, the tea-table shone with blue and white china, and silver, and glass jars of honey and jam. Behind the tea-table sat Martin's mother, smiling.

She was as clean and fresh, as white and pink and blue as her drawing-room. Her erect and trim little figure was crowned with white hair; her blue rather prominent eyes held the wistful appeal of the short-sighted as she looked into Judith's face to greet her. Her thin mouth smiled and went on smiling, happily, vaguely, with a kind of sweet and weak persistence. All the lines in her face ran upwards as if she had spent her life smiling. She had a white skin with a clear rose flush over each cheekbone. She was really very pretty in her white lace dress and fleecy pale blue wrap: a mother to take out to dine in her best black frock and her diamonds and feel proud of.

'So this is Judith that I've heard so much about,' she said charmingly; and put a hand on her arm to lead her to the tea-table.

Three black spaniels begged and adored at her feet; or rolled over, waving limp self-conscious devotional paws.

Over the mantelpiece hung the portrait of Martin's dead father. He had been Governor of somewhere: an important man. He looked reliable and kindly, with Martin's brown eyes and untidy features.

On the opposite wall hung a sentimental pastel portrait, life-size, of Martin at the age of three: golden-brown curls, pink cheeks, a white silk blouse with a frilly collar. There were some books in glass-fronted book-cases, some goodish furniture and china; one or two good water-colours and some indifferent ones; abundant plump cushions in broad soft chairs and couches. It was a house that shewed in every detail the honourable, conventional, deeply-rooted English traditions of Martin's people.

And yet not they, with their sober steadfastness, but that wild sister, the disgrace, Mariella's mother, had prepared, it seemed, the strange mould for the next generation: for all, that is, save Martin himself.

He was in high spirits. He smiled with all his white teeth, and threw sandwiches to the dogs, and teased his mother, and stared in a sort of delighted astonishment to see her actually sitting at tea with him in his home. He looked almost handsome in his bright blue shirt, open to shew a strong well-modelled throat rising cleanly from the broad shoulders.

He did not know that Judith was dead: that a dummy was sitting beside him. He had declared several times how well she was looking.

He said suddenly:

'Heard from Roddy, Judith?'

She was not prepared for that name; and she felt a faintness sweep over her.

'No, Martin, I haven't.'

'I had a letter from him this morning. It's pure agony for Roddy to answer an invitation, even, so I was flattered. He and I and one or two other chaps are going to do some sailing next month, off the Isle of Wight, and he actually wrote to make arrangements.'

'What fun that will be, Martin.'

She bowed her head over the plate in her lap, crumbling a scone to fragments.

'Why don't you come too, Judith? Do! It'd be perfectly proper wouldn't it, Mummy? We're her bachelor uncles.'

It was precisely at those words, at the unexpected recalling of all that light-heartedness, that happiest day of all, that the thing leapt to life within her, and fiercely, horribly pressed towards birth. Oh, now there was no hope. Roddy had arisen all in a moment from his false burial.

With a vast effort she prevented her eyes from closing quite; but to speak was impossible.

'Roddy says –' began Martin, glanced across at her, and stopped uncertainly, startled. He was silent, and then said:

'Tired, Judith?'

'A bit – after my journey – it's so hot to travel. Isn't it?' She turned to his mother.

233

'Yes my dear, it is,' she said cooingly. 'Come, I'll take you to your room and you shall rest till dinner.'

Martin had got up and was hovering over her, anxious and despondent. But she could smile at him now, and she said:

'I'd rather go out if I may, and get cool. The garden looks so lovely.'

'That's right then,' said Martin's mother encouragingly. 'Take her out, Martin darling, and shew her the rock-garden. Martin and I have been making a rock-garden, Judith – I may call you Judith, mayn't I?' She laid a hand again on Judith's arm. 'It's such fun. Martin and I are both ridiculous potterers and experimenters. Are you like that?'

'Not practically, I'm afraid.'

'Ah well, it's a delightful hobby. It keeps me busy and healthy, doesn't it Martin?' She looked up into his face, and he put a large hand upon her little shoulder. 'There,' she added. 'Run along now. Don't let Martin take you in the fields or up to his precious farm: you'll spoil your pretty shoes. Aren't they darling shoes, Martin? And such a *pretty* frock.'

With little pats and handwavings and vague benevolence she saw them out of the French windows down the steps into the garden.

Martin said:

'Wait. I'll take a gun. We're simply tripping over rabbits this year. It's awful.'

She did not hear properly; nor, when Martin came back to her, did she grasp the significance of the gun over his shoulder.

He led her out of the garden by a wooden bridge over a stream half-hidden in forget-me-nots, kingcups and iris plants; through the meadow where grazed the pedigree cows which, so he said, were his mother's pride; over a stile and up on to the chalky rabbit-pitted hillside.

She was standing among the willow trees, and out of the moonlight a voice was saying in a low hurry: 'I love you' – and saying another thing damnably characteristic: 'Lovely Judy! Lovely dark eyes!' His teeth gleamed as he smiled in the moonlight ... He closed his eyes ... It was all in such bad taste, in such bad taste ...

Martin was pointing out the marches of the estate. There were

234

beech-copses and farms and two gentle folds of sun-drenched sheep-strewn hill between them and its final hedge-rows.

'You know I do love it,' said Martin shyly. 'I worship the soil.' He hesitated and then said with a laugh: 'Funny: Sometimes I absolutely wish I were dead so that I could be buried in it and have it all over me and inside me for ever and ever ... Look at the way those slopes overlap ...' His eyes fastened on them, with a hungry expression.

Then this was Martin's secret bread. It was his land that nourished him at the source, and made of him this man with an individual dignity and simplicity at the core of his ordinariness. She made an effort to come nearer to him in mind.

'Yes ... I know, Martin.'

He turned joyfully.

'I always tell you everything, Judith. I suppose it's because I know you'll understand.'

'Which bit do you want to be buried in, Martin?'

'I don't care – as long as I'm well inside it.'

'Would you ever commit suicide?'

'Would I what?'

'Commit suicide. To – to get there quicker.'

He laughed and said comfortably:

'Well, I've never been tempted to so far ...'

'It's an old family place, is it Martin?'

'Oh yes. My father was born here, and all the others: Roddy's father and Julian's, and the only sister – Mariella's mother. She was very beautiful you know – and absolutely wild – almost mad I should think. She ran away from her husband and goodness knows what sort of life she led. I believe it simply broke my grandfather's heart. He died, and then Granny – you remember Granny? – couldn't bear to go on living here alone. All the children were scattered or married or dead. So she moved to the little place on the river – next door to you ... Poor old lady, she didn't have much of a time. She outlived all her children except Roddy's father: and he was never much use to her. He quarrelled with his father when he was quite a boy and left home. I don't know what about. Grandpapa was a terrible martinet ... Yes, they were an unlucky family.'

'And they all died young, Martin?'

'More or less. But we none of us ever live to be old,' he said cheerfully.

They had reached the top of the hill; and, suddenly, up went Martin's gun. Then, with an exclamation of disgust, he lowered it again.

'Wasn't ready for him. Once they get into that bracken –'

'What's that, Martin?'

'Rabbit. Didn't you see? Beastly vermin ... Never saw anything like them. Much as we can do to keep pace with them.'

He was muttering to himself in an annoyed way.

'But Martin – do you mean to shoot them?'

'Shoot them? I should say I do, if I get the chance.'

'I never have been able to understand how people can bear to shoot rabbits.'

'Hmm,' said Martin, grim and indifferent. 'You mustn't expect *me* to be sentimental about 'em.'

His eyes roved round alertly; his gun was ready to go up in a trice. He was not giving a thought now to Judith walking beside him.

Just over the crest of the hill came a sudden small kicking and flurry. A tiny pair of fur legs started away into the bracken, the white scut glancing and bobbing. But the bracken thinned away to nothing here: the small form was bound to emerge again in a moment.

There was a sharp crack.

'Aha!' said Martin; and he went forward to where something flipped in the air and fell back again, horribly twitching in a mechanical and aimless motion.

'Oh! Oh! Oh!' She stood rooted where he had left her, aghast.

He was stooping to examine it ...

She knew how it was looking – laid on its flat side and shewing the tender and vulnerable whiteness beneath its frail stiff paws. He was stooping just as a figure had stooped above that other rabbit ... What years ago! ... Roddy's rabbit whose death and burial had started this awful loving. Who was it devilish enough to prepare these deliberate traps for memory, these malicious repetitions and agonizing contrasts?

236

Oh this world! ... No hope, no meaning in it; nothing but per-versities, cruelties indulged in for sport, lickings of lips over helpless victims. Men treated each other just as Martin treated small animals. The most you could hope for was a little false security: they gave you that to sharpen their pleasure in the blow they were preparing: even the ones that looked kind: Martin for instance. As for Roddy – Roddy liked experimenting. He chose girls sometimes: that was more voluptuous. She saw his face, pallid and grinning, crowds of leering faces, all his. The hillside darkened. She sank on her knees, shaking and perspiring.

He was striding back.

'I buried it,' he called. 'It was a little smashed about the head.'

She had to lift her face towards him; but she made it blind. He came and stood beside her – he dared to, red-handed as he was.

'I'm afraid it wasn't one of the cleanest shots,' he said cheerfully. 'I got him at too long range. Still, – that's one less ... Come on.'

Her mind would frame only one sentence; and she tried over and over again to say it.

'I will not be a witness of your butcheries. I will not be a witness of your butcheries.'

But he would not understand. Perhaps it did not make sense anyway.

'Oh dear!' She sat there, tearing up turf with shaking cold wet hands, face averted, eyes staring, mouth open and out of shape, impossible to control. 'Oh dear! Oh dear! Oh dear!' The repetition was a sort of whine or mew.

'What's the matter?' he said sharply. He sank down beside her, and his astounded face came round her shoulder.

'The poor little thing, the poor little thing! ...'

'Do you mean the rabbit?'

She nodded.

'But Judith – good heavens! A rabbit ... Judith. I'd never have shot it if I'd dreamed you'd mind.'

She went on staring and pulling up the grass.

'Oh this world!' ...

'Judith ...' He was silent, completely at a loss.

'Still – it can't be helped ... I suppose one gets accustomed ...'

237

Her mind grew black again with formless and colossal conceptions of torture, murder, lust: and Roddy's face went on grinning among them. All was lost, lost.

'I'm very sorry,' said Martin helplessly.

'Oh I don't blame ...'

'It didn't suffer you know. Did you think it had? That kicking didn't mean anything: it was simply reflex action.' He thought he had found the clue; and added cheerfully: 'You'd do the same if I shot you dead at the back of the head.'

'I wish you had.'

She wept.

'Good God! Really, Judith ... I've said I'm sorry. I can't go on saying it, can I? I didn't know you were so – you oughtn't to be so – easily upset. Rabbits have to be kept down, you know. They destroy everything. Ask my mother.'

She went on weeping; and after a little while he got up and strode a few steps away, and stood with his back to her, shoulders hunched.

Worse and worse: he was deserting her ... She bit hard on her thumb till the pain of it steadied her, waited and then called tremblingly:

'Martin!'

He turned, saw her hand held out and came quickly and knelt beside her.

'What is it, Judy, what is it?'

'Oh Martin! It's nothing. Don't ask, *don't* ... Only – just – only –'

His arms went round her and she abandoned herself against him, pressing her head into his shoulder, groping for comfort, sobbing vast sobs, while he knelt beside her quietly and let himself be wept on; and now and then gave her shoulder a little pat.

After a long time she was so empty of tears that their source seemed dry for ever. She would never in her life weep any more. In the thin crystalline buoyancy of exhaustion she lay back on his shoulder and observed the gold light lying tender and still in the folds of the hills; and two rabbits skipping unperturbed not so very far away; and blue butterflies swinging on the long grasses; and all the evening shadows slanting beautifully downwards. Peace and comfort dropped upon her. The heavy ache for Roddy was gone. Now to make this no-pain permanent, to fix this languor and mindless calm, to smother the voice which cried and cried: 'I am cheap and shameful. I have been used for sport!' Now was the time to turn to Martin and see if he could save her.

She sat up and dried her eyes.

'There!' she said. 'I'm sorry. Thank you, Martin. You are a dear. You've always been very kind to me, haven't you?'

'Kind to you! Oh Judith, you know —'

'I think you must rather like me, Martin.'

He said with a deep intake of breath:

'Like you! You know I've loved you for years.'

She was silent, tasting a faint relief and satisfaction; and then said:

'Well, what would you like me to do about it, Martin?'

She saw that his hands were trembling, and he answered shakily:

'Do about it . . . I . . . What do you want to do about it? . . . I've said I —'

'Would you like me to marry you?' she asked softly.

'God! If there was a chance! . . .'

'Well — I might, Martin.'

She started to laugh and cry weakly at sight of the transfigured face he turned towards her; and a voice went on protesting inside her: 'No! No! No! It isn't true. I never will.'

'I'm so tired, Martin, I'm so tired!'

'Come home, my dear, come home.'

It was compassion and exultation and doubt and certainty, all mixed in an inarticulate eloquence.

He lifted her and brushed her skirt.

There was nothing to do but accompany him down the hill.

He left her at her bedroom door. His mother, he said, would come and give her aspirin and put her to bed, and see that dinner was brought up to her. His mother was splendid about headaches. Tomorrow there would be plenty of time to talk.

He had behaved perfectly.

She fell asleep that night in her white room with its cretonne wreaths of pink roses tied up with blue ribbon, and dreamed of Roddy. He sat on the hill, close to where the rabbit had been shot, and conversed in friendly fashion. He had come back from abroad, from some remote island. He took a puff at his pipe and said with apparent irrelevance: 'Not wives, my dear girl – mistresses. It's more convenient. When I return I intend to take Martin as my partner.'

'Martin wouldn't come. Not if it's mistresses . . .'

'Oh dear me, yes. He'll soon forget you over there. It's a very voluptuous clime.'

She said very humbly:

'Would you care for me to come, Roddy?'

'I fear you're supered,' he said with elaborate courtesy.

'I suppose so.'

He studied a notebook.

'Where do I come in your list, Roddy?'

'You're in the twenties, somewhere,' he said indifferently.

'Oh miles down –'

He seemed suddenly bored or suspicious, and shifted his position. As he did so, she saw his face for an instant, heavy-lidded and dissipated. She understood that he was thinking of voluptuous climes.

It seemed then there was no use in hoping to win him back. He was, obviously, bored to death with her.

'What's in here?' he said suddenly, and plunged his hand into the earth.

The rabbit! . . . the rabbit! . . . Everything shrieked, – and she started awake, sweating, in horror and desolation.

She leaned out of the window and saw the moon high in the sky. Beneath it, the trees had suffered their moon-change and were sculptured masses of dark marble, washed over with a silver-green phosphorescence. A tragic night, sleepless and staring beneath the urgent pressure of the moon: there was no comfort in it.

This house was full of ghosts . . . Perhaps Roddy's father had slept in this room as a small boy. He had grown up here and then shaken the dust of his home from his feet and gone away and begotten Roddy . . Charlie must have looked like the beautiful wild sister, and that

240

was why the grandmother had given him all that anxious and painful love.

The sister had given birth to Mariella, and then run away and led God knows what sort of life. Poor Mariella! She had never had the sun on her: she had lived from birth – perhaps before birth – in the shadow cast by her bright mother; and when she grew up she had not emerged from it. That was the truth about Mariella.

The family portraits were in the dining-room. Tomorrow she would see them, study and compare . . .

It was madness to have come to this haunted house.

Oh Roddy! She could not live without him. He must, he must come back and take her for a year – a month even. Perhaps he had found out by now that he did love her after all, and was too proud to write and confess it. Martin had said it was agony to him to answer even an invitation. She must write to him again, give him an opening.

Where was he now? If she could be transported to him now, this minute, she could make him succumb utterly to loving her. She would think of such ways of delighting him with caresses that he would never be able to do without her again . . . It was sheer stupidity to go on enduring this agony when it only needed a trifling effort to end it all. For instance, if you leaned a little further out of the window . . . But one did not commit suicide in other people's houses: that was the ultimate error of taste.

And then, poor Martin's feelings at the inquest!

Mr Martin Fyfe, who was overcome with emotion several times, stated that a few hours previously deceased had declared her willingness to become his wife. This avowal, made on her own initiative, had met with ample response on his side, and there seemed every cause for joy and congratulation. The coroner in returning a verdict of suicide while of unsound mind observed that this reversal of the customary procedure in betrothals was but another example of the lack of self-control so deplorably frequent in the young woman of today, and seemed to him sufficient in itself to suggest a distinct lack of mental balance in deceased. He tendered his sincerest sympathy to Mr Fyfe and absolved him from all blame.

And Roddy might depart from his habits and inclinations once again, and write Martin a letter of condolence.

No, no. She was going to show him she did not care, was not weeping for him: she was going to announce her engagement to Martin before long.

There would be a paragraph in *The Times*, congratulations, letters to write – (*I am a very lucky girl*) – a pretty ring – and almost certainly photographs in the illustrated weeklies.

Roddy would smile his cynical smile because she had behaved just as women always did behave: so long as they hooked some poor devil – no matter who – they were quite satisfied. And a damned fuss they made if a chap refused to be hooked.

Martin would probably insist on being married in church, and ask Roddy to be his best man.

No. Poor Martin was not going to be able to save her. Perhaps, instead, she was going to destroy him.

She went back to bed and tossed between her sheets till dawn.

6

Next morning Martin's face of suppressed excitement shewed only too clearly how deeply the web was tangled now.

She went with him after breakfast to visit his little farm.

There was something in the brown soft earth, in the dark warmth of byres and stables, in the rich smell of animal breath and hay and soil mingled, something in the many secret, silent heads lifting, snuffing, reaching tentatively out, then tossing away from the out-stretched hand; especially something in the clear golden-brown eyes curiously greeting you for a moment, then recoiling, relapsing into their animal aloofness: something that painfully suggested Roddy. He was like animals, electric and mysterious. The half-distrustful fleeting glance, the dark soft glossy head, the appealing grace: these were attributes he had in common with the farm dog, and the calves, the black kittens playing all over the stables, the dark chestnut colt in the meadow.

There was no escape from him in all the world.

She said to herself, moving her lips:

'Sick fancies. Sick fancies.'

If she could see Roddy as a natural human being, then only could she hope to be free of him.

She climbed a slope and sat on a stile at the top, waiting for Martin while he interviewed a farmer.

Below lay the house and garden she had elected to share with Martin all her life: lovely, intricate patterns of roof and wall in the morning sun; enchanting shapes of violet shadow spilt across the mellow brick; charming lavender smoke spirals from the chimneys; carefully-ordered paths and lawns, hedges and flower-beds; two cedar trees motionless in their great planes of gloom on green brightness, green on gloom; and beyond the fruitful walls, the enfolding patiently-productive land which was Martin's.

You would be thought lucky indeed to live here. Perhaps the land might compensate, drug the mind and give it slow contented musings. Perhaps you could escape from Martin and feel alone with it . . . But no: with its medium tints and mild companionable expression it was he himself. You could never get away from Martin here.

As he came running up the hill, eagerly, like a cheerful dog, she watched him coldly. With a faint distaste she observed his agile leap on to the stile beside her.

'Well?' he burst out happily.

'Well Martin?'

'What are you thinking of, looking so solemn?'

The unpardonable question. And he would always be asking it and she always answering sweetly with a lie; or else disagreeably with: 'Nothing.' No peace ever again, not even to think one's private disloyal venomous thoughts.

'I was thinking Martin, I don't believe you know a bit what I'm like.'

'I know enough to know I love you anyway,' he said with hearty confidence.

'You don't,' she said petulantly. 'Because you've never troubled to find out what I'm really like. It's never occurred to you there might be anything more than what you see. That's so like a man . . . Lord, how stupid! Everybody dismissed with a little label. Everybody taken for granted once they've passed a few idiotic conventional tests . . .'

'What on earth have I done now?' cried Martin despairingly.

243

'Nothing. Nothing. I'm only warning you.'

After a pause of non-comprehension he said gently:

'Of course I don't take you for granted, Judith. I could never do that. You're so clever and beautiful and marvellous – much, much too good for me. Oh my dear! – you don't know how I value you.' The tears came into his eyes. 'Whatever happens, nothing can alter my idea of you. If I *could* believe you had any faults, they'd only make me love you more.'

'Would they? Would they? You don't know what revolting ones they are.'

He laughed and said indulgently:

'It's no good trying to frighten me.'

'It's *true*,' she cried. 'D'you suppose I'm trying to be humble because I think it's the correct idea?'

He said nothing, and she felt him trying with perplexity to think out the proper method of dealing with her mood. Finally he said:

'Judy. I'll tell you what seems to me the only important thing – and that is, that we should be absolutely truthful with each other. Don't you agree? I think telling the truth is my only principle – besides washing. As long as I know exactly where I am, I can stand anything.' He drew her to him and turned her face so that his warm kind eyes could look into hers. 'I've always dreamt of finding someone I could tell everything to, and trust absolutely.'

Tell everything to ... Oh God! Was he going to say: 'My wife and I must have no secrets from each other?' Was he that sort of fool? He went on:

'Judith I might as well try to lie to myself as you. And I can't lie to myself. Why if I were to stop loving you even – if that *could* be – I'd have to tell you straight out. I couldn't pretend. I *hope* you couldn't either.'

'No, I couldn't.'

He went on with a shade of anxiety.

'And supposing there was ever anything worrying you — anything on your mind — please try to tell me. You needn't be afraid. I hope perhaps – you might think it was – rather nice to feel there was a person you could rely on always. Would you, Judith?'

He paused, breathless and deeply moved.

'Yes, Martin.'

'Please think of me as that person.'

'I will, Martin.'

'You're not worrying about anything now?'

'No, no.'

'That's right. As long as I *know*. I thought yesterday ... But I suppose it was the rabbit?'

She shuddered, and nodded her head, remembering her dream, unable to speak.

He said in an amused, tender big-man-to-little-woman way:

'You poor little thing to be so upset.'

She laughed in response, deprecatingly, drearily.

He tightened his arm round her, sighed happily and said:

'I can't believe it.'

'Nor can I.'

'I didn't sleep a wink last night.'

'Nor did I.'

'After all these years ... Do you know, I've been in love with you ever since I've known you? Never anybody else for a moment. But I didn't dare hope ... I wonder what Roddy will say when we tell him.'

'I wonder.'

'You know I was almost sure not so very long ago that if you liked any one of us specially it was Roddy.'

'Were you really, Martin?'

'Yes, and what's more I thought he was bound to fall in love with you. God, I was jealous!'

'Jealous of Roddy? Were you? How ridiculous!'

'Not really ridiculous. Roddy's so terribly nice and attractive, it seemed only natural you should prefer him to a dull chap like me.'

'He didn't ever *say* anything, did he, Martin?'

'Not he. Roddy's the darkest horse I know.'

'Yes, he is, isn't he?' She laughed. 'I suppose heaps of people fall in love with him?'

'Yes,' he said gravely. 'He's run after all right.'

'Does he – do you suppose he – falls in love himself, much?'

'Oh, more or less, I suppose.'

245

'Not seriously?'

He laughed and shook his head.

'Not very seriously I don't think.'

'Perhaps he *was* a tiny bit in love with me ... for a bit ...'

'I dare say he was. I don't see how anybody could help being,' he said with light tenderness, dropping quick kisses on her hair.

'And then I suppose he stopped ... And found somebody else ...'

'Perhaps he did. Don't let's worry about him anyway. He and I have different ideas about – all that sort of thing. He's rather naughty and spoilt I think – though he is such a good chap,' he added hastily, as if fearful of sounding disloyal.

She persisted, in anguish:

'How do you mean, naughty and spoilt, Martin?'

'Oh I don't know.' He was embarrassed, unwilling to give his friend away. 'A bit of a sensation-hunter perhaps.'

That was it then: she had been a new sensation: one that had quickly palled, because she had been so swiftly, so entirely yielded up to him. She should have whetted his appetite by offering only a little at a time and then withdrawing it: so, he might still be desirous of her. Instead she had satiated him at the outset.

She would know better next time ... But there would be no next time. Instead, there was Martin now who said:

'Won't you kiss me?'

She looked at him, aching with tears that were like an inward bleeding; and put her lips on his cheek for half a second.

'Listen Martin.' She took his hand and started to speak hurriedly, for fear of more kissing. 'About that truth business. What was I going to say ...' She steadied her voice. 'Yes. If you tried to – compel the truth you'd expect a lie, wouldn't you? That's logic. I'd always expect a lie anyway. I mean ... I shouldn't be at all surprised by it. I'd say it was my fault for not leaving you alone – not letting you be free enough – I'd think: well, I tried to coerce him, so he chose to deceive me. He was quite right.'

'A lie's a lie,' said Martin obstinately.

'A lie's a – What does that mean? It doesn't mean anything. Unless you believe God watches and writes down in his notebook: Martin Fyfe told a lie on Monday. If this goes on he won't get his harp.

Do you? Truth! What's truth? Why, half your so-called truths are built on lies. You can scarcely distinguish. I could – I bet I could – act a lie to you all my life and you'd never know it. *Be* a lie.'

He flushed swiftly at the last words and said in a stiff way:

'I dare say you could. You're clever enough for anything and I'm a fool. But don't try, please ...'

'But there must be no compulsion, Martin!' she insisted, horribly. 'You wouldn't try – to get at me – would you? You'd let me be, by myself? If you ever forced me when I was unwilling I'd tell lies and lies and congratulate myself for it. And I'd *never* forgive you.'

He lit a cigarette and said, close-lipped, eyes fixed on the grass:

'Does all this mean you want me to understand you've – changed your mind and wish to cry off?'

She threw out her arms dramatically, crying:

'Can't I say anything? Can't I say anything without being misunderstood? ... being ...'

'I've never seen you like this, Judith.' He got up and stood looking at her in despair. 'It worries me. I don't understand.'

'It's not customary I suppose, in an engaged young lady ...'

She shut her eyes, and the tears scorched their lids bitterly.

'Judy, what is it?'

'Oh Martin!' Hands pressed to forehead, voice a faint moan, she struggled on: 'Only there are – some things – aren't there? – there might be things which *can't* be told. Things one must forget – try to – at once –'

'Yes. Yes. If you say so,' he soothed and whispered.

'Because of the useless misery ... and because they've – withered up your heart – so that you couldn't recall them – even if you tried.'

'Yes, my dear.'

'I've had – one or two unhappinesses in my life. Everybody has, I suppose. I want to forget them ...'

'Of course, Judy, of course. You must *never* tell me anything you'd rather not.'

She put her arms round his neck for a moment.

'Thank you, Martin.' She dried her eyes and said: 'I won't be so silly any more.'

And if a doubt or a fear had begun to cloud his mind, his voice was none the less gentle, his eyes none the less trusting.

He took her back to the garden and gathered sun-warmed strawberries for her; and they talked cheerfully together until lunch time.

That afternoon Martin fished for trout in the stream, and she sat on the bank and read a page of her book now and then; and sometimes watched him; and mostly dreamed.

His small-boyish absorption was amusing and rather appealing. He was immensely happy, moving along the bank in cautious excited silence, casting deftly up and down stream. If he were to be disturbed or upset in his pursuit, he would say 'Ach!' and swear, and flush all over his face, just as he had in the old days. Even if she were the disturber it would make no difference. She knew better than to interfere, or to speak except when spoken to, and then briefly and to the point. That was in his eyes one of her most admirable qualities. He loved to have her beside him, behaving nicely and looking pretty, shewing interest, and smiling when it was seemly.

By the constant upward curve of his lips and by occasional dwelling glances, she knew he had thrown off the memory of this morning's unnatural emotional perplexities, and was content.

If only their marriage could be a perpetual sitting on a green bank by a stream, watching him tolerantly, almost tenderly, with quiet pleasure in his bodily magnificence, with a half-contemptuous smile for his happiness, and yet with comfort in the knowledge of it, and in the knowledge that her mere presence was sufficient for it, while her mind was off on its own, worlds removed from him! ...

It would be such an immense easing of the burden if only so much insincerity as was implicit in the acquiescent body was required, without the lies of the lips and the mind. She on the green bank always, with leisurely musings, and he moving past her, up and down, not touching her or demanding or possessing, but fishing for ever: it would be a pleasant enough marriage. He would look up now and then, smile approvingly, and say:

'Still there, Judith?'

'Still here, Martin.'

'Quite cheerful?'

'Quite.'

'Feeling safe?'

'Oh yes.'

'That's right. Well, I'll go on fishing then.'

'And I'll go on thinking.'

And he would smile again and send his line whipping and hissing through the air.

All the rest could go by, remain unsaid, with no falsehood at all. Perhaps, after years of patient sitting, even Roddy might be forgotten; or transformed into an object for idle pleasurable regrets.

In the midst of these speculations, Martin came back and threw himself down beside her.

'No luck, Martin?'

'Not a nibble ... I don't care. I'd rather talk to you.' He gazed lovingly at her and said:

'What are you thinking of?'

She clenched her hands; then answered softly:

'... of nothing ...
When I muse thus I sleep.'

He turned her face towards him with a hand beneath her chin, and gently kissed her lips.

'Dear Judith I'll try to make you happy.'

'And I'll try to make you happy, Martin.'

Perhaps in time ... Perhaps in time even Roddy ...

At that moment of wistful peace it seemed admirable to undertake the task of making Martin happy.

He said shyly:

'I wonder what made you say you'd marry me.'

'Because I'm so fond of you.'

'Ah! That's not quite the same as loving, is it?' His voice was wistful, but not disappointed.

She took his hand.

'No, Martin, not quite the same.'

He wrung her hand and said cheerfully:

'Well, it's something to be going on with. It's a great deal more than I deserve. Of course I don't expect you to feel romantic about me. Nobody could feel romantic about me, anyway.'

'Oh I think lots of people could. I'm sure they could,' she said; and felt suddenly ashamed. For indeed he was a man whom many women might love. What right had she to take him?

'Well I don't want them to,' he said. 'Your liking's more than enough for me.'

'Dear Martin! I promise you, at any rate, I wish I *were* in love with you.'

'Mightn't that be the first step?' he said smiling.

'No, no,' she answered lightly. 'I've finished with falling in love. I was in love once.'

'When?'

'Years ago! It doesn't amuse me. I reject it. Never again ...' She felt her lip start to curl and quiver, and stopped: then added in the same bantering tone: 'Foolishness. That's what it is. And as far as you are concerned, it would seem almost incestuous.'

'Don't use horrid words.' He sat up, amused but startled.

'Well it would. Not that I disapprove at all of incest, in theory. Yet I must confess my instinct's against it.'

'And so's mine,' said Martin firmly. 'Let's have no more nonsense.' He bent forward and dismissed the nonsense with a hearty kiss.

That was the last straw. Her mood, stretched finer and finer in the preceding few minutes, snapped. She rolled over away from him and stared into the water.

The tiny brilliant green water-plants and cresses grew up from the mud and pebbles and spread their leaflets below the surface in delicate array, motionless as if under glass. Oh, to slip into the water and become something minute and non-sentient, a sort of fresh water amoeba, living peacefully among their thin-spun tangle of whitish roots – now at once, before Martin noticed her disappearance! He would peer and peer into the water, with his red anxious face; and all in vain. In the shadow of his face her unimpressive form would be but the more obscured; and, unmoved, she would stare back at him.

God! – to go mad, crack-brained, fantastic, happy mad; or to be stretched upon a rack in a physical anguish which precluded thought!

'Tea-time,' said Martin. 'What a good afternoon it's been.'

In the hall they were met with a telegram for Judith. 'Decided go abroad this week instead of next. Come home tomorrow. Mother.'

Mamma had grown restless then, a trifle sooner than you had expected; and sent this peremptory summons. What an undreamed-of godsend!

'You can't go tomorrow, Judy,' said Martin, much upset.

'I must, Martin. There'll be such a lot to see to. I must go as soon as I possibly can. I ought to go tonight.'

The sooner she was out of the house the better.

'You couldn't possibly get there tonight by train. It's such a beastly journey.' He was struck with an idea and his face cleared a little. 'I tell you what. Wait till after dinner and I'll drive you back. If we started about eleven we'd be at your home soon after daybreak. Do, Judy, do. It'd be a marvellous drive. And I'll break in on Mariella and cadge some breakfast. There's so much to talk about. And if you're going abroad we shan't see each other for weeks. It's most infernally disappointing, isn't it?'

She agreed that it was. But as for the drive, that would be a marvellous arrangement. If Martin would send a wire to tell Mamma to leave the front door key under the mat, she would go and explain to his mother. As she left him, her heart felt almost light. Perhaps she could manage to wriggle out and escape now, after all.

7

Martin's mother stood on tiptoe to kiss her good-bye, while Martin went to fetch the car.

Her box was ready in the hall. She had given a last glance through the open dining-room door at the family portraits. She had been thankful to find them few and devoid of the likeness she dreaded. They were just anybody's respectable family portraits. Of the dead sister there was no likeness.

Martin's little sitting-room, with its photograph on the mantelpiece of a solemn Roddy in Eton clothes, its cricket groups including Roddy in flannels and a blazer, its painted green fire-screen decorated by Roddy with strange figures – that had been far more terrifying. She would not have to sit there now and look at Martin's photograph and scrap albums, as he had suggested.

'I'm sorry you must go,' said his mother, charming and abstracted.

'I'm sorry too.'

'But,' she said gaily, 'what a delightful idea, to drive through the night. Martin loves it, you know. I often hear him going off on a lovely night like this. Funny boy ... His horn sounds so dreadfully lonely it makes me want to cry. He likes to have a companion. I used to go with him sometimes, but I've had to give it up. I feel too old next day.'

She smiled sweetly; and suddenly, standing above her and seeing her so small and ageing, Judith felt no longer the great barrier of difference of generation, but the basic intimacy of their common sex; and with this an extreme tenderness and pity. She bent and kissed her – the poor thing, who must lie flat in her room thriftily husbanding her resources for the morrow, while she herself, coming thirty years of nights behind her, had the open dark for friend.

She knew well enough you did not love her son: she trusted you not to betray him by marrying him. It would be horrible to force her to hate you ... unthinkable.

Car-wheels grated on the gravel outside, and Martin sounded his horn.

In another few minutes they had waved good-bye to the small figure on the steps, and taken the road.

Into the deep blue translucent shell of night. The air parted lightly as the car plunged through it, washing away in waves that smelt of roses and syringa and all green leaves. The moon struggled with clouds. She wore a faint and gentle face.

'I shouldn't be surprised if there was rain before daybreak,' said Martin; and, reaching at length the wan straight high road, accelerated with a sigh of satisfaction.

'Faster, Martin, faster.'

Faster and faster he went. She settled herself close against him, and through half-shut eyes saw the hawthorn and wild-rose hedges stream backward on either hand. The night air was a drug from whose sweet insinuating caress she prayed never to wake. Soon, through one leafy roadway after another, the headlights pierced a tunnel of green gloom. The lanes were full of white scuts and little paws, paralysed; and then, as Martin painstakingly slowed down, dipping and twinkling into the banks. Moths flickered bright-winged an instant in the lamp-light before being dashed to their fried and ashy death. Once or twice came human beings, objects of mean and foolish design, incongruous in the night's vast grandeur; and here and there, under the trees, upon the stiles, in the grass, a couple of them, locked face to face, dis-quietingly still, gleamed and vanished. She observed them with dis-taste: passion was all ugliness and vulgar imbecility.

Now the moon looked exhausted behind a gathering film of cloud.

Soon came the rain, with a low murmurous hushing and whispering through the trees; and then a white blindness of lightning aching on to the eyelids.

'Shall we stop?' asked Martin.

'No, no.'

'I remember you hated lightning when you were a tiddler.'

'Do you remember that?'

'Yes. I shall never forget the day we were trapped by a thunderstorm in the old boathouse – you and Roddy and I. How you howled! And then you said you'd seen the lightning fall on Roddy's head and had he been struck dead. I kept on yelling that if only you'd open your eyes you'd see him in front of you, as alive as anything; but you only went on shrieking. And soon we all of us began to believe Roddy might go up in flame any minute.'

'Oh yes! I'd forgotten.' She laughed. 'I remember Roddy's face, so solemn and red and doubtful as he felt the top of his head. He was terrified I was making a fool of him and he wouldn't say a word. I asked him privately afterwards if he thought the Lord had visited him with a tongue of fire. He was disgusted.'

Martin threw his head back to laugh.

'You were a comic child. We used to think you were a little mad.'

'Did you, Martin?' she said, and doubt and sadness swept over her again.

Perhaps even in those days Roddy had laughed at her, thought of her as a joke, never as a companion.

'It's a pity really that we —' She stopped, remembering that she was going to marry Martin – on the verge of finishing her sentence:– 'that we met again after we grew up.'

Their relationship should have remained unspoilt in the mysterious enchantment of childhood, and then she would never have seen Roddy grow from that lovable small boy into the elegant indifferent young man who experimented in sensations.

No more lightning; and the rain came softly on to her face through the open wind-screen, blurring eyes and mind and all, until she sank into a half-sleep. Martin clasped her hard against his shoulder, once, as who should say: 'Sleep. I am here'; and she felt his enormous protectiveness flowing over her.

When next she opened her eyes, the darkness was taking back first one veil, then another. Purple paled to lilac and lilac wasted to grey. The sky was immaculate and without a glow. The country-side woke from sleep, gently staring and austere, each object upon it separately outlined without interrelation of colour and shadow under the uniform wan light. On the far horizon, a cornfield flashed out one moment in a pale flood of sunlight; but the sun was still hidden. The hedges frothed palely with meadow-sweet.

Soon came the beechwoods crowning the chalk hills. In the valley below ran the river, blanched and rain-flattened between its willows; and the road sloped gently down till it ran beside it. They were home.

Stiff and blinking, she stumbled out of the car, and stood on the steps of the porch.

'Thank you, Martin. It was marvellous. I hoped we should never get here. I thought we wouldn't – I don't know why. I got it into my head you'd manage a quiet smash without my noticing it. Every thing I passed I said good-bye to – looking my last on all things lovely; and when I finally dropped off to sleep I thought I'd never wake up. And after all you brought me safe home, clever boy. I *suppose* I'm grateful. But what an effort to have to start again in an hour or two!'

He did not answer at once; but after a few moments of fingering his hat looked away and said:

'Are you *very* unhappy, Judith?'

'Well – not very, I suppose. Rather. Not more than's good for me. I shall get over it ... I'm so sleepy I don't know what I'm saying. Don't take any notice.'

'I thought you weren't happy –' He stopped, overcome.

'It's all right, Martin. Don't you worry. I laugh at myself. How I laugh at myself!'

'Can't you tell me what it's about?' he said gruffly.

'I don't believe I can.'

He turned away and leaned despondently against the porch.

The sky was glowing now through all its length and breadth, like the inside of a shell. The dew shimmered over the grass and the greyish roses reddened, yellowed on their bushes. The birds bedazed the air with wild crystalline urgent repetition.

'You go in a day or two,' he said at last.

'Yes. And you?'

'I join Roddy next week.'

'Ah yes.' She turned to unlock the door, and fumbling for the key, lightly remarked: 'There's a person I shall never see again.'

'Who?'

He affected surprise; but he was only pretending. She could feel him saying to himself: 'So that's it.' And suddenly she hated herself for exposing herself, and him for guessing and dissembling, for forcing her to pronounce that name; and she added:

'I can't marry you, Martin, after all.'

Silence.

'Well, I've told you the truth at last. I thought I could pretend to you all my life, but I can't. You ought to be glad.'

He inclined his head.

'Aren't you going to say something, Martin?'

He shrugged his shoulders.

'Please forgive me,' she said; but she could not feel contrition: only a great weariness.

'Of course,' he said. 'There's nothing to forgive. I never really believed you'd marry me anyway.'

'Luckily I'm going abroad. You'd better forget all about me.'

'It's no good saying that,' he said, with a brief and bitter laugh. 'It was too late for that years ago.'

'You must try to hate me. I deserve it.'

'Oh, what's the good of talking like that?' he said impatiently. 'Do you *want* me to hate you? You know you don't.'

'No, I don't.'

'You know perfectly well I can't do anything except go on loving you.'

He still leaned with dejected shoulders against the porch, talking out into the garden. The eastern sky swam brightly, and the first beams of the sun shot into the garden; and the fluting clamorous chorus redoubled their enthusiasm.

'I haven't seen the sun rise for years. Have you, Martin?' She came near to him and put a hand on his sleeve. At the touch he turned round and confronted her in dumb despair, his eyelashes wet.

'Martin, I'm sorry, I'm sorry.'

'I can't leave you like this,' he said, and clung to her. 'Judith, is there nothing I can do?'

She reflected.

'Yes. Will you do something for me?'

'Of course I will.' His eyes lit up for an instant.

'Listen, Martin. Supposing he ever mentions me –'

She felt herself going white and stopped.

'Yes?' he muttered.

She went on breathlessly:

'I don't think he will, but if he should ... Supposing he ever starts to tell you something that happened – between him and me – please, you mustn't let him. Promise! If he begins, stop him. I shall never see him again; soon I shall stop thinking about him: but you mustn't know what happened. It was just a little silly thing – I shall see it quite differently some day ... but if I thought people knew I should *die*. Martin, don't try to find out.'

'All right, Judith. It's not my business.'

'Perhaps men don't tell things in the awful way women do? He doesn't generally tell things, does he?'

She could hardly bear to listen for his reply.

'No. I don't think so.'

'Make it be as if you'd never known me. Never talk about me!'

'I won't. I promise.' He looked at her; and she knew by his eyes how deeply she was making him suffer.

After a long time she added:

'One more thing. Of course I know that whatever he'd done you'd feel just the same towards him, wouldn't you? ...'

'I love Roddy ...' he said, his breath, his whole being struggling in anguish ... 'I've always had him – ever since I can remember ... more to me than a brother ever could have been. But if I thought –' His voice altered, grew terrible – 'if I thought he'd done you an injury –'

'It was nothing he could be blamed for,' she said slowly, with intense concentration: 'It was my fault. If I thought it was going to come between you I should be more unhappy than ever. Will you see that it doesn't?'

'I'll do my best,' he said in a dead voice.

She began to tremble violently.

'I must go in now, Martin. What shall you do?'

'I'll go straight back. I don't feel like – seeing Mariella – or anyone.'

'But don't you want something to eat?'

'No. I'm not hungry.'

It seemed unbearably pathetic that he should not be hungry – he who was always hungry.

'Good-bye then, Martin.'

'Good-bye.'

He took her outstretched hand and clutched it.

'Judith, if you should want me for anything while you're abroad – let me know. I'll come to you. Will you promise?'

'I promise, my dear.'

He looked a shade less unhappy.

'And please let me see you when you come back. I won't be tiresome; but I must see you sometimes.'

'When I come back then, Martin – if you really want to. But by that time you'll realize what a pig I am.'

He put his arms round her suddenly.

'Oh, Judith,' he whispered, 'can't you ever ...?'

'Martin, can't you ever not?'

'No.' He laid his head down on her shoulder for a few moments; then straightened himself and said with an effort at cheerfulness:

'Well, I hope you'll have a good time.'

'I hope you will. But you're sure to.'

To think he would be with Roddy for weeks, sharing work and talk and jokes and meals – seeing him sleep and wake; while she herself ... never again. If she saw him coming towards her, she must turn back; if she passed him in the street she must look away.

'Please take care of yourself, Judith.'

She nodded, smiling faintly.

He jerked round and went down the steps and she waited for him to turn his head again. But, when he reached the corner, without looking back, he waved his hand in a young quick awkward pretence of jauntiness, and strode on.

She stood and saw the fresh garden filling with light and shade; and thought: 'Poor Martin's crying'; and shut the door on him and the sun and the screaming of the birds.

8

The hotels and shops made a circle round the great *Place*; and to and fro all day went the people to their baths and douches and sprays. Bilious obese old Jews and puffy, pallid Americans thronged and per-spired; and ancient invalids came in bathchairs with their glum attendants. There was one, a woman long past age and change, with a skin of dusky orange parchment, black all round the staring eyeholes, tight over the cheeks and drawing back the dark lips in a grin. She was alive: her orange claws twitched on the rug. Perched high upon her skull, above the dead and rotten hair, she wore a large black sailor hat trimmed with a wild profusion of black feathers. Every morning, seated idly in front of the hotel, Judith watched for that most *macabre* figure of all in the fantastical show.

The sun poured down without cloud or breeze, and the buildings and pavements seemed to vibrate in the air. It was too hot to stay in the valley. She joined parties and motored up through the vine-yards into the hills – racing along in search of a draught on her face, eating succulent lunches at wayside inns, coming back in the evening to play tennis and bathe; to change and dine and dance; to hear a concert at the Casino; to sit in the open air and drink coffee and eat ices.

The hours of every day were bubbles lightly gone.

She was Miss Earle, travelling with her elegant and charming mother, staying at the smartest hotel and prominent in the ephemeral summer society of the health-resort. Her odd education sank into disreputable insignificance: best not to refer to it. She was adequately equipped in other ways. She had a string of pearls, and slim straight black frocks for the morning, and delicious white and yellow and green and pink ones for the afternoon; and white jumpers with pleated skirts and little white hats for tennis; and, for the evening, straight exquisitely-cut sleeveless frocks to dance in. She had them all. Mamma had ordered them in Paris with bored munificence and perfect taste, and an unenthusiastic ear for the modiste's rapturous approval of her daughter.

'If you were a little more stupid,' said Mamma, 'you might make a success of a London season even at this late date. You've got the looks. You *are* stupid – stupid enough, I should think, to ruin all your own chances – but you're not stupid all through. You're like your father: he was a brilliant imbecile. I never intended to put you into the marriage-market – but I'll do so if you like. *If* you haven't already decided to marry one of those young Fyfes ... They're quite a good family, I suppose.'

She appeared to expect no answer and received none.

Judith laughed at Mamma's epigrammatic dicta and was a social success. She motored, chattered, danced and played tennis, at first with effort – with Roddy rising up now and again to make all dark and crumbling; then gradually with a kind of enjoyment, snapping her fingers at the past, plunging full into the comedy, forgetting to stand aside and watch: silly all through – stupid even: stupider every day.

Demurely she passed through the lounges: they all knew her and looked her up and down as she went, discussed her frocks in whispers, with smiling or stony faces. In the streets they stared, and she liked it; she admired her own reflection in the shop windows. An elderly French count, with two rolls of fat in the back of his neck, entreated Mamma for her daughter's hand in marriage. It was a very good joke.

Then, one evening after dinner, while she sat in the lounge with Mamma and discussed the clothes of her fellow-visitors, she saw Julian walk in. He wore an old white sweater with a rolled collar, and his long hair was wild upon his pale chiselled forehead. His face, hands and clothes were grey with dust, his cheeks flushed and his eyes bright with extreme weariness. He stood alone by the door, unselfconscious and deliberate, his gaze roving round to find her among the staring, whispering company. Even before she recognized him, her heart leaped a little at sight of him; for his fine-drawn blond length and grace were of startling beauty after a fortnight of small dapper men with black moustaches and fat necks.

'It's Julian!'

She ran across the room and took his hand in both her own, joyfully greeting him. A friend from England! He was a friend from England. How much that meant after all! He had, romantically, kept his promise and come to find her, this distinguished young man at whom they were all staring. He and she, standing there hand in hand, were the centre of excited comment and surmise: that was flattering. She was pleased with him for contriving so dramatic an entry.

He had motored from Paris, he said, going all day over execrable roads in stupefying heat. He had found her hotel at the first guess.

He booked a room and went off to have a bath and to change. Judith went back to explain to Mamma, who asked for no explanations. It was, she remarked, pleasant to see a new face; and those Fyfes had always looked well-bred. She was glad Judith would now have a congenial companion while she finished her cure. If to her cat-deep self she said: 'So that's the one!' her diamond-like eyes did not betray her.

He came down half an hour later, elegant in his dinner-jacket, sat down beside Mamma and started at once to entertain her with the easy, civilized, gossiping conversation she enjoyed.

Then, when the band started to pluck voluptuously at the heart-strings with *Einmal kommt der Tag*, he turned for the first time to Judith, crying:

'We'll dance to it, Judith.' He jumped up. 'What a tune! We'll express our sentimentality.'

Mamma's rasping little laugh of amusement sounded in her ears as she rose and followed him.

He put an arm closely round her and murmured:

'Come on now. Perform! Perform!' – and they went gliding, pausing and turning round the empty floor, while everyone stared and the band smilingly played up to them. The rhythm of their bodies responded together, without an error, to the music's broken emotionalism.

'Once, Julian, you refused to dance with me.'

'Ah, you were a little girl then. It would have been no use. *Et maintenant, n'est-ce-pas, la petite est devenue femme?* We shall get on very well.'

After a silence he said:

'You wear beautiful clothes. You carry yourself to perfection. You have an air ... There is nobody in this room to touch you. What are you going to do with it all?'

'Oh, exploit it, exploit it!'

He held her away from him a moment to look down into her face.

'*Tiens! Tiens!* Is gentle Judith going to start being a devil? ... It would be amusing to see her try.'

'Oh, I will! I'd be most successful. You shall see.'

He laughed, watching her.

'May I help you? Shall we tread the primrose path together?'

She nodded.

'Well, start by looking a little more as if you were going to enjoy it. Have you ever been happy? No. Whenever you come near to being, you start thinking: "Now I am happy. How interesting ... Am I really happy?" You must learn a little continental *abandon* – I'll teach you.'

'You!'

'– and scornful as well! Oh, Judith, you're getting on. I like to see your mouth trying to be hard. It has such pretty points.'

The music stopped, and she disengaged herself. A few people

clapped, and she nodded and smiled to the band ... performing, performing; conspicuously self-possessed ...

'Good!' said Julian. 'Oh, good!'

She turned to him and said:

'Thank you, Julian. That was exhilarating.'

'Yes, you look as if you'd found it so.'

His eyes, brilliant with nervous fatigue, pierced her with a glance too penetrating.

'What a pity,' he said, 'you're so unhappy.'

'If it were so,' she said, starting to walk back towards her chair, 'it would be a pity ... Or perhaps that would be exhilarating too.'

'Oh don't be enigmatical with your old friend,' he said plaintively.

She laughed and gave him her hand.

'Good night, Julian. You go to bed. You're so tired you can hardly stand upright. Tomorrow we'll start enjoying ourselves frightfully. You'll stay a bit, won't you?'

'Oh, I'll stay,' he said. 'I think the moment is auspicious for me ... Didn't I always say I could await my turn?'

'Yes, you said so. You have a *flair* undoubtedly. You are full of *finesse* ... Good night.'

She waved a hand and left him.

Something was afoot ... He had come casting shadows before and behind him. Old things were stirring: the old illness of remembering was going to start again. And ahead was not a glimmer.

9

In that thick, steamy world, in the mingled soils of sickly heat, bilious faces, rich food, sensual dancing, heavy scents of women, applied bow mouths, soft perspiring flesh – sprouted and flourished her response to Julian. Rooted in reluctance, nourished by his skilful arts, it grew, a curious plant: stronger and more curious with every stab of reawakening memory.

Julian must save her this time: surely his wit and wisdom, surely the unknown world of sexual, emotional and intellectual experience which he held so temptingly, just out of reach – surely these would, in time, heap an abiding mound upon the past.

Neither by touch nor look did he seem to desire her. He wove his net with words: he understood her and she felt him coming closer, a step at a time.

He made himself the perfect companion – gossiping and exchanging cynicisms with Mamma, executing commissions for her, his car always at her disposal; taking them to hear music, to eat delicious meals; playing tennis with Judith and her hotel acquaintances.

He even went so far as to say tennis was good for his asthma and played in the tennis-tournament, with herself for partner; and they were barely defeated in the finals by the Brazilian brother and sister, amid scenes of hilarious enthusiasm.

His car was waiting outside the ground to whisk her away from the hot crowd.

Happy, perspiring, dazed with heat and fatigue, she climbed in beside him and lay back.

'We'll go and find somewhere to bathe,' he said.

'Yes!'

'And have supper at an inn, and stay out much later than we ought.'

'Yes. Oh Julian, we have done nice things together. I shall always remember them.'

She put a hand on his knee, and he smiled and nodded, all simple and brotherly ... He had tried his very hardest to help her win. She was grateful to him for fitting himself to her mood.

The car went spiralling up the vine–covered hills, and the electric air quivered away on each side of them in visible waves. The sun sank magnificently, without a cloud, a blood-red lamp. Its rays had long ago passed from the tortuous, steep and rock-bound way through which they now went; and a grey-green tranquil coolness blessed every sense. Then the road ran into profounder, wooded loneliness, and she espied a stream, leaping and plunging in little falls, far down in the gully below the side of the road.

'Stop here, Julian. We must bathe.'

She went springing down towards the water and he followed with the bathing-suits and towels.

The stream was shallow and broken up with boulders: no use for bathing.

'Let's follow it, Julian. We'll find something, I know.'

Soon it took a turn deeper into the wood's heart, and began to grow in depth and volume; then all at once plunged in a smooth gentle cascade into a wide rock basin. There it paused, deep and silent, magic ... What do you suppose lives here? It may put a spell column, and racing on downwards, and downwards again.

'Oh Julian, *what* a bathing-pool! Is it possible? Look at that colour I ask you. Is it limestone?'

The whole circular sweep of the rock shimmered in faint silver through the dim bluish depth of water.

'And deep enough to dive into, Julian – if we dare break into such magic ... What do you suppose lives here? It may put a spell on us ... I don't care! I long to be spellbound. Don't you think, if one plunged in, one might come out all silver-blue and cold and gleaming? I'd love to walk through the hotel lounge naked like that, with long blue dripping hair! Oh, come on, Julian – let's both try! I've had no luck for ages, have you? Perhaps it's turned today. You undress here and I'll go behind this bush and talk to you out of it, like God. Come – off with our lendings!'

And, in a flash, with the uttering of the last words, Jennifer came back, slipping the clothes down off white shoulder and breast, talking and laughing. A tide of memories; Jennifer's head burning in the sunlight, her body stooping towards the water – the whole of those May terms of hawthorn blossom and cowslips, of days like a warm drowsy wine, days bewildered with growing up and loving Jennifer, with reading Donne and Webster and Marlowe, with dreaming of Roddy ... Where had it all gone – Where was Jennifer? – Whom enchanting now? – How faintly remembering Judith? Compared with that tumultuous richness, how sickly, how wavering was this present feeling — what a sorry pretence. Would one ever be happy again?

Julian, lean and hairy in his bathing-suit, was already feeling the water with his toe when she emerged and, spurring her flagging spirits, leapt down through the bushes, paused a moment beside him, cried 'Ah!' and dived into liquid twilight.

He plunged in after her, and they came up together. 'You shouldn't have dived like that,' he cried. 'Don't do it again. There's a great jag of rock just below where you went in, – you might have hit your head. You're a very stupid girl.'

'Pooh!' She splashed and kicked round him, and went swimming close under the waterfall, feeling its weight press down and bubble upon her shoulder. The water was cold: the sun could never reach it save in light flecks through leafy branches. The pouring of the falls made a soft, full, lapsing speech. Nothing in the world was so smooth as the polished silk of their downcurving necks.

'Hey!' cried Julian.

She looked round and saw him near the further edge of the basin, trying to save himself from being carried over. She laughed, but he did not laugh back, and dragged himself out and sat on a rock in silence; and she saw that his legs and arms were grazed and bleeding. She went to him remorsefully and washed the blood away with palmfuls of water and sat by him, murmuring little sympathies until the stinging pain eased. He was not strong, she must remember: the shock and the pain had made him white about the lips. Poor Julian . . . How smooth and creamy her limbs looked beside his . . .

'One more dip before dressing, Julian. You sit there and rest.'

He sat and watched while she slipped in again and, lying on her back, pushed off vigorously from the side with both feet and floated in a great ruffle of water to the other edge. Then she climbed out and stood opposite him, dripping and smiling.

Something leapt into his eyes as they rested, for once, full on her: not admiration or desire, but something harsh and hostile, as if the sight of her exasperated him.

'Oh yes, it shows you off well,' he said.

'What does?'

'Your *maillot*. I suppose you weren't aware of it?'

'No!' She spat the word at him; and went quickly away.

They had supper at a white inn by the edge of the wood, about half a mile further on. The same stream flowed, sedately now, through the garden; and a dark plump Madame with great glossy raven plaits brought omelettes and trout and salads and fruits to their table beneath the plane-tree. Birds were singing the last of their songs in all the branches.

'Listen, Julian! – if that isn't a thrush? What is he doing out of England? Can you imagine a French thrush? Oh, he sounds homesick!' A sudden nostalgia overcame her. 'I want to go home too! I'm not a traveller. Sick for home – that's what I am. This thrush and our pool are probably the things I shall most remember about France – and all because they made me think of England ... There was a girl at College I used to bathe with ... You'd have loved to look at her. Her name was Jennifer Baird ...'

'I think I've met her.'

What was he saying so casually?

'You've met her?' Hands clasped, heart thumping, she stared at him.

'Yes, I'm sure that was the name. I was staying in Scotland with some cousins of hers.'

'When, Julian?'

She could scarcely speak.

'Last year, I believe. I remember now she was at Cambridge and said she knew you; but she wasn't very forthcoming about you. I'd never have guessed from her that you were bosom friends.' His voice sounded mocking.

'No, you wouldn't!' she retorted, stung and scornful. 'She doesn't tell just anybody when –' She checked herself; for perhaps after all it had been that Jennifer had not remembered her much in absence. She added quietly: 'She was a person I knew well for a time. Tell me ... What did you think of her?'

'Oh, mad as a hatter. But she was more alive than most people. A flame, let us say.' His voice was ambiguous, unkind.

'You didn't like her, then?'

'No, nor she me.' He laughed briefly. 'But she had a power, I admit. I intend to go and find her again some day. I dare say I might make her – like me.'

'I don't think you could!' She wanted to strike him for his cold-blooded self-assurance. 'If you think you could –manage her, control her, I pity you, that's all! I'd like to see you try! You'd think you'd got her easily – and then in another moment she'd have slipped through your fingers ... How I'd laugh! ... Personally I didn't need to make her like me: she just did.'

266

She felt that she was speaking wildly, and fell silent, weak before the flooding onslaught of the past.

It was too much pain. What was the use of trying to go on? You could never get free of the past. It came all around again at a word, and in a trice all save its shadows was trivial and insubstantial.

Julian was watching her; raising his eyebrows in a pretence of polite surprise and watching closely.

'Well, well!' he said. 'Calm yourself, my serpent. You have convinced me my best endeavours would be wasted.'

She hid her face, stooping it over the table with both hands across her forehead, feeling the nausea and sweat of faintness.

He helped himself to grapes and remarked:

'Not that I shan't be sorry never to see her on a horse again. She looked magnificent.'

'Oh yes! She . . .' Still with her face hidden she added, summoning a faint but steady voice: 'I'd go to her now, this minute, if I knew where she was. But I don't.'

There was a silence; and then he said gently:

'I'll find her for you if you like, my dear.'

She stretched a hand across the table to him.

'No. Help me forget her . . . and everything else . . .'

He stroked the hand; and without a word left her, to pay the bill. When he came back she was able to raise a calm and smiling face to him.

The stars were out when they took the road again, and the coming dark flowered like a field of pansies.

'Hadn't we better go home now, Julian?'

'No. I'm not going to take you home yet.'

She sat beside him, silent and dully apprehensive.

'It's a pity you're so unhappy,' said Julian. 'I think I said so before.'

She made no answer.

'You know,' he said, 'you're a fool to take on like this.'

Silence.

'You're simply destroying yourself over it and it can't be worth it. Why don't you tell me about it? I'll be nice.'

She shook her head.

'Do tell me, darling. You know, things have a way of swelling to monsters if we lock them up inside us. You see if you won't feel better after you've once got it out of you.' He spoke like a kindly father, and put an arm round her.

'I'm in love with someone,' she whispered. 'That's all. I thought it was finished ... Oh dear, dear, dear, how awful! ...' She drew deep choking breaths.

'Poor devil,' he said.

'You needn't be sorry.' She collected herself. 'It's good for me. Besides, it *is* finished really: I scarcely ever think of it now.'

'Does that yellow-haired female come into it, then?'

'Jennifer? No. Though she's gone too ... and that makes it all far worse ...' She added quickly: 'It's nobody you know.'

His silence told her that he was not deceived.

'Anyway,' she said lightly, 'there's one bad thing over in my life: falling in love, I mean. I'm *free* of it!'

'Oh, don't be ridiculous, my dear child! *Don't* be such a fool! Why, you haven't mastered your infant primer yet. *I* know! Do you mean to tell me this *unknown* fellow has absorbed all your powers of loving to the end of your life? I'm sorry then: you're less of a person than I thought you. Ah, you think I'm mocking, and you hate me. And I do mock. Yes, Yes! And I'm so sorry for you I –. But of course you won't believe that.'

He spoke with passion, slowing the car down till she scarcely crawled, then finally stopping her altogether by the edge of the road, beneath an overhanging rocky hillside. It was getting very dark: she felt rather than saw the tense expression of his eyes and mouth.

'You won't believe that,' he repeated, 'and you're thinking at this moment that such a brute as I never before existed.'

'No.' She felt dazed. 'I think you're meaning to be kind. But you don't understand.'

'Aha! Of course not. How can a coarse male animal like myself understand the feelings of a refined and sensitive young lady?'

'Oh, Julian – unfair ... unkind!'

'Well, *damn* you, don't you see I love you myself?' he cried in a perfect fury. 'Here am I, alone with you at last for a paltry ten days – after waiting years, mind you, *years* for my opportunity, and I find you moping and moaning over your lost schoolgirl illusions! Good God! Haven't you the guts to snap your fingers at a fellow who can't be bothered with you? Aren't you attractive and intelligent? Can't you laugh? Aren't there plenty of others? What am I here for? Go to the devil for a bit – I'll help you. I'll see you through it. But *don't moan.*'

He paused for breath, and went on:

'Here am I, as I said, with ten days of your company as my limit – ten days in which to make you *look back* into my eyes, not through them, to make you stop smiling and being polite and tolerant and sorry for me – oh, anything rather than your damned indifference! Why don't you hate me? I could do some good with you then. I thrive on hatred. Here am I, of all people, not able to sleep or eat for wanting to kiss you, shaking all over when I see you coming, raging when you talk to another man – and here are you, making a fool of yourself – obstinately wasting our time making a romantic fool of yourself.'

'Well, we're quits then,' she interrupted quickly. 'I love without being loved. You're another.'

He turned to her and said delightedly:

'You're angry. I've stung you up. You've lost your temper.'

'Oh, you're impossible.'

'No, no I'm not,' he said coaxingly. 'Look, I'll be so nice now. Listen to me, Judy darling. You're not the sort of person to have one abortive little romance and go to your grave an old maid. An old maid who's had a disappointment, Judy! – isn't that what it's called? There, I'm teasing again and I said I wouldn't. Darling, what's the use of being so damned constant? *Do* find someone else quick. You've no idea how delightful you'll find it when you're old to remember what a lot of people you've loved. And it's the *very* best remedy, Judy, for your indisposition.'

'Shall you employ it if –'

'If you turn me down? Probably. But don't turn me down – not without a trial. Here am I, ready to hand: you could do a damned sight worse than take me. I'll see we have a good time.'

Moths flittered and spun in the light of the head-lamps; beyond the two still long shafts of brightness the night looked very dark. How many miles from home?

At length she said:

'I take it this is not a proposal of marriage, Julian.'

He laughed.

'No, my dear, it is not. Nothing so grim.'

'Ah I see – your mistress.'

Her voice and her words made her wonder if she were not holding a conversation in a dream: there was the same feeling of having made a pronouncement of the first importance; but whose meaning she could not detect.

Julian's mistress ... The idea was for some reason profoundly shocking.

A French, an Austrian, a Russian; and now an English ... But perhaps he had been lying then. He did tell such lies about his experiences.

'I'm not made for matrimony any more than you are,' he said in a voice of gentle explanation. 'Can you imagine me as a husband? What hell for some poor fool! ... Yet,' he added with a sigh, 'I'd be fond of my children. I'd like to bring up a son. But I shall never have one.'

'If you would marry Mariella,' she said, still out of her dream, 'you could bring up Peter. She'd like that. I think she loves you.'

He took no notice; and she wondered if she had not spoken aloud, after all; or whether her small voice had not penetrated his absorption.

'Why, what would we make of each other married?' he went on. 'It would be one long succession of *agacements*. We're both so self-conscious, so fastidious, so civilized ... It would be appalling.'

'Yes it would.'

'But Judith, lovely delightful Judith,' he pleaded, his voice deep and beautiful, 'for a season, for a season! A clean leap in, and out again the minute it started to be a failure. Think what we could give each other!'

'It would be very good for us I suppose...' She held her head in her hands, trying to think. What could he possibly give her that she would want?

'It would, it would. We'd *live* a bit instead of thinking. I'd make you forget, I swear: and what things I'd give you to remember instead! – good things that have been my secrets for years, that I've longed for years to share, to offer to your nice quick intelligence. No one else has had them, Judith. They've been waiting for you: nobody else has ever come near you in my mind. Judith, it wouldn't be the irritating tiresome old bore you know: that isn't I! I've got secrets. Let me tell you them. So much beauty I'd enrich you with, and then I'd let you go. Isn't that fair? Isn't that worth having? Go and marry and breed afterwards if you must, but let me give you this first. Try me, Judith, try me. You can't refuse to try me. I want you so much.'

She wanted to stop her ears: for she felt herself helplessly yielding to the old syren of words.

'Julian – I couldn't give you – what you wanted. Oh I couldn't! It's such a step – you don't realize – for a woman. She can't ever get back – afterwards, and be safe in the world. And she might want to.'

'I'd see you got back if you wanted to. But I don't think you will. You won't want to be safe. That's not for you. Oh Judith, I know you better than you know yourself.'

'No. No.'

She was locked away from him and he did not know it. What he mistook for her living self was a mummy, with a heart of dry dust. He had not the perspicacity to see it.

He was silent, and then said:

'I wouldn't ask you for anything you – weren't prepared to give me. I hope – that might come. But for the present all I want is to help you live again – in better, more enduring, ways. Will you let me? Will you allow me to love you, Judith?'

'Perhaps. Perhaps, Julian. I'll try. I'll try to love you too.' The words broke from her on top of a great sigh.

'My dear!' She felt his triumph. He put an arm round her and lightly kissed her, and she thought: 'Now I've been kissed by all three of them.'

'But wait, Julian!' she protested, near to nervous tears. 'Don't say any more now. Take me home.'

'Yes, yes. I'll take you home now.' His voice was soothing and tender. He was letting her see that his patience was infinite. This time, she was caught.

The car glided downwards from the hills into the plain, through the lovely calm. Once she broke silence to say:

'Nothing's worth-while, Julian? It doesn't matter what one does? There's no point, really, in being alive?'

He laughed.

'Poor Judy! Give it up! You'll have to in time. Resign yourself, and the compensations won't seem so preposterously inadequate. There was a time ... But that's past. So long as there's a balance of happiness I'm content to be alive. That it's all futile has ceased to trouble me. It's not really difficult to be happy, Judith.'

'Well – you shall show me.'

But she felt crushed with melancholy to hear him; and his calm voice echoed drearily in her heart.

She bade him good night in the empty lounge, and went upstairs to the bedroom's rose and gilt harshness.

She was going to be Julian's mistress ... He was sure of her: she had noted his triumphant eyes and smiling mouth when he said good night ... Perhaps if she had offered to be Roddy's mistress he would have agreed with alacrity. He too was not made for matrimony.

She wished suddenly for Martin and sat down and started a letter to him; gave up after a few sentences, too heavy-minded to think; and went to bed.

10

The next day was *jour de fête*: there were to be grand balls, carnivals and exhibition dancing in all the hotels.

'We'll make the round of them, Judy,' said Julian. 'And afterwards we'll take the car and go up into the hills – shall we?'

And she thanked him and agreed.

He was debonair, gay and gracious: the lines in his face seemed to have been smoothed out, and the likeness to Charlie was strongly in evidence.

Dreaming ahead, she saw herself reluctantly, helplessly, plunging further and further into relationship with him. He would not weary of her soon. When once the thing started, the break with the past would inevitably be complete. Together they would be reckless, free; together they would snatch pleasure out of life's worthlessness; for Julian had promised faithfully that he was going to give her exactly what she wanted, that he had learnt precisely how happiness was to be come by, and would teach her ... She had given him leave to teach her.

Judiciously he absented himself for the day; and she spent the morning with Mamma, watching all the internally-disordered people pass, cup in hand, up and down the *Place* from spring to spring; and the afternoon with Mamma at the dressmaker's; and the hours between tea and dinner with Mamma in the hotel-lounge, glumly banishing and recurring to thoughts of Roddy.

Mamma sent her out to buy a copy of the Continental *Daily Mail*, which shrill-voiced women were excitedly advertising in the *Place*. Through her lorgnette, Mamma scanned the announcement of recent arrivals, the political outlook, the new French train smash, yawned, remarked that the holiday season in England seemed marked as usual by murders and drowning fatalities, yawned again and went upstairs to rest before her bridge-party.

An hour yet till dinner and nothing to do but sit and think of things.

Idly she picked up the evilly printed sheets. *Triple Boating Tragedy*. Why were they always triple? What must it be like to be relatives and friends of a triple boating tragedy? But that was a class disaster, like a charabanc death – not general.

Sailing Fatality off St Catherine's, Isle of Wight. That was where Martin and Roddy were yachting. They might have witnessed it. *Tragic End of well-known Young Yachtsman*.

She had an impulse to put down the paper; but a name caught her eye and she had to go on reading.

A dense fog in the Channel is presumed to be the cause of the death of Mr G. M. St V. Fyfe, one of the best known of the younger Solent yachtsmen.

According to information at present available, Mr Fyfe, who was an expert sailor and swimmer, had been out since early morning of the —th sailing his small cutter 'Sea Pink' single-handed. About noon a heavy sea-fog drove up from the Channel with great suddenness and in the evening his friends

273

became alarmed at his failure to return. Next morning a life-buoy and some other wreckage identified as belonging to Mr Fyfe's boat was found washed up on the shore near Brooke. It is thought that the boat must have been run down by a liner or other large vessel off St Catherine's Head during the fog of the previous afternoon. The body has not yet been recovered.

Mr G. M. St V. Fyfe, who was twenty-four years of age, was the only son of the late Sir John Fyfe, KCB, and of Lady Fyfe of the Manor House, Fernwood, Hants. Educated at Eton and Trinity College, Cambridge, he was among the most ...

There followed a few more words, but the type was illegible.

It could not be Martin, because he was Mr Martin Fyfe. Martin's initials were – Oh God! – forget you know his initials. She could see them now written in her own hand on an envelope: G. M. St V. Fyfe, Esq. Such dignified satisfying initials ... It could not be Martin because an unfinished letter to him was lying upstairs waiting to be sent. Martin was sailing safely with Roddy and one or two others. He would not sail a cutter single-handed in a fog, because that was so dangerous; and he never did dangerous things.

The body had not yet been recovered ...

If she read the thing through again calmly she would realize it was somebody else.

Perhaps better not.

Just the date though ... Two days old, this thing was now ... Mr G. M. St V. Fyfe – Martin Fyfe – *Martin* had been absent for two days ...

She thought: If I pretend I never saw it, it will be just as if it hadn't happened. I won't know it, and then it'll stop being true.

She folded the newspaper carefully, took it and went upstairs; and dressed for dinner with meticulous care. She was going to dine with Julian at the hotel which promised the best exhibition dancing; and she had agreed to wear his favourite frock tonight.

It was a very rich and expensive dinner that Julian had ordered; and a bouquet of red carnations lay beside her plate. Lobster and champagne. What a crowd of excited people! Bare flesh was very ugly, and all those waved heads of women were intolerable. The monotony of faces in a crowd! ...

274

Julian was studying her covertly, with flickering glances, though his attention was ostensibly for the company. He drank restlessly: the lines in his face were very marked. She would say something to him about the monotony of faces in a crowd; and then something about waved hair. After that she said:

'Julian, does anybody know you're here?'

'No, not a soul.'

'You left no address?'

'No. Paris is my headquarters. When I go off like this I prefer that the great world should await my return, not follow me.'

'Ah, you're wise.' She laughed. 'It must make you feel so free.'

'Why did you ask?'

'Because it just occurred to me.'

Because they might have sent him a telegram: he was the eldest of the family, and they might have wanted him for all sorts of reasons: for the funeral ... But the body had not yet been recovered. Soon she must say to him: 'Julian, Martin has been drowned.' He would not much mind: they had never been very intimate: but of course they had shared that blood-intimacy of the circle. She must really tell him soon.

They were dancing now. The room was full of smoke and light and sickly scent; and the heat was choking. Everybody was rising to dance.

One of the American young men from her hotel was bowing and murmuring in front of her.

'Not just now, thank you so much.' She flashed a smile at him. 'Perhaps later on ...'

Oh the queer marionettes bobbing up and down in their mechanical motions! How could people look so serious and perform such imbecile antics? But they were not real people.

'Look Julian, there's the Spanish boy we played against in the tournament. He's good-looking, isn't he? He's simply enrapturing that girl. Hasn't he got a lazy smile? ... You know, however ugly a Frenchwoman's body is at any rate it *is* a body and she's not ashamed of it. Those English people are just bundles of clothes. If you undressed them there'd be nothing. That's the whole difference ... Oh look, they're giving out favours. I'd like a fan. Let's dance.'

Threading her way through the crowded tables, she passed a party of fat elderly Frenchmen and heard one say to another, loudly and with drunken excitement:

'*Mais regardes donc un peu! En blanc – vois tu? Elle est bien, celle-là. C'est tout à fait mon type.*'

Their faces leered at her out of a dream.

Julian took her once round the room and then looked down at her and said:

'You can't dance tonight. What's the matter?'

She gazed at him in dread, dumb. There was a reason. Soon – soon she would have to tell him; and then, when it had been spoken, imparted, it would be true for ever and ever. Not yet.

After a little while Julian held her as if he had ceased to expect or desire any response or rhythm from the lumpish wooden body he had to push. It was no good trying to keep things going much longer ... All things were coming waveringly to an end. The end would come with her own voice saying: 'Martin has been drowned.' After that there would be a breaking-up and confusion, a going away to hide ... Not yet.

The dancing competition had started, amid loud laughter and applause. The couples, gradually thinning out, circled self-consciously. The little soft-eyed half-caste brother and sister – they were the ones. Their bodies were lithe and flat and sinuous, their proudly-carried small heads shone like black water, their eyes and lips were dreamy, sensual, sad, their limbs made poetry and music as they moved. They agreed, as prize-winners, to dance an exhibition dance.

Blushing, her teeth sparkling in a smile, she glided from the other end of the room towards her brother. He gave her his hand, she paused with a swirl of her long full yellow skirt, – and then they started swaying and circling together. They whirled; stopped dead; whirled again. He lifted her in the air and there she hung poised, laughing at him, pointing her tiny foot, then dropped like a feather and went weaving on.

Oh, let them dance for ever! While they danced, people could die, gently, easily, as a dancer sinks to earth, without pain to them or horror to others. Let them dance for ever! ... It was over. Hand in hand they curtsied and bowed, and ran off the floor.

'That was dancing,' said Julian. 'Nobody but each other to dance with you see, poor little devils. That's the way to learn.'

Roddy would have danced with that soft-smiling sidelong-glancing little dancer: he would have made a point of it, not out of pity. Martin would have left her alone with quiet distaste.

> Then, in a flash, saw the sea try
> With savage joy and efforts wild
> To smash its rocks with a dead child.

To smash its rocks with Martin.

Everybody was very gay now. Through the smoke, all the eyes and mouths laughed, excited with wine and dancing. Balloons and favours waved; the band blared. The musicians donned false noses and moustaches and stood up, leaping and shouting.

This place is Hell!

Yes, Hell. Grimacing faces, obscene bodies, chattering parrot and monkey voices; Hell's musicians, with vicious tunes and features dark with unmentionable evil ...

The lights were dimmed, the floor cleared. A dancing girl leapt into the middle of the space, throwing flowers. Her white ballet skirts spun mistily. The lights were extinguished altogether, and you saw that the outline of her bodice and her skirts, her shoe-buckles and the star on her forehead had been painted with luminous paint; so that now she was three stars and some circles and loops of light, wheeling fantastically in the dark.

Now was the time to slip out. Julian would not notice.

Half-way across the *Place* he caught her up.

'Where are you going?'

'There's something I must show you. Come with me.'

He followed in silence, into the hotel, upstairs, into the sitting-room 'Wait there, then. I'll come back.'

She saw that she was carrying a purple balloon. She dropped it and watched it go bouncing like a great bubble across the room.

In the bedroom she found the letter in the folds of the blotter. *'What a silence, Martin! I have been missing you ...'* Aghast, she tore it in shreds.

Now to go back to Julian.

He was standing in the middle of the room, waiting.

'Julian, what are Martin's initials?'

He thought.

'Something St V. – G. M. St V. – George Martin St Vincent.'

He raised his eyebrows – but grew pale.

'Ah yes.'

The paper lay on the window-seat; she went to get it. 'Take it away and read. There, where I've marked it.' She made a cross with her thumbnail.

She went back to the bedroom and locked the door; and, after a few minutes, heard him going downstairs again.

Then she flung herself upon the bed, weeping for Martin whom she loved: whom she had left crying for her sake; who should have lived to be loved by his children, and honoured and full of years; Martin who was kind when all else was unkind – Martin who had been dead two days, rolling about in the waves; Martin for whom poor Roddy had searched the sea in vain; Martin who had been comely and now was destroyed utterly and made horrible, – sea-water in his mouth and eyes and hair, sea-water swelling his shapely body to a gross lump.

Whom had he thought of while he drowned? Had he fought and cursed? Or had he welcomed death because of somebody's unkindness and deceit?

'Martin, I didn't mean it.'

Martin was almost in the room – quite in the room – standing just behind her, saying: 'I'm all right.' He had come to comfort her.

Martin had entered into everlasting life. Yes!

No. No. No. Dead. Unconscious. Nothing. Beyond sight and touch for ever.

Part Five

I

IT was the end of September. She had come home again, alone.
Morning, noon and evening she sat about or wandered by herself,
and watched the coloured procession of the days. Chill mornings
wrapped in bluish mist broke softly towards mid-day, bloomed into
shining pale yellow afternoons, died early, wistfully, in mists again,
in grey dews shimmering upon the leaf-strewn lawn and the fallen
apples, in motionless massed pomp of foliage burning softly beneath
sunsets of muffled crimson, in moonrises strange with a bronze light.

The river lay stretched like a silken substance, with an oil-smooth
sheen upon its dark olive surface; and all the poplars and willows
upon the bank grew both ways – into the air, and down through the
water with their long trunks shortened and their brightness tenderly
blurred.

Next door, the shutters were up, and the copper beech dropped
its leaves upon the deserted lawn.

In that deep-weighing, windless, mellow hush, alone in the house
and garden, by the river, and on the hills, she saw all things begin
to turn lingeringly, richly towards their end; and, at long last, felt
in herself the first doubtful stir of new awakening.

Mamma had not come home. She was in Paris now, and was to
remain there for the present.

She had been kind on that morning, when Judith had come to her
bedside, told her that Julian had gone, that Martin was dead and that
she herself was not feeling very well. She had asked not a single confidence, spoken no word of pity, but with merciful everydayness looked
after her, revived her body with the practical comfort of brandy and
hot-water bottles; and then, the next day, abandoned her cure and

279

taken her away. They had motored all over France and into Italy and Switzerland; and Mamma, between long intervals of silence, had talked light sharp surface talk of the places and people they encountered, of food and clothes: talk that could be listened to with adequate attention and answered with ease. Through the close wrapping of lead upon her mind Judith had understood the deliberate and painstaking scheme of help, and been grateful for it. But when, after three weeks, Mamma started to make plans for an autumn together in Paris, Judith had suddenly asked to be allowed to go home. It was the first spontaneous impulse from a mind diseased, so it had seemed, beyond hope of revival. Sluggishly it stirred, but it remained: she must go home, be alone, find work, write a book, something . . . Acquiescing, Mamma had not been able to conceal her relief. What a bore these weeks must have been for her!

Judith saw England once more with the senses of one waking before dawn exhausted from a nightmare, apprehending reality with shrinking and confusion, and then, gradually, with a faint inflowing of relief, of hope in the coming of the light.

Each morning she thought:

'Today I will begin to write – start practising again – apply through College for some post . . .'

But each evening found her still folded in the golden caressing solitudes of the garden, mindless and inert. There was no subject that could conceivably provide material for a book; no music that was not far too difficult to learn to play; no post that did not seem entirely distasteful.

Then, one afternoon, she paused by the grand piano, hesitated, opened it and sat down to play – Schumann, Chopin, Brahms, Debussy, Ravel . . . a little of each, stumbling, giving up, going on again. At the end of two hours she stopped. At first her hands had not obeyed her; but after a time they had begun to remember, she had forced them to remember a little. She must practise scales and exercises: it was too humiliating to be at the mercy of stiff clumsy fingers.

She looked round the drawing-room and saw that it was empty of flowers. She took a basket and went out into the misty sharp-smelling garden and gathered dahlias and late roses. The flower petals seemed to caress her cheek as she stooped to them, the stalks to yield gladly and fall towards her. They loved and welcomed her. She chose, picked, stroked them, held them against her face with voluptuous delight in their colour, form and texture. It was thrilling, living alone and gathering flowers.

She looked around her, up at the sky. The evening was like Jennifer. She went in to put her flowers in water.

Sheaves of cut lavender still lay drying on newspaper in the little room where the vases were kept. She finished stripping the brittle stalks, dividing the fragrant dried bluish heaps of buds and pouring them into bowls. The feel of lavender held in the palms and sifting through the fingers was delicious.

That day, years ago, when Roddy had come to tea, he had plunged both hands into a bowl of lavender in the hall and then buried his nose in them with a long 'Ah!' of satisfaction. This very *famille rose* bowl she was filling had been the one. She had said that, when the fresh lavender was ready, she would make him lavender bags to keep among his ties and handkerchiefs ... How long ago! ...

She longed for Roddy suddenly with a new and unenvenomed pang: she thought of him with tenderly regretful, half-maternal sorrow. He too would be lonely now. She would have liked to give him lavender, to walk with him in the autumn garden, quietly talking, sharing with him its loveliness and tranquillity. She would have liked to show him she wanted nothing now save to take his hand and tell him that she was sorry for him; they must be friends now, always, remembering whom they had both loved.

The evening post came just as she had finished disposing the bowls of lavender about the house. It brought a letter from Julian.

Judith,

Now that I know that my moment is over and will never come again, I must speak to you these last few words; and then be silent. If you reply to me, I beg you not to say you hope we may still be friends. We may not. I am not one who has friends.

That night I went from you and from that vile town raging, cursing God and man. I had been thwarted, so I thought, by a monstrous trick of chance in the very hour of my life's most delicious triumph.

281

I never could endure failure, as you know. I have generally succeeded in getting what I wanted. I have been very successful. That is because I am such a supreme egoist; and because in spite of all my window-dressing and general ambiguity and deceitfulness I don't – often – deceive myself. I know very well what I want: I go straight for it in spite of my path's apparent twists and deviations; and indeed, indeed, Judith, I wanted you. I say to myself: 'Fool! There are plenty of others worth the wanting'; and yet – and yet it does not seem so. No! Despite a life's endeavours, I am not proof yet against the slings and arrows. And when at last they do cease to assail me, it will, I begin to fear, be merely because I have become moribund, not philosophical.

God, I raged! – against Martin for dying, against you for being so foolish as to care, against myself for being made uncomfortable and ridiculous; for I was ridiculous in my own eyes because I had declared myself – shewn all my cards and lost.

Now I have become sane again.

Looking back on it all, I think (with surprise) that I was mistaken. It never would have done. You were not for me, or I for you. I never could have made you passionate – and that was essential. You were all dark within. If anything flashed in you it flashed hidden: you never would have let me warm all myself at you. I see now how you would have given me nothing but the polite, faintly curious attention which I have had from you since our first meeting. It would have been a tedious game trying to knock a spark out of you. I should soon have wearied of it. But before that I should have hurt you. I am not an unaccomplished mental sadist. It would not have done either of us much good.

About Martin: I thought you would like to know. They found his body on the beach two days later; and took him home and buried him beside his father. He had been cheerful all the time, enjoying his sailing; and went out in high spirits on the day of the accident. You must not grieve about him. He doesn't know he was young and loved life and now can't love it any more. He won't get old and past loving it. He'll never miss dead friends and lovers and long in vain to follow them. Fortunate Martin to die before he wanted to . . . But there! These are empty consolations. I also loved my Martin. We shall never see him again. It's little comfort to tell ourselves we shall stop missing him when we're dead too. I am told his mother is calm and courageous, fortified by a complete faith in a loving God. Roddy I saw at the funeral, but had little speech with. He looked unhappy. A brief note I had from him yesterday, concerning the disposal of some of Martin's things, remarks that it is easily the worst thing that's ever happened. This is the only comment he has made or is likely to make – to me at least. He will get over it. He is now in Scotland with friends, shooting. I give you these tidings of him because I surmise that – you will like to have them. But *I know nothing of all that* ... nor do I wish to know ...

Ah, Judith, in spite of all I am very romantic and sentimental, and I say to myself that I have my memories; and they cannot be taken from me. You were very charming, very kind and tolerant. We did some good things together – good vivid things: though I suppose the fact of my physical presence never made them to you what yours made them to me: a superb excitement and intoxication. Twenty years hence when you're long since married and have indulged your deplorable philoprogenitiveness, and are stout, Judith, stout, comfortable, domestic, I shall write one sentence upon a blank page and send it to you:

> Do you remember an inn, Miranda,
> Do you remember an inn?

and perhaps – for one instant – you will stir in your fat and almost, *almost* remember? ... But no! There spoke indeed the sentimental egoist. For the inns you remember will not be those you visited with me; and you have made it clear – haven't you? – that I may never call you Miranda. Besides, for my own part, like enough I shall by then have forgotten the amenities of bathing and omelette-eating and motoring by night, and disremembered all my apt quotations. You will be a placid matron and I a gaunt, stringy and withered madman: one of the kind with livid faces and blazing eyes, who dog young women down lonely lanes. So *never more, Miranda, never more* ...

I read this through, my Judith, and I say to myself: words, words, words! And I think: for whom, for whom shall the close dark wrappings of your mind be laid aside and all the flame come leaping out? I sit and consider how in all these years I never so much as kindled a little glow to warm my hands at; and dream of how happily things might have fallen out if I hadn't been as I am, and all had been different; and I feel lonely and wonder what I shall do without you. Don't for God's sake pity me. I shall forget you. But oh, Judith! you were a pleasure: never quite real. And still, still persists this ridiculous feeling that I should like to do something for you. There is nothing, I suppose?

Next month I go to Russia. For what purpose? I know not. To hear some music, and learn a smattering of the language; to write newspaper articles ('Impressions of an Unprejudiced and Unofficial Wanderer'), to pick up a few acquaintances, to forget you; to contract, perchance, some disease and die of it ... At all events, to Russia I go. Farewell.

J.F.

2

That night she woke from a deep sleep and knew that Martin was dead: not an object of horror tossed about decaying by the waves; not a thing alive somewhere in some nightmare form, appalled at its own death, watching, accusing, reproaching, desiring, reading the secrets of her heart; not a Martin going on obliviously in another, beatific life – but a dead man whose end had chanced upon him swiftly and mercifully, whose bones were in their grave beside his father's, quietly mingling with the earth he loved. Martin had not died out of spite, or because her crookedness and Roddy's had somehow wrought upon him like an evil charm and driven him to be drowned. He had been in high spirits, full of interests in which she had never played a part and so could never spoil; and in the midst of his enjoyment he had died. Drowning was a good death, so people said. Now neither happiness nor unhappiness was possible to him any more: that was all death meant. He had loved her, and now she was nothing to him; he was insensible to her remorse and her regrets. She dared at last to sink in that deep well of sorrow; but its waters were pure now, and in the end she drew herself from them refreshed.

Tomorrow she would be able to write to Martin's mother.

3

She wrote, briefly; and when she had finished, the paper was spotted here and there with irrepressible hot tears; but they were for Martin's mother. She would never shed any more for Martin now.

She dried her eyes and wrote to Julian.

My dear,

I was extraordinarily glad to get your letter. I thought I had lost you as well as everybody else. You have done something for me, Julian: the thing I thought no one and nothing could do. You have made my imagination stop shrieking like a fiend in hell about Martin. It's not only what you so wisely say about a young man's death: it's the knowing that he was found again, and buried in the earth as he wanted to be: that he isn't a derelict, our beloved Martin, in the unfriendly sea. It has all stopped being monstrous to me; it is a natural grief and now I can bear to live again. He was in love with me and I was unkind to him and longed too late to tell him I never meant to be. That was the trouble. But it is all over now.

Thank you from the bottom of my heart for what you have told me of Martin – and of Roddy whom I shall never see again, to whom I may not write and say how I grieve for his sake. You have done a great thing for me: so now it will be easier than ever – won't it? – to dismiss me from your mind.

Ah Julian, you wrote to me in a softened mood. Now you are regretting it, perhaps, or laughing at yourself and me. No, it never would have done. You imagined me: you say so yourself. Thank your stars you were spared the boringness, or worse, of seeing me come true. What coils and glooms and sickened moods poor Martin perhaps saved us! But I hope and believe we'd have ended it and parted, laughing, before we'd even thought of crying. I wish you much success and joy with all the not-impossibles who are to follow me.

What a year this has been, and how we grow up! Shall I really never see you again? It would be bathos after the elegant farewells we are now exchanging: but it may happen.

My harmless Julian, you would not dog a fly – let alone young women in lonely lanes. I do like you very much and I have the greatest respect for the high quality of your morals, and if I die a widow with lots of children I shall bequeath them all to you to bring up. You will have so many of your own that a few more will make no difference. Think how happy you'll be instructing, admonishing and advising them.

What of Peter and of Mariella? – sad, strange, lovable Mariella and her child? Their pathos weighs upon me; but I can do nothing. *Only you can, Julian.* I should have liked news of them. Rumour has it that the house next door is to be put up for sale.

I am all uprooted, and don't know what I shall do. I must begin to make plans. I suppose I shall never emerge from obscurity in any way. I used to think it a certainty that I should. I see you smile unkindly.

Yes, I will be Miranda to you, Julian. What we shared meant as much to me, in a different way, as it did to you; and it will never come again.

Perhaps there will never be any more inns, with anybody, in my life. Enchantment has vanished from the world. Perhaps it will never come back, save in memory. Perhaps I shared with you the last gleam I shall have of it.

Judith.

4

Martin's mother answered, in a large, old-fashioned feminine handwriting, by return of post.

Dear Judith,

Of course I remember you. I do not forget pretty and charming people with sweet voices; and as a friend of Martin's you are dear to me, as all his friends are, because they were responsible for so much of his happiness.

It was kind of you to write. I miss my darling boy every moment of the day. Never was a better son born. But he would not have wished me to grieve, and so I try not to. He is in God's keeping and I feel him very near to me; please God there will not be many years in store for me before he and I and his dear father are reunited.

It is a great comfort to think how happy his life was. His nature was all sun, and from his birth till the day he was taken from us I verily believe not a cloud came over him. Should not that console us?

Thank you again, dear Judith, and believe that Martin's mother remembers you affectionately.

Eleanor Fyfe.

'Not a cloud came over him.' She would believe that and smile ageing, stricken, lonely as she was, till her life's end.

Perhaps after all it was so. Perhaps he had not allowed one woman's petty favours and denials to make a shadow across the large and perpetual sunshine of his way. How little, after all, they had been together, how few words exchanged; how insignificant a figure she must have been, when all was said and done, among all the figures in his thousands of days!

Slowly, the darkness was lifting. Soon now, Jennifer's letter must come, and a new beginning dawn out of this end of all things.

5

It came, one morning when the first gale had started to sweep in upon the season's painted picture; a day when lights, shadows, leaves and wings of birds moved, flew, shone, flickered, paused in a restless harmony.

Darling,

Something makes me write to you now. I have often nearly started and then given it up, but now it feels as if I must, it feels rather like an evening that perhaps you don't remember but I do, when I *had* to come and see you after not having been able to for ages – that time you were ill.

I have felt such a sort of disgrace to myself, and you, and College, and English girlhood, going away like that, that I decided I'd better keep quiet for a bit. I *couldn't* write. But now I must. Have you been waiting and waiting for a letter, and thinking I'd forgotten you? Darling, I haven't forgotten you. Perhaps you've forgotten me. But I don't think so. It is most damnably difficult writing to you. As you see, this is more illegible even than usual with the effort. College does seem so far away. Higher Education for Women never did me any good – except it gave me you and you are an angel and so lovely. I feel very old and different. You remember my hair – you liked it – I have had it all cut off. Just because Geraldine's was short I thought I must have mine the same. Just like me. Mother can't get over it, she now thinks my morals are past praying about, which is a step in the right direction. It all waves and curls and it is marvellous to be without the weight of it and the bloody hairpins prodding my scalp under hats. I thought getting rid of it would be a good way to cut off the past as well. I thought I'd be a different person, more adapted to Geraldine, if I did it. And anyway I couldn't bear her brushing it after you. You remember Geraldine. It was because of her I left College.

Darling, do you hate me now, you ought to. Oh, that last term and the night when I said good-bye to you. I try never to think about it, because it makes me feel so awful. I promised I'd explain everything, didn't I, but it's not much easier now than then because I suppose whatever's been happening to you you're still an innocent baby, while I feel like the most corrupt disreputable I don't know what. Have you had a tremendous love-affair yet? I always used to think there was a man you were on the verge of loving. Perhaps he's made you understand by now what it really means being in love. I loved you frightfully from the very first. I used to think about you night and day. I was in a fever about you. I began to be absolutely afraid of my feelings for you, they were so extremely strong. I couldn't understand them. Then I met Geraldine, and I realized a lot of things. You know what I am – she swept me off my feet. I was too excited to think. She dazzled me. I simply let everybody and everything else go. *And all the time I loved you more than ever.* You may not believe it but it's true. But I couldn't explain to you how I felt – I didn't care. You'd have hated it really, wouldn't you? You are pure and ethereal and I am not. Nor was Geraldine. You used to look after me and kiss me as if you were my mother (not *really* mine of course, who is quite awful, one of those lipless women. I suppose Nature wanted to readjust the balance of mouth and that accounts for mine.) I got into such a ghastly muddle over it all, I thought the best thing I could do was to go away. Geraldine clung rather – I knew she'd always be coming up, and I didn't want her and you to meet, I knew she'd be jealous (she's the most jealous person I ever knew). And I saw things could never be happy between you and me again. Oh it was a hellish muddle. It doesn't bear thinking of. I *had* to go away and try and forget. Just like me. I'm such a coward. I went abroad with her and she gave me a marvellous time, I must say. I was absolutely fascinated by her to start with, almost hypnotized, and we went all over Europe. You know I can't help more or less enjoying life frightfully, especially when it's being rather wild and queer – and it was. But then one or two people I met fell in love with me and I suppose I fell a bit in love with them, I always do, and she got jealous and more and more full of accusations and reproaches. I was so sick of her I could hardly bear to look at her. She never could see a joke. So in the end I left her and came home. She goes on writing me reproachful letters, but I don't answer them.

Oh dear, you seem to be very far away from me now. I shall never find anyone who understands like you again. Why did you ever waste your time over me? I'm rotten and I always shall be. As you see I'm at home now, but I shan't stay long. There are far too many raised eyebrows and disapproving chins about. I'm only waiting till I can raise some money and then I expect I'll go abroad again. I always prophesied I'd come to a bad end, didn't I? I seem to like nearly all the vices.

I suppose we shall never meet again. What's the good? You're probably full of new things and people by now, and I dare say I'm changed for the worse. Quite a Fallen Woman. And you wouldn't like me any more. I simply couldn't face it. But write to me once and tell me everything. Tell me if you understand. Tell me I was right to go away. Oh I'd like to be back with you in Cambridge – just for a day, even for an hour – just you and me. There'll never be anything like that, again.

Darling, have you cut off your hair I wonder. It was lovely too, parted in the middle, so smooth and thick and dark purple. You can't have changed it. You will never change, will you, only get more and more deep and clear and yourself. I shall change, but you must always remember I love you.

Jennifer.

She sat down clasping the letter between her palms, feeling the familiar glow steal over her, rising from the very sheets close-written in that sensitive erratic hand. Now, while her heart still beat with relief, joy, surprise, now while Jennifer seemed to have drawn near once more of her own accord, to be inquiring, holding out hands, hinting that she needed her – now it seemed plain at last what was to come. Whatever Jennifer had done, would do, they two must be together again.

She took up a pen and wrote.

My darling,

I knew your letter would come, because I wanted it so badly.

There are no new things and people. There is nothing. I haven't got on very well without you and being happy seems to belong to a far-back time when you wore a green straw hat with a wreath of pink clover.

You have explained everything at last. Thank you darling. Perhaps if we had both explained things more to each other, there wouldn't have been such blanks and failures.

I am at home, alone, wondering, like you, what to do next. I am quite free. I want to be with you again. Let us meet and think of something to do together. I shall go to Cambridge for a day at the beginning of next term. Meet me there. I'd hate to find you again for the first time in a different setting. I promise not to remind you of the past or of things you want to forget. I too only want to see a future now.

I am living in an utter solitude, which is thrilling but insidious.

This time of year always reminds me of you. I wish you were here to bathe at midday, when the haze is warm and golden, to share my fruity meals, and drift on the cold white-misted moony river after dark.

Tell me a date and I will come.

To think of you without your hair! Mine is exactly as it used to be.

Judith.

6

Some days later, the same post brought two letters. One was Jennifer's answer, scribbled all but illegibly across a half-sheet of notepaper, dashed off, it seemed, in wild haste.

Oh it would be too lovely to see you again, darling. I can't seem to make plans, or think at all. You are alone and you sound as if you had been so terribly unhappy. Oh, poor darling. Yes, it would be marvellous to do something together, but what? You know you know *you know* what I'm like. Why do you want to be bothered with me again. Remember how miserable I made you. But I must see you again – just to set eyes on you again would be heavenly. October 24th. Will that suit you. I will come to our teashop where we always went. Sit in the front room in the corner under the window. I'll come for you there about four o'clock. *Don't wait for me after five.* I shall get there by car somehow. I thought if I didn't come till the afternoon it would give you time to go out to College and see people if you want to. *I don't want to.* Perhaps we could stay the night somewhere. What do you think. I can't say anything more definite than this. I will *try* to get there punctually. But if I wasn't there – (here several words were so thickly inked over as to be indecipherable – and the letter ended in a desperate-looking scrawl) – It will be too too lovely to be with you again.

J.

The other letter made a bulky package. She opened it and saw many sheets of round unformed handwriting. At the top of the first page some other hand had written something minutely in pencil: Julian's hand. She read.

You asked me for news of Mariella. Here it is. I think you guessed what I was neither perspicacious nor interested enough to suspect; or did even she fall into the common habit of 'telling Judith'? There is something about this document which has made me feel far from flattered in my vanity or elevated in my self-esteem. What I send you is for you and no one else. After you have read it destroy it. You are discreet; and for some reason you care what becomes of us; and, last but not least, you have the artistic conscience, a sense of dramatic values. It seems to me this rounds us off nicely.

Tchehov? Turgenev?

J.F.

And underneath she read in Mariella's childlike hand:

Dear Julian,

I think this is the first letter I have ever written to you. I've often wanted to write to you when I couldn't bear it any longer. I've often nearly started and then I haven't dared. I don't know why I do now except that Martin dying does make me feel rather desperate. I've nobody now and he was allways nice to me. I think he guessed a little but never said. I could allways rely on him. I didn't think unhappiness could ever last like this. I've had it for years and I've allways thought, well it must get better soon, something nice would happen, but it seems to get worse and worse and I must just get used to it now. Dont you think there must be a Devil to account for all the damned misery in the world, I do. What am I to do with myself, I haven't got anybody. If I beleived in God ever listening to us and minding what happened to us Id say it was him telling me to write to you, because it came to me last night all in a flash I must do it, I should be sort of saved if I did. I was deciding to kill myself but once Ive written all this out I dont think Ill want to. Ill go away and never see any of you again but Ill go on living.

What Im writing to you about is this. Will you take Peter and look after him – you will do it better than me, and you love him and you have always thought I didn't know how to look after him. I expect its true. I feel very helpless and worried about him. I hated it when he was born, I didn't want him. I never ought to have married Charlie, you told me so, and then to have the baby – it meant I could never forget the awfull mistake and poor Charlie, and I wanted to forget him. I thought I could never love Peter – I *hated* him at first – me to have a baby of all things, but after a bit I began to love him, he was so sweet, and instead of making me remember miserable things he seemed to be going to make up for everything and I thought perhaps I should be happy after all, bringing him up. And then that day you came back on leave and saw him when he was a baby I saw how you looked at him and I knew you were going to love him too. And I thought, if he cares for Peter prehaps he will like me better, but instead of that you seemed to dislike me more. I understand why of course. You couldn't help loving him for himself and because he was Charlies, but because he was mine too you couldn't help allways remembering the gastly quarrel whenever you saw him with me. That's why you wanted to have him to yourself away from me and allways told everybody I couldn't look after him and oughtnt to have had a baby. You did tell everybody didn't you? Poor little Peter I suppose it was true because bit by bit I got jealous of him. Oh what a devil I felt being jealous of my own son. And I adored him too but I couldn't bear to see you with him and you trying to take him away from me and him getting to love you better than me. I used to go away and as for crying, I've cried enough in the last few years to make up for all the years of my life when I never cried. I didn't cry at all when poor Charlie was killed, I suppose I was numb and then there was this horror of the baby coming. I felt turned into stone.

And then began the time I thought you would marry Judith. I know you were in love with her, I suppose you still are, she is so pretty and clever as well. I was allways very fond of Judith, she was sweet to me, and I used to think Id try hard not to mind if you married her because it was so suitable and shed make you happy if she loved you. But I dont think she will love you, it wasnt you she wanted. It is awful to think she has your love and doesnt want it. The waste, I cant bear it! If only all the people with unwanted love could hand it on to the people whod die for it and there were none

of these gastly gaps – everybody loving someone who loves another
person. It seems so funny it never struck you I was the one who could
make you happy, that Id always love you and look after you, but of
course its silly to talk like that. I know Im stupid. I never read books
or had any education. I have always exasperated you but I think if
youd loved me I might have been different. Id have learned from
you, Id have done anything to please you. I know I could have. But
it never seemed worth while making an effort. I was allways your
but and you expected me to be a fool. Its terrible how I irritate you.
Why did I marry Charlie. He begged me and begged me and I'd
always been so used to giving way to him. Besides I was so young then
he told you and the revelation of how contemtable you thought me.
I thought if I went and anounced to you I was going to marry Charlie
youd realise I wasn't a baby any more, that I was grown up, and
youd say no, I must marry you not Charlie. And then your fury when
he told you and the revelation of how contemtable you thought me.
I think you were jealous too, because Charlie had done a thing without
telling you and of course youd got him out of so many scrapes you
couldnt bear him turning to someone else, especially a person like
me who I suppose you thought too stupid to mannage him at all.
Poor Charlie I know you loved him and tried to be like a father to
him but honestly I dont believe you managed him quite the right
way. I suppose it was my damned pride that made me go through
with marrying him. When he came and told me hed sworn never to
speak to you again, his only brother, I felt it was all my fault and
I couldnt desert him. I couldnt help loving him in a way, he was
very lovable and he did depend on me so. I vowed to myself I'd stop
him drinking etc, and then perhaps youd be grateful to me and thered
be a reconciliation. Poor Charlie, prehaps it was best he died, he was
so weak. It was funny how he fell in love with me when he grew
up. Somebody in my life has loved me anyhow. He really did. He
longed so to have a son before he died too. Poor Grannie, she thought
it was so wrong cousins marrying, but Charlie said no, he knew wed
have wonderful children.

Prehaps Peter will be wonderful. Hes got his music, and he hasnt
got Charlies wild histerrical temper. Hes a very good unselfish little
boy, very afectionate. Will you please take him and bring him up.

You will do it better than me. I couldnt write like this if I hadnt quite given up hope of you ever turning to me. When Martin died I thought perhaps it might bring us closer, you were the one person I wanted to see, it would have been such a comfort. But no, my last hope is gone. I must think only of Peter now. I dont see how I can do it, the one thing Ive got, but I know its best. Ill know hes getting the best chance, which will be a great weight off my mind. I know you dont want to send him to school till hes much older, Im glad because hes rather dellicate and not a bit like other little boys – you mannage all the money, so youll know how much there is for him. Quite enough I think. Prehaps you will let me have him now and then for little visits, and when he grows up prehaps Ill be able to explain to him – if I'm alive. I dont really think I shall be. I promise Ill never interfere or bother you, but please you must remember its not because I dont love Peter Im giving him to you, *but because I love you* and wish he was yours. It will be wonderful doing something for you. Itll make me allmost happy. Dont let him quite forget me, but I know he really loves you better than anyone. Oh before he was born I used to think if this was only Julians baby how happy Id be – I love you so much I would love to have your children and sufer pain for you – even though Ive never wanted children for myself. I know people allways say I am so cold and dull and sexless, so I am to everyone else because ever since I was very young you have absorbed me intirely. To you I would have been more like a flame, to burn you up. But you were allways so cold and uninterested, you never thought I was atractive to look at even.

Oh I shiver when I think of having produced Peter perhaps only to be as unhappy as me or to die young like Charlie and Martin. But if you look after him hes more likely to be alright. Please if you marry get someone who will be nice to him. Oh this is awfull. What am I doing. Please take him soon. Dont write me an answer but just say if you will take him and when and I will send him with the governess, but you will sack her wont you and educate him yourself. I never did like her. Well I have written it all, I feel very exhausted but Im glad its written. I shant ever need to pretend again, the strain was awfull. I dont quite know what I shall do. I think I shall sell the house. I couldn't bear to live in it ever again after all thats happened. It was an unlucky house so I dont want to keep it on for Peter. I dare say I shall go on with this vet business, or anyway looking after dogs somehow. Im not stupid with animals if I am with people.

Oh darling Martin, it is terrible without him. Why wasnt I with him in the sailing boat, it would have saved so much trouble. Do you really think we never meet the people we love again. I know youll say never, so dont answer. *Sometimes* I feel it must be alright, I feel allmost a certainty this isnt the end.

I shant read this over. I've written in such a hurry I expect its full of spelling mistakes etc. and youll laugh when you read it. I cant help it.

You mustnt dispise me for telling you I love you.

Good-bye from

Mariella.

Beneath her signature came Julian's pencil again: 'I have sent for Peter.'

7

In the early afternoon, the taxi drew up beneath the archway of College, and she saw once more the red-tiled floor, the cold polished walls, the official bleakness and decorous ugliness of the entrance hall.

The portress had been her special friend. She opened the door of the lodge, expecting a joyful smile: but the elderly woman sitting at the table was unfamiliar.

'Is the portress out?'

'I'm the portress, Miss.'

'I don't think I remember you.'

'No, Miss. I only came this term.'

'Ah yes. How do you like it?'

'Well it's all a bit difficult to get into, Miss. Hard like.'

'Yes. I found that. I used to be here.'

'Oh yes Miss.'

Her eyes looked bored behind her glasses. She was thinking there were any amount of girls always coming and going. You couldn't be expected to take an interest . . .

Judith looked around her and was seized with panic. The whole place was unfamiliar. Nothing recognized or greeted her.

A menace of footsteps drew near, resounding harshly on the tiles. A group of girls in gym tunics passed and stared. They must be first-year students. She could not remember one of them. She shrank from their curious glances and went swiftly down the corridor to the foot of the stairs.

A girl came running down, two steps at a time, saw her and paused, smiling shyly.

'Hullo, Judith!'

'Hullo!'

What was her name? Joan something? You could never have exchanged more than a few words with her. She was fair-haired, ordinary, rather shapeless and untidy, like so many others; but her smile was reassuring.

'Have you come up to stay?' she said.

'No. Just for the day . . . to see one or two people. How are you getting on?'

'All right. How are you?'

'Oh, all right.'

'Well – I must fly. Good-bye.'

'Good-bye.'

She was alone again.

She went up the shallow spiral staircase, and stood still at the top. There was scarcely a sound: it was the usual afternoon hush. She crept up to the mistress's door and knocked; but there was no answer: then on to one or two other rooms, where the grave faces of dons would look quietly pleased to see her; but no reply came. Everyone must be out in the well-remembered October weather.

There was still Miss Fisher's door. She had sent a note to Miss Fisher, her own don, saying she might come, to inquire about a possible job of some sort, to discuss her prospects, and ask for a written testimonial: so behind this door there would be someone who expected her.

But when she drew near she heard the sound of several voices raised

297

as if in argument, and another shiver of panic took her. She let her raised hand drop to her side again and went quickly away; and the voices of a great crowd of unknown people seemed to come after her, questioning her intrusion, while she ran up the next flight of stairs.

Here was the familiar corridor and her own door, half-open, with a strange name on it. There was nobody inside. She peeped in. Nothing, nothing of her that remained. Instead of blue, purple and rose colour, black and orange stripes everywhere; an array of un-prepossessing photographs on the mantelpiece, and some dirty pink plates and cups strewn about.

Only the window remained unchanged, holding up its great autumnal tree-tops to her gaze; but their unmoving pageant stared back and did not greet her. She was dispossessed entirely.

There on the corner was Jennifer's door fast-closed, and bearing an unknown name. The sunshine sloped across to it in a dusty beam.

A maid came round the corner carrying a tray of crockery. She stopped, blushing with delight. It was Rose, who had always been so pretty and coy and smiling, and who had once brought a hot limp bunch of wallflowers from her mother's garden, and laid them on her table. She was quite well thank you, and pleased to see you again. She and some of the other girls were only saying the other day they quite missed you. She wasn't staying much longer now: she was leaving to get married.

Even Rose would soon be gone.

Now she must get out again as quickly as possible without being seen. She had meant to pause again and listen at Miss Fisher's door; but now that was impossible. When now and then on her way down a footstep started, coming closer, a voice was raised, her heart beat in a wild terror of detection. Nobody must see her slinking out again from the place where, in her presumptuous folly, she had returned unannounced, expecting welcome. The place was terrible – a Dark Tower. She must escape. How had she been deluded for three years into imagining it friendly and secure – a permanent dwelling? In four months it had cast her off for ever.

Out again into the courtyard and quickly into the waiting taxi. Jennifer would appreciate the grimness of the story when she told

298

her. She sat back weaving it into a dramatic recital for Jennifer's sympathetic ears.

The town lay shining and smiling secretly in the sunlight, windless, its buildings, spires and streets caressed with a dusty golden light. Here, too, all was quiet. They were playing games. Where had been so many familiar faces, all seemed strange; and the few undergraduates she passed looked commonplace, dingy even, and schoolboyish.

She hesitated on the threshold of a bookshop and then passed on. To be recognized was now as great a dread as not to be recognized. What would people think of her, wandering about alone? How should she explain her presence to inquirers?

Trinity Great Court grieved in the sun for Martin. It had not yet quite forgotten him. It did not like its handsome young men to die.

If only Jennifer would come soon she could clasp her hand and feel a voluptuous stir at the heart of her perturbations; but to flit and pause alone like this, obliterating herself with a sort of shame, looking out for a chance familiar face and yet fearing to see one – this was appalling. It happened to people visiting their university with twenty years between them and youth.

Tony must still be in Cambridge. He was a Fellow of his College now ... Suddenly conscious of his being very near, somewhere round the next corner perhaps, she dived for shelter into the teashop.

The young waitress came towards her with a smile; at sight of the pleasure and greeting in her face, Judith felt a weight lift.

'Your usual table?' she said in her soft voice.

'Yes. I'm expecting my friend. You remember her.'

'Yes indeed I do. That's nice.'

She led the way to the table in the corner, beneath the window, lingered a little chatting, and then was called away.

Nearly four o'clock. Jennifer might be late: she always was.

The room was empty save for two women in the opposite corner, engrossed in the usual whispered teashop confidences. What warmth and colour Jennifer would bring with her when she came! Judith thought:

'I won't look towards the door; I'll look out of the window; and then suddenly I'll turn round and she'll be there.'

299

Where she sat, the purple curtain obscured her conveniently from the street; if she craned her neck forward a little she could just see round the curtain and out of the window. Over the large shop-front directly opposite, on the other side of the narrow street, the blue blind was drawn down; and the plated glass made a dark mirror. Within its space she watched a shadow-show of people passing to and fro.

The clocks chimed the hour.

The street was filling up now. It was amusing to keep one's eyes fixed on the blue blind, to see only an insubstantial noiseless world of human forms, cars and motor-bicycles, and be blind to the confusion of human and mechanical reality collecting outside. She would look only at the blue blind and see Jennifer's reflection approaching before she saw her self. Her heart beat at the thought.

The room was filling up now. She tipped Jennifer's chair against the table, for fear it should be taken; resumed her watching.

The space of glass cleared suddenly, was empty of all its shapes. She stared into the dim blank, waiting.

Then two shadows slid slowly in and paused. She watched them calmly, knew them without shock of alarm, or surprise. Roddy bent his head to light his pipe. She knew the individual set of his feet, his long legs, the slender rather round-shouldered line of his back. She could almost discern his curious blunt profile, with its upward sweep of brow and eye. Tony was with him. His short figure had its hands in its pockets, its head raised towards Roddy, nodding slightly as if in earnest conversation. The noise in the street seemed to die away, and in the long hushed breathless space of a minute, Roddy lit his pipe, threw away the match, passed a hand over his hair in a familiar gesture, nodded and laughed, it seemed, looking down at Tony with that queer half-turn of the head; and then moved on, slipped with his companion towards the edge of the pane; and vanished.

He had come to see Tony then, just as if nothing had happened: as if he had not searched the sea for dead Martin; as if there were no reason not to go smoking, laughing, talking past the great court of Trinity.

Did he miss Martin? Had he put from him the memory of the tragedy with a characteristic shrug of the shoulders? Did he ever think with momentary discomfort of Judith?

300

Tony would have him all to himself now: no Martin, no Judith to interfere. He would be happy. They would come closer to each other; and never again would Judith be able to step in between them; for there was no more Judith. What were they talking of so earnestly – what, what? The old yearning to know, to understand, returned for a moment, and was followed by an utter blankness; and she knew that she had never known Roddy. He had never been for her. He had not once, for a single hour, become a part of real life. He had been a recurring dream, a figure seen always with abnormal clarity and complete distortion. The dream had obsessed her whole life with the problem of its significance, but now she was rid of it.

She had tried to make a reality out of the unreality: she had had the power to drag him once, reluctantly, from his path to meet her, to force a convergence where none should ever have been; and then disaster had resulted.

She seemed to wake up suddenly. Roddy, Roddy himself had been passing in the street outside. She could have seen him, and, instead, her eyes had not wavered from his reflection. A shadow laid on a screen and then wiped off again: he had never been much more; it was fittingly symbolic that she should have allowed him to pass thus for the last time from her eyes. For it was certain that she would never see him again.

Half-past four. She would not watch the window for Jennifer any more. For the first time it occurred to her that Jennifer might not come. She beckoned to the waitress and ordered China tea and scone.

'I won't wait any longer for my friend. Something must have delayed her.'

She sat on, crumbling the scone, sipping tea. She counted twenty three times over very slowly; and then looked at the door. Then she counted again. She took an illustrated paper from the window-sill and studied it. If she went straight through its pages without looking up, Jennifer would come.

Quarter to five. Jennifer might have made a mistake about the tea-shop: perhaps she was sitting waiting somewhere else. But that was impossible. Perhaps she had confused the time, the date . . .

She took Jennifer's letter from her bag. October 24th. Four o'clock. 'Don't wait for me after five.'

What was it that she had scratched out? She scrutinized the thick erasure; but there was no clue.

The clocks struck five When the last one had finished chiming she rose, paid her bill and went out again into the happy-looking streets, where there was nothing more now to fear or to desire.

The train steamed out of the station.

Farewell to Cambridge, to whom she was less than nothing. She had been deluded into imagining that it bore her some affection. Under its politeness, it had disliked and distrusted her and all other females; and now it ignored her. It took its mists about it, folding within them Roddy and Tony and all the other young men; and let her go.

Darkness fell, and the ploughed fields went wheeling and slipping by, the smoke-white evening vapours laid low and heavy over their dim chill violet expanses.

She was going home again to be alone. She smiled, thinking suddenly that she might be considered an object for pity, so complete was her loneliness.

One by one they had all gone from her: Jennifer the last to go. Perhaps Jennifer had never for an instant meant to come back; or perhaps her courage had failed her at the last moment. Wise Jennifer shed her past as she went along; she refused to let it draw her back to face its old coils and perplexities and be tangled in them once again. She did not want to return to Judith and love her and be troubled by her once more; or else return to find that all was different, that in this ten months' interval life had separated them beyond hope of reunion. Yes, Jennifer had escaped again. She had never intended to come back.

Yet it was impossible to feel self-pity. Perhaps it was the train's monotonous reiterated motion and murmur that benumbed the mind, soothing it to a state that seemed like happiness.

When she reached home she would find that the cherry tree in the garden had been cut down. This morning she had seen the gardener start to lay the axe to its dying trunk. Even the cherry tree would be gone. Next door the board would be up: For Sale. None of the children next door had been for her. Yet she, from outside, had broken in among them and taken them one by one for herself. She had been stronger than their combined force, after all.

She was rid at last of the weakness, the futile obsession of depend-ence on other people. She had nobody now except herself, and that was best.

This was to be happy – this emptiness, this light uncoloured state, this no-thought and no-feeling.

She was a person whose whole past made one great circle, com-pleted now and ready to be discarded.

Soon she must begin to think: What next?

But not quite yet.